UNCOMMON DREAMS

Jill Cristao

COPYRIGHT

Uncommon Dreams
Published by Jill Cristao
JillCristao.com
Copyright © 2022 Jill Cristao

All rights reserved.
No portion of this book may be reproduced in any form without permission from the publisher, except as permitted by United States copyright law.

For permissions, contact: jillcristao@gmail.com
ISBN: 9798418423337

To my Heavenly Father, with gratitude for always being consistent, loving, and faithful each day of my life. Even when I turned my back on you, you led me home again.

To my husband, Frank, for his support throughout the writing of this book.

To my children, because my own story of abuse has intersected yours in ways you didn't ask for and didn't always understand, but you've loved me anyway.

To my sisters, because so much of my story was your story, too.

To all the women who have trusted me throughout the years with your precious stories, may this story remind you that you are deeply loved by your Heavenly Father.

Overture

Wiley - June, 1942

Mama shooed away the chickens as she walked to the vegetable garden to pick just enough beans for dinner. Inevitably, a fresh crop of weeds distracted her. She just pulled the last of the weeds and reached for the beans when she heard the slam of the screen door behind her.

"Mama, Mama! They're moving out! They're sending Karl to Virginia Beach and then overseas. I've got to go!"

Mama put her hand on her sore back and slowly straightened up. Ellie, nineteen and every bit as pretty as Mama had been at her age, handed her the telegram with her big brown eyes pleading. Mama read it quickly and then handed it back.

"Well, if you've got to go then you've got to go. But Papa isn't going to like you going out there. He won't like it one bit."

"I was fine when I visited Karl at the base in Cheyenne. The troop trains are safer than the old tractor he drives."

"It's not the trains he worries about," Mama said. "It's the troops and Karl in particular. Now go tell him lunch is ready. Don't ring the bell, he's over at the Brenner's, something about a calf that's in trouble. He said he'd be back for lunch. You go find him and tell him about the telegram. If he says no, then leave it be. We'll let him sleep on it and see if he doesn't change his mind in the morning."

Ellie gave Mama an exuberant hug and ran to find Papa. Mama filled the skirt of her apron with the beans and carried it close as she walked back in the kitchen and spilled the beans into the sink to rinse them. Then she sat down heavily on the red stool. She was tired and her feet were swollen from standing on them all morning. She'd baked four pies and six loaves of bread and had two chicken casseroles in the oven. Plenty to share at the potluck tonight. Those casseroles should just about be done.

But instead of checking the oven, she pulled a handkerchief out of the pocket of her blue and white gingham apron and gave in to the cry she'd been holding back for Ellie's sake. She'd half expected Ellie to come home married three months ago when she visited Karl at the training camp in Wyoming. Ellie would come home from Virginia Beach with a ring on her finger, of that Mama was certain.

Angrily, she blew her nose. Karl Little wasn't worth it. He thought he was too good for his family's farm, and what would his parents do, seeing he was their only son? No, he wanted to build things, be a famous architect someday. Filled Ellie's head with all kinds of ideas about moving to the city and being successful. Why, it would take years to save up for college and here he was going off to war. Signed up right away, a good thing, but still, what about Ellie? What if she came back from Virginia Beach expecting a baby? Who was going to pay for that?

She gave a deep sigh. At nineteen Ellie wanted nothing more than to be married and have a family of her own. She was a good girl, always had been. She was pretty too, pretty and ready and waiting for her time to come. But she was waiting in that day-dreamy way she had that bothered Mama, painting picture after picture of pretty little houses and flower gardens with swings. They were nice pictures, but they didn't put food on the table nor money in the bank. They were dreams, not reality.

Mama went to the large porcelain sink and washed and trimmed the beans. Through the white ruffles of the dotted Swiss curtains she could see the bedsheets on the clothesline blowing in the breeze and Papa's overalls looking stiff as boards. It was time to get the laundry in and those chicken casseroles out.

She put the beans on a slow boil and with two worn potholders pulled out the casseroles and set them on hot plates on the kitchen table. Surrounding them were the pies and breads already cooling. Ellie should paint that, she thought. That's what's satisfying. Not some pictures of dreams but the work of a woman's hands, the fruit of her labor.

She went outside and plucked the clothespins from the hanging laundry, dropped the pins into the same clothespin bag she'd kept hanging on the line for more than 30 years, then carefully folded the sheets so they didn't touch the ground too much, and as she always did, brought them close to her face so she could breathe in the sweetness of summer in cotton.

With the clothesline empty, she carried the heavy wicker basket inside and set it down in the kitchen. Then she turned off the beans and went to the big window in the parlor to see if she could see Ellie and Papa coming up the cowpath. Not yet. She went back to the kitchen. Could Ellie be caught up in a conversation with Tommy Brenner?

Now that was a pleasant thought. Tommy wouldn't be drafted due to his II-A deferment as necessary to farm labor. He helped his father manage their large farm with more animals than most around them, enabling him to stay home and help feed the nation.

Mama pulled the blouses from the laundry basket and sprinkled them with water, rolled them up and put them in the clean, empty vegetable bin in the refrigerator to keep them damp until she could get to ironing them, all the while considering the possibilities of Tommy. He was his father's son, a farmer through and through. He wasn't tall, blonde and handsome like Karl, no, he was barely the same height as Ellie, and his wavy brown hair wasn't unlike Ellie's wavy brown hair. They actually made a good match physically. But further than that, Tommy was hardworking, helpful, cheerful, one of those young men that gave you confidence that the world wasn't completely upside down and there was hope for future generations of farmers.

She took the rest of the laundry upstairs to put it away. To his credit, Tommy had tried hard to get Ellie's attention. Seemed like Ellie looked at him more as a nuisance than anything else. Maybe they were too familiar. Maybe she just didn't see Tommy as the man he was becoming.

"Smells good!" Papa yelled from downstairs and then she heard Ellie, too, "Papa said yes, Mama! I'm going to Virginia Beach!" The door slammed accordingly. Mama went downstairs. Papa was bent over the sink, washing his hands. Ellie twirled Mama around and ran upstairs.

"Wash up and then come back down here," Mama yelled after her. "Lunch is on!"

"I can't, I have to pack!"

Papa dried his hands on the old towel. "What could I say?"

Tears filled Mama's eyes. "Things are going to change, Papa."

His rough hands brushed at the tears on her soft cheeks. "It's just life, Greta. We've still got each other. I gotta go up and change these overalls, they're too smelly for lunch. I'll be back down in a minute."

Mama sat down yet again on the red stool. Her baby girl, the youngest of three and the last one home, was really leaving. She was going to learn how hard life can be and there was nothing Mama could do about it.

"God, please don't let Karl hurt my baby," she prayed. "Help them be wise and not impulsive. He's ambitious but I don't know that it's good for him or for her. Keep your hand on them no matter what comes, and don't let them get too far from you. And help Ellie grow out of that day-dreamy stuff. It's not good for her. Watch over my baby, Lord. I know she's your baby, too."

Wiley - November, 1955

The tornado wasn't as big as some that rip through tornado alley in central Illinois, but this one destroyed several farm buildings and one farmhouse. It was late on a November afternoon when it came through. Mama was in the kitchen putting the finishing touches on supper and Papa was helping her set the table. They knew the wind was bad and were considering taking supper to the cellar and eating down there when suddenly they heard the roaring train of the tornado and their world spun upside down and their lives were taken.

Their daughters and their families picked through the rubble but everything was just destroyed, impossibly turned into a million indistinguishable bits and pieces. Mama and Papa and all the years of living and everything associated with a memory, good or bad was gone. Completely gone.

After the funeral the three daughters sat down in the farm kitchen of the oldest, Charlotte, who lived just a few miles from Mama and Papa. Ellie sat on the yellow chrome stool because it reminded her of Mama's red stool. In fact, she had her own red stool in her own kitchen in town. At the gray formica table with matching chairs were Charlotte and Ruth. Ruth was the middle sister who'd driven in from Indiana with her husband and six children. They were busy playing outside with Charlotte's six children. The men were out there, too, wisely giving the women room to sort things out.

"Chuck and I would prefer that whoever wants the farm buys me out," Ruth said. "We don't want to have responsibilities here in Illinois. I'm sorry if that puts a burden on either of you, but we have enough to take care of in Indiana."

It was Charlotte's turn. "Irv's doctor told him he's going to have to find another occupation soon. He needs back surgery as it is, and we've been talking about putting our farm up for sale." She hastened to add, "Don't tell anyone, we don't want word getting out before we're ready. But this means we can't take on Mama and Papa's farm. We need to sell."

Ellie shook her head, "Honestly, I don't know what to do."

"You can't possibly be thinking of farming it," Charlotte said.

"Karl has never hated farming, he just had other ideas. Since they haven't worked out, he's wondering if we should consider buying the farm."

Ruth was just as surprised as Charlotte. "You've been living in town for years! You don't remember how hard it is. You've got a nice modern house with everything you could want. Why would you go back to farming?"

"I guess the grass is always greener," Ellie said. "Life in town hasn't been easy. Karl is getting fed up at the plant. There's no future for him there. He could be his own boss if we farmed."

Charlotte crossed her arms across her chest. "I hope you don't mind my saying so, but while you may not need the money," she glanced over at Ruth, who was nodding, "Ruth and I do. I'm sure that even with that VA loan you've got a good-sized mortgage. If you sell your house, how can you afford to buy us out and build a new farmhouse?"

"Maybe we could give you a portion of the profit at the end of the year. How about that? We could pay you off over time. We'd need to talk with Charlie Walker at the bank. It's all so sudden," she stopped. "It might be difficult financially, but you know we had a wonderful childhood there." Then she added softly, "There's no better place for children to grow up."

Neither sister replied.

Ellie looked at them. They were being kind. "There's still a chance," she said.

Ruth put her hand over Ellie's hand. "There is. Of course. But do you really think you can afford to buy both of us out in a reasonable amount of time and keep the farm running smoothly?"

"No," she said, "I don't think we can afford that."

"Then we sell it," Charlotte said. "The sooner the better. You'll be glad you have the money, Ellie. The Brenner's, we should give them first offer on it; Mama and Papa would want that. Let's sleep on it and then talk to them tomorrow afternoon. Are we agreed?"

Ellie and Ruth agreed.

"My sisters want to sell it," she said to Karl when they got in the car. "They're not interested in being paid back over time. We'll have to sell the farm."

She could tell by the extra spray of gravel beneath their tires as they pulled away that Karl was not happy about this. She went on, "You've put in almost ten years now at Atlas and you're bound to get that promotion anytime. It would be silly to walk away now."

"Ellie, I don't know why you're so eternally optimistic." Karl pushed the head of the cigarette lighter in with his left hand and pulled a cigarette out of his shirt pocket and brought it to his lips. Deftly, he pulled out the lighter and applied the glowing coils to the end of his cigarette and put the lighter back in the dashboard, all with his left hand. He did all this while what was left of his right hand held the steering wheel steady.

"There was another opportunity for a promotion," he said. "I didn't get it. I didn't want you to worry about it so I didn't tell you."

"When was this?"

"I got a phone call this morning from Hank. There was an announcement today. Brooks promoted his son Pete. He's the new Vice President of Production."

"Is he just going to keep promoting his sons?" Ellie exclaimed. "This is not fair. You're the better man!"

Karl held up his scarred right hand with its missing digits. "A veteran with just one working hand may be a hero but apparently not being able to shake hands or play golf won't cut it in the big leagues."

"You're worth two of Pete. You're smart and you work hard and your hand has never been an issue when it comes to your work. Managing may not be what you wanted to do but it's a good job. You do it well. You know that."

"That grenade has cost me more than I care to think about."

"No, it hasn't, Karl. We have a beautiful house and you've provided a good living."

"Being a manager at Atlas doesn't give you the life I wanted to give you."

"Well, I haven't been able to give you the children we both wanted," she said. "You've never blamed me for that. Just as I've never blamed you for getting injured. I've been proud of what you can do, and we've never looked back at what we wanted before the war. I'm just so glad to have you home."

"Don't you see, Ellie?" he argued. "I don't want mediocrity. I'm tired of being passed up for promotions. I want to be my own boss. I just need some time to put together a sound business plan. I could turn the farm into a well-run, profitable business. You've always loved it there. I know that. The doctor says if we can relax, you'll get pregnant. You were so happy growing up. The happiest girl I ever saw. The farm is the place for us. It might take a few years but we could be self-sufficient and not wait for the next raise or the next promotion."

"Oh, no," she said, remembering Papa's dinner table discussions. "We'd be worrying about whether there's enough rain or what the price of corn will be or what insect is destroying our crops, or how we're going to pay for the next piece of equipment or what's wrong with the soil or a million other things we can't begin to control! At least now we know what our challenges are."

"I'll never get anywhere at this job, Ellie. On the farm I can do it my way. I won't be reminded every day of what could have been."

"Mr. Brooks trusts you. He's giving you new responsibilities all the time."

"I have all the responsibilities of a vice president but the salary of a manager."

"Eventually he will see how valuable you are. At some point he's got to see that."

"Then why do I still feel like I'll never be good enough?"

She grew quiet. "I don't know. I can't fix that, Karl. I wish I could, but I can't."

He looked at her. "If anyone could, it would be you."

His words were loving, as always, but he was not being honest and she knew it. "I think, sometimes, that somehow I make it worse. I feel as if you must live up to something for me. As if just by being me I push you too hard. I think it's deep inside you," she went on, "and I can't touch it. It's up to you to know what it is and why it is."

They pulled into the garage of the brick ranch home he had customized himself. It was their pride and joy. He put out the cigarette in the ash tray and they walked inside. He pulled Ellie to him once they stepped inside the back door. "Maybe just being with you is enough, Ellie. Maybe it's not what I do with my hands, such as they are, but what I do with my heart."

"I love it when you talk like that," she said, her voice muffled in the jacket of his suit. "I love when you want to make me happy." She lifted her head. "But the farm won't make you happy in the long run. You have ambitions. You still want to succeed out there, in the world, I know you do."

"The farm life is a good life. I never hated it like your mother thought. I just wanted to save you the work. Give you something better."

She thought of Mama and her work, up with Papa at the crack of dawn, cooking, tending the garden, feeding the chickens, helping with anything and everything that came up, canning in the summer, sewing throughout the year. Her life had never settled down, she'd never wanted it to. It was hard work but Mama always seemed to gain a few pounds every year despite the labor and somehow the weight had kept the years from telling her age.

She could be Mama and Karl would become Papa. She softened. "I understand you didn't get the promotion, and I understand we couldn't have predicted that my parents would die so suddenly and we'd have this opportunity. I'm not sure this is a good idea but I love you and I trust you. Charlotte's going to call Tom Brenner in the afternoon to see if he wants to buy it. His son Tommy will be sure to want it if Tom Sr. doesn't. Go to the bank first thing in the morning and ask for Charlie Walker. He oversaw their accounts. He'll give you some good advice."

The next morning Karl was at the bank when it opened. Charlie invited him into his office.

"I understand you know all about the Jenkins' farm and the finances," Karl started. "Ellie and I have talked and we'd like to see if by any chance we can swing buying out her two sisters and rebuilding and investing in some more land and cattle to make the farm profitable again."

"I remember your mother and father," Charlie said. "Good people. As I recall they moved to Florida."

Karl's face flushed. "They did and they're doing fine. Now, I know I wasn't ready to be a farmer when I came home from the war. I had some things I'd hoped to do. But I'm more realistic now. I like the idea of being my own boss. I've worked hard and I've done well as a manager at Atlas Manufacturing. Mr. Brooks, the president, he would give me a good reference, I'm sure of it." He was talking fast, he knew it, but he couldn't stop himself. "I'll have to reconnect with the farming community and get a feel for where thing are at. I'm still good with my hands, well, hand, and I can fix anything, just like my father could. I've got a good head for numbers. I'll put together a business plan just as soon as I can but before I do that I'm hoping you can give me some idea of what it takes overall, and what the bank can do to help us out."

"I see," Charlie nodded. "I know you haven't had a lot of time to prepare to buy the farm, but I hear your enthusiasm and I respect that."

Karl looked at him uneasily. "I know it will take a lot more than just enthusiasm, Mr. Walker. I'd like to make a success of it, a real business if you will. We would buy out Ellie's sisters, build a new house, maybe even put up a new barn so we can get more cattle and buy more land."

Charlie nodded. "Today our prairies are producing like never before. That's swell, but that means the land is worth a great deal and you'll pay a pretty penny to buy them out. Then how will you build your new house? Sell the one you own? I'm guessing you bought it with a VA loan and you don't have much equity in it yet. If you don't sell it and instead try to stay in town and come out to take care of the animals every day, you'll run yourself ragged in no time. The fact is, you might want to sell off most of those cows. Commercial fertilizer is the way to go these days. Your father-in-law was resisting it because he didn't want to have to buy the equipment to apply it."

"I didn't realize that," Karl admitted.

Charlie went on, "Now on the other hand, if the Jenkins daughters sell those acres, they'll get a significant price for them. I know several buyers right now who would be happy to get in a bidding war over it."

"I see," Karl said. "Well, it does sound like it would take some time for me to get up to speed on this. And it might take more money than I realized, too."

"You're a humble man, Mr. Little. I respect that. I think this is more about timing and finances than anything else. It's not that you're not capable, it's just that financially it would put you in a great deal of debt and you'd be hard pressed to repay it for several years. Do you and your wife want to live under that kind of pressure?"

Karl felt his face flush again. If Mr. Brooks had given him that raise and promoted him years ago he might have been able to swing it. Then again, if he'd gotten the promotions he wouldn't be thinking about buying the farm. His feet felt restless suddenly. He stood up. "Thank you, Mr. Walker. You've been a great help."

"It was good to see you, Karl. You're welcome anytime."

He didn't go directly to the plant. Instead he went out to the farm. His own parents had long ago sold their farm when he came home from the war with a mangled hand. They'd moved to Florida for his father's health. This was his last chance to say goodbye to the life he and Ellie had known as children.

The enormous pile of rubble was still there but the barn stood and the animals were still being maintained by Tom Brenner and his sons. Karl walked over to what had been the kitchen garden. The dry dusting of last night's early snow was easily pushed away with the toe of his shoe. He bent down and dug his fingers into the chilly earth. It was good and fertile, like the earth he grew up on just a few miles south.

He let the dirt trickle out of the bottom of his fist and onto his shoes. The last of the dirt fell and he opened his hand and brushed away the dust. They would not sell their house and try to farm. He would have to stay at Atlas. Being family owned, with Brooks' sons holding all the executive positions, it wasn't likely he ever would be a real success, but they had a good life and he made decent money and they watched every penny. Ellie didn't have to work while she waited to become a mother.

He walked slowly down the path towards the pond where he and so many other farmer's kids had come to swim while their parents talked. For a moment he was taken back to those days and heard, for just the briefest of moments, the high-pitched shrieking and giggling of girls.

He spun around, expecting to see them, remembering a long-forgotten late afternoon when his father and Mr. Jenkins were talking in the barnyard and the girls came flying out of the house towards the path to the pond. Ellie was maybe twelve and he was thirteen, and her hair was flying free from the braids she wore at school. She was the prettiest, happiest girl he'd ever seen. "Come on," she'd said. "Come join us!" And he had, untucking his shirt from his denim shorts and running after them, then plunging into the water with them. He couldn't get over how easy it was to splash and frolic with the three sisters. But Ellie, she was so free and sure of herself. And so pretty he couldn't keep his eyes off of her.

The memory hurt. He squinted his eyes, trying to think why it would hurt to remember this, but like when his feet felt like bolting earlier at the bank with Charlie, he didn't understand it. He just had to keep moving. He abandoned the path and walked back to his car.

Wiley - May, 1956

One morning the following May, Ellie ran into Tommy Brenner's wife, Alice, at the grocery store.

"Tomorrow's the day," Alice told Ellie. "The men will be clearing your parent's yard and getting it ready for our new house!"

Ellie's eyes grew wide. "But you have a house next-door to Tommy's parents."

"We decided to rebuild on your parent's foundation. You see, we're expecting baby number five in the fall. We need more room. We hope to have the house ready by then. " She absently rubbed her stomach. "The new house is going to have five bedrooms and a big wrap around porch."

Ellie tried to smile. "Congratulations, Alice, it sounds just perfect."

The next day she drove over to the farm and parked her car behind a thick hedge of wild raspberry bushes where no one would see her. She walked to the small orchard of fruit trees in bloom and climbed the cherry tree so she could see the Brenner men working on the rubble. Shovel after shovel went into the cavernous dumpster.

She didn't want to think about the prayers Mama had prayed for her daughters and their husbands. She didn't know what remnants of them remained as the Brenners threw away the million pieces of her childhood home into a huge dumpster. She didn't know that God looked down on her as she sat in the tree among the sweet cherry blossoms and he remembered the prayers Mama had prayed all those years ago.

She closed her eyes to create a memory of what the house had looked like, tall, white and square with dark green shutters, sheer organdy curtains in all the upstairs windows, the clothesline full of sheets and overalls and dresses and slips and unmentionables, Mama's roses and peonies all white and pink against dark green leaves, the big barn clean as whistle and the corn, only five or six inches high but a beautiful green, full of promise, with the black dirt still showing even rows as you looked out at acre after acre. Oh, how glorious the earth had felt on her bare feet as she walked the newly turned furrows. She imagined the pond behind the orchard cool, waiting as the sun hung lazily in the sky on hot summer days.

Ellie realized she had been wrong in thinking of those years as her own. Those years belonged to Mama and Papa, really they did. Those were Mama's years of being a wife and a mother, she did it all and had it all, and Ellie missed her and ached for her all over again. But Mama was gone. She knew now she would never be Mama and Karl would never be Papa. Mama and Papa had lived and died. It was her turn now, and baby or no baby it was up to her and to Karl to live their own years, these years, as best they could with what they had, and what they had not.

She looked up at the blue but silent sky. God didn't seem to care how much she wanted a baby. God had taken Mama and Papa, brutally. Karl's dreams, he was wounded much deeper than just the remaining scars where his thumb and fingers used to be. His dreams of being an architect were blown to bits along with most of his hand. God had allowed that. What good was it to pray?

Resolutely, she watched until the pile of rubble was completely gone. This is life, she thought. All you have is what's in your hand at any given moment. What you can see. No more praying for what she couldn't have. No more trusting that God was good. Karl, he was good, their love was good, and if Mama and Papa could create such a wonderful world of their own, a legacy that lived on despite the fact there were no heirlooms, then she and Karl could, too.

Wiley - August, 1959

On top of each neatly ironed and folded shirt she placed a matching tie. "You have five shirts for three days," she said. "Is that enough?"

"It's plenty," he replied.

"I can put in another shirt and tie if you want them."

"The suitcase won't close if you try to put one more thing in there."

"What about your robe?"

"I'll be fine," he said, and lifted the top of the suitcase over the bottom and fastened it before she could slip in one more thing. Outside a horn tooted. Karl looked up. "That's my taxi."

She leaned up for his goodbye kiss. It was surprisingly passionate. "I think putting you into sales and flying all over the country with you is Mr. Brooks' best idea yet," she said.

"Not all clients have second homes on Martha's Vineyard where they insist on signing their contracts," he said, "but I sure am glad this one does. I can't wait to see it."

"I'm almost jealous," she admitted.

"You love it when I'm gone so that you can paint all you like."

"I'll miss you terribly!"

He kissed her again. "I know. But I think at last Brooks is seeing how versatile I am. I have to go. Vice President of Sales has a good ring to it, don't you think?"

"Are you serious?" She walked him out to the taxi in her housecoat.

"This is the twelfth major account I've brought in this year and it's only August." He swung his suitcase into the open trunk. "Brooks told me he's got some important news to discuss on the flight to Boston. I don't know what else it could be."

"Promotion or no promotion, we'll celebrate when you get home. I'll pick you and Mr. Brooks up from the airport Friday afternoon, four o'clock like you said. We'll drop him off at home and go out to eat."

"It's a date," he said and kissed her again.

She waved goodbye. She went back inside and surveyed the house. It was already as neat as could be. With a smile, she did what she had done the other times he had left on business trips. She pulled out her paints and supplies and got to painting. She skipped supper and stayed up late and woke up when she felt like it. The hours passed by without even noticing them.

Friday came quickly and with their plane due to arrive just before supper time Ellie had her hair done in the morning and had time to dress carefully for dinner before leaving for the airport. She arrived at the airport just a tad early to watch their plane land. Having never flown she found it thrilling to watch the flights take off and land.

She was outside at the gate when she spotted Mr. Brooks. She stood on her tiptoes to scan the crowd. Where was Karl?

With her gloved hand, she waved to Mr. Brooks. "Yoohoo!"

A stout, rather short man, he marched over to her, suitcase in hand, sweating in his 3-piece suit in the humid ninety-degree heat.

"Hello!" she said pleasantly. "Where is Karl? I don't see him." She scanned the crowd again.

"I have some rather bad news," he said, his eyes searching her face.

Her heart skipped a beat. "Where is he? Was there an accident? Is he okay?"

His face grew red and she noticed the large round bald spot on his head turn red, too.

"Nothing has happened to your husband, at least not yet." He saw her confusion and impatiently exclaimed, "He isn't hurt, if that's what you mean. Though by the time I'm through with him, he might be!"

She could barely contain her growing impatience. "Mr. Brooks, I'm asking you a plain question. I would like a plain answer."

"Where's your car? I'll tell you in the car. Give me the keys," he said. "I should probably drive."

"No," she said, as calmly as she could. "I can drive my own car."

She drove carefully, all the while trying to understand what he was telling her.

"He must have been planning this all along. I had no idea. I never saw it coming. I never dreamed he was that kind of man." He pulled a cigar out of his pocket. "Don't mind if I smoke? It settles my nerves."

"It's fine." She rolled down the window for fresh air and gave her finely set hair one last look in the rear view mirror before the wind blew the curls out. "I still don't know what you're talking about."

"She looks just like you. I never realized it but you could pass for sisters, you could."

"*Who* are you talking about?"

"Bridget, my daughter. She's barely twenty-two. Beautiful, young, innocent. Half your age."

She looked at him, trying to ignore the distracting fact that she was still several years away from forty. "What are you implying?"

"I'm implying nothing!" He pulled the cigar from his lips. "I'm saying he ran off with a young girl almost half his age—my daughter —and he's not going to get away with it!"

She hit the brakes.

His hands flew to the dashboard to brace himself. "I told you I should drive!"

She pulled the car over to the side of the road, battling the anxiety in her chest. "I want to know exactly what happened."

Brooks opened his window and threw the cigar into the ditch. "I told him my youngest son is going to take over as Vice President of Sales for this new division."

"Your youngest son, Rick? He's what—twenty-five?"

"Yes, with an MBA in business."

"Has he brought in the same amount of highly profitable new accounts as Karl has in the same amount of time?"

"I don't deny that Karl is good at sales. I'm pleasantly surprised. That's why, after giving him time to prove himself, I offered him the sales management position in our new division and I gave him a raise."

"Sales *Manager*? *Again*?"

Brooks had the decency to squirm, "Yes."

"Just what is it you have against my husband, Mr. Brooks? He's worked for you for fourteen years, given you the best years of his life, and you can't make him more than a manager?"

"He never wanted to work in a manufacturing plant and we both know it. He came to me and I hired him because I felt sorry for him. He turned out to be a good manager, and now he's doing well in sales but he doesn't have that aggressive edge he needs to be a vice president! I have to think of my business first."

"You put your family first, Mr. Brooks. That's not always fair."

"It's *my* business," he boomed. "I'll promote whomever I want to promote! And may I remind you, this was all *before* he ran off with my daughter? It's not even relevant anymore!"

"Or maybe he's just patient and hard-working, wanting to please you! You have given him responsibilities that your vice presidents have not had because they can't follow through! Karl's character traits would make an excellent vice president!"

"Mrs. Little, may I remind you that your husband has just left you? The man you are defending is a liar and a cheat and you need to face the truth."

She leaned back against her seat. It couldn't be, it just couldn't be. At last she started the car and drove on. It wasn't until she was a few blocks from his home that she spoke again.

"I'd like to know more details."

"Did he even tell you Bridget was his new secretary? As of last fall?"

Ellie nodded, "Yes, he did."

"I watched them, nothing seemed amiss. I asked Bridget to come with us. I wanted her to learn the ropes. I had hopes that someday she might become a leader in our company like her brothers. Being a woman she had a chance to learn the company from the ground up from a different perspective. I thought she could be quite an asset.

"We landed in Boston Tuesday afternoon and drove down to Cape Cod. That night we were tired but we went over the contracts to make sure everything was in order for the next day. Discreetly, I made sure they went to their separate rooms.

"Wednesday we took the ferry over to Martha's Vineyard. We checked into our hotel, found our client's house, had some drinks, and we walked around the property, which was right on the ocean, absolutely stunning.

"Anyway, we went back to our hotel and in the morning I'm expecting to go over the paperwork with Bridget and run numbers with Karl before we head back over to the client's, but instead nothing. They don't come down. I call their rooms. Nothing. I go up to their rooms. Nothing. They're gone. Both of them. It doesn't take a rocket-scientist to see what happened, but the clerk at the desk gives me a note."

He pulled it from the inside pocket in his jacket and read it aloud. *"Dear Father, Do not try to follow us. We're both adults and we know what we're doing. Give my love to Mom. Do try to forgive me. Love, Bridget."*

"Does that sound like a smart girl to you?" He pounded the door panel. "What was she thinking? What was Karl thinking?" He looked at her.

"I can't explain it."

"You will let me know if you hear from him? You will call me. She's my only daughter."

"I can't promise you anything at this point. I don't understand it myself."

"If she's pregnant, I tell you, if she's pregnant I'm going to disown any child that comes from this!"

Ellie winced. A child? No, no it couldn't be.

He tucked the note back into his pocket and pulled out his wallet. For a moment she thought he was going to try to give her money. Instead he pulled out a photo of a beautiful young girl who did, unmistakably, look a lot like a younger Ellie.

She looked away but her eyes still saw it. Every day that went by she saw it. Every night as she fell asleep alone she saw it. Every time she tried to take a deep breath and breathe, really breathe, she saw that picture and her breath caught short in her chest. A weight was on her chest, heavy, suffocating the life out of her.

Charlotte tried to talk to her. "Ellie, I heard the news from Helen of all people. She got it from Mrs. Brooks herself. Why didn't you tell me before the town gossip did?"

Ellie's voice was flat and dull. "I have nothing to say."

"Can I do anything? Do you need anything?"

"No"

"Did he take your savings? Tell me he didn't touch the money from the sale of the farm!"

"He didn't take anything. Just two suits and five shirts and ties. Didn't even take his robe."

She could hear Charlotte's sigh of relief. "I was so afraid he'd taken your money!"

"There are worst things than taking money."

"Like what?"

"I don't know, such as getting her pregnant."

Charlotte gasped. "Oh, Ellie, I didn't think of that. Do you think she's pregnant?"

"I don't know. Her father mentioned it. He's afraid she is."

"Don't think about that, Ellie. It may not be true. You don't know. No need to worry about it if it's not so."

"It's impossible not to think about it. It's a very real possibility."

"You need to think about taking care of yourself now. Are you going to file for divorce?"

"I don't know. I can't even think that far. It's too final."

"Leaving with another woman is final, Ellie. It doesn't get much more final than that."

"I'll think about it."

"What about a job? Or painting? I've always said you could sell your artwork. You're really, really good."

"I can't paint now. In fact I already threw most of them out."

"No! Ellie! You've got to try to remain calm. You need time to let things settle down."

"Settle down? Do you remember when we went to look at the farm the morning after the tornado? Walking around trying to make sense of the house and everything in it just being gone, reduced to a pile of rubble? That's where I am, Charlotte. That pile of rubble, that's me. My life is not going to settle down for a long, long time."

One day, it was almost Christmas, just after she got home from the drugstore where she worked now, the phone rang. She picked it up on the first ring. "Hello?"

"Ellie, it's Karl."

She couldn't speak.

"I'm sorry, Ellie, really I am."

Still, she could say nothing.

"I miss you. I've made a mess of things."

At last words came out, "Where are you?"

"We're on Martha's Vineyard."

"What are you doing there?"

"I'm a caretaker. I look after people's homes for them, their summer homes, while they're gone."

"You have a house?"

"A caretaker's cottage. I've fixed it up nicely. We live in it as payment for taking care of an estate here. It has a big kitchen. Bridget started a catering business."

"They must be wealthy people."

"There are lots of wealthy people here. Powerful people."
"Is that what you always wanted, to be wealthy and powerful?"
"I just work for them. I'm not one of them."
"Did you plan it with her?"
"No, it was impulsive. I was angry at the time and she was there."
"Do you love her?"
He paused. "I didn't."
"And now?"
"In a way."
She knew. "Is she pregnant?"
"Yes."

Words would not come, only dark angry feelings that had ugly tentacles that went deep inside and wrapped around her mind and heart.

"I failed you," his voice cracked. "I have failed you most of all."

She found her voice again. "No, it was me. I failed you. We know for sure now, it was me."

"No, Ellie! You could never fail me! Do you understand that? It's me. I fall short in everything. I just couldn't take it anymore. I was letting you down, us down. It's not you."

Instinct made her take another risk. "You're not happy. Even with this child. That's why you're calling."

"I love you. It's always been you."

"No," she said decisively, despite the pain. "It has not. Not when you left with her. You may not have loved her but you were doing what felt right to you. You were protecting you. Not me, not us. You love yourself. You made your choice but you're not happy now and you feel guilty and you're testing me to see if you can come back. This way you can stay with her if I don't want you back."

She could tell by his silence that she was right. "You should have just come back." And with that she hung up the phone.

Wiley - September, 1963

He came back, four years later, at night. He just opened the back door with his key and slipped into bed beside her. She opened her eyes and for one split second she panicked, and then he covered her mouth with his kisses and held her to him. As much as she hated him, she felt the weight slip off her chest and the tentacles release her. She could breathe again.

Nine months later, when she was 40 and Karl 41, they rejoiced in the birth of a healthy baby girl. They named her Greta, after Mama.

1

"Greta, it's Mom. Call me when you get home from work." Greta looked at the time the message came in on the answering machine. She pushed the stop button, picked up the phone and dialed her mother.

"Mom, it's me. What's wrong? Your message sounds strange."

"Something's come up."

"The machine says you called at ten o'clock this morning. Why didn't you call me at work?"

"I didn't want to bother you."

"You're never a bother, Mom. I've told you that." Greta picked up the bottom half of the phone and carried it to the living room so she could sit in a more comfortable chair. "Now, what's going on?"

"Can you come down this weekend? Do you have plans already?"

"I'm supposed to work tomorrow, put the finishing touches on the Lakeshore Drive apartment I told you about."

"I was hoping you could come home for the weekend. It's important, Greta."

"What's it about?"

"I don't want to talk about it over the phone."

Greta rubbed her forehead. "Okay, okay. I'll come down tomorrow afternoon and spend the night. I should get there about two or three o'clock. Okay?"

"Okay. Thank you. I love you."

"I love you, too."

She called Jonathon. "Jonathon, I've got to cancel our job for tomorrow. I'm sorry. Something's up with my mom. I need to drive down and see her tomorrow."

"You have a life outside of work?"

"I'm a terrible example, I know. Is there's any chance you're able to meet me at the Lakeshore Drive apartment early on Monday morning?"

"How early are we talking?"

"Six-thirty?"

"Six-thirty in the morning?"

"I know, but if today you can drop off the purchases at the apartment and I meet you there early Monday, we can get everything arranged before the couple returns from their vacation. They said they'd be back early in the afternoon."

"I have a meeting with Carol at eleven o'clock Monday morning. I need her update on my internship."

She calculated quickly, "If we get there by six-thirty we should be done with the accessorizing by ten. If not I can finish on my own. Okay?"

"Okay, fine."

"Thank you! You really are the best intern we've ever had. I hope you know that."

"I'm living for the day when I'm done with late night cramming and the panic of finals and project deadlines at work. I had no idea interior design was this demanding. I just want eight hours of sleep a night. I think you sleep less than I do."

"I sleep nights."

"Will it reflect negatively in your review of me if I state the obvious?"

"What's that?"

"I don't believe a word you say."

Laughing, Greta hung up the phone.

By the time she pulled her Jeep into the driveway of her childhood home on Saturday, some of the stress of the week was behind her. The long drive was at least worthwhile in that regard. She took out her overnight bag and walked in the back door without knocking. "I'm home!"

Ellie came up the basement stairs, her arms full of clean laundry. She looked tired, Greta thought. And thin. And her coloring was odd.

"You look tired," Ellie said.

"I was thinking the same thing about you," Greta said as she hugged her mom, laundry and all.

"Let me put this away and I'll put out our supper. It's already on plates in the oven. You're hungry?"

"Sure." Arguing about food with Ellie was pointless. Besides, Greta suspected the only cooking her mother did was when she had company.

They had meatloaf, baked potatoes and peas for dinner, with bread pudding for dessert. Ellie put two big bowls of the pudding, each with a splash of cream, on the coffee table in the pine-paneled family room. "Let's eat dessert in here, it's more cozy."

Greta gladly curled up on the sofa next to her mom. "It's a perfect fall day for bread pudding, that's for sure. Now what's going on?"

"It all started a few months ago. I wasn't feeling well and I noticed my eyes looked a little yellow, and my skin did, too. I looked jaundiced, like you did when you were born."

Greta nodded and tried not to be obvious as she looked at her mother's skin that indeed had a yellow cast to it. "Did you see Doc Peterson? Or is he retired now?"

"He's semi-retired. He ran some blood tests and sent me to a specialist."

Greta nodded. "And?"

"The specialist is an oncologist. A cancer doctor." Ellie stopped aimlessly stirring her pudding. "It's not good."

Greta froze mid-bite. "Wait. What? Cancer?"

"Pancreatic cancer."

The words echoed hollowly in Greta's head, looking for a landing place. "How bad is it?"

"It's not good at all, Greta. In fact, the doctor thinks I won't make it a year."

The world receded and spun away. She felt empty of all else except this horrible news. She stared at her mom, trying to grasp the news. "You should get a second opinion. The best hospitals are in Chicago. You can stay with me, I'll take you. Or go up to Mayo in Rochester. It's the best. I'll go with you."

Ellie took a deep breath. "No, it's already been confirmed."

"Mom, second opinions are critical. I know that much. I'll find you the best doctor. I have several friends who are doctors in the city. They can tell me who to see."

"Honey, I appreciate this, but I've already gotten two opinions from highly recommended doctors."

"Oh. Then what about treatments? We have university hospitals in Chicago. You can get in on a clinical trial. Jacqui, at work, her mom is participating in one right now."

"I don't want to argue with you," Ellie said. "This is not what I need right now."

Greta tried to slow down. She realized she was still holding her bowl of pudding. She put it down and moved over so she could fiercely hug her mother. "I'm so sorry. I'm in shock. I can't even imagine what you're feeling." Her mother's petite body had never felt smaller and more frail. Her vulnerability was frightening.

It was hard to stop hugging her. She sat back but still held her mom's hand. "How much time do you have?"

"I don't know. Doc said less than a year, maybe six months. If it's spread then not long at all."

"You have to find out. "

"I don't want surgery. The doctors said they would only know for sure if they opened me up. Besides, any treatments would only delay it a short time."

"Mom, you have to have surgery. Don't you want to do all you can to live longer?"

"No," Ellie said resolutely. "I have seen my friends with cancer suffer too much from the interventions. They start with surgeries and then the chemotherapy gets them sicker and the radiation burns them. They die sooner than they would have otherwise. No! I don't want any of it."

"But you don't know that, Mom. People live for years sometimes. Sometimes the cancer completely goes into remission!"

"It could only delay it a few months. That's what I've been told."

"Mom, you have to fight this!"

"I've fought enough in my lifetime."

"That is not who you are."

"You're the fighter now, Greta. I don't have the energy for it. I'm not well."

"Please, just consider it. Let me research this and find out more options."

"Greta, I did not ask you down here to argue with me!"

"I want you to live. I don't want you to die," she said weakly, feeling tears burning behind her eyelids.

"This is my choice. I want to die with dignity."

Be strong, for her. "I'll try hard to respect that."

"Thank you."

"You're sure you don't want another opinion?"

"You have always been hardheaded," Ellie sighed.

"Spoiled rotten."

"We wouldn't have had it any other way."

Greta started to cry, and her mother wrapped her arms around her and held her to her chest. Then Ellie started to cry, too. They cried together for a long time.

The next morning as they ate breakfast Greta's mind started to think ahead. "What do we need to do? Do you want to do something fun? Do you have a bucket list? Are there things you need to take care of that I can help you with? Anything I should know? I don't even know where to start."

"I don't have anything in particular I want to do. I just want to take care of things so you're not left with too much to do. In fact, I've spoken with my lawyer about transferring things into your name before I die."

Greta looked around. "You mean the house and personal things? What do you want done with them? Do you want anything to go to Aunt Charlotte or Aunt Ruth?"

"Yes, the house goes to you but we need to get you on my bank accounts too, and there are some stocks I need to transfer over to you, too. As far as my personal things, I can't think of anything my sisters would want. They both downsized years ago. I know you don't have space for anything. You could consider keeping the house as a place to get away. I've always kept up with repairs and it's in excellent condition."

"The house is amazing, Mom. Nothing has changed in all these years and yet it still looks pristine. But I don't need a second home. I can't imagine selling it, but I don't know how I'd take care of it like you do."

"House values are low right now. You won't get much if you sell it."

"I can't even think about selling it right now."

"Next time you come down we'll get things signed and done legally. Everything you need right away will either be in the metal box on my closet shelf or in my safe deposit box at the bank. You'll want to go through them, especially the Atlas Manufacturing stocks. I've had those for years, when your father worked there after the war. I've only recently found out they're worth a great deal now. I also have the money from the sale of my parent's farm. I kept it as an emergency fund. I never needed it and it's increased over the years."

"Atlas Manufacturing? Isn't that what Brooks International used to be called?"

"Yes, back in the 1950's."

"And you never sold them? Dad didn't take them?"

"No, he never took money."

"He never took money? What does that mean?"

"Nothing. He just wasn't like that. In fact, I still get monthly deposits into our savings account. I used the monthly deposits to pay off the mortgage and put the rest towards your college. I always wished I could have paid for all four years. Looking back I could have used the emergency fund. But I was so proud of how hard you worked to pay your share. I knew then you would be successful someday. I think you work too hard now."

"Oh, Mom," Greta started to cry again. "I'm sorry I grumbled about having to pay for college. I really am. I can see now it was good for me."

"You never grumbled for long, Sweet Pea. It was just normal teenage stuff. Now about the money, you put it towards something special. Maybe a house of your own, or a special project."

"I don't need the money, Mom."

"Yes, you do. You need a home of your own. You can't keep renting that little house forever. I don't know what you see in it."

Greta wiped her tears onto her sleeve. "What is it with you and the carriage house? My front yard is Lake Michigan for goodness sake! The interior is being featured in *Architectural Digest*'s piece on design firms next year. Features on it from local Chicago magazines have brought me more clients than any other interior I've ever done. All because I recreated the fairy tales Dad told me at bedtime. He really should have been an architect or a designer. Many of the great architects design interiors as well."

"You're father was good at many things. He did most of the interior of this house. Unfortunately, none of what he did made him happy for long."

"What I don't get is why it should bother you so much that you keep telling me I should give up my home?"

"It's the style," Ellie said. "I don't like it."

"English Country is my thing. Designers like Mario Buatta and Mark Hampton have built their careers on it. It's timeless and I'm building my career on it, too."

Ellie changed the subject. "I want you to tell me what things you'll want to keep. I can box them up and then give away or throw out what you don't want. You won't want to deal with that when I'm gone. We need to be practical."

"This is just a little too practical for me right now. "

"How about we start with my paintings? Let me know if you want any of them. I'll throw out whatever you don't want."

"Don't throw out a single one! By the way, you said last year you were going to do a painting of Grandma and Grandpa Jenkins' farmhouse for me. Did you ever get around to it?"

"I'm sorry, I know I kept saying I would, but I kept procrastinating. It's too late now. I haven't painted in years. Even if I could paint, I can't concentrate enough to paint anything now that my days are numbered."

Greta tried to keep the disappointment out of her voice. "Don't even think about it again. You do what makes you happy now. I'll come out every weekend to help you with whatever you need. And if you need me during the week, I'll be here then, too."

"For now I'm okay. If—when—I start to get weaker, I'll let you know."

Sunday afternoon came too quickly. Ellie stood at the end of the sidewalk by the mailbox and waved as Greta drove away. Slowly she walked up the front steps and closed the door behind her. She felt exhausted. How many more times would she be able to have weekends like this with Greta? At this rate, not many.

With this realization, she walked through the house. What else needed to be done right away, before it was too late? Immediately she remembered her commitment last year to paint her parent's house for Greta. She had painted it once before, before Greta came along, but in the hot anger and deep depression of those early days when Karl first left, it had indiscriminately gone in the garbage with the others.

Perhaps there was enough time to rectify a few regrets. Ellie found herself walking to the spare bedroom with the pull down ladder in the ceiling to access the attic. Tentatively, she tugged at the stairs. A muscle in her back pulled as she did so.

"Ouch!" She rubbed her back and paused to get her breath back. She carefully climbed the steps. Even in the dimly lit attic her eyes knew right where to look for her paint supplies despite the decades it had been since she last used them. If she could still hold the brush steady, she would make sure Greta had her painting of Mama and Papa's farmhouse.

The next day Ellie's back hurt so badly that she called Doc Peterson.

"Hi, Maureen, it's Ellie Little. I'd like to see Dr. Peterson today if he has an opening."

"He's completely booked today, but Dr. O'Sullivan, his new associate, is in and he does have an opening due to a cancellation. Would you like to meet with him?"

"He has my files, right? He can see what Doc Peterson and I agreed on?"

"Any notes that Dr. Peterson included in your file will be available to Dr. O'Sullivan."

"Fine. I'll see him."

She impatiently waited for him in the examination room. He wouldn't, she hoped, ask a lot of questions that Doc had already covered with her. Additionally, she hoped he wouldn't try to contradict her wishes. She wouldn't stand for that.

"Mrs. Little," he smiled as he stepped inside and closed the door. He reached out his hand, "Aidan O'Sullivan."

He was a good-looking man, she granted him that, but he looked so young.

"I've been coming here a long time," she said, shaking his hand. "You can see that in my file."

"Yes," he said, his smile wider and warmer.

"I've got cancer. Pancreatic cancer."

The smile disappeared quickly enough. "Yes," he said. "I'm so sorry. I read over your file before I came in. The latest report from the oncologist just came today."

"I'm here because I think I need to start some pain pills."

"What kind of pain are you experiencing?"

She told him. He examined her back, probing gently. He finished his exam and leaned against the small desk. "Are you ready to ask hospice to come in?"

"I'm not dying tomorrow. I just want some pain medicine."

"Yes, I understand. It's just that hospice specializes in managing pain. They can be a big help."

"I'm not ready for hospice. I told my daughter that yesterday. Doc guessed it might be less than a year, more like six months. We agreed I would let him know when I'm ready for hospice. Today I just want something for the pain."

Slowly he pulled the prescription pad out of the pocket of his white coat. "I'll write you something today and talk with Dr. Peterson to let him know. If you need something stronger, then you may want to talk with him about bringing in hospice sooner rather than later."

She walked into the drugstore, the same one she'd worked at years ago when Karl left. It was remodeled now and no one working was familiar to her. The pharmacist was nice enough but she felt rather angry as she took the bag and walked out. Everything was changing. It would keep on changing, without her. And that was fine, that was the cycle of life, but six months was six months. True, she had unfairly pushed Doc to get any kind of timeframe out of him, so who knew how reliable his guess was? But hospice now? This young new doctor, what did he know? Rushing things, that's what he was doing.

Still, when she got home she took a pill and sat down to paint. If she didn't have a lot of time left, she better get to work.

She stopped only when the phone interrupted her just before dinner time.

"Ellie, it's Doc Peterson. I heard you were in today. How are the pain pills working?"

"They're taking the edge off. Enough that I can get some work done."

"Good. I just wanted to check."

"I know you were just guessing, but less than year, maybe six months, that's what you said. You still think so?"

"I think so."

"Six months or closer to a year?"

"I don't know, Ellie. It's impossible to say. I'm sorry."

"Your new associate, he said I may need to consider hospice soon if this pain keeps up."

"He's right."

"He's very young."

Doc laughed. "So were you and I once. He grew up in Wiley and he's the cream of the crop if you ask me. I think he's got all the makings of a great doctor. I trust him with my patients. He's that good."

"Okay. Well, thank you for following up. That was nice of you."

"You're welcome. Like I said before, I'm cutting back my hours, but I told you I will do my best to see you through this and I meant it. Have a good evening."

Dying isn't going to be easy, she thought as she settled the phone in the cradle, but if good people keep being good then maybe it won't be too awful.

Greta came down the next weekend, and the next, and the next and every weekend into the holidays and then beyond them. Ellie said nothing about all the painting she was doing and kept Greta distracted by talking about her organizing and things she'd need to know about the house, and she made sure they both stayed out of the spare room where her work was hidden.

It was a good rhythm for several months. But finally the week came early in March when her arm could no longer hold her hand up. Her strength was failing quickly. Through sheer determination she managed to finish the last of the paintings. Carefully, she made room for them in the closet and packed up her paints one last time.

Greta stayed that weekend and into Monday and was there when hospice came and papers were signed and the reality of death loomed nearer. Ellie hated the stronger pain pills, they often made her quite ill but she could still talk with Greta and Charlotte, who was always bringing food though Ellie couldn't eat anymore. She was losing weight rapidly and her skin was now a deeper, unsightly yellow.

The following weekend Greta brought work with her so she could stay indefinitely. Her boss, Carol Fitz, had agreed to her working from home as much as possible. Jonathon called Greta every day to say hello and encourage her. And it was Jonathon, not Carol, who sent her mother a huge gift basket with flowers, a candle and snacks.

One afternoon when Ellie became even more uncomfortable and hadn't slept in several nights, she had Greta call Doc and ask him to stop by and give her a once over to see if there was something the hospice nurse was missing.

Greta made the phone call and shortly the phone rang with a response. Greta hung up the phone. "Mom, Maureen from the doctor's office called. Doc is on his way over."

"That was fast," Ellie said.

"A definite plus to living in a small town where you're one of the doctor's favorite patients," Greta smiled.

Her mother nodded. "I remember when he came to town and set up practice. All the women swooned over him. Best looking doctor Wiley ever had. By the way, hand me my lipstick, it's on the dresser."

Trying not to smile, Greta handed her mother her favorite red lipstick and held a mirror to her face so Ellie could apply it. She did amazingly well.

Greta stayed close by as Doc gently checked Ellie's lungs and pulse. Then he sat on the side of her bed for a few minutes.

"I don't see anything unusual," he said. "It looks like the nurse is doing just fine. If you can hold off from sleeping early in the day, you might be able to sleep better at night. But, that's not always possible if your body is telling you to sleep." He stopped and looked at them both. "I think it's time to move on to morphine. It's more effective in dealing with the pain. It will, however, make you much sleepier. In fact, as time goes on you'll want to sleep more and more."

"I'll go in my sleep, is that it?"

"Likely" he said gently. "That's the way it often happens."

He looked up at Greta. "You've been a gift to her, especially these last several months. She's blessed to have you here."

"I wish there was more I could do," Greta said, tears welling in her eyes.

"You're doing all any of us can do. You're loving her well." He looked back at Ellie. "Now, before I go, may I say a prayer for you?"

Ellie appeared as surprised as Greta but her answer rang out clear, "Yes."

He took her hand. "God, we know that you are sovereign. Our times are in your hands. The days of Ellie's life were ordained before she was even born. I pray you would give her faith in your love for her. Give her great courage and may peace be in her heart. And we ask that mercifully you would keep her from great pain. We ask these things in Jesus' name. Amen."

Greta walked him to the door and said goodbye and then went back to her mother's bedroom. "What was that all about?" she asked.

Ellie shrugged weakly, "It was nice."

"Do you believe in God? I thought we were atheists." She helped her mother turn on her side. "I didn't know you even prayed."

"It was nice, Greta. Leave it be."

"I'm not saying it wasn't, I'm just surprised, that's all."

"He was telling me it's time I made my peace with God."

Greta climbed up on the other side of the bed so she could be close to her mother while she slept. "How does one do that?"

"I think I just need to pray. That's what I need to do. Just pray." She closed her eyes and appeared to doze.

Greta sat there for sometime, listening to her mother's even breathing.

"I have to forgive him," Ellie said suddenly, her eyes wide open.

Greta practically jumped off the bed. "I thought you were sleeping!"

"I was praying." Ellie reached out, grasping Greta's hand. "You must forgive him, too."

"What are you talking about?"

"Your father. We have to forgive him for leaving us. All the past, we have to let it go."

"I'm fine, Mom. I'm okay, I'm not holding onto anything. But if you need to let it go, it makes sense to do it now."

"There are things you don't know, Greta. Things I should have told you a long time ago. Please forgive me."

Greta smiled softly, "Of course I forgive you."

"You won't say that so readily once you know."

"Sure I will," she said. But inside she wasn't quite sure that was true. "Can you tell me now?"

"No, I'm too tired. In the morning."

Ellie had just fallen asleep when the phone on the bedside table rang. Lightly, Greta sprang up to grab it quickly in the kitchen instead, "Hello?"

"Greta, it's Carol. How is your mother?"

"I'm not sure how to answer that. She's in a lot of pain and she's sleeping more and more every day. I think the end is close."

"I'm sorry to hear that. I'm also sorry to bother you, but have you spoken with Janna Harris lately?"

"Yesterday. She mailed me their blueprints here and I'm working on the design already."

"When are you planning on actually seeing the house?"

"She also overnighted me photos."

"So you're working on it already. Where's the contract?"

"Carol, have you talked with her? Is that why you're calling? Is there something I don't know?"

"The point is you're working without a contract again and that is clearly against company rules."

"I called it in to Sophie this morning. I left a message asking her to draw one up and I gave her the terms."

"Sophie called in sick this morning. We have the machine taking the calls for now. I have no idea of the status of your work if you don't tell me directly."

"I'm doing the best I can, Carol. I can't help that you weren't in when I called and Sophie is sick today. I always get the contracts signed and I submit them to you right away with an overview of the scale of the work."

"Yes, and you're supposed to give me the status of all your jobs. I know this is a bad time, Greta. I know it. But at the same time I have to keep this business afloat. I hope you understand."

Greta clenched her jaw and said nothing.

"Have a nice day," Carol said, and the phone went dead.

With a sigh, Greta pulled out the blueprints and the files and sat for the rest of the afternoon in the dining room, working on the design plans for the Harris house. Her mother slept and slept.

The next morning, Greta helped the hospice nurse as she changed the sheets, brushed her mother's hair, fluffed the pillows behind her, got her fresh moisture sticks for her mouth and cleaned her glasses.

"I can give you your morphine now," the nurse, said.

Ellie shook her head. "I need to talk privately with my daughter. Are you able to come back in an hour or two?"

"I have another patient just a few blocks away. I can go there and be back before noon. How is your pain level?"

"I'll be okay. I have to be clear for now."

"Okay, that's fine."

Ellie waited for the sound of the front door closing. "These nurses are just wonderful. I can't believe how helpful they are."

Greta piled up the pillows on the other side of the bed so she could sit next to her mother again. "There, we're all set," she said, settling onto the bed. She couldn't wait to hear what her mother had to say.

Ellie eyed her warily, "Even without my painkillers, you have much too much energy for me."

"Sorry, I've had a lot of coffee this morning," Greta admitted.

Ellie smiled weakly. "I really don't think you're going to like what I have to tell you."

"I think I'm ready."

Ellie's breath was shaky as she started. "You know your father could do anything. He inspired me, like he did you. I fell in love with him because he had a way of talking that convinced me anything was possible. That was before the war. Before we got married. Then he was injured, and he came back a different person. They warned you that could happen. He got a job at Atlas Manufacturing. They had really grown during the war and your dad, he got a job right away. He was so good with people and so capable at just about everything that he became a manager. Those dreams of being an architect kept chasing him though. He was capable of much more responsibility, much more, but he couldn't draw, he couldn't be the architect he wanted to be.

"As the years went on all five of the Brooks sons were joining the company as vice presidents in the different departments as the company grew. They weren't half as smart or effective as your father.

Your dad saw how it was. I kept thinking they would see how good he was. I know now it wasn't realistic. Your dad was so discouraged that when the tornado hit and my parents died, he thought about taking over their farm and making that even more successful. He looked into it but it would have taken more money than we could afford at the time so he walked away. That was another disappointment. I don't think I understood how important it was to him to succeed."

"But being a manager wasn't so bad, was it?"

Ellie's voice was getting stronger now. "He made a good living but it wasn't fair, Greta. Your dad was devoted to that company. When Mr. Brooks wanted to expand the business even further he brought your father into the sales division. It was the perfect fit. Your dad had a way with words and he could sell anything to anyone. He brought in several big accounts from around the country in just a few months. He thought at last Mr. Brooks would see he was worthy of becoming a vice president. Now I know your father could never be a yes man to the president. He was his own man, a leader.

"Towards the end your dad told me he had a new secretary, Mr. Brooks' daughter, Bridget. Why she didn't become the secretary of one of her brothers I can only guess was a family thing, but it was a disaster for us. She went with him on that last trip, when they closed a big account with the owner of a company who owned a second home out east, on the island of Martha's Vineyard. It was August so he invited your dad and Mr. Brooks to the island to sign the contracts there. Brooks told your dad he had some good news for him. Your dad thought Mr. Brooks was finally going to give him a promotion, with the new division it was perfect timing. But no, he just made him the new manager of their sales division."

"That's awful," Greta said.

"It was the last straw," Ellie said. "Your dad just cracked. He was so angry, so hurt, so disappointed. That's when he ran off with, literally, the boss's daughter. Apparently she convinced him, maybe seduced him, that she could offer him the comfort and encouragement he needed."

"Dad left you before I was born?"

"We'd been married almost 15 years by then."

Greta sank against the headboard of the bed. "I had no idea."

"Funny thing is, I forgave him once. He came back four years later and I just let him back in and a miracle, an absolute miracle happened. You."

Greta's mind whirled with questions. Unsure of how long this unexpected energy of her mother's would last, she wanted to think of all the right questions so she wouldn't have regrets later. "How long before you asked him for all the details?"

"I'm ashamed to say I was too terrified of the truth for the first few years, and besides, I was enthralled by you."

"What did Mr. Brooks do when Dad came back? What about the daughter, Bridget? Did she come back, too?"

"Brooks made sure your dad couldn't find work in the entire county. That's why your dad had to commute to Sears in Chicago. I never heard what happened to the daughter…"

Greta looked sharply at her mother. "What does that mean?"

"What?"

"Your voice kind of trailed off at the end there. What does that mean?"

"This is the hard part, Greta. I don't know how to tell you."

She took her mother's hand. "I can handle it. You're here with me."

Ellie looked at Greta full in the face. "Your father and Bridget lived on the island for four years. They had a little girl."

It took more than a few seconds to register this fact.

"Yes," Ellie squeezed her hand. "You have a sister. I thought when you grew up I would tell you. But then I was afraid you'd find her and your father and move away. I would be alone all over again. You were all I ever wanted and I had waited much too long for you. I didn't think I could handle it if you left me."

All Greta could do was blink. "I don't know what to say."

"I was selfish. I have carried this guilt with me your entire life."

And kept from me a sister. My own sister. She did not say it.

She leaned over and kissed her mother's yellowed, sunken cheek. "I love you, Mom. No matter what."

"I love you, too." Tears began to roll down Ellie's cheeks.

"It's okay," Greta wiped the tears, "I'm not going anywhere, I promise you."

"Your father," Ellie said, "he told me they lived in a cottage, on the ocean. He told you fairy tales about them, Greta. You've rebuilt their home. That's why I don't like it."

"What?" She could hardly swallow. "That's their house? Why would he do that?"

"He loved his daughters. Both of you."

"But listening to that must have been so painful for you!"

"He thought I couldn't hear him."

"Where is she? Where is her mom? Is that where Dad is?"

Tears coursed down Ellie's sunken cheeks. The burst of energy was running out. "I don't know. I never wanted to find out." She reached out to Greta. "You should find them. When I'm gone. They're your family now."

"Oh, Mom!" Greta held Ellie gently on her own chest, as they both cried.

"I'm tired now," Ellie managed, sinking into Greta's arms.

"You must be exhausted. The nurse will be back soon. Will you be okay without anything for the pain until then? I can beep her if you want."

"No," Ellie said. "I'll be okay. Thank you." With great effort, she reached up and gently caressed Greta's cheek. "You made it easy for me to tell you the truth. Forgive me."

"I do, Mom. I understand, I do. I just love you so much."

"I love you," Ellie said, her eyes saying more than even her words did.

Greta helped her lean back on her pillow and then she straightened the sheets around her mother's chest. Ellie's eyes were closed already and her breathing labored.

Greta went out to the living room to see if the nurse's car was in the driveway. No, the nurse wasn't back yet.

She rinsed out her coffee cup and freshened the water in the plants and flowers from family and friends. "I have a sister."

The nurse tapped gently on the front door. Greta let her in. "She's sleeping."

"It will only take a minute," the nurse said. "I'm glad you had your talk. It's much more difficult once the morphine kicks in."

They walked into Ellie's room. "Mom," Greta said softly, bending down, "the nurse—*Mom!*"

There was no mistaking the stillness and staring. Ellie was gone.

The nurse stepped back and let Greta hold her mom and cry as long as she needed.

The coroner and his assistant came almost immediately, and they moved quickly. Greta stood guard just outside the bedroom, watching their every move.

"Ma'am," the young man in the black suit and crew cut said to her, "we recommend loved ones don't watch us transport the deceased. You might find it disturbing."

"I'm fine," she said firmly. "I insist on staying with her."

The two men looked at each other.

"I'm staying with her until she leaves the house," she said.

They gave her a curt nod and began to do what they had to do.

Aunt Charlotte came just as the coroner's black vehicle pulled away. Greta was never happier to see her aunt. "She went much too fast," Greta cried as Aunt Charlotte hugged her.

"She loved you, Honey. She loved you more than her own life."

"I know," Greta sobbed. "I don't know what I'll do without her."

"You made her so proud. You just keep doing what you do and know that she would love to know you're happy."

"I'm lost without her."

"No, no you're not. You've got her gift of creating. You're every bit the artist she was. You just keep that going. Keep that alive."

When Aunt Ruth arrived the next day from Indiana, she and Charlotte helped her plan the funeral.

"She wanted it to be simple," Greta told them. "She didn't get specific. I think she thought she'd have more time to talk about it."

"We'll just have a simple service at the funeral home then," Aunt Ruth said.

"I'll invite our pastor to speak," Aunt Charlotte offered.

"She was an atheist," Greta said. "We both are—were."

Aunt Charlotte shook her head. "I never believed that for a minute."

"It was just her anger," Aunt Ruth agreed. "About, shall we say, certain things."

So they knew, too. "She told me about my dad and how he left her before I came along. I also know I have a half-sister somewhere."

"She finally told you," Aunt Charlotte sighed. "I wondered when she'd get around to it. Are you okay?"

She could only nod.

Aunt Ruth added hastily, "But then you came along! You were a miracle, Greta. A gift straight from God. Your mother knew that."

"I'm not saying she wasn't grateful for me, I clearly know she was. I'm just saying she did not follow God."

Aunt Charlotte smiled. "God followed her. I'm convinced of that."

"I don't think so," Greta replied. "Doc Peterson came just two days ago. He prayed with her before he left and she was completely surprised. You can't tell me she believed in God."

"What did she say when he asked her to pray?" Aunt Ruth asked.

"She said yes, it was okay."

"Anything else?"

"Well, honestly, I thought she'd fallen asleep but then she scared me when suddenly she opened her eyes and said we had to forgive my dad. She said she'd been praying."

Aunt Charlotte spoke up, "Your mom was raised by the same Mama and Papa we had. I can tell you she knew all about what happens when we die and our need to be forgiven for our sins and to forgive others. And that would include forgiving your dad. *Especially your dad.* Considering all the prayers that have gone up for her soul through the years from just us two sisters, I can tell you we are not surprised to hear she was praying. In fact," she dug a tissue from her pocket, "you couldn't have given us better news."

Greta was dumbfounded. "What are you two talking about? My mom didn't believe in God. She never once took me to church or read a Bible. She made it clear there is no God."

"Honey, to whom do you think your mother was praying? How could she forgive your dad if not for God?"

"I have no idea," she admitted.

"I would just like to ask that my pastor be invited to say a few words at the funeral home and to pray at the graveside," Aunt Charlotte said. "Is that okay?"

"I don't mean to be ungracious, but I want to do what I think my mom would want. Up until she died, I doubt she'd prayed in years."

"It doesn't take but a moment's sincere change of heart to make all the difference in the world," Aunt Ruth said.

Greta looked at her aunts, seeing much of her own mother in them. "I just want to honor my mom."

"Your mom was facing the end of her life, Greta. It's times like this when what we believe happens after death really matters. There's an urgency to make things right with those we've hurt, and with God. I think Doc Peterson knew that. I think your mom knew that. Your aunt and I know that. We're just asking you to consider it, too."

Greta sat upright. "Wait, how did this become about me? I'm talking about my mom."

"You're quite adamant about this, Honey," Aunt Charlotte said. "You sure you're not angry at God?"

She tried to laugh but it just wasn't there. Enough of this. "I have no idea. Yes, Doc did pray with her, and she did say she was praying and she does want me to forgive my dad. But I don't have an issue with my dad. I haven't seen him in almost twenty years, so I don't even know him anymore. And, yes, I'm understanding what you're saying about my mom. Maybe she did have a change of heart that made her want to make peace with God. It's okay if your pastor says something at the service. But I don't want it over the top religious. That's not okay; that was not my mom."

It was not over the top, in fact, most of it was a blur of cousins and their kids and old friends she hadn't seen in years and at some point she just felt like it simply would not end. But there she was, the funeral behind her and now just the graveside formalities, sitting with her aunts by her side and the flower covered casket in front of her.

The pastor had come there, too, a younger man who did not look like whatever she imagined a pastor would look like, and he was reading the twenty-third Psalm. She couldn't get past, "He leads me into green pastures, he leads me beside still waters. He restores my soul."

He restores my soul, he restores my soul, he restores my soul. She closed her eyes. What would that feel like, for just a moment, to rest like that? And then she heard, "Amen." She opened her eyes. It was over. She had to walk away from her mother's side.

Deep in her chest, where she already felt the exhaustion of loss, she felt a burning sensation. There was no way she could go back to the house and stay there another day. It was full of too many memories and messed up lives and news that was still hard to comprehend. It was much too much to deal with right now. Forget the house and her sister, and her dad, forget the will and the paperwork and the mail and bills and whatever else she had to do. In the fifteen minute drive from the cemetery to the house, she made up her mind. She would toss her work things in the backseat of her vehicle, put all her clothes and her mother's metal box with all her important papers into suitcases, stop by the post office to cancel the mail, and then she was leaving Wiley. For a long, long time if at all possible. She had a life to get back to. Her sanity depended on it.

And so she did.

2

As Greta put her things away, she couldn't help but look at her cottage in a different light. Somewhere on a little island, decades ago, a version of this house had existed. How could that be?

There was no time to dwell on it; Carol called for the third time since she walked in the door. How much longer could she avoid her? Angrily, she picked up the phone. "Carol, I have one more day off, just one. I really don't want to discuss work yet."

Carol's voice was cool. "I know you've had a rough time of it, but what you don't know is that we have more than three dozen new clients who insist on working with you and you alone."

"Three *dozen*?"

"The April issue of *Architectural Digest* with their feature on the country's top design firms came out yesterday. Photos of your house are front and center. Sophie is inundated with phone calls. We can't keep up with them. I'm afraid she's going to call in sick again if it keeps up."

"My house is front and center? Wait, they said we'd be in the May issue. It's early," she said weakly. "I haven't even gone through my mail yet to see the magazine."

"Originally it was May, but they changed it to April six months ago, after the photo shoot. I must have forgotten to tell you. Anyway, it's here now and we need to discuss how you're going to manage the attention you're getting."

There would be no break, not even for a day. She wanted to whimper. Like a puppy who is sad and overwhelmed and can't do a thing about it. But not with Carol on the other end of the phone. Quietly she took a deep breath, "Okay. I'll see you tomorrow."

The growing list, several pages now of those hoping for an appointment with Greta, was being held hostage on Carol's desk.

"It's important to know what you're planning on telling these potential clients so we don't lose any of them," Carol was saying. "If you allocate a certain amount of time with each of them, that might be best."

"You know I can't begin to know the scope of their projects," Greta said. "Allocating ahead of time would be career suicide."

"Then we need to determine at what point you'll begin referring them to me, Jonathon or Jacqui or even Edward. By the way, Edward met an American couple who hired him do their Paris apartment. Fitz & Winton Design," she leaned forward, "is now international!"

"It's quite a month," Greta said.

"Yes, but it means Edward won't be back at least for another month. Keep him in mind for fall appointments. And, you'll want to check out the shipment of antiques he's sending. He said he found some marvelous pieces that you asked him to look for."

"That's exciting. I can't wait to see what he found. Meanwhile, I need to get to work."

Carol shook her head and tapped the long list of people waiting for a call back. "I was afraid something like this would happen. If anything, they should have highlighted my designs or Edward's over yours."

Greta glanced at the dozens of copies of the magazine piled high on Carol's worktable. Her own copy at home had revealed the layout with Greta's design front and center. How that got past Carol, Greta couldn't imagine, but it had. Wasn't Carol getting calls, too? If she wasn't, she was being extremely gracious all things considered.

Carol went on, "I want to go over how far out you're going to be booking some of these people and how you're going to keep them interested if you can't get them in soon enough to suit them."

"I wish you would trust me. I will figure this out and pass along those I can't get in but who have urgent needs."

Carol laid her hand over the pieces of paper. "We're the foremost design firm in Chicago. We have standards that must be met. While this list may look to you like success, it's the reputation Edward and I have built that has given you this opportunity. I don't want that endangered by this scale of notoriety. I'll expect to see any names you're unable to engage as a client, along with the reason, what they need and who you recommend to follow up with them."

Ah, perhaps she was crediting Carol with graciousness too soon. "Finding the time to do what you're asking is going to seriously interfere with my ability to meet the client's needs."

"I talked with Jonathon. He's almost done with his internship with us but I've extended an offer to him. I don't know that he's going to take it, but if he does, he'll be a big help to you. He's already spread thin between you and me and Jacqui, we're all extremely busy, but I think he will help you stay on track and keep things from becoming chaotic. I've been down this road with other designers over the years, trust me. I know how to manage this."

With that she handed Greta the lists.

That afternoon Greta took Jonathon to a quick lunch at Berghoff's. "Thank you for the gift basket and flowers you sent for the funeral. They were beautiful."

"You're welcome. It's so good to have you back," he said. "But is it too soon?"

It occurred to her that in her office Carol had never even mentioned her mother's passing. She smiled at Jonathon, "What's that song? Nat King Cole? *Stay as Sweet as You Are?*"

He blushed. As always, he was dressed in subtle tones. Today it was a tan wool suit with a white shirt underneath a cream colored cable knit vest. His fair hair was receding already, but it suited him, as did his round wire glasses. He was an Army brat, well-traveled, well-educated and incredibly smart in a quiet way, much older than his 23 years.

"You really are one in a million, Jonathon. You have an incredible future ahead of you. Which reminds me, Carol tells me she made you an offer."

He sighed. "That she did. Am I crazy to take it? I don't know. I may not get another one with such an important firm."

"That tells me it wasn't generous. Is it even adequate?"

"May I ask—was she generous with you when you were hired after you finished your internship?"

"Not at all. But I was so happy to be working for them that I didn't care. That didn't last long when I realized how poor I was going to be. Still, I'm not sure if the worst thing is the pay or how she micromanages everything,"

"It's suffocating," he stated honestly.

"Don't get me started."

They ordered and she discreetly slipped off her high heels. Dressing up for work was fun at best, extremely uncomfortable at worst. "You know, as much as I want you to stay, because you really are the best intern we've had in years and someday I'll probably be asking you for a job, I think you could work anywhere. New York, L.A., you name it."

"Really?"

"I've seen a lot of interns come and go, and I've seen a lot of designers come and go, too. You came in humble and hungry to learn. That's why we all love working with you. Personally, I know that you respect me and my work, while at the same time you have your own style and you're incredibly good. Design is innate with you. You get it, and you have a clarity, a focus that's clean and pure and unique. It's that uniqueness that sets you apart."

"Thank you for that. I think everyone else at the firm wants me to design like they do. I get that, but you're so versatile. I've seen the modern rooms you've done. They're such a contrast to the traditional side of you. You inspire me to push myself in every style."

"Good design is always pleasing, no matter what the style. I also know that while I love English Country and hope it will never go out of style, it will have its day and then something completely new and fresh will come along. It's that pendulum. And that, my up-and-coming brilliant designer friend, is where you'll shine. Give the clients what they want, but if they're open to new looks, design from your passion. Find people who will trust you and let you do your thing whenever possible. And someday, hopefully in less than ten years, you'll be associated with a look and you can do your thing to your heart's content."

"Like you," he smiled and lifted his water glass.

"Thank you," she returned, and lifted her water glass to his. "Here's to you, to success whatever you decide."

"I'm just glad I can at least help you now," he said, and they clinked glasses.

Over the next several weeks conversations repeated themselves with little variation, "Ms. Little, it's so exciting to talk with you! I saw your house in the magazine and I just love it! It's exactly what I want you to recreate for me. What do you charge and how soon can we meet?"

Not for a moment did she take any of it for granted. This was her dream come true and she wasn't going to let a little thing like sleep keep her from doing the best she possibly could. Her calendar filled, spilling over into the following year and it showed no signs of stopping as daily she took time to talk with each new person who called.

Her new clients adored her and her current clients felt more special than ever. Her head spun as she tried to keep track of them all and their unique needs. Each one wanted something special, something no one else had, yet had that "Greta" look.

Jonathon measured walls and windows, took pictures and sketched and kept notes as she interviewed the clients and surveyed their needs. He was her right arm when it came to managing the work crews. She poured over fabrics and antique stores, showrooms at the Merchandise Mart and flea markets in the burbs. She worked with paint colors and supervised drapery installations and managed delays and road blocks and tried to keep everyone happy.

She worked through summer without a break. The warm weather extended well into fall but Greta never noticed. Her whirlwind continued into November and then her mother's lawyer kindly called to tell her the deadline for taking care of her mother's estate was nearing. Reluctantly, she did her due diligence in taking care of the tedious legalities. Though this included driving down to Wiley to meet with the lawyer and empty the safe deposit box, she managed to avoid driving past the house. It was one responsibility she did not want to be reminded of. Aunt Charlotte's grandson, Ben, mowed the lawn in the summer and would shovel the walk and driveway in the winter. Any bills were sent to her address in Glencoe. It was quite a nice arrangement.

In December a favorite couple, longtime clients, invited her for Christmas. Their family and friends plied her with questions and asked her to work on their homes, too.

If Valentine's Day came that year, she conveniently was too busy to notice it, and then it was Easter and somehow summer came in full swing and the pace did not relent. Jonathon helped her a great deal since his own list of clients was still small. Together they were creating a stunning list of finished homes, extraordinary rooms and beautifully detailed offices scattered across the country. No longer was she just popular in Chicago, her work and reputation was truly spreading across the country.

One summer afternoon as she came back to the office to get some paperwork done, Sophie handed her a fresh list of messages. "Here you go. Looks like another busy season is ahead."

Greta stopped. No one knew all that went on at Fitz & Winton like Sophie did. "What's up? What do you mean?"

"You'll see."

On top of the stack of messages was a call from *Traditional Home* magazine. They wanted to highlight the work she had done on a musician's home in Tennessee.

She shrieked with delight. "Sophie!"

"The editor called for you. She's a fan, believe me!"

"This is so exciting! Now I just have to figure out how to replicate myself!"

For a few minutes she sat at her desk and just stared at the phone. It was heady stuff, to be sure, but the pace, could she keep it up? Was she ready to double this craziness? Then again, by the time the feature, if indeed they wanted a feature, was ready for publication it could easily be six months to a year out. Perhaps it was doable.

Absently she picked up the next message on the pile. Another request for her design skills. She didn't recognize the area code, but that was nothing new. Taking care of this would give her time to think before she called the editor back.

"Hello, I'm Greta Little from Fitz & Winton Design, calling for Denise Arthur."

"This is Greta Little?"

"Yes, it is," she replied. "I have a message that you'd like me to help you with your home."

"I do! I just love your style. My mom recently passed away and I inherited the house from her. It's been in the family for more than three generations. It's unique and special and I think you're just the right designer to bring it into the '90's."

"Where do you live and what can you tell me about the house?" she asked.

"We're on the East Coast. Martha's Vineyard. It's a special old house, about one hundred years old. I think you'll love it. Please tell me you're able to come out here!"

"I see, well, I'm booked solid right now but if—." She stopped. "You did say Martha's Vineyard?"

"Yes, we live in New York but this is my family's summer home. I just know you're the one to help us. Please, please tell me you can do this."

Suddenly all the rush and excitement of each day of the last year stopped so suddenly that in her mind's eye she could see the squares of days in her planner just colliding with each other like animated figures in a cartoon.

She felt a strange paralysis set in, accompanied by a disconnected, surreal feeling. "I'm sorry," she managed to say. "Something has come up—suddenly. I—I have to go. I will call you back when I—when I can." She hung up the phone.

Unnerved, she sat there for a moment, waiting for the feeling to pass. It was as if she was above herself, watching herself at her desk, overwhelmed by the very mention of the island where her father had lived. Slowly she blinked several times and took deep breaths to calm down. It didn't help.

Whatever this was, it wasn't good.

She got up and walked to the water cooler for a cup of water. Still, she felt shaky, as if she was floating. Back and forth she walked in her office, eyeing the things that grounded her: her beautiful captain's desk, the floral chintz sofa, the leather wingback chair, the surprising lace and chintz on the office windows, the gorgeous buffet that was really a filing cabinet with shelves and locks added. Lastly, she looked at her worktable. For the first time in her ten year career the pile of new fabric books from Schumacher looked unappealing. The samples of wood from Highland House weren't half as beautiful in the afternoon light. None of it was reassuring.

There was important paperwork on the table, a pile of work done in the last month that needed to be given to Carol to bill out. Carol would have a heart attack if she knew it was just sitting there, buried under a measuring tape and sketchpad. She winced as she looked past it at the stacks of files on current clients, each bulging with samples and notes and drawings. Her eyes moved to the boards of tassels and trims in the corner that needed to be sorted through and the discontinued ones eliminated but Jonathon was already too busy to help with that.

She muttered, "It's all stressing me out. It's not just the call, it's everything. How can I keep going at this pace?" She turned and paced some more. "I need another assistant. I absolutely must have another assistant. That will help." She peeked out the door. Carol's office door was open. She took a chance.

"Carol, I need another assistant."

"I'm gathering all the billing for the end of the month," Carol said, continuing to type furiously into her computer. "Do you have any more work for clients yet to be billed?"

"I'll check. Look, I really need another assistant. Another assistant could stay on top of that for me."

Carol glanced at Greta. "I thought you said you could handle this notoriety."

"I am. I can. It's just getting busier all the time. It's not slowing down and I could use some more help."

"We can't afford to hire anyone else. Does Jonathon need to step up his work?"

"Jonathon is doing a fantastic job. He can't be spread any thinner."

"Maybe next year," Carol said, getting back to her paperwork. "Keep up the good work and we might be able to swing it."

Keep up the good work? If she kept going at this pace she would end up in the hospital or be committed.

Greta went back to pacing and muttering softly to herself in her office. "Maybe it's time to go solo. Could I hire Jonathon full-time? And another designer? Get someone to do all the billing? And maybe someone like Sophie to run the office? Could I swing it financially?"

Her head began to ache, painfully. The image of her mother's house flashed through her mind. "Oh," she said. There was that. It was all hers now. Every bit of it. Her mother's lawyer had done a fine job with the estate. Everything was in order. She hadn't really looked at the bottom line yet, how much she now owned. Funny how little it mattered now that she was bringing in a great deal on her own. If she sold the house she could swing those salaries at first, maybe just long enough to get her feet on the ground and real money coming in, enough to launch a new business at least.

She slowed her pacing. It wasn't just the house and legal affairs. The entire remains of her mother's life were waiting to get packed up and put away or dispersed.

Don't forget Martha's Vineyard. You need to connect with your father and meet your sister.

She stopped and closed her eyes. "I am not up for that. Not now!"

Everything she'd been ignoring felt like it multiplied exponentially. That floaty feeling came again.

"Come on, you're strong, you can do this," she whispered to herself.

She thought for a moment. Here she was, talking to herself in her office, hoping her coworkers couldn't hear her. Craziness was already setting in! So what could she do? Now? Today?

Hardly able to swallow the growing dread of facing the realities she'd been ignoring for too long, she grabbed the pile of paperwork and walked back over to Carol's office.

"Here," she said, firmly slapping them down on Carol's desk. "I apologize for getting them to you so late." She sat down before Carol could say a word. "I need to take some time off. Like now. As on Monday, for a week, maybe two. I think two."

Carol gave her full attention. "You're burning out. Take the time off. You need it."

"Burning out?"

"No one can do it all, Greta. It's impossible. Take a nice vacation."

"Have I been showing signs of burnout?"

Carol looked at her evenly. "No one can do it all."

"I've been doing great up until this point. I just want to take some time off."

"This isn't an argument. I'm agreeing with you. Take a vacation." She looked at Greta's stack of paperwork, gave Greta the side eye and turned back to her keyboard. "Give Jonathon your appointment book."

Back in her own office, Greta waited for Jonathon to return from a house call. When he arrived, she followed him into his office. "Jonathon, I need you to listen closely."

"I am," he said, looking at her cautiously.

"I'm heading to Wiley. I need some time away to get some things in order there. I'll email you a copy of my calendar for the next two weeks. My appointments are now your appointments. Okay? You deal with them and their needs however you deem best. I trust you completely. I'll make sure you get paid in full for them."

"You're not okay," he said. "No designer does this."

"Yes, they do. They just don't tell their clients why and they never give credit to their assistants. I promise you, you can take full credit and you can tell them I said so. I will back up every call you make. Just don't tell them I need a break. Tell them something personal has come up."

"I'll do exactly as you say. Thank you. I mean that."

"You're welcome, but I'm the one who is grateful. I love my clients and I know you'll do a great job. I'll be back in two weeks. Tell them I'm so sorry. In no time they'll forget about me and love you. Just leave me a few to come back to," she smiled.

Two weeks wasn't long, but it was a start in facing grief and dealing with the house. She took a deep breath in and was pleased to find she had her feet on the ground again. It felt a little shaky still, but much better than an hour ago. She made copies of her appointments for Jonathon and put them on his desk, and emailed him copies as well. Then she grabbed her purse, her keys and locked her planner in her desk. Panic seized her yet again. It felt like her entire life was in that planner. Every moment of her past and future was set in stone there. Resolutely, she ignored it and walked out the door.

3

A summer storm blew in forcefully, the rain just beginning to pour down as she pulled into the driveway of her home. The sprawling ranch looked beautiful with the mature trees and the roses in bloom despite the lack of care, and the lawn neatly cut. Once inside the sounds within the house gradually rose above the storm outside. At first she tried to ignore them by busying herself with little things like flushing out the faucets, checking the refrigerator to make sure it was running just fine, but the sounds inside rose, insistent. The ticking of the kitchen clock, the hum of the refrigerator; there was no shelter from them.

She was there to clean, to pack, perhaps throw out some things, and, she knew, to process her grief as she worked. Another look around and she realized that for the first time in her life she could see the house, smell the house, but she could not feel it. A barrier existed, an impasse that would have to be crossed. She considered this.

From her practiced eye, the mid-century house was well-preserved. The pine paneling in the family room still gleamed from years of polishing. The pink and green linoleum in the kitchen was worn in spots but only she knew where to look to find them. The pink boomerang print on the countertop was still as bright and cheerful as she remembered it. The starburst light above the pink formica table with black legs and pink vinyl chairs was still pristine, if a bit dusty. The charming vintage appliances spoke of years of memories of her mother baking.

She stepped down into the living room with the slim green sofa and orange chairs, the stereo that came out of the wall with the touch of a button and still worked despite the many times Greta had almost blown the speakers when left at home alone with her rock-and-roll albums.

The pink-tiled bathroom, the blue-tiled bathroom, the Lucite towel racks, the inset soap dishes, the door of the laundry chute, all so full of years and years of memories. No, it wasn't the house and the furnishings that were the problem, they were a comfort. It was her mother's eyeglasses on the end table by her bed. It was the jewelry box on the dresser and the perfume bottles with familiar scents and the dresses in the closets and the shoes and the medicine cabinet. All of her mother's personal things.

A migraine, a regular occurrence of late, stabbed at the back of her head. She went to what had always been and still was her bedroom but doubled as a guest room. The nubby white chenille bedspread with the pink fringed flowers still felt like an old friend as she stretched out on it.

Outside the thunder continued to rumble. How long had it been since she took the time to listen to a storm? She gave herself to it now, trying to ignore the growing migraine that encased her head and exhausted her so early in the day. For a long time the thunder rumbled above, and it rose louder than the sounds within the house, stronger than her headache. Then slowly, the storm receded, abating gently, gradually, until she couldn't hear the rain against the window. Leaning across the bed, she opened the window, much as she had done as teenager, longing for the world outside to distract her. Warm, moist air filled the room with its sweetness. Raindrops splattered on the driveway from the towering oak above it. In the distance she could hear the drone of a small airplane.

The slow, droning plane succeeded in taking her thoughts from the present back to a summer afternoon long ago. A child again, flat on her back in the thick grass of the backyard, looking up through the heavy black branches of the elm tree with its leaves touching the brilliant blue summer sky. She can hear the plane approaching and waits patiently for it to come into view. She does not worry that the plane will not cross the path of her gaze for she is confident that the plane is there for her to see as it passes overhead.

Slowly, the plane approaches and she watches it carefully. But the plane is so high up in the sky that she is sure the pilot cannot see her after all. Disconnected, she feels disconnected because he cannot see her, and she is saddened by the realization that she is there only to see and to watch, not to be seen.

He disappears from sight. The little girl closes her eyes and burns the sound and sight of him into her mind so she will remember him. Maybe next time he will see her. She will be waiting, remembering.

Greta sat up on the bed, aching head in her hands. *No one sees the real you. You don't matter.* She still felt lonely, unseen, and disconnected from everyone.

Don't think about that. Get to work. That's what you're here to do. She stood up but the ache of the migraine sat her down again. Something had to get done about these migraines or she wouldn't be able to function at all. Impulsively, the only way she could do it, she went to her mother's room. Doc's number was still on a slip of paper on the bedside table.

"Hi, I'm a patient, formerly, of Dr. Peterson's. Does he happen to have an opening this afternoon? I'm in the middle of a terrible migraine and I really need help."

"Can you get here within the hour? I can squeeze you in."

"I can. Thank you." She hung up the phone, grateful she could get in right away.

Her reflection in the mirror made her freeze. She was in her mother's room, using her phone, and yet she looked, for that split second, like it was her own room, her own phone. And then she realized further, it was her room, it was her phone. All of it, it was hers now. What was no longer was.

Sobs racked her body, and burning pain seared through her from head to toe. Only the fact that she had to get to Doc's office kept her from letting it all out. Her head pounded as she blew her nose and tried to pull herself together.

Doc handed her several foil packets of pill samples and then sat down behind his desk. "Losing your mother is one of life's worst losses."

Greta nodded and did her best to listen to him. He looked different, a little less hair, a little less strength, another year older but something else, too, something in his eyes, something defeated.

"The best thing to do is allow yourself to grieve," he was saying. "Don't stay too busy and don't fall into depression. Try to find a balance. And pay attention to those headaches. If you feel one coming on, by all means take the medication. But try to find out what is triggering them and avoid that stress."

She gave a quiet laugh and shook her head. "You have no idea the kind of stress I've had in recent years."

Doc looked right through her. "I just lost my wife four months ago. I know what I'm talking about."

She swallowed hard. "I'm so sorry. I had no idea."

"It's been the longest four months of my life," he said quietly. "The first few weeks I stayed home; I couldn't think clearly enough to take care of my patients. I tried to force myself into working full-time again. Fortunately, my associate didn't let me do that. Almost ruined our friendship, but I got over it. I'm learning to pace my life differently. I'm adjusting to being alone. Trying to grieve the gaping loss of my wife of more than 50 years. It's a full-time job right there."

Greta saw the tears in his eyes and looked away.

"Oh, I know you're hurting, too," Doc went on. "After taking care of my wife and my patients all these years, I have to take care of me. No one else will do that for us. I know you took care of your mom, drove down every weekend and then just stayed with her at the end. Your mother never stopped talking about how proud she was of you and how hard you worked to make her proud."

She dabbed the tears threatening to fall. "I forget how personal it gets in small towns."

"I'm glad your mom's not suffering anymore. I'm glad my wife's not suffering anymore. Now we have to figure out how to heal and get back to living."

"I've been very busy at work. I couldn't help it. It's been such a demanding year."

"Is that what you want for the rest of your life?"

"I do, just maybe not at this pace. With the timing, coming right after my mom died, it seemed like the only choice. But right now, I know I have to begin to take care of the house, her things. I have to figure this part out."

"You didn't mention grief in there. It's hard work, necessary work."

"I hate it. It hurts."

His eyes narrowed. "I haven't made friends with it either. I hate death and what it brings. The guilt, the anger, the loneliness…"

This time when she saw his tears she could not hold back her own. She reached out to the desk in front of her and took the tissues so conveniently placed. "Surely you've seen death hundreds of times, and yet you still feel how insidious it is. Thank you for being honest about it. It helps me be honest, too."

He nodded and clumsily wiped the tears from his own eyes.

"You know, " she said, "you know."

Doc stood up and walked over to her. "Yes, I know. I know death; I know grief. I know what I *should* do, but that doesn't release me from the process. I still have to go through it. And so do you." Seeing she had run out of tissues, he handed her some more. "You might consider getting some counseling to talk through your grief."

"I can't squeeze any more hours into my days," she said. "I'm already working evenings, too."

"What about journaling a little every night, or maybe every other day or even once a week?"

She wiped her nose yet again. "I used to journal, back in high school."

"Journaling is an excellent way to process feelings and work out problems. Why not set aside some time at night before you go to bed or early in the morning?"

"I'll think about it," she said. "Thank you for everything."

"You're welcome. I'm glad I was in today. May I pray with you before you go?"

She blinked several times.

"I don't usually do this," he said. "But every so often, like when your mom was dying, I ask. It seems that something's weighing heavily on you. Like you're at a crossroads of some sort and you need some extra encouragement. Would it be okay?"

This sounded more welcoming than she would have thought. "Yes, that would be fine."

"Heavenly Father, I thank you that I happened to be here today and could talk with Greta. Jesus, please comfort her as she grieves her mom. Give her space and time to do this well. Bring good people alongside her to help her, and give her wisdom to make choices that will bring her life and healing. May she have joy again in her life, and may she feel your love restoring her day by day. Amen."

There was that word again. *Restore*. She hadn't thought of that since the funeral. In an entire year how much restoring had she sought? Avoidance yes, but work, as much as she enjoyed it, sure wasn't restoring to her soul. Maybe she could journal about that, about what restoring might look like.

She gave the doctor a brief hug as she walked out, still lingering on that word and feeling grateful for his kindness.

As she walked to the elevator, she worked on opening the sample of medicine, The elevator arrived quickly. She punched the button for the first floor and tried not to drop the sample at the same time. Finally the foil peeled away and she could pop the pill in her mouth. It was bitter. Now she needed some water.

To her surprise, the elevator kept going past the first floor and opened up into the basement. She had pushed the wrong button. The door opened on what looked like a small cafeteria for staff. Several people in scrubs were eating at the tables. She saw a pop machine, a small lunch counter and some tables.

She set her purse down on the table and dug for some change. She eyed the orange-flavored pop. Her favorite. She hadn't had one in years. Did pop help with restoring?

Seated with her pop at the formica table to rest for a minute, she noticed the pale blue walls sorely needed fresh paint, much as the rest of the big old building did. The lunch counter held thick white restaurant ware in neat stacks. By the aging coffee machine were more white cups and saucers. Her eyes drifted upwards, where she could see yellow stains on the ceiling behind the fan that lazily spun above their heads. She could imagine how the room looked from up there and took in her mind, a photograph. The timelessness of the space became clear as it developed. She escaped into it. It could have been the '40's, her mother's prime, World War II, husband off in the China-Burma-India theater, when Ellie still lived in her old bedroom on the family farm. Or several years later, her husband safely returned, a new house in a town where factories offered jobs to the returning heroes, still no children for Ellie and Karl but they were a family nonetheless. Had Ellie known Doc back then? Had she been here, in this building asking him to help her find out why she couldn't have a baby?

How Greta wanted to be in the old photograph to know what their lives had been like all those years before she came along. Tears burned against her eyelids. She closed her eyes tightly, trying to think of something else. A wide lens on a camera, she pictured herself from the ceiling again, in that room right now, burning a negative onto a photograph no one but she would ever see. Sadly, she realized no one would ever wonder or care that she had ever been here, too.

In her mind's eye the picture came sharply into focus, she in the center. The frame moved slightly and Greta saw a man behind her, against the wall opposite the vending machine. He had been there when she came in but now she could see him clearly. Stark, in a photograph of pale blue and gray and yellowed white, he had black hair, black jeans and boots and a white shirt that was crisp and bright. The camera clicked, and for a moment she could only see the two of them.

She whirled around as she realized she was the negative exposed, he was watching her, had been watching her the whole time. His eyes quickly looked away but then just as quickly looked back.

The longer she glared at him the more he looked familiar. Was this Aidan O'Sullivan? The guy two blocks over from her own house? The one she went to kindergarten with? Who bought her ice cream every day in fourth grade? Wow, he was good-looking. Her face flushed.

She laughed out loud. Despite the awkward moment, despite the headache, despite regretting she hadn't put on any makeup that morning, she laughed. He hadn't changed, not really. He grinned, too, more to himself than to her, and looked down to hide it, crossed one boot in front of the other, the toe dragging on the dingy floor. So he was still cocky, the attitude was still there, evidenced in his dark hair just long enough to press convention, and the cowboy boots, and the shirt-sleeves rolled up rather sloppily, and most of all in that teasing glint in his eyes as he looked up at her, his head still bent but his eyes searching hers.

She pushed away from the table and walked over to him.

"Hello, gorgeous," he said softly.

She smiled. Funny how childhood friends who had shared ice cream and bike rides and softball games on summer days with the other neighborhood kids could get away with this.

"It's nice to see you, too." His blue eyes were much more intense than she remembered. And his dark lashes, they just weren't fair.

"You okay?" he asked.

"Just got a little lost and then figured I would get a pop while I was here. Want to walk me out to my car?"

"Sure."

Outside the air was thick with humidity from the rain. Aidan took two quick steps in front of her and walked backwards in the parking lot, facing her while he talked. "It's almost time for dinner. Want to go to the hamburger joint and eat at the park?"

He was still a quick thinker and didn't waste time. "I just took some meds. It might be a good idea to get something in my stomach."

He turned around then and pointed to an old blue boat of a Buick. "Here's my car." He opened the door for her.

"Didn't this use to be your brother Davey's car?"

"It still is. I'm just keeping it running for him."

A memory flashed through her mind as he got in and started the car.

Davey and Aidan and a cousin who looked just like Aidan and often came from the city to play with them, only they were older, in high school, and they were wearing almost identical navy suits with wide lapels. Where were they going, to a disco, a court appearance? She couldn't recall if she had ever known.

"I heard your mom passed away. I'm so sorry," he said. "It must be difficult."

"Thank you. It is."

"I understand you work in Chicago?"

"I do. I live in Glencoe but I work downtown. You live here?"

"I do. I live with my mom."

She looked at him.

"Hey, I lived in the city, too, went to school there and got a job, but I moved back last year to work and I haven't gotten a place of my own yet."

"I didn't know you were in the city! Where did you go to school?"

"Northwestern."

"Northwestern? That's a tough school to get into! I had no idea what happened with you. Actually, well, for some reason I thought you got in trouble with the law."

"That's a topic for the park," he said. "Let's get our food first."

They got their food and found a picnic table under a tree by the gazebo in the city's spacious park.

"So tell me what happened to you after high school."

"You didn't hear about it?"

"I really didn't stay in touch with too many people. My mom never cared for gossip so I was out of the loop."

"I don't know if it classified as gossip," he said. "It was all true."

"Why am I sure this isn't good?"

"Because you knew Davey. He dealt drugs all throughout high school. He kept selling them after he graduated and I got pulled into it after I graduated the following year. Long story short, he sold drugs to some cops and when he realized it, he tried to get away. Pulled a gun and shot one of them, killed the officer. He's in jail for twenty years."

"I can't believe I didn't hear about this!"

"It was all over the news for what felt like years."

"I'm so glad you weren't involved!"

"I was, but that's the long version."

She sipped the last of her malted milk as she waited. He didn't budge. "Come on, you can't leave me dangling."

"It's ugly."

"Life is ugly."

He eyed her again with those blue eyes. "I don't go around telling everyone the whole story."

"Who am I going to tell?" she asked. "Seriously?"

"It's not that I don't trust you. It's just more personal, that's all."

"Oh. Well, I get that."

"Okay, now it's your turn. What kind of exciting and crazy things have happened in your life since high school?"

"Just the normal stuff. College, and then work. A lot of work. But I love it."

"What do you do?"

"I'm an interior designer. I wake up every morning and can't wait to get to work. I wouldn't call it fun necessarily, but I get to be creative and add beauty to people's lives. I love every minute of it."

"You must be good at it."

"I hope so. It's been a long ten years but I feel like I'm finally reaching my dreams."

"You just lit up like a Christmas tree."

She couldn't hide her smile. "I really love what I do."

"What brings you back to Wiley? Vacation?"

"No, I have some things to figure out. I've been stressed out at work and though my mom passed away just over a year ago, it's finally dawning on me that her house is my house now. I'm having a hard time wrapping my head around that. I have some big decisions to make. I've been putting them off for too long."

"I'm sorry for your loss. Is there anything I can help with?"

"No, but thanks. I think most of it's a matter of figuring things out in my head. There's been a lot going on."

"If there's any packing involved, I can pack boxes, I can even lift some furniture if you need it."

"You're sounding very helpful."

"I'm trying."

Those blue eyes really were too much. She gathered the wrappers and empty drinks and put them in the paper bag. "Where's the garbage around here?"

When she woke up the next day without a headache, she felt like she had her life back. She threw on a t-shirt and shorts, found the scrub bucket and cleaning supplies and set out to deep clean the entire house. Despite the fact that there was no air-conditioning, and it might possibly be the hottest day of the year so far, she was determined to clean from top to bottom. She opened all the windows in hopes of getting a breeze, set the old wire fan on the kitchen table, and proceeded to clean out the drawers and cabinets. Except that they were already organized and spared the dust behind closed doors. She cleaned them anyway. It was as good as pacing and felt more productive. The fact that she was alone helped, too. She could talk to herself all she wanted.

She eyed the canned goods. It would feel so good to throw them out. With that she started whistling and in no time at all the kitchen cabinets were completely cleaned out of expired food. The satisfaction made her grin.

The doorbell interrupted her exuberance.

A rather delicate looking little girl with mousy brown hair and brown eyes stood outside. "May I come in?"

"Hi, I'm Greta," she said, stepping outside. "What's your name?"

"Trissa."

"Trissa?"

"No, Trissa."

She thought for a moment and tried again. "Trista?"

The little girl nodded and bounced on her toes. Bare toes, Greta noted.

"How old are you, Trista?"

"I'm seven and I live next door. I used to come in sometimes for tea."

"Oh, I bet that was fun! I'm sorry, I don't have any tea ready today but I found a packet of Kool-Aid. Would you like some?" Kool-Aid never expired, did it?

Trista nodded and followed her into the house. "She was your mom?"

"Yes, she was my mom and I used to live here when I was your age."

"She used to watch me ride my bike."

Greta got out the sugar and let Trista stir in the sugar and mix it all together in her mother's pitcher.

"How about we take our drinks outside and we can sit on the steps and then when you're done I'll watch you ride your bike?"

Trista nodded. "Yes, please! My mom says your mom is watching me now. She's my garden angel."

Greta didn't know how to respond to that. "Really?"

"And she has wings and I can talk to her anytime."

"I think you mean guardian angel, like someone who guards you. But I don't think...," her voice trailed off. Was it her job to correct her on this? She decided she was not an authority herself on this, no need to pretend otherwise.

Trista took a sip of her drink and then she was off on her bike. A rusty bike it was, with the plastic on the pedals broken and her small feet wrapped around a single metal bar as she pedaled furiously. She was a determined little thing. Kind of reminded her of how she used to be at that age—serious and very determined. Being an only child probably hadn't helped with that.

A thorough look at the aging exterior of Trista's house gave no clue as to whether anyone else was home. Trista meanwhile had made it to the corner and for a moment Greta feared she would disappear down the next street. Did mothers really let their children out of their sight like this these days? How had her own mother done it?

Up and down the street Trista pedaled. Greta stretched out her legs and sipped her drink. It sure was a quiet neighborhood. Trista finally rode her bike back up the sidewalk to the steps. "I'm tired."

"You have very strong legs, Trista! You're a very good bike rider."

Trista gave her a fairly toothless grin. "I know."

Just then a woman in scrubs stepped out of Trista's house. "Trista! Come back in here!" She waved to Greta. "I hope she hasn't been bothering you."

"No, not at all!"

Trista waved goodbye and rode her bike across the lawn into her own yard.

A lazy weight of tiredness hit Greta as she walked back into the house. For only a moment she debated getting back to work, but then reconsidered. Instead she went to her room and pulled back the white chenille bedspread and took a long nap.

Twilight was falling when she woke up. The house was silent and dark. She listened for a few minutes, waiting for some clue as to what time it was. She guessed eight-thirty. It was after nine.

Though she knew she hadn't shopped yet, she went to the pink Philco refrigerator with its V-shaped handle that opened either direction and looked inside. It was empty. A rush of cool air brushed against her face. It felt good.

She closed the door. She could go find some fast food. She could also go to the grocery store and buy some healthy food. She put on her gym shoes, brushed her hair and grabbed her purse. A trip to the grocery store would have to do.

As she walked out to the garage, she heard a car driving by and turned her head. She was sure she saw the large tail end of a blue Buick. And then she heard the brakes, the engine put in reverse and the car backed up.

She laughed and walked to the end of the driveway. "Are you driving by my house on purpose?" she asked Aidan through the open window.

Sheepishly, he nodded. "You caught me."

"I'm feeling very sixteen at the moment."

"That sounds like it has some possibilities," he said.

"I should rephrase that. You are acting very sixteen at the moment."

"Touche."

"Actually I'm hungry. I need to make a grocery run."

"Then hop in. I can help with that."

"Here you go trying to be helpful again," she said as she slid in.

He was also helpful in putting away the groceries, and helpful when it came time to eating the omelet she made them and in opening the wine bottle, which they had to have because wine at least somewhat elevated the humble eggs.

He looked around. "You know, you really need to get some air-conditioning in here."

"I don't know if I'm going to keep the house."

"A window unit wouldn't hurt."

"Trust me, aesthetically, it would hurt."

"Hadn't thought of that. I get it from your perspective, but this is Wiley. We're pretty humble people."

"I admit I'm a snob. Welcome to my world. Besides, my mom has plenty of fans."

He stood up and took their plates to the sink and rinsed them off. "Would you like to go out for dinner tomorrow night?"

"I don't really date."

"You are single?"

"I'm single. I just don't have time to date."

"I'm just asking you to dinner. You had time for dinner tonight. It's kind of late, but still, a person has to eat."

"No."

He dried his hands on the towel and came back and sat down opposite her. "I think you usually don't have the time. But now, while you're here, you might have some time. I'm just asking as a friend."

"I want to stay focused."

"Maybe we could talk and I'll just listen. I'm good at that."

"I'm not a talker. I need to get this house in order. It's not really home anymore, but I'm beginning to understand it's really mine. I don't know if I'll sell it now or not. At the least I need to pack up my mom's clothes and throw out old paperwork and make sure the house is kept up. I've been completely negligent with it this past year."

"What about grieving?"

She gave him a sharp look. "Yes, I need to grieve, which is not something anyone can help me with."

"I know. It's hard work."

"Have you…?"

"My dad. A heart attack almost five years ago now. I was right there. I tried to save him. I did all the right things but he was gone."

"I'm so sorry." She frowned. "That must have been rough. You were at the clinic—are you in the medical field?"

"I sure am. I joined Doc Peterson's practice over a year ago."

"You're his associate?"

"I really did have some brains back in the day, I just didn't use them."

"I'm so sorry, I didn't mean to be rude—."

He interrupted her. "It's okay. I surprised myself when I decided to go to med school."

"Now that's a story I'd like to hear, but I want all the details — the long version."

"It's tied into what happened with Davey. You'll get two stories in one. Let's go get comfortable in the family room."

"You're not working tomorrow?"

"Tomorrow is Saturday."

"I lost track."

The windows on three walls were all open, and the evening breeze carried on it the sound of crickets.

"Do you hear the crickets?" she asked. "They sound particularly loud tonight. It brings back memories of chasing fireflies and watching the stars. I'd like to turn off the lights and pretend we're outside." She looked at him. "Just don't get any ideas, this is not a romantic move. I'll keep this small one on for some ambience."

He stretched out on one end of the sofa and she curled up on the other. For a few minutes they just listened to nature sing.

"Life sure gets simple at times like this," he said. "Like when we were kids."

She decided to bring it up, in case he was having a hard time figuring out how to start. "How old were you when you started using?"

He took a deep breath and sat up a little more. "I was in high school, my freshman year."

"And what happened after graduation?"

"After graduation I didn't know what I wanted to do. My parents had never mentioned college and I didn't know how to go about it. Davey and Travis kept telling me they needed help and I could make a lot of money with them."

"That's it—Travis! I was trying to remember your cousin's name. He was from Chicago and came to visit your family on the weekends."

"We were supposed to keep him out of trouble. Well, he's the one who showed us the ropes. He sold to us and we sold to our friends. We made more money than we knew what to do with. We kept it stashed in our parent's basement, where I still lived. The amount of money coming in was crazy. Davey and I kept accumulating it, afraid to do anything that would draw attention. Every week it seemed like the deals were getting bigger and bigger. Then one day, the end of August, Travis pulled us into a deal that involved so much cocaine that he was afraid to leave it at our usual drop-off site. Instead, he wanted to hand it off directly to Davey, so he brought it to Davey's apartment. He thought no one would anticipate a deal this size in our hick town. I was supposed to meet him there with the money, but I was late. My mom picked that day to clean the basement. I couldn't get the money without her noticing. By the time I got it, I was an hour late.

"What we didn't know is that an undercover cop had befriended my brother. Davey hinted to him that he had a deal coming down, so the cops were monitoring Davey's apartment. They thought it was just a small town drug bust, nothing big. They thought they knew me too, because I hung out with him so much. But when they saw Travis arrive, they mistook him for me. We looked a lot alike back then. They waited around a bit, to see if anyone else showed up, and then they raided his apartment. They had no idea Davey had a small arsenal in there; he was terrified of getting caught. The police went in completely unprepared. Davey shot first, caught an officer right in the chest. Bullets flew and Travis got hit in the spine. I had just driven up to the building and I could hear the shots. I drove off in a panic. I found a motel a few hours away, rented the room for a week and stashed the money in an air vent. I left it there and came home a few hours later, like I didn't know a thing.

"My mom was hysterical. Davey was in jail, both the officer and Travis were in critical condition. Then the officer died. My dad went on a drinking binge. I went to Chicago and stayed with my aunt and uncle so I could see Travis. Day after day I sat in the hospital waiting room with his family. His parents never stopped praying. I watched them and felt such guilt. I told God that if he would save Travis, I'd do whatever I could to turn my life around. Travis made it, but he's paralyzed."

"I'm so sorry," Greta said, trying to wrap her head around this.

"I offered to stay in Chicago and help him. There wasn't anything I could do about Davey. That was cut and dried, manslaughter. He went to prison. My parent's marriage just fell apart. My aunt and uncle let me stay with them and I helped Travis through rehab and stuck with him when he moved back home.

"That didn't go so well. Travis' mom wanted to baby him too much, so he ended up getting an apartment and I helped him get settled and in the process we became roommates."

"When did you begin to think about becoming a doctor?"

"It happened over time as I watched so many medical professionals come into Travis's life and do their thing. Each did what they were trained to do and one by one, sometimes team by team, they helped him both physically and emotionally. They cheered him on as he learned how to live a life that is completely off script. It took years and years of these professionals showing up every day but without them he could never live on his own and have the life he has today."

"It must have been powerful seeing Travis heal."

"It made me realize I could show up and have something to offer, and if I can do it every day, just do my thing like they did, maybe I can watch people's lives change over time."

Then it dawned on her. "You used the drug money to get into college."

"I sure did. I thought about giving it to the wife of the officer who was killed, but I was afraid that would implicate me and land me in jail. I figured maybe I could at least redeem it by using it to save the lives of other people. The amount was enough to get me in the door, and from there I got scholarships."

"What about Davey? Was he angry that you used it?"

"No, he's still the protective older brother. He never implicated me in the drug deals, and he didn't want me getting caught with it. He thought using it for school was a great idea."

"How's he doing now?"

He rubbed his fingers absently against the nubby fabric of the sofa. "I guess you could say he's trying to make the best of it. I see him regularly. My mom does, too. But it's hard. He's broken, kind of lost. He's developed a persona in prison to survive, but behind that is a guy who wants the opportunity to live a normal life. He had no idea how his actions when he was young would completely change his future."

"Travis never said anything about the money? He wasn't angry? No one came after you for it?"

"Travis wanted nothing to do with it. I tried to ask him if he wanted it. He said, and I quote, 'I don't know what you're talking about and I don't want to know. You understand?' That was the end of it."

"I don't know that I've ever met anyone who has done what you've done."

"Which part of what I've done?"

"You literally turned your life around! Look at all the good that has come from a terrible situation."

"It wasn't me, really. It wasn't anything I did."

"What do you mean? Of course it was."

"No," he said. "I think it was God. I think he heard me praying in my car and at the hospital outside of Travis's room. I think he gave me a second chance."

"You think so? You think there really is a God who listens to you?"

"Am I the guy you grew up with?"

"No," she reflected. "So this God stuff, is that why you joined Doc? I notice he prays a lot."

"In my first interview with him he mentioned that every so often he prays with a patient. He said he's seen more healing come from prayers than from his own hand."

"That's quite a remarkable statement, if it's true."

"I've never known the man to lie," he said. "His humility in depending on God, it made me want to learn from him."

"You're really not that different from Doc." She stretched her arm across the back on the sofa. "A general practice seems to suit you."

"The intensity of school and residency was enough to convince me I wanted a real life again, where I could still have relationships outside of work and be who I want to be rather than who my job makes me to be."

She raised her eyebrows. "That's why I was surprised when you said you're a doctor. You come across low-key, so different from the doctors I know."

"What about you? How does your job impact you?"

"Me? Well, I live in a world where you need to be the best at everything."

"I'd like to hear the long version if that's okay. Fair is fair."

"Your story is a tough act to follow. Mine is much different."

"I'm a good listener."

"In my field success is based on performance. Good design is considered mediocrity. There are a million designers who can put together a nice, safely designed space. Competition is fierce at the top. A designer has to be extraordinary to get the attention and the clients that can really make a career."

"Does one have to be excellent to start with or can you build up to that?"

"When I started out I thought it was all about building a portfolio. I had to have the best designs that would get me the best clients. I worked hard but in college you're just starting and you don't have clients. At that point I thought if I worked hard enough for long enough, that I had a chance at being successful. But, like in many fields, I learned that it's not just what you know, it's who you know."

"So who did you know?"

There was along pause. "I knew Geoffrey Tate. He's a rather famous artist—."

He interrupted, "Hey, I've actually heard of the guy! I went to an exhibit he had in Chicago while I was in college!"

"Seriously? Then you probably saw me there. Little black dress, pearls, hair up in a twist, hanging on his arm."

"Every girl there was wearing a little black dress and was hanging on his arm."

They laughed together.

"But," she added, "I was the only one who went home with him. I lived with him for several years."

Aidan gave a low whistle. "A little age spread there?"

"I had just started my senior year of college when I met him at his gallery. He saw me coming a mile away. Young, blonde, naive, gushing about his paintings. I didn't have a chance. Of course, all the while he let me think he didn't have a chance. Was I ever naive."

"How long were you with him?"

"Five, almost six years."

"From what little I know about him I would guess for him that's a long time."

"I thought who we were together was special enough to change his pattern. He introduced me to all the right people. Through him I met Carol Fitz and Edward Winton of Fitz & Winton Design, the design firm where I've worked ever since. I gave him a fresh, youthful perspective that he needed at the time, seeing he was fifteen years older than I and his work was getting a bit stale. Eventually the alcohol and drugs just tore us apart. It's an old story among the creative types."

"How did it end?"

"He had an affair. Really messed me up."

"How messed up?"

"I had nothing when I left him. Emotionally, I was a wreck. Financially, I had my job but my money had all gone to support his lifestyle. One of my clients offered to rent me their carriage house which is right on Lake Michigan. They wanted to remodel their main house and the carriage house so I did them for free, so for the first year I didn't have to pay rent. I've lived there for about five years now. I had no idea that living on my own would be so peaceful."

"Life with Geoffrey wasn't peaceful?"

"It was craziness. I don't know how else to explain it. But the good news is I have so much more energy for work when I'm not in a relationship. My career just took off. I have no regrets."

"No more serious relationships?"

"I still go places with guys. I just make sure they know it's just as friends. And most of the time, they get it. You have to be seen in the city if you want to meet new people and create new business. I have a friend, Kyle, he's my jogging partner, we call each other first if we need a guest to attend an event. We've been doing this for years."

"Privately he dates guys, right?"

She stared at him. "How did you know?"

He leaned towards her. "Because any guy that can go out with you without wanting to date you doesn't date women."

"Very funny. Hey," she said, as she smacked his outstretched leg. "Didn't you tell me—what, all of thirty minutes ago—that you wanted to go out to eat as *friends*? Am I smelling some hypocrisy here?"

He looked at his watch. "Look at the time! I really should say goodnight now." He swung his legs around to stand up.

"Wait a minute," she said, briefly touching his leg to stop him. "Let's talk about this."

"What?"

"Let's be upfront about what this is. This is really nice, talking with you. Come to think of it, it feels like the first real conversation I've had with anyone since my mom died. Mom and I had gotten to the point where we could talk about anything." Tears filled her eyes and began to run down her cheeks.

"A year's a long time to not have a real conversation," Aidan said quietly.

"I've been going on adrenalin, focused on work but I'm beginning to feel so disconnected from everything. It's the strangest feeling." She breathed deeply to calm down the tears. "It really scared me to feel so overwhelmed. I really needed to get away and begin to deal with things. I feel like I can just be myself around you. You're making me think I might be a talker after all. You really are safe to talk to."

"I think it also might be because I'm not like your other friends who live with that same pressure to perform like you do."

She was taken aback. "You think I'm driven to perform?"

"It's the circle you move in, too. It might be something to think about. Is any of that pressure internal?"

"I would much prefer to blame the people around me, especially my boss."

"It's getting late," Aidan said. "Before I tread any further into dangerous territory, I better go."

She walked him outside. "Thanks for your help tonight."

"I just happen to be available tomorrow if you need any more help. And tomorrow night. Dinner again?"

"I don't know. I just want to sleep in and then maybe pack some clothes up, it might be kind of emotional. You don't want to be here, trust me."

"I could come over later in the day. You might be ready for a distraction."

"I'll think about it."

He put the car in reverse. "You do that."

To her dismay, she woke up early the next morning and couldn't get back to sleep. With a deep sigh she got out of bed and began her day.

Her mother had been able to dispose of some of her clothes before she became bedridden. Still, the majority of what was left were her mother's favorites, along with some older outfits, some dating as far back as the sixties. Her fingers ran along a pair of bright green and white floral poncho pants and the matching shirt. How could she give this to the Salvation Army? No one would appreciate them.

Her heart ached as she put them in the bag to give away. She could see her mom wearing them, so pretty and stylish, her brown hair pulled back in a pony tail with a pretty matching scarf tied around her head. Always, always, so pretty.

She couldn't give them away. Back she went to the bag and pulled them out and set them on the bed instead. And so she started the "keep" pile. Each choice hurt, ached, simply ached. By the time the closet was empty, the keep pile of bags was every bit as large as the pile to be given away. Emotionally, she was wrung out.

She went to bathroom to splash her face with cool water. "One bedroom closet down, two more bedroom closets to go," she said to the mirror.

Her own bedroom closet wasn't any easier. Being the current guest room, half of it was empty, but the floor held several boxes that looked interesting. In the first one she pulled out some notebooks and school newspapers from high school. Another box held all her report cards and school photos. In another were photos, all neatly organized by decades in photo albums. She debated for a half a second. "Not today." Instead, she carried it to her mom's room and set it on the floor next to the keep bags.

When her closet was empty, she got the broom and swept it clean. Out of nowhere came a rush of memories. Her parents arguing, yelling so loudly that she wanted to hide. Countless times she had hidden in that closet, on that floor, on that wood right there, pushing out her shoes so she could sit flat, knees bent to her chin, hands over her ears so she couldn't hear them.

Because she didn't know if she would ever be caught up in such a moment again in this house in this room, she bent down and sat on the cool wood and went there. The last year her dad was there, her mom and dad were both so angry. Was that because they loved each other or hated each other? They were each so kind and gentle with her, but with each other they were sharp and pointed, hurtful.

"Stop asking me so many questions!"

"I have a right to ask you questions!"

"Your accusations have to stop! You're acting like a crazy woman!"

"If I'm crazy it's because of you! You've put me through hell. I can't trust a single thing you say!"

"I haven't lied to you, ever."

"You lied when you left with her! You lied to her when you came back to me! You're a liar through and through."

The back door slammed and his engine started with a roar. Then she heard their bedroom door slam shut and her mother sobbing. Surely the neighbors could hear it all through the open windows.

Her head bent on her knees, she cried. She cried for the little girl that she was, frightened by these two strangers fighting so viciously, completely unaware of her and how much it hurt. She cried for the loneliness she felt and the truth that she couldn't do a thing about it then or now. It hadn't made sense then, though now it was beginning to. How much of their fighting had been about his family on the island?

Some time later she lifted her head. What was that? The ringing phone sounded distant. It rang many times before she got to it.

"Hello?" she said, her voice cracking. She coughed to clear her throat. "Hello?"

"Are you okay? It's me, Aidan."

"Yes, just finished cleaning for the day."

"May I come over?"

She looked around at the bags and boxes. "Give me an hour. I'll shower and get cleaned up. We can go for a drive."

"Maybe we can get a bite to eat first?"

The starburst clock on the wall said five pm. She hadn't eaten all day. "You pick the place."

An hour later he knocked on the door. She answered it wearing an airy, white cotton dress with side pockets in which she'd just thrown her earrings and watch. Her straight blonde hair was still wet but pulled back into a smooth ponytail with a simple ribbon. She'd managed to put some polish on her nails and she thought her toes looked particularly pretty in her favorite Lagerfeld sandals.

He shook his head when he saw her. "How do you look this good after cleaning all day?"

His green polo shirt and navy khaki shorts made his tan stand out and his hair and lashes were still damp, which made them even darker, which made his blue eyes even more intense. She tried to ignore all of this. "You look nice," she smiled.

They drove an hour to get to Bloomington and found an Italian restaurant that was pleasant, cool, and dark, with small candles lit on each table. Through dinner they talked about their favorite clients, his and hers, over a shared dessert they talked about their memories of school, and over multiple cups of coffee they talked about all the times their paths had surely overlapped in Chicago.

Greta noticed first, "I think we're the last ones here!"

They looked at their watches. It was almost eleven-thirty in the evening.

"How did it get so late?" Greta asked as she got into the Buick.

"No idea! This never happens to me!" Aidan started the car.

"You know, I think it's your turn to tell me about your love life."

"There's not a lot to tell."

"Details."

"I'm telling you, most of my adult life I've avoided women. I just haven't wanted to have a serious relationship."

He pulled out onto the highway. It wasn't long before the lights of the city receded and they drove in the moonlight. Though she waited, he didn't go any further. She decided to dig. "Okay, so why don't you want a serious relationship?"

"I have too much I want to do. I don't want to be tied down and then not be able to commit to my work."

"I have to say," she said with more than a little admiration in her voice, "that is a refreshing answer. I've met so many men who never admit that's the truth behind why they won't get serious. I think you just nailed it. But now that I'm in my thirties, I'm beginning to see guys who thought they'd never cave, they've played cool and focused on their careers, until they meet that one girl and it's all over. And they don't go reluctantly, they jump in and they pursue her and you can hardly recognize them anymore."

Aidan nodded, "It's all about the career until that one. *The one.*"

Greta sighed, rolled down her window and rested her elbow on the edge of the door above the recessed window. She leaned her head into her hand.

Aidan looked over at her. "You okay? Did I hear a sigh?"

She shrugged. "Yes, I just don't know; I don't know if there's really *the one* out there for everyone."

"I'm not sure what you mean."

She lifted her head. "From what I know my grandparents on my mom's side—I'm named after my grandmother Greta—they loved each other very much. They raised my mom and her sisters on a farm outside of town. Together they were a team, stable and secure, and they gave their kids the perfect childhood. They died together in a tornado that destroyed their house back in the '50's. But my mom and dad, they were not like that at all." She looked at him. "Did your parents fight?"

"They fought so much I thought they would kill each other sometimes."

"Who can do that to kids?"

"They weren't worried about how it would affect us. We were to be seen and not heard. If we tried to speak up my dad would smack us on the head."

"That's awful!"

He shrugged, "It's just the way it was. It didn't matter how old I was. My dad smacked me when I was 18 years old. I take it your parents fought, too?"

"My parents didn't start until I got older. They never got angry at me, not really. I have good memories of my early years. But as time went on they just couldn't stop fighting. I'm starting to understand it better now, but for most of my life I thought it was me. Classic kid stuff I guess, thinking their world revolved around me. Now I know they had other things going on. It's starting to make sense."

"Did your mom dying have anything to do with that?"

It was dark inside the car, yet still she looked hard at him and studied him for a moment. "Just before she died she explained some rather painful things."

He glanced at her as he drove. "Sounds like some unexpected news."

"I have a half-sister I never knew about."

Without thinking he decelerated and looked at her. "Are you serious?"

"I only know a little bit. I think she was born on an island out east. My dad lived there for a few years when he left my mom before I was born, which was news to me, too. My dad could be dead. I haven't heard a word from him in twenty years but my mom got deposits into her savings account every month. He could be alive, but I have no idea where he might be, other than out on the island of Martha's Vineyard which is where he went when he left the first time."

With that Aidan pulled the car over onto the shoulder in front of a field with towering green corn stalks. "Are you okay if we just park here and talk for a few minutes?" he asked. "Will you feel safe?"

"Of course," she said. "But it's not that big a deal." She wiped the tears falling down her cheeks.

"Greta, it's a really big deal. I want to be able to look at you and listen to you but I just want to make sure you're okay being in the middle of nowhere."

"I feel safe with you, Aidan. It's okay."

He turned off the engine and rolled down his window. The soft sweet smell of corn and the sound of crickets and frogs filled the car.

She swiped again at the tears that continued to fall. "I have no idea how to process this. For the last year I've just pushed it out of my mind. I could hardly grieve my mom's death, let alone deal with all that she told me just before she died. And I do mean, literally, just before she died."

"That's shocking news for anyone, let alone to learn this as your parent is dying."

"I don't know if it's possible but I think I've been in a shock for a year. I'm just now able to talk about it."

"It's not surprising, Greta."

"It's painful, I can tell you that."

Quietly, he sat there with her.

"I think I'm angry more than anything right now. All my life I've wanted a sister. And somewhere out there I have one. I can't wrap my head around it. And that my mom would keep her from me. I mean, I get it that she would have been jealous or hurt if I found my sister, but that was so selfish of her to not let me know, to not let me have the joy of having a sibling. I just can't comprehend this. I thought I knew my mom. I didn't. I really, really didn't."

Aidan opened the glove box and pulled out some fast food napkins. "Here," he said.

She blew her nose. "It's like you said, it wasn't about the kids. Even me, her only child, whom she spoiled rotten, she wouldn't give me the one thing I really wanted. Because it would hurt her."

"Even when you grew up it was still about her because she could have told you as an adult and let you make up your own mind."

"Ouch," she sniffed.

"Sorry."

"No, I need to hear the truth. I'm ready."

"I could be wrong, and I'm no therapist, but it sounds to me that not only do you have to grieve the loss of your mom, but you have to deal with the grief of all the years you never had with a sibling you never knew about. On top of that, there's the loss of what you thought to be true about your mom and your parent's marriage. That's a lot of grieving."

"I haven't done any grieving. I got back to work after the funeral just as a magazine released a feature story they did on design firms and included pictures of the interior of a house I rent and designed. I've been inundated with work ever since. It's everything I always wanted. Everything. Except it feels empty now. I don't have any time to enjoy it. And sometimes…."

"Yes?" Aidan said. "Sometimes?"

Her voice came out small and timid, "You touched on it before when you said something about having relationships outside of work. I don't have anything left at the end of the day. Sometimes I just feel disconnected from everything. Like I'm this fake person creating and designing and I find myself forcing a smile or faking my way through a conversation and I'm not even there, not really even listening. I'm just pushing myself onto the next project, the next conversation so I can keep running.

"Only I hit a wall one afternoon. I had this crazy feeling like I just couldn't be a part of it anymore. It was too much. I could see myself looking down at my office with me in it. I disconnected from myself and my life. That's when I knew I had to start dealing with everything I kept pushing to the fringe. I've been chasing success and escaping reality. I can't keep it up anymore. It's too costly."

In the darkness the breeze blew softly through the windows as she dropped her head into her hands and just cried.

After some time, and many more napkins used as tissues, Aidan asked her, "Is it okay if I just hold you?"

She nodded. He moved to the middle of the vinyl bench seat and reached out his arms. She bent her head against his chest and alternately cried some more and blew her nose and wiped away at the mess of mascara on her cheeks so it wouldn't get on his shirt. At last, exhausted, she stopped crying.

Gradually, her breathing grew regular. He loosened the grip of his arms around her and pressed his cheek against her hair. "I'm glad you got it out."

"I'm afraid I've got a lot more to go."

"You probably do. But it's a good start, a really good start."

For a long time they just sat there. They sat there as the crickets quieted, as an owl hooted from a large tree down the road, and as the night deepened and they grew tired. The dew fell and the car felt cooler, damp and almost chilly.

At last she reached up and brushed his cheek with her hand. "Thank you," she said, looking into his eyes. "Being a safe person for me is the kindest thing you could have done. I think it's the first time I've ever cried with someone other than my mom. I have always cried alone."

The intensity of his eyes bothered her. She leaned forward and disengaged herself. "I need to stretch my legs," she said. Deftly, she opened the car door and stepped outside. Aidan did, too.

"Look at the stars," he said, his head tilted back. "They're magnificent."

The sky was full of a million twinkling stars. If there had ever been a more beautiful night, she could not imagine it.

She walked over to him and tucked her arm around his elbow. "Let's walk."

Slowly they walked down the road, breathing deeply of the fresh, sweet air. They walked until it felt too far, too disconnected from the Buick and safety. They turned around.

"Shall we go home?" he asked.

"Yes," she said.

Her window rolled down still, she leaned out and her hair, long free of the ribbon, glistened as it lifted and fell in the wind as Aidan drove. Every so often she felt his eyes on her. Once home, he walked her up the sidewalk and waited while she walked up the steps and unlocked the front door with its three triangles of windows at the top.

"Sleep well," he said as she pushed open the door. She turned back and leaned down to give him a light kiss on his cheek. She felt the bristle of his cheek, the realness of his skin on hers and it was all she could do to pull herself away. "Good night," she said.

"Good night."

The days went by and each day Greta found herself sleeping in a little later, feeling a little more rested. The day came when she awoke feeling completely refreshed. It was close to noon. She almost danced to the shower, so happy she was to feel strong again. Dressed, she did not feel like cleaning out one more space in the house. She wanted to go do something. Anything. She went to the garage and pulled out her mother's bike. An old green and cream colored Schwinn from the 1950's, it had thick tires and a basket attached to the handlebars. She jumped on and could not resist the urge to head towards Aidan's street just two blocks away. She had no good excuse for this should she get caught. Thankfully, no cars were in the driveway when she slowly rode past the white-sided ranch where he lived. It was, however, much neater and prettier than it had been years ago. A basket of red geraniums hung by the front door. Flowers bloomed underneath the windows and the evergreen bushes were neatly trimmed.

The clock ticked on once she arrived home. The bike ride had not relieved her restlessness.

It had been a few day since she had heard from Aidan. She felt strangely irritated with him when he did call. The fact that she had been cleaning up the attic and had to dash for the phone didn't help.

"Hey," he said. "How are you doing?"

"Fine."

"Well, good. Any chance you'd like to go for a walk?"

"Umm…you know, I think not. I have some things I need to do."

"Alright. What about tomorrow night?"

"Go for a walk?"

"Yes."

"Okay. That's fine. About seven o'clock? I don't want to interfere with your dinner plans."

He hesitated, "Is something wrong?"

"No, no, everything is fine."

"Then I'll see you tomorrow night around seven."

The next day her plans to attack the third bedroom, the room that was more for storing stuff than a bedroom, despite the maple bedroom set, no longer seemed appealing. Emotionally, she didn't want to deal with any more memories.

Instead, she brought a garbage can over to her mother's desk in the family room and began to toss old bills and unnecessary paperwork. Then she made a list of her mother's assets that had been transferred to her own accounts. She called banks and confirmed current balances. That done, she made several phone calls to friends in the city and then reached out to a highly recommended financial advisor. She was put through to him directly and after a long talk with him she had more information and an appointment made for once she returned home.

All this done, she began to make a list of numbers. She added, and added again, and yet again. With her pencil she circled the bottom line several times. Not included was the unknown value of the stocks from Atlas.

She had tried, in all the sorting through of things so far, to find something that surprised her. A private note in a pocket perhaps, a ring among her mother's jewelry that she didn't know about, that kind of thing. Instead, her mother's greatest secret was here. Her mother had been a wealthy woman. Through the years she had lived simply, using only the interest of investments and savings and slowly but surely it had doubled, and tripled and grown exponentially. And she had never said a word of it to Greta.

She pushed back the chair and with the paper in hand she began to pace. This paper held reality and she held it tightly to make it more real. She looked at it again and again as she paced.

She talked it out, "I love my job. I don't love Carol. I really can go out on my own, start my own design firm. Would I stay in the city? It would be foolish not to stay where my client base is so strong. But, I could go anywhere! Anywhere? East Coast? West Coast? South? Paris? Edward and I get along great. He would help me get established there. What about travel? Now? No, not when things are going so well right now. But still, I can go anywhere I want to go."

Her pace increased. "Focus. Think clearly. You have to get this house in order. You have to…" What came after that she did not know. She waited. For the first time in years and years no next step came to the surface. Nothing.

She opened the desk drawer and set the paper inside and shut it firmly. Her brain hurt. Perhaps for now planning would be best done in small doses. She turned around and put her hands on her hips as she surveyed the room.

"What next?" She caught herself and laughed out loud. She was chronic when it came to staying busy.

By the time Aidan came for their walk she was even more restless.

"How was your day?" she asked, as they began their walk.

"I've had better days, " he admitted. "Had to let a patient know he has cancer."

"Ugh. Here I am at last beginning to deal with my mom's death and some other family has to go through this all over again."

"Everyone's journey looks different, but you know what? The death rate is still 100%".

"Isn't that a little cavalier for a doctor?"

"I'm just keeping it real," he said. "Life and death health issues are a constant in my profession—*constant*. It hurts every time I have to share bad news. Still, it's the bottom line of every single thing I do."

"I never thought of it that way, " she said.

"So how was your day?"

"It was a good day. A little crazy, but good."

He waited.

"I don't even know how to say this," she said. "It's kind of awkward. It looks like my mom was in a good place financially. Much better than I realized. Much, much better."

"Much better?"

"Much better."

"That sounds exciting!"

"It is!" She gave a skip to her steps. "I don't even know what to do with this news."

"You'll get an advisor, right?"

"Of course! I've got that lined up. I just don't know what to do with the myriad of options suddenly available. I tried to think of some this afternoon."

"It sounds like you're open to change."

"I didn't get too far. Considering how long it's taking me to deal with the realities I have right now, I can't imagine trying to take on more."

"But what if change helped you alleviate some stressors?"

"Like what?"

"You were telling me how stressful your job is. Could you see yourself having your own business, working for yourself?"

She lightly punched his arm. "That's exactly what I was thinking earlier today! When I think about how wonderful it would be to run my own business the way I think it should be run, I just get so excited I want to jump up and down and act crazy!"

"That sounds entertaining."

"Oh, stop! I am so happy about it that I know I have to look into what it will take to wrap things up and start my own business."

"Will it take time to develop a plan?"

"Actually, I already know what it would take. My brain just automatically strategizes and prioritizes things. Well, usually. I tried to do that today and I could only get so far."

Aidan looked at her. "Being able to strategize, that's a gift, not everyone can do that."

She shrugged. "Once I learned to trust that, it made my work so much easier. I can focus on the design end of things, the creative part, and invest my energy there. The execution is just a matter of solving problems. If there's a problem and something's not quite the right shade, or the table arrives and the scale isn't exactly what I thought it would be in the room, I just add that to the list of things to be solved.

I'm not immune to mistakes. I just have to get through the checklist until everything is perfect."

"Do your clients remain so unruffled by mistakes?"

She laughed. "That would depend on whether the mistakes are mine or theirs! When I do exactly what they want me to, trust me, there are even more mistakes! Sometimes they just won't listen to my feedback until it's too late. Then they let me do what I recommended in the beginning. As far as my own mistakes, clearly I don't do it often or I wouldn't be where I'm at, but it still happens now and then and I think it's harder on me than on the client. I know I'm a perfectionist. I think it makes my work better, but at the same time it's a lot of pressure. I do that to myself."

"That," Aidan said, "is no doubt what makes you so good. By the way, I really like your house."

"What?" She stopped.

"I found the magazine issue with your house in it."

"Are you serious? You looked it up?"

"Sure, why wouldn't I? Isn't that what friends do? Support each other? Encourage each other?"

"I guess so," she said slowly. "I just, I mean, you're a guy. Most guys wouldn't be interested."

"Maybe I'm not most guys."

That, she thought, is the problem.

She offered him iced tea back at her house and he took her up on it. They each sat in an orange chair in the family room with their glasses.

"These chairs are really cool," he said, swiveling. "Early '60's?"

"They're mid-50's, original to the house. This is a time capsule. I think that's one of the reasons I'm reluctant to let it go. I don't know if anyone else will really appreciate it."

He lifted his glass, "Here's to having a second home in Wiley."

Half-heartedly, she lifted her glass. "I don't want to sound ungrateful but it's not really home."

"Sure it is."

"I haven't lived here since I left for college. Unless weekends and breaks counted."

"You could make it home."

"There's absolutely nothing here, Aidan. For me," she hastily added. "I know you enjoy Wiley. Your mom is still here and you have a great job doing what you love. My dreams are elsewhere."

"What do you dream about?"

She leaned back in her chair and looked up at the ceiling. "I think it would be exciting to create rooms that become classics for years to come. One of my favorite designers is Sister Parish. She began designing in the 1930s and her American country look became iconic. Her work is still studied and copied today. Can you imagine? Sixty years later and her work is still considered extraordinary. When I look at her rooms I can imagine myself living there. I can imagine it's my house. I want to give that same feeling to people who see my work."

"I don't get it."

"I'm not explaining this well. I want people to look at my work in a magazine or wherever, and see themselves in that room. I want to be able to listen to them and their needs and create a space that makes them excited to come home. I want them to be able to create there if they love creating, or have a haven of rest, or a beautiful place to entertain, or a home that functions smoothly yet still feels warm and welcoming."

"I get it now. I'm impressed by your passion around it."

Greta sat up straight again and crossed her legs. "I am passionate about it but so are thousands of other designers who are working just as hard and dreaming just as big. I have plenty of competition."

"This is reminding me of our prior conversation about you being driven. Do you recall that?"

Her laughter belied her angst. "Touché, my friend, touché."

"That's not what I meant. I meant to point out that the world you live in is indeed demanding."

"Aren't most things in life that are worth having demanding?"

"It's a lot of pressure, Greta."

"You may have found the perfect life for yourself here, but Wiley is not the place for me. There is absolutely no need for designers here, nor is it a great place to vacation. If I didn't have to get this house in order, I sure wouldn't be spending my time here."

"Where would you go if you had a proper vacation? What was that island on the East Coast that you mentioned? Where your dad lived? Is that a great place to vacation?"

"Martha's Vineyard? It's for the extremely wealthy."

"They need designers more than most of us."

She swirled the melting ice in her glass and thought a moment. Should she tell him? Could she go there? She decided she could. "Actually, I got a request to go out there and work on a second home for someone. It sounded like a young couple. What I wouldn't have given to go there before my mom died. But now it's all mixed up with my dad and my half-sister. If I go out there, I'm too afraid of what I might find."

"I'm confused," Aidan said, leaning forward. "The other day you said that growing up you wanted a sister more than anything else. Now you have an opportunity to actually go to where your half-sister might be, the person you wanted more than anything, and your dad might be there, too, and you don't want to go?"

Her chest tightened. "For what? To see my sister and my dad having some fantastic relationship that I never had with him? All these years he could have reached out." She was so angry she stood up and began to pace, glass in hand. "They're probably one big happy family. Maybe my dad and that woman had more kids! Do I have to meet her and all their kids, too? The woman who did this to us?"

"It sounds like your worst fears are talking right now."

"Yes!" She slammed her glass down on the end table. "I do not want to deal with all this when my mom has just died!"

Aidan leaned back in his chair and said nothing.

Greta got a towel from the kitchen to wipe the splashed iced tea and the considerable condensation on her glass. She tossed him the towel so he could wipe off his glass, too.

"It's hot as Hades in here," she said. "I'm angry, which I know is a normal part of grief, and I'm also, embarrassingly, more stressed out than I realize because clearly my mom has been gone for a year. She did not just die." She thought a moment. "Wow. It's her birthday today." She sat back down to let that sink in. "I thought I could talk about this with you. I had no idea I was so angry and my worst fears came right to the surface."

"You're processing, Greta. You're doing hard work."

"All these bits and pieces of my life feel like they're converging on me. I feel like I should just know what to do."

"Sounds like what you were saying about your work, how you can see everything all at once. Only now you can see what has to be done, but you're not sure how it all goes together."

"That's exactly how I feel." His blue eyes were especially intense. She had to look away. "Yes, well, not a fun way to spend an evening. I'm done with this conversation."

"It's not even dark out yet. Would you like to go to the cemetery and visit your mom's grave?"

"No, I'm not prepared for that today. We could go out? Find some mini-golf or a movie?"

"We don't have to go out. It's nice just hanging out here."

She looked around. "I have an idea! We could find an old game. My mom has a closet full of them."

"Like?"

"*Mille Bornes*?"

"Never heard of it."

"*Password*?"

"It's a board game?"

"*Parcheesi*?"

"Nope."

"*Sorry*?"

"I think we had *Sorry*."

"*Sorry* it is. Come on, help me dig it out," she said. "Maybe there's one you'll like better."

The spare bedroom was not a mess, exactly. It was just "full" with a bed, dresser, sewing machine cabinet, and old TV.

Greta opened the closet door, expecting to see the pile of games stacked from the floor up. Instead, to her surprise there stood three canvases, one in front of the other. She covered her mouth with her hands, eyes wide.

"Are you okay?" Aidan asked, putting his hand on her shoulder.

She could only nod. At last she took a breath. "I cannot believe this."

"What is it?" he asked, slightly impatiently.

With trembling hands she lifted the first canvas. "It's the farmhouse, my grandparent's farmhouse! I asked my mom if she ever got around to painting this, and she said no. She must have done this in those months before she died! I didn't know she did it!" She started to cry. "It's so beautiful! And I find it today of all days." She set it down on the bed.

The white farmhouse was clear and beautiful, as it must have looked at the height of her grandparent's strength. To the side of the house you could see the rich black furrows with the green of the plants showing the even rows. The dirt looked so moist you could almost feel it on your bare feet. Sweet white priscilla curtains hung in the windows framed by green shutters, and in the front of the house were the bright contrasting colors of the pink, white and burgundy peonies.

Her eyes drank it in. This was her mother's childhood, her memories, alive and more real than Greta could ever have imagined.

"Look at the path there on the other side of the house," Aidan said, "by the barn. Look how she made the grass look worn and so realistic."

"There are children on the path, running! She used to tell me about the path and a pond they swam in with their friends. I bet it leads to the pond! And look here, chickens! And a horse, She said sometimes they'd take the horse and a cart down to the pond and it would wait for them until they were done swimming and the horse would take them back again. Doesn't it just make you want to go there? Like it's still there?"

"It sure does," he said.

She looked up at him and as she did so her eye caught the colorful canvas of the second painting. "Look!" she pointed. "It's this house!" Carefully she lifted the next canvas to the bed.

"Wow," Aidan said, as he sat down on the edge of the bed. "She was good."

Tears were running down Gretas cheeks unchecked as she examined the strokes that had captured much more than the physical presence of the house. She bent down to examine it closely. "That's my mom, sitting on the swing with me on her lap. I had forgotten all about that swing. Look at the car in the driveway. That's my dad's old car. He was home, but not in the picture. Isn't that interesting?"

"Do you think it's recent? That she did it at the same time as the farmhouse?"

"I do. She put them all together here." She turned around to look at the last canvas and froze.

Aidan drew in a sharp breath and held it as he looked at the large canvas with its dreamy swirl of ocean, sky and clouds and the beautiful little blonde girl in a pink dress playing in the wet sand.

"It's got to be my sister. My mother painted her. Why would she do that?"

Neither said a word for a long, long time. The silence was interrupted by a rather loud, repetitive beeping.

Aidan jumped off the bed. "Sorry, it's my beeper." He pulled it out of his pocket. "May I use your phone?"

"Sure, there's one in the kitchen on the wall with the stove."

He came back in a few minutes. "All done. Just had to phone in a prescription. You doing okay?"

She shook her head, her eyes remaining on the paintings. "I have that floaty feeling again. Like I'm just overwhelmed and need to distance myself from everything."

"It's quite a jolt," he said. "Take your time."

Turning her head, she said, "When you talk like that I feel like one of your patients."

"I'm sorry. I'm feeling overwhelmed right now, too. I guess I'm resorting to a familiar way to react. I'm sorry about that."

"It's okay," she said. "This is a whole lot of crazy right now. Just when I think maybe I'm getting on the right track, something comes up and everything goes upside down again." She pointed at the canvases. "Talk about surprises! It's been a surprising day all around. And in the middle of it all, there's you."

"Is that a good thing or a bad thing?"

"I have no idea."

His eyebrows raised. "Really?"

"As close as I can tell, you're a friend that has just come out of nowhere and I can't even believe how lucky I am to have you here right now. Isn't it something how our lives can suddenly open up and accommodate new people?"

"I don't believe in luck or happenstance."

"There's no sense behind the mess of my life right now, I can tell you that."

"Sometimes it looks like that. But I think there is a purpose in the timing. Looking back, we can usually see why things went down a certain way."

"Is this going to be more about God?"

"I would like to point out that God does orchestrate things in our lives for a purpose. The Bible is full of accounts of people whose paths God directed."

"I've never read the Bible."

"That doesn't mean they're not still there, speaking truth."

"What about you? How do you fit in all this? Coming into my life and playing psychiatrist or doctor, like I need to be fixed."

"Is that what you think I'm doing? Really?"

She stood toe to toe with him, her hands on her hips. "I don't know. What would you call what you're doing here?"

He blinked. "Being a friend."

"Exactly. Only sometimes it doesn't feel like just a friend, Aidan. We've been hanging out together for almost two weeks—just two weeks—yet sometimes I see you looking at me and I don't think friends look at friends like that."

His chin jutted out but he said nothing.

"That's what I thought. You," she poked his chest, "you have no idea what you're doing here either, do you? You're in way over your head. That's what I think. You walked into my life out of the blue and you're scared to death."

He gave a little laugh and scratched his neck. "Maybe."

She turned and walked out of the room. "I can't even. No, I can't even." She opened the front door and just started walking.

For a moment Aidan stood there, and then he followed her outside. "I'm sorry."

"Whatever!"

"No, I really am."

"Exactly why?"

"For being confused and adding to your confusion." He shoved his hands in his pockets.

She turned to him. "Thank you. That is the truth. That is something, however small, that is clear right now and maybe I shouldn't be too grateful for it, but I am. Thank you for being honest."

For several minutes they just walked on in silence. Finally she turned to him. "So what's up with this? With us?"

"Greta, I don't know if this is the time to have a conversation about us. You've had quite a day. Really. I don't want to add to it."

"I'd like to be the judge of what I can handle," she said. "I'm asking for some clarity and some honesty before I go back to the city."

"Okay, I just have to say something. But first, I'm not avoiding your question. It's a fair question and it deserves discussion, though I honestly don't have answers. What I want to point out, however, is that I got beeped and came back from answering it, and suddenly you're all upset at me. When I left minutes earlier, you were staring at that last painting. It looks like you just avoided dealing with that and jumped all over me."

She thought carefully. "I didn't realize I did that but I got that weird floaty feeling I get sometimes and I wanted to get away from it, to deal with something more concrete."

"Thank you." And they resumed walking.

She felt tired. Exhausted. As if she was completely out of shape and trying to run a marathon, which wasn't completely inaccurate as she considered the amount of grieving she had done in the last two weeks.

"I wonder why I do that," she said. "What is that floaty feeling?"

"Do you really want to know?"

"You have an answer?"

"It's called dissociation. It's exactly as you described. You're overwhelmed and you disconnect in order to back off and get some relief."

"Am I crazy?"

"Not at all. It's a coping mechanism. It's your body and brain working to try to help you. Does it happen often?"

"No, it just started. That's why I took some time off of work. It freaked me out."

"For what it's worth, I think you might want to consider taking a real vacation."

"That's not going to happen. These two weeks feel like a luxury I'm going to regret when I get back to work." Tears welled up in her eyes. "Aidan, are you okay if I just take your arm right now and walk closely with you for a while? I'm really tired."

"Is it going to confuse you more?"

She sighed. "I hope not. I just really want the comfort of a friend right now."

He put his arm around her and drew her close.

Together they just walked and walked until the sun set and the night world descended on them and the old neighborhood ran out of streets to walk and so he walked her back to her house.

"Are you up for going out to for dinner tomorrow night?" he asked.

"Sure," she said. "You pick the place."

They exchanged a brief hug and said goodnight.

The next morning Greta couldn't wait to get to the store. She was on her way out the door when the phone rang. It was Aidan.

He got right to the point. "Change of plans. Let's have dinner at my place tonight instead of going out to eat."

"That would be your mom's place?"

"Technically, yes, but she's going to an all-night Bingo and I thought it would be fun to grill some steaks, just the two of us."

"That sounds fun," she said. "Casual then? May I bring something?"

"No, but thanks! But not casual, dressy. See you around seven o'clock?"

"See you then."

Dressy? Really? Somewhere, in the pile of bags and boxes was a pretty pink sheath of her mother's, very Jackie Kennedy. She rummaged through and found it and a pair of black kitten heels, too. They would do.

She got back to her errand at last. The local farm and feed store, she was glad to see, still had an excellent sporting goods section. She immediately saw the pink and purple bike she wanted. It took a bit of persuading for the manager in that department to give her the display model, but in the end he softened and she bought it and put it in the back of the Cherokee. Then she stopped at the fabric store and bought a huge roll of pink tulle ribbon and she stopped at the gift shop for a card. Once at home, she pulled the Cherokee into the garage, unloaded the bike and proceeded to wrap it in a bow of tulle ribbon. She set it on the side of the garage by the workbench.

Next she loaded into the car several boxes and bags full of items she wanted to bring home. Donations had already been made to second-hand shops in town. The kitchen remained stocked with all the small appliances original to the house: the original mixer, the chrome toaster, the beehive blender. In the pink metal cabinets were the atomic melamine plates, the colorful Pyrex bowls, ample Tupperware for any family, though she did pack the frozen popsicle molds to go home with her. Every surface had been cleaned or polished. The attic had been sorted through and the rec-room, too. There was really nothing left to do.

Aesthetically, of the three beautiful paintings her mother had made for her, the one by the ocean would look the best over the carved wooden mantle in her carriage house, especially because she lived right on the shore of Lake Michigan. The painting of the ranch straight out of the mid-century would not go at all, and the farmhouse didn't quite have the look she would have chosen for her English Country decor, but considering the emotional weight of the oceanside painting, the picture of the farmhouse was going home with her. The others would remain in the closet for now.

Carefully, she set the painting of the farmhouse, wrapped in a sheet, on top of the boxes in the Cherokee. It fit just fine.

Room by room she surveyed her work, trying to be objective. With most of her mother's personal things either boxed up or given away, the clean, modern lines of the sleek furniture, the warmth of the many woods, the bright spots of oranges and blues and greens in pillows and upholstery, they all spoke loudly of their timelessness. How can it be, she wondered, that things last longer than people?

Despite the close proximity of Aidan's house, she wasn't about to walk there in her dress and heals. Instead, she drove to his house and parked in front of it. Only the Buick was in the driveway.

She knocked on the door. Had she ever knocked on his door as a child? Maybe on Halloween.

He was wearing a white shirt and black trousers, and she was sure she caught a muted hint of cologne.

"You look beautiful," he said, his eyes flicking over her hair in a french twist. "I like your hair that way."

The house was small and overflowing with overstuffed furniture that did not match. On the wall were pictures of the Pope and John F. Kennedy and Bobby Kennedy, with a rosary hanging alongside them. She tried not to widen her eyes.

He didn't miss a thing. "My mom has a thing about the Kennedy's. It's an Irish thing."

"They're right up there with the Pope I see."

"That's a Catholic thing. Again, my mom."

She nodded and followed him into the kitchen. A boom box sat on the kitchen table, playing classical music. "Vivaldi?" she asked. "Seriously?"

"I'm trying to have a little class," he said. "Continue on through the patio doors, please."

She stepped out onto a large, fairly new wooden deck. Lights twinkled in the branches above the deck. A small card table with a lace cloth on it sat in the middle, complete with candles, creamy white china and a bottle of wine. In the corner a heavy grill was smoking and the smell was amazing.

"Lovely," she said sincerely. He pulled out the chair and she sat down. She ran her hand across the tablecloth. "Irish lace. She let you use her best cloth no doubt."

"She did. With warnings not to spill and to serve white wine instead of red. I tried to tell her we're having steak, but she refused to listen. White wine it is."

"I'll be careful, I promise," she smiled up at him.

A strong breeze picked up the edges of the tablecloth. She smoothed it and looked around as Aidan brought out a basket of bread and a plate of cheese. The neighbor's houses were close and there was really no privacy at all.

They had just managed a toast to friendship when she felt a large plop of water on her arm and then another on her forehead and back.

"Do you feel that?" she asked.

He held his open palm up to the unexpected rain. "I did and I do." With a deep sigh he grabbed the bottle of wine. "I'll get the food, you get the dishes."

She moved the boom box to the coffee table in the front room, and spread the lace cloth on the kitchen table while he rescued the steaks from the sizzling grill. It was only a matter of minutes before they heard the thunder and it began to pour. By this time they were seated at the kitchen table, toasting again and eating his delicious meal while the front blew in.

With every bite, with every sip of wine and laugh they shared as they ate, she wanted this evening to last forever. "This is fun," she said. "A great way to end my vacation."

"You have one more day, right?"

"No, I decided to leave in the morning and have some time to get sorted out at home before work on Monday."

He carried their empty plates to the counter. "I didn't realize that. I was going to invite you to go to church with me tomorrow."

"I don't do church."

Aidan scraped their plates and put their dishes in the sink. "Why is that?"

She crossed her legs and quietly tapped the toe of one of her mother's black kitten heels agains the table leg. "I feel like we've been beating around this bush for the last two weeks." She tilted her head. "Which reminds me that we have also not gotten any clarity on our relationship, other than last night which wasn't much." She looked outside at the yellow lights above the deck, twinkling magically through the warbled, rain drenched patio door.

He held up the nearly empty bottle of wine. "Would you like more wine?"

"No," she said, her toe tapping increasing. Then she stopped. "They wouldn't be related, would they?"

"What?" He poured some dishsoap in the sink and turned on the faucet. "I'll let these soak."

"Your religion and our relationship."

He wiped his hands on a terry cloth towel hanging on the oven handle. "Let's talk about this in the front room," he said.

"I don't want to," she replied. Unbidden, tears filled her eyes. *You're not good enough.* She looked up and blinked to make them dry up and go away. When she looked at him, he was leaning against the stove, one foot crossed over the other, much like he had that first day at the clinic. Only now he wasn't looking at her. His arms were crossed and his eyebrows were furrowed as he looked intently at the floor.

Her heart hurt. It would burst if she didn't speak truthfully. "It's true, isn't it? You—us—this really special thing we have, you're holding back and the only thing that we don't have in common is your religion. I'm not good enough for you."

She stood up and walked over to him. He stood up straight. Her hands slid up the chest of his shirt, which was still slightly damp from the rain.

"This dinner, the lights, the music, the china, the wine, you're wooing me. So, don't tell me you aren't feeling what I'm feeling right now."

His eyes flicked over her hair and she felt him draw in his breath.

"You want me to take my hair down, don't you? Yes, you do. You want to hold me and kiss me and give into this, too, don't you?"

Lightly, she clasped her hands around his neck. She could feel his body automatically lean into hers, though his hands settled lightly on her shoulder blades. She had never felt so much like she belonged in a man's arms as she did at this moment.

"I can't do this," he said, his intense eyes looking back and forth into hers. "I do want you. More than I can say. This is killing me."

"But you can't give in. You *won't* give in."

He nodded. "I believe in waiting until marriage. I also believe that if we don't share the same faith, it won't work, no matter how good the sex is."

She flushed with anger. "How do you think that makes me—" She stopped, shocked as she saw tears fill *his* eyes and spill onto his shirt. She unclasped her hands and stood back. "What on earth?"

"You think it's easy for me to say no, to turn you down? You have no clue how hard it is. I tried to tell you." He walked out of the room, brushing the tears away.

She followed him into the front room. "Tell me what?"

He turned around. "Can we talk in my car? Or go for a drive? I don't want to argue in here."

She reached for her purse. "I'll leave if I upset you this much."

"Please don't, I want to talk."

She glared at him, frustrated by the confusion. "Fine. I'll drive."

"Okay."

The force of the storm was spent but the rain continued, gently but steadily. Apparently he felt as spent as she did, for she drove in silence, unsure of what to say or even where to go. She decided, spur of the moment, to head towards her grandparent's old farm. The roads twisted and turned. The houses grew further apart and then the cornfields and soybean fields spread out on either side of them.

"There," she pointed. "That drive right there is where my grandparents lived." On impulse, she turned up the long drive. She had done this just once, a long time ago, with her mother.

When she pulled in they could see lights on a large porch that wrapped around a big, green house. A dog barked.

"The barn looks just like it does in the painting," Aidan said.

She nodded and tried to envision the old farmhouse there. Her mother and the grandparents she never knew, how happy they were, how good their marriage and their life was. Except she couldn't imagine it now. The reality was not as good as the painting.

Slowly she turned the car around and headed back towards the main road, the wipers beginning to catch on the drying windshield. Once on the main road, she parked alongside the soybeans. She rolled down her window and turned to just look at him. He looked, to her satisfaction, as miserable as she felt.

"What are you doing? I know that neither one of us was planning to rekindle a childhood friendship, let alone begin to have feelings for each other, but despite the bad timing, I'm really hesitant to just walk away. It's not like me, but I don't want to just say goodbye."

He started slowly, "I don't know what to do. What we have *is* special. You are an incredible woman and I don't think you were expecting it any more than I was. But here it is. The bottom line is, I happen to have a relationship with God that is really important to me. I can't set that aside. I can't do it."

"Who is asking you to set it aside?"

"Greta, I'm totally committed to God. He has turned my life around and I am so grateful for that. He's the most important thing in my life."

"So now you're a priest?"

"It's not like that."

"The other day it was all about your career. You didn't want to be distracted. Remember that? Which is it?"

"I haven't gone looking for a relationship because my work has been all-consuming. I figured someday I'd get past this season and settle down and see if I could find someone who shares my faith. This—*this* is because I do have feelings for you and I'm trying to not hurt you by building more into this relationship when we don't share the same faith. That's the most important thing in my life, and we don't have that in common. Without that, I don't know that what we do have will last."

She sat there thinking about it. "I'm trying to understand. I haven't come across anyone like you before. That's pretty special, to me it is. It's a big deal. Why is the difference of our faith so important, compared to a rare connection? I don't get it."

"Do you see how much I've changed? That's not because of education or any career path. It's about God changing me from the inside out."

"I thought it was about Travis. You watched what he went through and that changed you."

"God used that to help me change," Aidan said. "Remember when I told you about stashing the drugs in a hotel? That car ride to the hotel and then the entire way back, I just prayed. I mean I literally cried out to God as I drove. I have never been more scared in my life. I had messed up big time. When I got back and found out what happened to Davey and Travis, I knew, *I just knew*, it was no accident that my mom was down in the basement that morning and made me late in getting to Davey's apartment with the money. Can you imagine how different my life would have been had I been there when the police came in? I could have been hit with a bullet. I might have panicked and picked up a gun. At the very least I could have been arrested for drug trafficking."

"So God rescued you and let you off the hook? That's why you follow God?"

"It's not like that," he said. "I can't tell you how often I felt guilty and almost wished I had been there. Why was I protected from that? I suddenly saw how much my family—my mom and dad, my aunt and uncle, and Davey and Travis—how destructive my choices had been to all of them. I was young and stupid, but that was no excuse. I didn't deserve a second chance, but when I reached out to God that day God was right there ready and waiting to help me. *Me.* A young, stupid kid with no future and no regard for anyone except myself and God was real for me, he was there for me."

"What do you mean he was there? How did he help you?"

"I didn't realize it at the time, but looking back from the moment I cried out to God, God began to take what was a desperate situation and turn it for my good rather than my destruction. Like I said the other day, I think God gave me a second chance. What made me decide to go see Travis instead of staying home with my parents when Davey was arrested? What made me think it was a good idea to then stay in Chicago with my aunt and uncle and end up helping Travis every single day for months and years? Where did that come from?"

He went on, "All I know is that I kept talking to God every day and began to read my Bible and go to church, and slowly I began to make different choices, choices that would please God instead of me. I began to try to implement what I was reading and learning before I understood it all, just because I believed it to be right. As I did that I kept getting stronger. My priorities changed. I began to be less selfish and more compassionate. I began to really care about people. Who I used to be, I didn't want that anymore. I felt horrible about the things I had done and so grateful that I no longer had to feel that shame and that guilt. I felt clean, like my mistakes and my parent's mistakes didn't define me or muddy me any more. For the first time in my life I had hope for my future. I didn't do that by myself. I'm not capable of that on my own."

She looked out the windshield where every so often a raindrop fell from the tree over them and trickled slowly down the glass. "I'm not a bad person. I'm not selfish. I try to be kind to others. I go the extra mile for people. My priorities are just fine."

"But you think you don't need God."

"Why should I?"

He leaned forward and put his hand on her knee. "Because he loves you. Because he knows all the things you've done that have pushed him away and all the ways you need him but don't want to admit. He knows what your parents have done that hurt you, and he wants to heal you. He loves you and wants a relationship with you."

"I'm feeling rather cynical," she said, looking him square in the eyes. "If there is a God, why would He love *me*?"

"God wants a relationship with you, Greta. He wants that for all of us. That's why He sent Jesus to die for everyone's sins, so we don't have to have our sins separating us from God. We're accountable for our sins, but Jesus came and said, 'I'll pay the price for their sins. God loves us so much that he let his only son go through all that for our sake. That's their gift to each one of us. It's a gift we choose to take, or leave."

"So that's where Jesus comes in. I never understood that. What is it about Jesus? There is so much controversy over him. I don't even feel comfortable saying his name."

"Jesus is both God and man. He gets how it is to be tempted and vulnerable and weak. Yet he would not sin, he had to be unblemished, sinless."

"That makes no sense."

"Yet the Bible confirms everything I've said in a thousand different ways. Wise men have studied it for centuries and found it to be absolutely true. I don't deny for a minute how hard it is to wrap my mind around this. Yet, I believe it to be true because the Bible says Jesus is the only one who has paid that price for us. Without accepting him and what he did for us, we can't be in relationship with God. That's why some people object to Jesus. They want to think they have another way to being close to God. But Jesus is it. He's the only way."

"And you think God and Jesus, they want to help me. Seriously?"

"He does, Greta. Before you were born, the Bible says he knit you together in your mom's womb. He knows how much you need him. You may not realize that today, but at some point in your life, I believe you will see God at work and you will either choose to trust him to do as he promises or choose not to trust him."

"I'm already not trusting him, though I can't say I've ever really needed him. I don't even know what that would look like. Besides, from what I know, my birth was actually quite a surprise."

"It was no accident, Greta. I believe that you were born for a purpose at that exact time, and the timing of all this, including you and me, it's all a part of God's plan for your life."

Tears pricked her eyelids. She refused to let them out but she could not deny the impact of his words. *You matter to God.*

"What is it?" Aidan asked.

"Nothing," she said.

"What you do with your life right now, it's important to God, Greta."

"I don't know what to do with my life," she said, trying to think clearly. "I'm feeling pretty foolish after telling you my brain just automatically strategizes everything. I've cleaned up my mom's house and I have to go back to work. It's all I know to do. But you want to know the truth? I'm going back a day early because I'm afraid that if I don't get to Chicago tomorrow, I won't make it into work on Monday. I don't want to deal with Carol ever again. I don't want to see my clients, or even have my house featured in another magazine." She looked at Aidan. "Can you believe it?"

His blue eyes were so kind. "I told you, I think you need more time off."

"I don't even know where I'd go! I can't think straight at all. In fact, I'm probably going to be mortified that I came on to you tonight, but you are the only thing that feels good and right in my life right now. Only I don't measure up to your religion. Well, I sure don't know where God figures in all this. To me, that's adding in one more complication and messes me up further."

Aidan said nothing, he just looked at her with more sympathy. This irked her. "And I don't know what to do with *you!* I didn't go looking for you! You're a complication I do not need on top of everything else. But here I am, telling you I think we have something special. I think you don't know what to do with your feelings for me. I think you're afraid of me. Which is ridiculous, by the way." She looked at him, willing her eyes to be as intense as his.

Apparently it worked, for he was the first to look away.

"I just want that clear," she said, reaching for even more clarity, "that I didn't go looking for you. I would also like it clear that when I did begin to have feelings for you, I did not pursue you. You have pursued me. I haven't called you, you've been calling me. You've said it was friendship but we both know better. Tonight, in your kitchen, I did that because I wanted it out in the open. I wanted you to admit that you are just as aware as I am what's happening here. And," she pointed her finger at herself, "I want it clear that I had the guts to admit it first."

HIs voice was so soft she had to lean forward to hear him, "I knew it the first time I saw you," he said.

"Knew what?"

His voice grew stronger, "The moment at the clinic when you walked in and sat down, I put down my coffee and I looked up and there you were. I knew who you were. I remembered you. I had a crush on you back in the day, but so did a lot of other guys. You were always way out of my league. I took one look at you that day and I knew…"

"Knew what?" she asked again.

He shook his head.

"Knew what?"

"I realized I was in way over my head. Who was I that you would look at me? Yet there you were, just a few feet away and I thought, 'If she doesn't see you, then just sit down and don't embarrass yourself. But if she sees you and says something, go for it.' So I did. You know, I don't think I even touched my coffee after that. I saw you and nothing else after that."

She sat up in her seat. "You admit you feel this—what we have every time we're together—and you don't want to pursue it? You're willing to walk away. Why now? If you think we're so far apart in our goals, why didn't you walk away before this? Shouldn't you have walked away if you value your faith so highly?"

"I kept telling myself we could just be friends."

"Yet tonight you set up a romantic evening."

"I did. I told myself it was just easier and nicer to eat at home. But really I wanted to have a special evening with you before you left. It's what I want, even though I know that ultimately we are very different and we will end up hurting each other."

"Yet you go ahead and send me double messages, which is hurtful right there. You're doing that. Even after we talked last night. In fact you're doing it right now."

"Yes. I'm sorry. I'm sending you double messages and confusing you."

"You are messed up."

"I am. I'm so sorry."

"It makes me feel like I'm garbage. Like I'm some temptation to you that is bad. Who does that?"

"I did that."

"Yes, you did!"

"I'm so sorry. You are not garbage," he apologized. "You're a woman way out of my league and I am messed up and I want to protect you from getting hurt and yet selfishly I want to be with you every minute of every day."

"I'm telling you I'm willing to get involved for the first time in years. Does this mean nothing to you? This is completely out of character for me."

"I know," he said, looking down.

She leaned over and lifted his chin so he could see her eyes. "I am not the kind of woman who throws herself at a guy. This connection we have is something special, Aidan. This is the last time I'm going to say it. This—we are—*really, really* special. Do you not see that?"

"I do see it. I would love nothing more than to—to slip back into old ways. But I know that we would connect over sex and how would we know then if we really could make it work without sex? That can't be the glue that binds us together. Our faith in God has to be that glue. That way, no matter how bad things might get down the road, we would do the right thing, love each other well in the end, despite our imperfections, because God would be helping us."

His eyes were pleading with her. "You know how you can look at a client's needs and see exactly what you have to do? I see that with us. I know how good this is and I know how much it will hurt if we don't have the same love for God. It will hurt that much more because we feel this way about each other."

She sat back behind the wheel. "*Whatever.*"

"Greta, if we begin a serious relationship and trouble comes, which it will, where will you go for help? I watched my parents fight and make a mess of everything because they had no answers, they had no idea what they were doing. I don't blame them for having troubles, I blame them for their reaction to them. My dad always turned to alcohol and my mom turned to perpetual discontent. She became bitter and angry and a victim. I grew up in a house without hope. Nothing changed, it just grew worse."

"What about the Pope on the wall? Didn't that help?"

"A picture on a wall does not equate with a life lived trusting and following God."

"How do you know that? Maybe to her it does."

"My mom doesn't pray or know what the Bible says. She's only heard it in Latin and she doesn't care what it says in English. She would rather hold onto her bitterness than learn more about how God can help her move on."

"That's getting personal."

"Faith is personal. It transforms us from the inside out. That's why people are called Christians, they follow Christ, they become Christ-like. If you and I don't have that transformation and hope as our common goal, we will end up messing up our lives and the lives of our kids."

She grew quiet. "Isn't that what all parents do?"

"I do not want to be at odds with my wife or my kids, or my God. I want to be side by side with my wife, a real team, with the same goals of pleasing God and living with a common hope that at least shows our kids that God is good and His ways are helpful and meaningful."

"I don't know what to say. I've never thought about this and clearly you have. It's a much different perspective on marriage. I have to admit that I respect you for thinking that far ahead. I will have to think about all of this."

"You're an incredible woman, Greta, incredible."

Her laugh was short and angry, "If this is where you try to let me down easily, it's not necessary. I don't need it."

"I have messed this up so badly, I don't know what else to say. I'm trying to be absolutely honest and transparent because I think it's the right thing to do but I'm afraid I'm just making it worse."

This level of honesty, it should hurt more, she thought. But it doesn't. It just makes me want him more. Another painful reminder of how good together they were. She started the car and headed back to his house.

"Good night," he said as he got out.

"Have a good life," she said.

He turned as if to look at her. And then he stopped, turned and walked away.

4

The first thing she did the next day when she arrived at her home in Glencoe was to take down the Impressionistic painting above the mantle and replace it with her mother's painting of the farmhouse. It represented her grandparent's lives, her heritage, and her mother's love and her mother's incredible talent. She loved it there.

Next, she checked her voicemails. She was not surprised when Carol's voice greeted her, "I'm calling you at home because I don't want to bother you while you're on vacation. However, I do want you to get this as soon as you return. A woman keeps calling here, Denise Arthur. She says you called her but got sick or something and had to hang up. Is that correct? What is she talking about? Let me know. And for Pete's sake, call her back."

And the next message, "Greta, it's Carol again. This woman, Denise Arthur, she's driving Sophie nuts with her nonstop calls. Please call her back right away. "

The third message stunned her. "Greta, Vincent Morales just called me. It's Sunday morning about ten o'clock. You may recall Vinnie is from the mayor's office. He's a lawyer, one of the many who represents Mayor Bailey. Edward did the design for Vinnie's law offices about two years ago. Remember that? Denise Arthur knows the Baileys. Apparently she spoke with Phyllis Bailey, who remembered we did Vinnie's offices, and Phyllis called Vinnie and told him to make this happen. You're being requested to go out to the Arthur's house as soon as possible."

Greta dialed Carol's number immediately. "Hi, Carol, it's Greta."

"Am I ever glad you're home!" Carol said. "Have you called Denise Arthur back yet?"

"No, I just finished listening to your voicemails. I'm stunned."

"I can imagine. Vinnie told me Denise Arthur's father is a senator in New York. Senator Arthur has vacationed several times with Mayor Bailey and his wife. Not only that, her father is a close friend of the President."

Greta was taken aback. *"The United States President?"*

"Yes."

She exhaled loudly. "I had no idea."

"I understand the house is on Martha's Vineyard. I recommend you call Denise to confirm and book your flight today. Don't worry about the expenses, but at the same time, make sure we make a good profit on this. I think you better clear your calendar."

"You're aware of how full my calendar is right now?"

"I do. I acquired another intern last week and I'm looking at hiring someone else full-time."

"Carol, that's great news."

"Yes, well, the connections this Arthur woman has could help us tremendously. Whatever she wants, you make it happen."

Of the hundreds if not thousands of home consultations she had made in her career, finding Denise Arthur's house in the town of Gay Head on the island of Martha's Vineyard promised to be the most challenging. Flying from O'Hare to Boston had not been a problem. Renting a car and driving from Boston to Cape Cod and then driving to the town of Woods Hole was not difficult. The reservation for the rental car on the ferry to Martha's Vineyard in the middle of the busiest month for tourism, a reservation Greta could not obtain from the Steamship Authority because they said it was completely booked, forcing her to call Denise to let her know how impossible it was, apparently wasn't completely impossible if you had the right connections, thank you, Denise. Getting in line at Woods Hole and waiting for the ferry was not really difficult. She felt a bit special knowing strings had been pulled to reserve her rental car a space on the ferry.

Parking the rental car like a sardine among the other cars on the ferry was harrowing. Sitting outside on the upper deck for the 45 minute ferry ride to the island was thrilling and worth the tangled, humid mess her hair was becoming in the sea air.

Fighting the traffic and almost getting killed trying to get out of the mangled mess of cars, bikes, and motor bikes in Vineyard Haven, where the ferry docked, was alarming and a jolt after her romantic visions of a bucolic island waiting to greet her.

Following the map to go up-island to the furthermost tip of Gay Head was no simple task either. For one, she wanted to take her time and look at all the houses. She could not. Not only did she not have time, the farther she got from Vineyard Haven the fewer houses were visible from the road. Apparently people named their houses out here, a charming custom, because there were all kinds of rustic signs with enticing names on them that led down mysterious dirt roads, but the houses were well-hidden behind pine trees and scrub bushes and years and years of undergrowth.

In fact, the farther from town she got, the more the island looked like the woods of Wisconsin, only definitely more quirky. When she finally found the road that Denise had described as their driveway, it was hard to believe anyone could possibly call it a road. It was as smooth as the proverbial bumpy old washboard. She grimaced as the rental car bounced along this way and that, down bend after bend of skinny pine tree groves that never seemed to end.

Ahead, the drive narrowed and then circled and she could see the gray shingles of a huge house. Behind it the horizon was all blue sky, unbroken by trees. She turned off the car and got out. No, that wasn't just sky, it couldn't be. Indeed, it was ocean, too, beautiful beyond words.

She grabbed her bag and camera. Her car door wasn't even closed yet when a woman bounded out of the house, followed by a golden retriever and a husband. The dog got to her first.

She took a deep breath as she leaned down to pet the dog. *Talk about feeling out of your league. Nothing for it but to give it my best.*

She stood up tall and straight. "Hi," she waved to the couple. "I'm Greta."

Denise was slight, with curly brown hair that skimmed her shoulders. She was not quite pretty, but her makeup-free skin was fresh and healthy. She appeared to be a little older than Greta, yet her voice had a distinct little girl sound to it.

Her handshake was warm and firm. "Hello, welcome to the Vineyard! This is my husband, Pemberton DeWitt, but please, call him Pem."

"Nice to meet you," Greta smiled. Pem's handshake was cool, reticent, but his smile was friendly. He was tall and thin, and his light brown hair was a mass of unruly curls.

"And your dog? What's its name?"

Denise laughed, "She's not ours. Goldie belongs to a neighbor a few houses down. She comes and goes as she pleases around here. We all love her."

"Come on in," Pem said. "We can't wait to show you the house."

"How long has it been in the family?" Greta asked, taking in the worn gray shingles of the large two story house.

Denise led the way to the door, "My great-grandfather bought the property in the late 1800's and built on it right away, but it's been added on to several times since then."

As they stepped inside the years fell away and it took Greta no more than a few seconds to get a sense of just how special it was. The wallpapered walls, comfy arm chairs, braided rugs and Windsor chairs, watercolors and oils of ships and boats, a fireplace flanked by sagging chintz loveseats that were decades old. Still, it was the warmest, most inviting home she'd ever seen.

"I can see why you love it," she said sincerely.

"I knew you'd see it," Denise said. "I just knew it! Even though some of it has never been updated, it's kept its charm. Come, we'll show you around."

They walked through rooms filled with priceless antiques and worn furniture, rich paintings and yellowed childish drawings and aging popsicle stick birdhouses alongside polished silver pitchers filled with flowers. She spied nothing in the entire two floors, the addition for the maid's quarters and the addition of the sunroom, that screamed wealth, yet nothing was cheap or useless or unloved.

"My mother summered here as a child, too. They came in June and left in September. This was her favorite place in the whole world. She left it to me when she died. I'm ready to bring it up to date but as you can see, it's overwhelming. I don't know how to make it cohesive and fresh. We really need your help."

Greta was taking notes as fast as she could. "What are you hoping it will look like and feel like when we're done?"

Pem spoke first, "I get claustrophobic in here. When we have friends over the rooms are much too small to entertain the way we like. People are scattered everywhere because other than the lawn and the beach, there's no one room large enough for us to gather."

"I'm a little nervous about tearing down walls," Denise said. "I wouldn't mind taking down the dining room wall, as it would open up into the living room, but Pem thinks the wall separating the kitchen and dining room could go, too. What do you think?"

"Let's take a look," Greta said, and headed for the kitchen.

For a few moments she assessed the many details and factors. "It does appear to be a viable option, and if you like to entertain and cook, it's always nice to have your friends in the kitchen with you. They can help and it's much more congenial," Greta said. "At the same time, your kitchen is quite large already. If we open up the kitchen, dining room, and living room, the scale of this portion of the house will be much different from the scale of the other side, with the library, den and sunroom. I'm afraid it would feel like two different homes. That's defeating your desire to make the house more cohesive. We possibly could open up the den to the library, though I would hate to see that, as the paneling in the library is gorgeous. We'll never be able to accurately match it to make it blend with the den. Also, if we tried to do that, the sunroom won't feel balanced unless we expand its footprint, too. Then I think the lower level of the house as a whole would be cohesive, but it will change the character of the lower level. It would lose some of its charm, and that must be considered."

Pem jumped in. "I think opening up the entire downstairs would be brilliant. It would be so much more expansive and contemporary."

"But it would feel no different from a house anywhere else," Denise said. "This is the island. It's not suburbia. I don't want to lose everything that makes this place special." She turned to Greta, "What do you think?"

"Let's start from a different perspective. Generally speaking, first I recommend removing the wallpapers and going with paint colors in soft beiges and whites with some differing shades of blue on the first floor. It will really bring the sky and ocean colors inside, and we can carry those colors into the smaller rooms to help them feel larger and tied in with the other rooms. But the library with those paneled walls is just a treasure. I would change very little in there. Taking down the wall between the dining room and living room will be sufficient in opening up the main floor. Taking down the kitchen wall, too, would create a domino effect of changes that may not really be necessary. As far as any further more specific recommendations, I'll need time to put them all together for you."

She glanced at Pem to see his reaction. His eyes flashed in anger and then it was gone so fast she wondered if perhaps she had misread him. Neither one of them said anything. She could only assume they wanted to discuss this later, in private.

Greta went on in hopes of minimizing any conflict. "Is the house just for use during the summer?"

"Oh, no," Denise said. "I come out as often as I can. We always come out in August, and for several long weekends in June and July and even September. Pem can't always make the weekends, his job is so demanding. But we do try to come out for Thanksgiving and sometimes even for a break in the winter."

"So you don't just want a summer house, you want it to be enjoyable year round."

"Yes," Denise said. "We really need your help with that, too. We don't know how to make that bridge between a summer home and a year-round home. It has always looked like a year-round home with all the old-fashioned curtains and rugs and furniture. How do we make it look fresh for summer and yet warm enough for year round?"

"The lighter paint colors will help tremendously in making it feel fresh for summer. Then finding just the right fabrics for the sofas and chairs and window treatments will be important. The correct texture and weight of those fabrics, and then layering them in the fall and winter, that will make all the difference. I highly recommend swapping out a lightweight area rug for a more traditional, heavier one, in the fall, and maybe even switching out a painting or two, as well as seasonal accessories of course. It used to be quite common to do these things, but I think some trends have traded style for convenience. With an island home such as this, one that you want to use for all seasons, I recommend taking a morning or afternoon to swap things out in the fall and then again in the spring, or perhaps after the new year, depending on how often you'll be here in the winter. It can be lots of fun with the easier items, like bringing out heavier throws and quilts and pillows and candles to make it cozy."

"That's simple enough," Denise said. "I can do that."

"Yes, you can," Greta said. "It just takes getting into the habit of looking at the rooms as each new season approaches and then planning out what you're going to do."

"We have another issue," Pem said. "The views up here are spectacular. So many ocean-view houses have nothing on their windows. I don't want the view blocked, but Denise wants privacy."

Denise nodded, "I do like my privacy. Our beach below is private, but it's right next to a public beach. We don't get many strangers up here but when we do, I like the option of shutting them out. As we improve the house, I don't want everything we have to be on display."

"We have an alarm system for that now," Pem said. "No one is going to break in again."

"Last winter we had someone break in," Denise explained. "It was the strangest thing. They slept in our bed and used food we had in the freezer. We had some things stolen, small things, nothing too valuable. There was no sign of anything destroyed or vandalized. We didn't find out until we came in May. We hadn't been here since the beginning of January. We had an alarm company come out right away and install a system." She shuddered. "It still feels creepy."

"I'm sorry to hear that," Greta said, thinking of her mother's house. "It sounds like leaving the house empty is risky."

"Our caretaker says it happens all the time. It's just one of the hazards of owning a vacation home," Pem said.

"No," Denise said slowly, "he said it only happens maybe once or twice a year on the entire island. If the vandals live on the island, they know that most of the nicer homes have caretakers who regularly check them. That's why it was unusual, because our caretaker regularly checks the house. It's as if they knew his schedule and avoided him."

"Regardless," Pem said, "I would like to see the windows bare so the view is appreciated."

Greta's heart skipped a beat as she recognized the power struggle playing out in front of her. She hated this part of the job, but it was a constant. "I understand," she nodded. "I'll see what I can do. We may need to take it on a room by room basis. I'll find some options for you. But first we need to talk details like budget and timelines."

They sat at the kitchen table and went over the definite must-haves. It was good to know even the ultra-rich and connected had budgets, even if their budget was doubtless one of the most generous budgets Greta had yet encountered. Carol, she thought, will be quite happy.

However, when it came to the timeline it was a much different story. "Done by November 1?" she repeated in astonishment. "That's quite ambitious, even if we just stick to taking down the one wall."

"We want to have Thanksgiving here," Denise said, her eyes filling with tears. "My mom died last year on Thanksgiving, and we want this year to be special. All our loved ones are coming."

How could one say no to that? "Considering all the work on the walls and floors and kitchen, we'll need several reliable crews," Greta said, nervously addressing the one aspect of this job she couldn't control. She had no contacts of her own out here and dependable crews were critical to meeting deadlines. "Do you have contacts with crews here, on the island, who can help make this happen?"

Pem said, "We have several people we can call, depending on the work we need done. They live here year round and they're good craftsmen. You won't find better anywhere."

She was still doubtful. "Won't they be booked this far into the summer? I imagine everyone would want to get work done while they're out here for the season."

"I can usually pull some strings," Denise said, smiling.

"That you can," Greta laughed. She assessed quickly. "If I work onsite for several weeks, I can oversee the major installations and changes and then come out for a few days weekly or bi-weekly in order to have the rest done. If you can extend the deadline to just before Thanksgiving, that would give me an extra three weeks. I will need it. It may be close but if we get enough crews and they stay on schedule, we can do it."

"Marvelous," Pem said. "That will work."

Denise nodded. "Yes, I agree." Then she reached out her hand towards Greta. "If you're going to come out here often, we want you to stay with us. I think you'll love the Daggett House Inn, but we could only get you in there for this week. If you would like, you're welcome to stay here after that. You saw the maid's quarters. My mom had them built. We won't be using them. You are welcome to use them as your own apartment and office for as long as you're here."

Pem agreed. "It's the least we can do considering how hard we tried to get you here."

"I appreciate your offer and I can see how important this house is to you," Greta said. "I get it."

Denise blushed. "I'm sorry I went overboard getting you here. Somehow I just knew you were the one to help us. I may have been a little overenthusiastic, but this means so much to me. I'm so happy you're here and can do this for us."

"This is a such a special project," Greta said. "I'm happy to help you. Staying here while I work looks like a perfect solution."

"Now," Denise said, "before you get too focused on all the work ahead of you, come outside and see the ocean."

Greta tried not to show her excitement. "I would love to see it."

They walked outside through the old French doors in the kitchen. The patio led to an expansive yard that was surprisingly plain but the view was absolutely stunning. "We're going to have the patio and yard redesigned," Denise said. "Our friend next door is coming out to the island shortly and will give us some ideas. We want to tie it into the path here that leads down to the ocean. Let me show you."

The lawn gently sloped down to a path that was hidden from view above. Below it, Greta could hear the loud waves hitting the shore, much louder than the gentle waves of Lake Michigan in her backyard. A wooden boardwalk lined the steep incline to the beach below. Beach roses and tall grasses grew along the boardwalk all the way down to the beach. As they approached the end of the walk, she lifted her eyes. The vast ocean spread across the entire horizon before her.

The power and beauty of the water, sky, and clouds just poured over her. She could not get enough of it.

"Wow."

"It never gets old, trust me," Denise sighed.

She wanted to feel the water on her legs and even dive in and feel the rush of the waves. She settled with slipping off her shoes and walking to the edge of the waters as they flattened across the stones and sand. It was heavenly. Maybe her restoration could begin here. She looked at Denise, who had done the same and was standing beside her. "You know," she said to Denise, "this is really a tough job but someone has do it. I'm so glad you have good connections in Chicago!"

The three of them laughed together. Greta noticed how Denise's face lit up when she smiled. She was pretty; here by the water she seemed to come alive.

By dinnertime Greta was exhausted from all the measuring and drawing she had done. She was anxious to get to her hotel room. Kindly, Pem pulled out a local map from a drawer in the kitchen filled with tourist information. He highlighted her route to the hotel in Edgartown.

The drive to downtown Edgartown was longer than she realized and finding a parking spot for the Daggett House Inn took several turns around the same block before she got a lucky space.

The young girl who led her to her room gave her a brief history, "This inn has roots from before the Revolutionary War. The dining area here used to be a tavern. Your room is the special hidden staircase room, used to hide people during the war. The access is hidden. Can you guess where it may be?"

Greta nodded towards the row of bookcases. "It must have something to do with them."

Sure enough, the hostess pulled on a bookcase, the door opened and everyone seated in the low-ceilinged dining room stopped talking and watched as the hostess led her up the winding narrow staircase that led to her small, quaint, sunlit room.

As soon as the girl left, Greta dropped her suitcase and bag on the floor and dropped herself on the four poster bed. Though the room was charming, she didn't bother looking around. Instead, she kicked off her shoes, pulled out a pillow from beneath the blue plaid bedspread, and turned onto her stomach and fell asleep.

Was it the sounds of laughter drifting in through the windows or the wonderful smells of food wafting up the staircase that woke her? She wasn't sure. Her watch said it was late, almost ten o'clock. Her stomach rumbled. She really needed to eat. Quickly, she washed her face, brushed her hair and found her sandals. She went downstairs, slowly opened the secret door, then tried to ignore the curious stares of the few remaining dinner guests as she slipped through the dining room. She found a waitress.

"Do you happen to have any openings for dinner?"

"Sorry," the waitress said, "the kitchen is closed. If you want to eat here you really need to make a reservation in advance this time of year."

"Next time," Greta sighed.

The Edgartown lighthouse was not far away at all. As beautiful as it was, what she really wanted was food. Crowds of people browsed through the stores and milled on the sidewalks, even this late at night. Pretty things were plentiful but food was not. She had to settle for some gourmet crackers and jam from a little shop filled with rather touristy items. Though several more stores tempted her with pretty clothes and jewelry, it was not the time.

She took another street back towards the Daggett House and she was glad she did. A beautiful row of Greek Revival houses lined the street with hydrangeas nodding gently over picket fences. The glow of lights within the homes tempted her to stand and look into their beautiful rooms but she minded her manners and didn't stare. The sea air was cool and salty. In a word, it was all quite heady and kept her vividly aware that she really was on an island surrounded by the Atlantic ocean.

However, as she climbed the stairs to her room, all she could think of was her last dinner with Aidan in his mother's small kitchen while it rained and she looked at the warbled lights in the trees through the rain-streaked patio doors. That was heady, too. She shook her head to dispel the image. It was a world away, despite the fact it had been just days ago. Still, the memory lingered.

By the week's end she felt like one of Denise's and Pem's family members. They gave her a key to the house and she had permission to come and go without needing to knock. Both made sure she had lots to eat and let her set up office in one of the bedrooms in the otherwise empty maid's quarters. Pem even hooked up an old computer for her in case she needed it. When they left to run errands or go down to the beach, she had the house to herself. Room after room she sat down in and contemplated and drew in her sketch book. She brought her paint samples to every room and debated and debated. Several times while engrossed in her work she was surprised by the soft fur of Goldie at her feet. Often the retriever followed her and engaged her to play fetch with soggy tennis balls.

She was engrossed in a sketch of the redesign for the master bedroom on the second floor when she heard Goldie barking and an unfamiliar voice below calling out for Pem and Denise. She went downstairs and found a man walking through the kitchen.

"Hi, can I help you?" she asked.

"I'm looking for Pem and Denise," he said. "I live next door."

Goldie jumped on him and licked his face, tail wagging. Clearly, she knew him well.

"They shouldn't be too much longer but I don't know for sure when they'll be back," she said. "I can tell them you stopped by."

"That would be great." He extended a hand to her. "Jake Bernstein."

She shook his hand. His brown eyes were warm and friendly. "Nice to meet you, Jake. I'm Greta Little."

"I told them I would help them out with the design of their patio, so I'll show myself out and take a look. I may be here a while but I'll be outside."

"Oh, that's great!" she said. "I know they're anxious to get that going. Do you design outdoors spaces? Is that your business?"

He chuckled and patted Goldie. "Not really. I mean, yes, I do, but I'm better known for buildings. I'm an architect. I just offered to help them out because we're close friends and our families have lived next-door to each other for eons."

"Oh," she said, "I'm sorry. I didn't know."

Jake Bernstein, did she know him? His name sounded familiar. She was thunderstruck. "You're *Jacob* Bernstein! You designed the Garrison building in downtown Chicago! I met you at the grand opening three years ago!"

He looked her up and down. "We've met before?"

"It was just a brief introduction. I'm an interior designer. I did the design for the Garrison penthouse."

HIs eyes widened. "Yes! I remember now! You did!"

"You know that?"

He smiled and scratched Goldie's ears some more. "Originally, I was supposed to design the penthouse. I backed out when Keith Garrison got behind in paying his bills and Olivia Garrison kept arguing about the vision for the penthouse. I'd had enough."

"I did hear some rumors to that effect."

"Did you ever get paid?"

"Eventually. I didn't have to go after it, my boss did."

"How did you like working with the Garrisons?"

"Never again."

"Exactly my thoughts! I must say, your design was impressive. You gave them what they wanted and at the same time you honored the space. You walked a fine line. I respected you for that. Olivia enjoyed showing me your work."

"That means a lot coming from you! But," she added, "it's one of those projects that I didn't want to advertise, you know? The final result was definitely more a reflection of her taste than mine, which is fine, but I don't want people thinking I was responsible for all of it."

"Oh, yes, we've all been there."

They turned as Goldie ran barking to the backdoor where Denise and Pem were coming up the path to the house. Jake went outside to greet them. Through the kitchen window, Greta watched in amazement as the friends hugged and greeted each other. Jacob Bernstein, *the Jacob Bernstein* was right there with his tousled brown hair, in shorts and a t-shirt, and Birkenstock sandals. He looked like the guy next door, nice-looking, normal and easy going. Except he was a genius. Who had just complimented her design of the Garrison penthouse. *Inconceivable.*

While he got to work outside, Greta continued to work inside. Part of her itched to go out there and listen to their conversation. She wanted to hear his ideas, the way he processed and created. Surely he would know that she had studied his work intensely as she worked on the Garrison penthouse. One couldn't design the penthouse without trying to honor the architect who created it. Which had he graduated from, Yale or Harvard? She couldn't recall, but she did remember that after graduating he was invited to work at Rem Koolhaas's Office of Metropolitan Architecture in the Netherlands, known for their innovation and exceptional pool of talent. He had long since left there and established his own firm but his roots were clearly evident.

She scowled as she sketched. Their outdoor space should be an extension of the interior. How did one interject themselves into a conversation with Jacob Bernstein?

Just then they came back in. "Greta," Jake said from her office door, "I'd like to hear your ideas for the interior and see how we might collaborate. Would you be comfortable with that?"

"I thought you'd never ask," she smiled.

They walked the yard several times. His questions about her vision for the interior were respectful. As she had tried to honor his design for the Garrison building, he was being kind and honoring her design for this home.

"Stay for dinner," Denise insisted at the end of the day. "Jake is getting some lobsters from Poole's. I've got fresh fruit and veggies from the farmer's market and Pem's going to make some of his famous frozen cocktails. We'll eat down at the beach."

"I don't want to intrude," Greta objected.

"You're not," Denise replied. "It will be fun! Plus, we've got a whole closet full of swimsuits and beach coverups in the bedroom by your office. Go find something that fits. We'll all go swimming."

By the time Jake came back with the lobsters she had wrapped up her work and changed into a simple black swimsuit and wore a white embroidered coverup over it. She helped Pem carry down an armful of towels and tablecloths to the beach. In the sand was a freshly dug pit loaded with wood.

"We'll be glad for the fire later," Pem said. He helped her spread out the towels and tablecloths. Denise came down the wooden boardwalk with a tray of fruit and crackers. "Pem," she called, "There's a phone call for you up at the house. It's a woman, I didn't recognize her voice."

"Okay," he called. "I'll get it and bring back some sand chairs."

Denise set the platter down on a tablecloth. "Do you like to swim?"

"I love to swim," Greta said. "I was on the swim team in high school."

"Then let's go!" Denise said.

They left their sandals and coverups on the towels and ran towards the water. The salt water felt like heavy silk on her legs. She dove under and surfaced on the other side of an incoming wave. Denise surfaced beyond the wave, too. The two of them dove again and began to swim together. At last they stopped and Greta flipped on her back. "I want to just float awhile," she called to Denise. Denise flipped over, too.

Lazily they floated apart and then one of them would paddle closer again and then float side by side, only to drift and repeat again and again.

Greta glanced towards the shore. "Except for Pem and Jake, the beach is completely empty!"

Denise kicked her feet a little. "It's so private here."

"It's gorgeous," Greta said. "Absolutely gorgeous."

"I don't take it for granted. I never have and I never will."

Greta looked over at her with growing admiration. "I believe you." She looked away again, rather taken aback. She hadn't realized how thin Denise really was.

"We better head back," Denise said. "It looks like Jake has steamed the lobsters."

They swam back to shore.

"It's a feast!" she exclaimed as she looked at the spread of food atop baskets and the tablecloths. Jake threw her a towel. "Come on, sit down. The lobsters are perfect."

Glasses clinked as they toasted the night and the ocean and good food. They ate slowly, digging every morsel of the rich meat out of the lobsters. Whether it was the salty air, the goodness of fresh seafood or the laughter and camaraderie surrounding her, Greta had never enjoyed a meal so much.

Afterwards, they cleaned up and then the four of them ran into the waves together, splashing and screaming like children. They came out a long time later, exhausted and breathing heavily from the playing and the constant push of the ocean waves. The tide was coming in and the sun was getting low in the sky.

"You know the sun turns green here, just before it dips below the horizon," Jake said to her.

She pulled her coverup over her damp suit. "Really? Is that exclusive to the island?"

"It is. I make sure I catch it every night while I'm here."

"I'm looking forward to seeing it," she said, and sat down next to him on the sand. "I would love to learn more about your work," she said, hoping she didn't sound like a groupie.

"His firm just won a competition in Switzerland," Pem offered. "What are you building there?"

"An international bank of course," Jake replied. "Speaking of, how is your father doing?"

Denise leaned forward, "Greta, Pem and his father are in banking in New York. "

"Father hasn't been out to the island once this summer." Pem drained the last of his cocktail. "He's too busy making money with the merger. More anyone?"

They declined, but Pem unscrewed the metal mixer resting in the ice bucket and poured himself another drink.

"Hey, let's go for a walk," Jake said. He stood up. "The guys at the fish market were saying some lobster traps are loose. Let's see if we can find them."

Denise moved closer to Pem on the blanket. "I'm going to stay here."

Jake reached out his hand to Greta. She let him pull her up, then she brushed off the damp sand. They walked a while in silence.

"How well do you know Pem and Denise?" he asked.

"I just met them this week," she said.

"Are you staying at their house?"

"I work from there, but I'm thinking about staying with them, too. They did invite me. Honestly, I don't know if I have much choice. I'm at the Daggett House until next Tuesday. Getting a last minute reservation for any length of time anywhere out here is impossible."

He looked ahead, down the long, darkening stretch of beach. "Let me guess. Denise insisted, last minute, and the money, no offense, was such that you were persuaded to try to accommodate her."

"The money and her connections. My boss insisted."

"Just be careful."

"What do you mean?" She noticed his eyebrows furrow and the frown on his face was disconcerting.

"I just want to give you a—a heads up to, to well, be careful."

She tried to laugh. "It seems like you're trying to tell me something without telling me something."

He stopped walking and turned to look at her, crossing his arms as he did so. "Look, they're my friends. I hardly know you. I think, however, from one professional to another, I owe you the courtesy of giving you something of a heads up. In our work we get to know people on a deeply personal level, maybe designers even more so than architects. So with this couple, keep some distance."

"Thank you, but don't you think I deserve to know what you mean by that?"

He relaxed his arms and kicked the sand. "You're right, you do. There's a lot of booze and a lot of dysfunction between the two of them. I love Denise, she's like a sister to me. I'd do anything for her. She and Pem have been together since college. He's an addiction to her. But he isn't aways kind."

"I must say, this is quite a surprise."

"I don't want to betray their friendship, but I feel like I need to warn you."

"They've been wonderful so far. I saw a little power struggle at first, but that's normal."

"Well, the closer you get, the more you'll see."

"I can't leave. They want everything done by Thanksgiving. I need to be onsite for at least a few days of the week. We've got crews scheduled already. I can fly back and forth but that has its drawbacks, too."

"You'll figure it out," he said. "Just be careful. Hey—look—there it goes!"

She looked out across the water at the red opaque sun sliding into the ocean. "Ah, nary a touch of green," she noted.

"Maybe tomorrow night."

When they returned, they found the fire glowing but no sign of Pem and Denise.

Jake reached for a blanket and shook off the sand. "I'm not ready to go in yet. Would you like to sit for a while?"

"I would," she said, her calm belying the excitement she felt at the surreal scene around her. A fire crackling in the sand. Waves breaking just feet away from them. An empty stretch of stunning beach. And *the* Jacob Bernstein her companion. Never in a million years, she thought. She looked up. Oh, and moon rising and the stars beginning to shine. She sighed more loudly than she intended.

"I'll second that," Jake said. He laid down and stretched out his long legs and folded his hands behind his head to support it. "It's been a week."

"What did your week look like?" she asked, leaning back on her hands, knees bent.

"Let's see, I left a team in Switzerland on Monday. Left another team in Japan on Wednesday night. Spent a few hours in California with my folks on Thursday, arrived in New York this morning and flew straight here."

"You're still functioning?"

"Barely. If I fall asleep, I apologize. Tell me about your week."

"A week ago I was back in central Illinois closing up my mom's house. She passed away a year ago and I just had too much going on to get it in order. So, I just spent two weeks trying to catch up on that. I got back to Chicago on Sunday and found out Denise had convinced my boss I needed to be out here on Monday. I made it on Tuesday. Now, here I am. This may not be as far as California or even Switzerland or Japan, but it's a long way from the cornfields of Illinois, I can tell you that."

"I'm sorry about your mom's passing. Were you close?"

"We were."

"Is your dad still alive?"

She caught her breath. She'd been trying not to think about him. "I don't know. He left twenty years ago. I understand he lived out here for a few years, back in the early 60's. He might still be out here, who knows? I may look him up someday, but for now I want to focus on the work."

He turned towards her on his side. "What's your father's name? My family has been out here for decades."

"Karl Little. He was a caretaker for several families."

"The name isn't familiar," Jake said. "I'll ask our caretaker if he knows of him but I know my guy is newer out here."

"Thanks, that would be nice."

"Sure. Are you up for another log on the fire?"

"I could stay out here all night," she laughed. "You sure you can stay awake?"

He threw a log into the flickering coals. "Oh, I think I so."

They made it through two more logs before she caught him yawning. "That's it." She got up and poured sand on the fire. Then she reached out her hand to encourage him to get up.

Reluctantly he let her pull him up. "I'm going, I'm going."

They shook out the blankets and slowly headed up the boardwalk. She kicked something in the dark and stumbled. His hand on her waist caught her. "What was that?"

She bent down. "It's an empty bottle. It looks like vodka."

They looked up at the house. Through the wall of windows they could see into the living room but it looked empty.

"Here," he said. "I'll throw it out."

"Was Pem down here?" she asked softly.

He answered just as quietly, "I didn't hear anything."

She felt his hand lightly on her waist again as they approached the house. "Be careful," he whispered.

"I will."

"Do you see that path there? On your left."

She squinted in the pale light. "Yes."

"That goes to my house. If you need anything I'll be there. I just came out here to recharge and help Denise with her patio and yard. I have no plans so I should be available anytime."

"Is it really that bad between Pem and Denise?"

"It can be."

Inside it was quiet. There were several half empty bottles of liquor still on the counter in the kitchen.

"I'll walk you to your car," Jake said.

"I need to change. I'll be just a minute."

She changed quickly and gathered her things together.

He walked her to her car and they said goodnight. When she looked in the rearview mirror he was still watching her brake lights as she tried to avoid the worst of the bumps and finally turned out of sight.

When she arrived Saturday, Pem and Denise were sitting at the kitchen island eating breakfast.

Denise jumped lightly off her stool. "Let me fix you an omelette!"

"I ate already, but thanks. The Daggett House makes an incredible bread and the scent just wafts up the stairs to my room. I couldn't help myself."

Denise settled back on the stool. "I know we had planned on working with you today but I think we should hijack your morning. You haven't seen the island yet. You need to take a break."

"If you're still up for it, I'm still up for going over some of the plans with you today and starting to finalize them." She lifted her sketch book out of her bag and waved it in front of them. "I've got some really good ideas!"

Pem looked at Denise. "I think she's turning us down as tour guides. And we were willing to do it on a Saturday!"

"The traffic is unreal today," Greta said. "I'm sure you're secretly glad I said no! Besides, I'll take you up on it another time if you'd like. I'll go set up the sketches for the living room. We can start in there when you're done with breakfast."

She could feel their excitement as they listened to her and looked at the drawings. Included were paint choices and swatches of fabrics from the books Jonathon had shipped to the Daggett House before she left Chicago. Pem was definitely more detail-oriented than Denise and asked many more questions. Thankfully, he liked her answers. Room by room they went. By late afternoon they were done with the details for the first floor. Only the bedrooms upstairs remained unaddressed.

Elated, Greta went to her office and typed up her notes for the first floor rooms.

"I hear it went well," Jake said.

Greta jumped in the chair. He was standing right next to her. "Hello!"

"Sorry about that! I just wanted to congratulate you. I saw your sketches. You nailed it."

"Thank you. It's been a productive day."

"Are you almost done? It's Saturday evening. You're not in Chicago, you know, you're on the Vineyard."

The cursor on the computer screen blinked patiently. "I really want to get my notes written up so I can pick up again tomorrow."

"Do you ever rest?" he asked, crossing his arms.

She lowered her voice, "I'm trying to get this done so I can minimize the time I need to be here. Someone told me it would be a good idea."

"How'd it go today?"

"Fine. Completely fine."

"You still need some time to just relax."

"Not right now," she smiled.

He walked away. "You're no pushover, I'll give you that."

"*Whatever*," she whispered to herself. But that reminded her of Aidan. She pushed away thoughts of him and went back to her notes. She wanted more than anything to begin the punch list. Instead, she bit her lip and pushed herself away from the desk.

A half hour later she was in the ocean, strongly swimming parallel to the shore, getting in touch with her body again. It had been too long since she had pushed herself hard. She started to get a rhythm to her strokes. Thump, thump, thump, the rhythm set her pace. She smiled at the way her muscles remembered how to do this. It was different in the ocean, that was certain, and her muscles were objecting but she pushed on. She stopped and turned back towards their spot on the beach and then she paused. There, in its own clearing on the edge of the slope next to Denise's house, it had to be the Bernstein house. It was raised on what looked like a sleek cement platform, three glass fronted rectangles floating above the ground. It was glorious.

They ate dinner in the kitchen but took their drinks to the beach, where Pem again had a fire going. This time he did not drink too much and the evening conversation was much lighter. Greta listened with delight as they shared some of their earliest memories of each other, many of which happened on that very beach. Then the lapses between comments grew longer as the sun steadily dropped.

"I saw green!" Pem shouted. They laughed together and toasted the sunset. The clouds were beautiful and Greta was sorry to see them darken. But then the stars began to glitter and she laid back on the sand. "How do you people ever leave this island?" she asked.

"You can leave," Jake said, moving so he sat beside her. He handed her a folded blanket. "But the island never leaves you. It gets in your blood."

She put the blanket beneath her head. "I can see why."

He stretched beside her and put a blanket beneath his head, too. "Do you see Orion?"

"I'm terrible with the stars," she said.

"There it is," Pem said, pointing.

Denise leaned her head against Pem's shoulder. "I see it."

"I can see the Big Dipper," Greta said, "And there, the Little Dipper. That's about the extent of it for me."

Jake pointed out several more constellations. "I had posters of the constellations on my bedroom walls. My dad drilled me on them from an early age."

"You were such a nerd about it," Pem said amicably. "You had the constellations memorized."

"How did you manage that?" Greta asked.

"We lived all over the world and no matter where we went, we studied the stars. My father was an ambassador in several different countries through several administrations."

"Oh," Greta said, trying to wrap her head around that piece of news.

"You know, Pem, you were hoarding quarters and keeping books on your piggy banks at age five," Jake gave back. "You were the nerd."

"We were all nerds," Denise said.

"How were you a nerd?" Greta asked Denise.

"I was born with my nose in a book."

"I confirm that," Pem said. "She still does. Only now she gets paid to do it."

"I'm an editor for Simon and Schustser.," Denise explained. "What about you, Greta, what were you a nerd about?"

"I drove my parents nuts rearranging things in our house. I couldn't figure out why they didn't understand that certain things just belonged in certain places."

"Definitely one of us," Jake said.

Denise put another log on the fire and snuggled against Pem. "What do you want to do tomorrow? It's supposed to be chilly. I can feel it already. I can make some soup."

"Kale soup?" Jake asked.

"It's too early for kale soup," Pem said. "October, yes, August, no."

"I don't know," Jake said. "I may not be out here again in the fall. Please Denise, make kale soup."

"No," Pem repeated. "It's unthinkable."

Greta looked at Pem. There was an edge to his voice that made it seem like he really meant it.

"Oh, Pem, stop it!" Denise said. "I'm going to tickle you until you say yes."

"Stop it you two!" Jake yelled. "You've got two single people over here who don't need to hear this."

Greta laughed out loud. "We could go for a walk again?"

Jake jumped up. "I thought you'd never ask."

And so they walked and talked.

This repeated itself the following night, and the next and the next. That particular night was Tuesday night, and Greta had moved her personal things into one of the bedrooms in the maid's quarters.

"Everything seems fine between them," she told Jake late one afternoon as they came in from the ocean after a strenuous swim before dinner. "I haven't seen anything odd. They are so incredibly kind and fun and generous."

"They are all of that," Jake said. "I'm glad to hear it. It sure is convenient for you to stay here. I think you're probably good for them, too. I was thinking, let's make dinner for them tomorrow night."

"What a great idea! I would love to."

"I have ulterior motives. I need some red meat. They never eat it."

"Surf and turf?"

"Yes. Do you like scallops?"

"Yes!"

They each grabbed a towel.

"Come with me to Poole's fish market tomorrow afternoon," Jake said. "You'll love it. In fact, you can walk over and pick me up when you're done with work. I'll show you my house."

"I'm dying to see it," she confessed.

"Really? Why didn't you say so? We'll go now. Dinner won't be ready yet. They'll never miss us."

"Are you sure?"

"Of course. Come on."

Wrapped in their towels, she followed him up the path, their suits still dripping.

"This used to be my parent's property," he said. "They retired to California and rarely used it anymore. It made more sense for me to take it on and make it mine. I kept the main house and added two wings that match it in size and shape. Zoning by-laws out here are strict. I wanted to do glass walls all around but I was lucky to get permission to have glass on the three walls facing the ocean. So, the original house is now the kitchen, dining and living area. The wing on the left has an office and library, and on the right is the bedroom wing."

Hidden among trees and well-placed landscaping, she first noticed the infinity edge of the pool and then the subtle levels of wooden patios with scooped hollows of recessed seating, level after level escalating to the three tall rectangles that made up the house. She felt mesmerized as he led her up the levels to the alcove with the outdoor shower where they both rinsed off before going in.

She tried to dry off completely but Jake didn't seemed too worried about the sand or water. "Come on." He slid open a wall of glass. It slid smoothly over another glass wall and the house immediately opened up to the outdoors.

When she stepped inside she had to stop. Her eyes swept the room, gathering detail after detail. Light bounced off white walls and the shiny black of large square floor tiles. A large white area rug centered two modern black leather sofas and a large silver-edged glass coffee table in the center of the large expanse. Behind it, along the far wall and under what were the windows facing the front of the house, was another seating arrangement of white side chairs and round metal and glass tables. A small, freestanding bar was tucked into the corner there. To the far left was a wall of white bookcases filled with books and dotted with photographs and artifacts from travels. In front of the last one, at an angle to the bookcase, stood a gleaming baby grand. A tall, two-sided fireplace separated the sofas from the kitchen. Far to the right in the kitchen polished smoked glass kitchen cabinets blended with sleek black and chrome appliances. A black quartz countertop covered a black island of cabinets. Above it hung three glass and iron modern sculptures that were lights. On the opposite side of an additional half wall of cabinets was a large white rectangle of a dining table surrounded by slim black molded chairs. On the center of the table was a glass tower filled with lemons.

This was not a woman's house, nor was it for children. It was at once a space for entertaining and living a life apart from the norm. It made no apologies for being different. It was a space to escape into, a space to relax in and reflect on intellectual pursuits. The view, when she remembered to turn around, with the bright green of the lawn and the deep blue of the ocean seemed more vivid and more stunning by the stark contrast of this interior. And that, she realized, was the point.

For a moment she just closed her eyes and breathed it in. She could feel this house. It beckoned her to appreciate its perfection.

"Go ahead," he said, nodding in each direction.

Her damp feet padded silently on the cool tiles. Her eyes measured the height of the ceilings, her fingertips ran across the crisp upholstered fabrics and smooth leathers, the silks and nubby cottons of the comforters and pillows in the bedrooms though her hands still clutched the towel around her. In her mind's eye she was sitting in every chair, walking each hall early in the morning and late at night, rinsing in each sink, sleeping in each bed and entertaining and eating and dancing. Dancing? Yes, as she returned to the central space, she could picture their dark silhouettes dancing in the cool shadows of a summer night, much like tonight.

Her mind raced as she tried to think of a word for this, this knowing. *Destiny*. Did he feel any of this? He was studying her but his face was impassive.

"Words fail me," she confessed. "All I can think of are overused superlatives that you've surely heard a thousand times before. This may sound strange, but I feel your house right here," she tapped her heart. "It is the highest compliment I can give you."

He smiled. "I can see that. Thank you."

Outside she paused in front of the exquisite pool with its infinity edge, taking in the sheer beauty of its design, how well it went with the house and how extraordinarily it blended into the landscape. Another work of art. His genius was unmistakeable.

Just then Denise's voice, distant but clear, called their names.

"Be right there," Jake shouted back.

She followed him back through the winding path to Denise's and Pem's house.

"I have to head back to New York next Sunday," Jake said. "Are you planning on being here much longer?"

"I'm going to leave Thursday and then I'll be back the following Thursday and Friday. I have a lot to find yet. I can do that best back in Chicago."

"I've really enjoyed our time together," Jake said.

She kept her voice light, "You've been so generous in welcoming me into your circle of friendship."

"If you know what dates you'll be coming back over the next several weeks, perhaps we can coordinate our calendars. I can arrange to bring some work out here and we can continue to have some of our walks at night time. What do you think?"

"I thought you couldn't extend your stay?"

"I think I can rearrange a few things. If you can do the same that is."

"I would like that," she said.

5

September and October flew by. It was now the beginning of November though the weather was still surprisingly mild. The house was coming along splendidly. Thanks to multiple crews hired from across the island and the Cape, the rooms were stripped of decades of wallpaper and painted in fresh tones of white, beige and blue. The worn kitchen cabinets had been replaced with new white cabinets and a white center island with a top of white quartz became the focal point of the kitchen. The aging french doors were replaced with new, white french doors that would someday, if the planning commission ever approved of Jake's now complete plan, lead out to an expansive patio and pool. In the foyer, halls, bathrooms and kitchen on the first floor, slate tiles with radiant heat were installed.

The wall between the dining room and living room had been removed, opening up the space as a great room. With only blinds covering the windows now, the resulting room was flooded with light and felt fresh and inviting. The wood floors of both the rooms had been refinished and gleamed after being made to look as one, as if there had never been a wall between them. She had yet to find the right area rug for the space, but several perfect lamps had just been ordered. The custom sofa and several arm chairs were being made and were due to arrive the week before Thanksgiving.

Meanwhile, the ancient painted maple dining room table and leaves had been stripped to their original warm golden grain and now made an inviting place to gather for food. Black Windsor chairs surrounded it and above it hung an old chandelier with black painted arms. Detail by detail it was all coming together.

The four of them were into the rhythm of the weekends at the house. Greta arrived early on Thursdays and got a tremendous amount of work done on Thursdays and Fridays. Friday afternoons Jake would fly in and Pem and Denise came in on Friday nights or Saturday mornings, and the four of them were their own family: close, familiar, joking, at once helpful but in the way, and always coming back for more.

Greta stayed through the weekends, soaking up the camaraderie. The work and friendships were a wonderful diversion from thoughts of Aidan that continued to unsettle her. During the early part of the weeks, as she worked in Chicago, Aidan's words and ways still ran through her mind. His views on many things played over and over and she had numerous conversations with herself as she considered them.

On the island however, this special project and these special people were a fine replacement for thoughts of another man. Loneliness was not an issue. She had no desire to look for her father or his family, if indeed they were still on the island. Managing this job and her work in Chicago was taking every bit of mental fortitude she possessed. Besides, Pem and Denise and Jake were fast becoming the siblings she'd never had.

Or so she thought until one Friday after an early dinner as she and Jake cleaned up in the kitchen while Denise and Pem ran to the video store for some movies.

"Let's make dinner for them tomorrow," Jake said.

"Surf and turf again?"

"Sure. I'll get the steaks and we can see if by any chance there are some bay scallops yet at the fish mark"

"Sounds delicious."

"I've never seen Pem so relaxed and happy," Jake said as he handed a washed dinner plate to Greta.

"I was wondering about you," Greta said as she dried the plate. "Are you always this relaxed?"

"My New York team is wondering what's changed," he said. "They've never seen me so pleasant."

"And what do you tell them?" She dried the pan he passed her.

"I finally told them there's a gorgeous blonde I'm crazy about."

Her heart skipped a beat. "Oh."

He rinsed the soap from the sink and his hands. "That was the last pan."

She handed him the towel so he could dry his hands while she put away the rest of the dried items.

"Aren't you going to say anything?" he asked.

She looked over her shoulder as she placed the plates in the cabinet. "I'm speechless."

He came up behind her and put his hands on her shoulders. "I'm crazy about you. Do you know that?"

She tried to laugh.

His face brushed her neck. "You've been driving me crazy for three months now. I think it's time we talked about this."

"I don't want things to change," she said, still facing the cabinets, keeping it light, hoping he would, too. "It's been a lot of fun and we've become good friends."

"Never in my life have I waited for a woman to show me she was interested like I have waited for you. Every time I think you're being kind or thoughtful to me, I see you being just as kind and thoughtful to Denise or Pem or a construction guy or a neighbor. It's who you are. I love that about you. But I need to know if you feel the same about me as I do for you."

She turned around and looked at him, her hands resting lightly on his upper arms. "I didn't know you felt this way."

His dark eyes ran over her face. "Now that you do?"

"I don't know where this will go. It could change everything."

He put his arms around her. "That's what I'm hoping. You'll be out here, what, two more weekends and then the house is done? Then what? Do you know I've put my life on hold for you? I'm delegating work in Switzerland and Japan that the perfectionist in me would never do. I'm pulling all-nighters in New York, just like in college, in order to make it here for the weekends. Because of you, I've been here every single weekend. I haven't missed one."

"And that's all about me? You haven't needed the rest?" She noticed the fine lines around his eyes and felt the warmth of his body so close to hers.

"I've needed you."

"You're not always an easy man to read," she said.

"All you have to do is ask."

Still, she felt a reluctance to go further. He must have felt it, for he released her.

"Let's walk down to the beach," he said.

For the first time he shared personal details of his life as they walked. "I met my former wife in the Netherlands," he said. "She was

French and an architect, too. We were married ten years and we've been divorced ten years. I still see her sometimes, our paths cross and it still hurts. I've had some long term relationships and a few not so long term. I'm not involved with anyone right now. I've been busy with my work and yet I'm disciplined, too, I know when I need rest. I admit when I first saw you I thought it would be nice to get to know you better while I took some time off. I soon realized it could not be just a casual affair. I think you know what I mean."

She pushed a lock of hair away from her eyes. Who did she think she was? Despite her aspirations, at most she was a midwestern interior designer who caught a few features in some magazines. Jacob (she could not think of him as Jake when reflecting on his brilliance as an architect) would have books written about him. She had never traveled outside the United States, unless visiting the Canadian side of Niagara Falls counted. Jacob's firm had offices in three different countries. She didn't know senators, let alone presidents. He grew up with them.

Then there was the reality that back in central Illinois was a guy she had been ready to give her heart to just a few months ago. Their conversations still played over in her mind as she went to sleep at night. She was beginning to think that Aidan was right about a lot of things. All that he had done right was beginning to outweigh her anger at his conflicted feelings and how he had led her on when he shouldn't have. He was also the most compassionate guy she'd ever known, and an incredibly good listener who let her be honest about how broken she really was. She had done more grieving those two weeks in Wiley than she had the entire year prior. Besides that, the chemistry between them was off the charts, even if he did reject her. What kind of a person was she if she moved on to another relationship when she'd been so ready to get serious with Aidan after years of protecting herself?

Speaking of past love interests, what about Jake's ex-wife? Just how much did he still hurt from their divorce? And *French? French?* How did one possibly compete with *that*?

Yet, he was interested. If she admitted she was uncertain about many things and at a crossroads, would he be okay with that? Wasn't it better to be honest now than deal with his disappointment later?

She looked over at him as they walked, searching his face for any reason not to speak plainly. He was wearing no masks that she could see.

She put her hand on his arm to stop him, so they could talk and look at each other, so he could see how sincerely she meant this. Her eyes never left his face. "I've been looking to make sense of the disjointed pieces of my life. I thought I had it all together and yet this last year has been overwhelming. This project has been the best diversion, but it doesn't change the fact that I have had this feeling lately that the time is coming to make life-changing decisions. I've needed something tangible to tell me, 'This is the way.' I was not anticipating it to be a relationship. I don't even want a flirtation. I had one of those recently and I'm still feeling upside down about it."

"A flirtation?"

She held up her hand. "I'm not done yet. My interest in you has been wholly platonic and based mostly on the fact that I wish I was a student again and could follow you around and immerse myself in your world to learn from you. You are so brilliant that you're at once fascinating and terrifying. Somehow I feel quite young around you though granted, we are twelve years apart, which is reminiscent of my one long term affair out of college, which makes me rather nervous.

"However," she took a deep breath, "the moment I stepped into your house everything changed. Everything just fell into place. The order I crave, you crave it, too. You know exactly what needs to go where and you know how it will make people feel when they walk into your spaces. You beckon them in and they have no clue they've just walked into you but they react and you know it. Your buildings will speak to them long after you're gone. But if someone comes in and changes anything in your original design, they will have lost you. You get it like I get it. We are more alike in that way than anyone I have ever met before. I feel like I know you, I know every inch of your house and even worse than that, I feel like I belong there. I could see myself in there, with you, and even, curiously, dancing with you. As in Ginger Rogers to your Fred Astaire. Now is that enough to convince you I'm completely bonkers? And by the way, bonkers is a Midwestern word, there's no French translation."

"Then we're both bonkers as you say, because I felt the exact same thing."

"Even the Fred Astaire thing?"

"No, not that. But close to it. You don't want to know."

She raised her eyebrows and they continued to look at each, each as honest and exposed as they could be.

"I'm nowhere near your equal," she said, sharing her worst fear. "I'm afraid I'm going to feel intimidated by you."

"Greta! Jake!"

They turned to see Pem waving two wine bottles while Denise bent over a fire at their usual spot.

"I heard you," Jake said. "We will pick this back up again."

She tried to exhale all the nervousness she felt that would not be resolved with Denise and Pem there, but she couldn't seem to stop her heart from pumping so fast.

Around the fire each took a turn discussing their day and what they had accomplished. They talked about how the sun was setting earlier and earlier, the ease of getting around the island now the day-trippers were gone, and the price of lobsters. All but Pem sipped their wine. He was drinking heavily.

Greta listened and talked but mostly she waited, her heart going *thump, thump, thump*. At last the sun began its slide again but this time Jake pulled her to her feet.

"Greta and I will be awhile," he said, startling Pem and Denise.

Denise asked, "Is everything okay?"

"Very," Jake said, and they took off running before Pem could yell "Green!" again.

"This sunset is ours," Jake whispered into her ear as they ran. They ran as far down the beach as they could in order to have some privacy and yet not miss the setting of the sun. "Here," he pulled her down and sat behind her, his legs with his jeans rolled up on either side of her legs, arms wrapped around her.

"You have no idea how much I am smitten by you," he said as they looked at the sky. "What if I told you I feel intimidated by you?"

All she could do was shake her head in wonder.

The white foam just barely swept over their toes as it pushed as far forward as it could before receding. The sky was streaked with clouds of pink and orange, purple and gray. The huge sun, ever powerful, smoothly slipped behind them.

"Make a wish as it goes down," he said.

Out of nowhere thoughts of Aidan overwhelmed her. "I can't," she said, her eyes surprisingly filled with tears.

He squeezed her gently and bent his head to the back of her neck. "Come on, make a wish. We can say this is where it all started, with these wishes."

She smiled and tried not to think of Aidan, tried not to want his arms around her, tried not to want this moment with him.

Lower and lower the sun sank and then suddenly it was going too quickly and it disappeared. Jake's hands pulled her around. She felt the warmth and strength of his lips on hers, searching for a response. She responded with all the passion she had wanted to give to Aidan, but quickly she realized this man wanted nothing less than all of her. Why not be loved by a genius of a man who did want her, who didn't hold back? Her passion turned into surrender to Jake. As helpless as she had been to shape her future with Aidan, whatever her future held, it was being created here and now.

She awoke to hear Pem and Denise in the kitchen. Rolling over, she looked at the clock on the bedside table. It was the middle of the night. The bedroom door was shut but she could hear them much too well, they had to be fighting.

"Who is she?" Denise yelled.

"You're being paranoid again," Pem yelled back.

Greta reached for the extra pillow and pulled it over her head. The muffled voices continued to filter through the door for some time. Then she heard a crash. She threw the pillow aside.

"Stop it, Pem, you're scaring me!"

"If you weren't so stupid and cloying I wouldn't do this! What will it take to get you off my back? Yes, I came down here for a few minutes of peace and quiet without you holding on to me. A man can do what he wants in his own house. This is my house, too, just remember that. We're using our money on this remodeling. That makes it mine, too. Oh, and by the way, I'm not cleaning this mess up. You clean it up!"

"Stop being so hurtful, Pem, please, stop it. How can you even think like this?"

"I said leave me alone!" Another crash and she heard Denise cry out.

With that Greta jumped out of bed and threw on the jeans, sweatshirt and clogs she'd been wearing earlier. She also grabbed her keys and wallet from the dresser top and tucked them in the pocket of her sweatshirt.

She swiftly walked down the hall to the kitchen.

They looked at her in surprise.

"We thought you were at Jake's. We didn't know you came back," Denise managed, her eyes still wide with fear.

Pem wore a pair of striped boxers, his hair askew. His eyes, heavy with alcohol, looked back and forth between Greta and Denise. On the new slate floor in front of Denise's bare feet were two crystal tumblers, smashed to bits. Pieces of glass were scattered across her feet and there was an ugly bruise forming across the bridge of her foot where a cut was beginning to bleed.

"Don't move!" Greta cried out. She grabbed some paper towels and one of the stools tucked under the counter of the island, noticing as she did so the faint lines of fine white grains on the countertop. Pretending not to see this, she set the stool next to Denise, who was wearing a thin, sleeveless nightgown. "Sit here." She looked over at Pem as Denise carefully stepped up onto the stool.

"She dropped her glass," he said, looking Greta straight in the eye.

The cold in his eyes reminded her of the eyes of a dead fish washed up on the shore. She shivered and tried to hide the terror she felt looking at him. "Why don't you go sleep this off?" she said quietly. "I'll take care of Denise."

With relief she watched him walk upstairs. She turned to Denise. "Are you okay?"

Denise's thin, pale body was shaking. She looked twice her age. "I'm fine. I'm just so embarrassed."

Greta frowned. She bent down to pick the shards off of Denise's feet and blotted the bleeding cut. "You have no reason to be embarrassed. Pem should be embarrassed. There, I think I've got it all. I'll get you a damp paper towel. It will pick up anything I missed. Where's the broom?"

"It's in the closet over there," Denise said. "Please don't tell Jake about this. It's nothing, Pem just had too much to drink, that's all. I shouldn't have come down looking for him. It's my fault."

Greta found the broom and swept carefully. "It wasn't your fault in any way. Pem should never frighten you like that. He could have thrown those at your face instead of your feet."

"He's just under a lot of pressure right now."

She shook her head as she swept the glass into the dustpan. "It's not okay under any conditions."

When the floor was wiped and completely clear of glass, Denise stepped down, wincing as she did so, and then she picked up the stool and put it back underneath the counter island while Greta put the broom away.

"Thank you," Denise said. "I'll be fine. It won't happen again, I promise."

"I just want you to be safe, Denise. Is there someone you can talk to about this? I'm sure the island has people who can help with things like this."

Denise shook her head. "It's fine, I'm fine."

Denise headed upstairs, and Greta turned off the lights, but not before noticing the grains on the counter, just above where Denise had replaced the stool, were gone.

The next morning Pem was at the counter in the kitchen making a green smoothie. "Would you like one?" he asked.

"No thanks," she said. His generosity offended her now. She wanted nothing from him. She filled her mug with coffee. "How is Denise today?"

"She's fine. We both are. She's out swimming. About last night, these things just happen. We forgive each other and move on."

"She's out there swimming? The water must be cold, she shouldn't be swimming alone!"

Pem shrugged. Greta took her coffee and went down to the beach to watch Denise.

Denise waved from the water and headed for shore. Greta met her with her towel and wrapped it around her. "How are you doing?"

"I'm fine," Denise said as she rubbed down.

"It's November!"

"Usually the gulf stream is no longer warming the water but it still feels warm to me."

Greta's stomach tightened as she looked at the ugly bruise and cut on Denise's foot.

"Is this the worst that he's hurt you?"

Denise shook her head.

"Can you tell me more about it?"

"I think he's seeing someone else," Denise said quietly. "I think that's why he's been so happy lately. Last night I thought I heard him on the phone downstairs, that's why I came down."

Greta's mind raced, trying to think of the right questions. "If he's hurting you and unfaithful, why do you stay?"

Denise looked away, a pained expression on her face. "You don't understand. He loves me, he needs me."

"If he loves you, then why does he do this to you?"

"He can't help himself. If he would just get help with his drinking, he would be okay. I almost had him persuaded to go for help last week. There's an AA meeting right down the street from us in Manhattan. But then he got a call again, from a woman I don't know, and he got angry when I asked him who it was." She looked back at Greta. "I'm scared."

"That you're in danger?"

"No, that I'll lose him."

"Oh, Denise, he's not safe. I'm worried about you. Do you need help—money, a safe place to go—anything?"

"I don't need anything. Pem and I have a special bond. I couldn't make it without him. I don't expect anyone to understand that."

"Do you have someone you can talk to about this, someone who understands abuse?"

Denise turned, her eyes hard and her voice sharp, "Abuse?" She looked back up at the house where Pem stood outside, watching them. Though they were quite a distance away, she lowered her voice even further, "He loves me. He would never abuse me. He's a lost little boy whose father treats him horribly. I've been nagging him too much about his drinking and I'm paranoid about who he is talking to on the phone. I shouldn't have pushed him so hard."

Greta's mind ached as she tried to make sense of what she was hearing. "None of that is an excuse for hurting you, Denise. He should be grateful that you care enough to want him to get help. And he shouldn't be cheating on you!"

At that Denise began walking ahead of Greta. "I'm not crazy! Everyone treats me like I don't have a brain, as if I'm some stupid woman who doesn't know what she's doing. No one appreciates how hard I'm working to keep my marriage alive!"

With a heavy heart, Greta followed Denise up to the house.

"Nice swim?" Pem asked as Denise stepped into the outdoor shower stall to wash off the sand and salt.

"Yes, but probably the last one of the year," Denise said cheerfully as the water ran over her skin and suit. "The weather forecast is calling for a drastic change. I'm going upstairs next to take a shower and get dressed."

"What are your plans for the day?" Pem asked Greta.

Anything without you. "I'm going to see if any of the antique shops are still open. I'm hoping to find a special something for the center of the kitchen island."

"I think there's a new one in Oak Bluffs that's still open," Pem said casually, following her inside. "Do you know where Circuit Avenue is?"

"No, I've only been to Oak Bluffs when we went to Illumination Night."

He went to the desk in front of the window by the front door and pulled out a map. "I'll highlight the route for you."

He was back to being kind, friendly Pem again. Except she knew better.

"Here," he said, "I marked the roads and wrote down the name of it, The Yellow Whale. Look for the yellow painted whale above the door. Can't miss it."

"Thanks," she said, feeling like a child avoiding boy cooties as she took the map from him. She went to her room to get a sweater and her purse.

She was pulling out of the driveway when she saw Jake come from the path between the houses. "Hey!" he called.

She rolled down her window. "I'm heading to Oak Bluffs. Would you like to come?"

He was already half way around the car before she finished. He sat down next to her and buckled up. She pulled away.

"I have to talk to you," she said.

"Is this about last night?"

"Not about us, it's about Pem and Denise," she said grimly. "Their arguing woke me up in the middle of the night. He scared her good. Threw two of those heavy tumblers at her, hit her feet. One cut her foot and bruised it badly. That's when I went into the kitchen to help her. I wish I had gone in earlier, maybe it would have stopped him. Thankfully he left us alone, but I'm telling you, Jake, it was scary. His eyes were just dead, like a dead fish. It was awful."

His mouth was a thin red line and she could see an angry flush rising from his neck to his face. "He's always controlled her. In previous years she's come over to my house for help several times in the middle of the night. I think he's had to control himself more with you here."

"It sounds like she suspects he's cheating on her."

"It wouldn't be the first time."

"Also, there were lines of cocaine on the countertop."

"That wouldn't be the first time either."

"Why on earth doesn't she kick him out? Does her father know all this? I can't imagine he would put up with a son-in-law who treats her like this."

"Her father has been absent most of her life. Her mother practically lived out here, except when it was an election year. Then she and the children would follow him around for the photo ops. Denise craved his attention. She has two younger brothers. One is a lawyer and the other one is mentally challenged and lives in a special home now that her mom is gone. Pem refused to let Denise take custody of him when her mom died. He has no patience for any kind of weakness."

"Oh, Jake!"

"There's nothing I can do to persuade her to leave him, I've tried."

"Have you seen bruises, broken bones?"

"I haven't seen physical abuse, but the emotional abuse is killing her. If you knew her before they married, you wouldn't recognize her today."

"I believe you. Sometimes when she smiles, I can see how beautiful she is. But at other times, I think she's aged beyond her years. What gets me is how well Pem hides all his anger and control. Is it the alcohol that brings it out?"

"I don't think so. It's always there. He just chooses who he takes it out on, and that is Denise. It always has been."

She pulled the map from her purse. "Which way do I turn up here? I'm looking for an antique store in Oak Bluffs."

"There's a good one in Edgartown," he said. "I don't know of one in Oak Bluffs."

"Pem said there's a new one. He wrote the name of it on the top there. He was back to being his helpful self this morning. He even highlighted the route."

Jake peered at the map. "Shops come and go all the time here. I'm surprised it's still open since the season is over. Turn right at the next intersection."

"You know, I hate to leave Denise alone but I can't stay here with Pem like this. I think it would be best if I come out next Wednesday and Thursday and leave on Friday before they get here."

"You can still come out as planned, just stay with me."

"I don't think we're ready for that," she said. "Besides, it wouldn't be professional."

"Pem and Denise would understand."

"No," she shook her head, "It doesn't seem right."

"You realize what you're saying? When are we supposed to see each other? What happens to us?"

"I realize this will impact us. Is that what you mean?"

"Yes."

"For Denise's sake I would like to stay but it's just not safe. The crews have done their work in record time, but I'm still waiting on shipments to arrive and I have to be here for them. I need to finish this well. I have an obligation that has to come first."

"Why not stay in a hotel again?" He added, "You'll have no problem getting a room this time of year."

"That's not a bad idea. It would be rather awkward, but I could do that if you really want me to keep to our schedule. I know you've gone out of your way to make these weekends happen."

He breathed a sigh of relief. "Thank you. This is a good reminder that we need to figure out how we're going to make this work long term."

Circuit Avenue looked deserted. They found the Yellow Whale without a problem. A delicate bell jingled as they entered.

"Good morning!" The cute young clerk was certainly perky for what had to be her first, if not only, customers of the day.

"Hello," Greta said.

"Is there anything I can help you find?" the clerk asked.

It's a matter of knowing it when I see it," Greta smiled.

"Ah," the girl nodded knowingly. "I understand."

"Are you gong to remain open year round?" Jake asked.

The girl nodded, "I just moved to the island in August and got a late start opening up the shop. I plan on staying open through the winter."

"Oh, so it's your shop?" Jake asked.

Greta looked up from the shelves she was perusing to glance at the girl. Small, with short dark hair cropped closely to her head, she looked all of eighteen.

"I interned at Sotheby's," the girl smiled. "I've always wanted to own my own antique shop. This store is a lifelong dream come true."

Jake raised his eyebrows, "Congratulations, I wish you every success."

He walked over to Greta. "Lifelong?" he whispered. "I can't believe she's even twenty-one!"

They both slowly perused the store. "Really," he asked, "what are you hoping to find?"

"I told Pem I was looking for something for the center of the kitchen island, but truthfully I'm looking for something special to give them as a gift when I'm done."

"What might that be?"

"I really am hoping I'll know it when I see it. I do have a backup plan though. I've made some unique serving trays for clients in the past. I use antique picture frames and mirrors, and sometimes I'll use fabrics or photos under glass. Considering all the layers of wallpapers we removed, I'd like to use the scraps I saved to make a collage and put that under glass."

"That sounds like something Denise would like," Jake said. "I'll keep an eye out for frames."

They looked around for a while, making sure they saw everything. Jake picked up a colorful paperweight. "I've seen this before," he said.

Greta looked at it. "A millefiori, right?"

"Yes." He turned it over. "Look at the price tag."

"Wow. That must be quite special."

He set it back down. "It looks like one Denise used to have."

Greta walked on and then slowed down and turned back to Jake. Softly she said, "When I first arrived, Denise told me their house had been broken into. She said some family things were missing. You don't think…?"

He went back to get the paperweight. He walked up to the counter and the girl behind it. "I'd like to purchase this," he said. "Can you give me some history on it?"

"No, I couldn't say. I have a partner, we both find items to sell. We might have found it at an estate sale, something like that, I couldn't say for sure." She rang up the sale.

They left soon after and headed to Edgartown. The ocean between Oak Bluffs and Edgartown was calm and a soft shade of pale blue. The horizon blended with it, white in places, surreal.

"This is my favorite shade of ocean," Greta said.

He reached across the seat and took her right hand from the wheel to hold it. They drove on in comfortable silence.

Thankfully, the store in Edgartown had several old frames in a box. Each was prettier than the next. She chose several for future projects, too.

Jake looked at his watch as they got in her rental car. "If we want to see if there are any bay scallops yet, we should head up-island to Menemsha."

"I almost forgot about dinner tonight. I don't know that I feel up to it."

"I'll be there. I'll stay as late as you want me to stay."

Little gray shacks dotted the wharfs of Menemsha, and each wharf was full with well-used fishing boats. A black lab bounded over and greeted them as they walked up the gravel of crushed shells to the small building.

An enormous chunk of a fresh black sea bass lay cut open on a small metal counter. The wizened fisherman set down his knife. "What will it be today, Jake?"

"Any chance you have some bay scallops?"

"You're in luck. How many do you need?"

"Two pounds will do just fine," Jake replied.

"Could we walk up the jetty?" Greta asked as they left the shack.

"Sure." He set the wrapped scallops on the floor of the car and then took her hand. They walked as far out on the huge stones of the jetty as they could while the black lab barked excitedly and ran just a few feet ahead of them.

"I haven't seen much of the island at all," she said, looking out into the ocean.

"It will take years. Every part of it is beautiful and different. It's always changing, too."

She took his hand in hers. "What's your favorite time of year here?"

"It's hard to say. I love the height of summer, swimming, hanging with friends, napping in the shade. Or when it's foggy and moody and you can't see your hand in front of you, or early summer when everything suddenly bursts into bloom. I've been here several times in winter. The taverns offer good beer and not so bad food and you're best friends with everyone before you leave the place. I really like it when a good nor'easter rolls in and you stay inside with a good book and a roaring fire and have kale soup for a week."

"You're making me want to stay year round."

He leaned over and kissed her soundly. Her footing teetered on the slippery rocks and they clung to each other and laughed through the kiss while the lab barked at them. He kissed her again and this time there was no laughter and if the dog barked, they didn't hear him.

"About living out here year round," he said as they headed back, "the people here are rather particular. They're wary of tourists and keep to themselves. It can take some time to build trust with the islanders. They're good people. Resilient. It's expensive to live here and most of them work several jobs, whether the tourists are here or not. Others have come out here to escape one thing or another. They come to lick their wounds, to get a fresh start, to escape their past, to hide from something. I've seen it all."

"Don't we all do that at times?"

"It happens more often here. There's a lot of alcoholism and drugs and New Age religions, fire walking, you name it. Don't get me wrong, it's still safe. My parents never locked their doors. I do because I've traveled so much it's just a habit."

He opened the car door for her. "Let's stop at my house on the way back. I've got a platter of steaks in the refrigerator and everything we need for a salad. We can bring it over all at once."

She pulled in his driveway and followed him inside. "I wanted to ask you about the baby grand. You play?"

"My mother insisted."

"Constellations, piano lessons, what else did they make you do?"

He opened the refrigerator and pulled out the steaks and vegetables all neatly prepared. "Tennis, golf, lacrosse."

"Polo?"

He looked at her. "Are you being serious?"

She laughed, "Not at all."

"What about you?"

"In high school I was in French Club and on the swim team and in student government. In college I stayed away from sororities and spent every weekend scouring the Art Museum and galleries. I toured all the historic houses within a hundred miles of the city."

He pulled a six-pack of beer from the refrigerator. He held it up. "For tonight? What do you think?"

"Don't do it. I may not have another drink around Pem ever again."

His face clouded over as he put the beer back and firmly closed the refrigerator door. "Promise me you'll call me if anything happens in the middle of the night? Every bedroom here has a sliding patio door. I'll leave mine unlocked. If you or Denise need anything you can come there and I'll hear you. I'm dead to the world when I sleep. I won't hear you at the front door or the sliding doors off the dining room."

She hesitated. "Can we leave through your bedroom now, so I know how to get to it if there's an emergency?"

"Sure."

They picked up the food and walked down the long hallway to his room. The bed faced the windows and the view of the infinity pool against the ocean in the distance was stunning.

"I still have no words," she said.

"Words aren't necessary in here," he said as he bent down to unlock the wall of glass that was another door.

She pretended not to hear him and instead looked once again at the crisp white bedspread tucked neatly into the platform bed and the colorful splash of paints across the canvas about the bed. Its colors were repeated in the tiny squares of tiles in the bathroom visible to her left. The bathroom counter had a small tray of lotions and bottles. She wanted to go smell every one of them.

He coughed politely. "This is the way out," he said with a sweep of his hand.

She stepped across the track and onto the patio, assessing the placement of this particular door to the shared path.

"There's a motion censor that lights up when you come within twenty feet," he said. "You'll be able to find it without a problem. Just be sure to keep a flashlight by your bed. You know what? Hold on, I'll go back and get one for you."

"That's a good idea."

He came back shortly with a heavy silver flashlight. In the car she slipped it into her purse to avoid any questions from Pem or Denise.

"Is it my imagination or is it getting awfully gray out here?" she asked as they walked up to the house.

Jake looked up at the darkening sky. "That's ominous."

They went to the kitchen to put the food away. Pem stood at the open French doors with a drink in his hand, Denise was by his side looking out onto the ocean. Just then a huge clap of thunder sounded and a bolt of lightening lit up the sky.

A shiver ran down Greta's spine. "Where did this come from?"

"A cool front came through from the northwest. The conditions are perfect for a good storm," Pem said. "It's moving fast."

She looked at him carefully. Was he slurring his words?

"I was just going to put a movie in the VCR," Denise said. "We were going to watch it last night but you two stayed out on the beach a little late for us."

Considering how the middle of the night had gone, Greta really didn't want to talk about it at all.

Pem turned to Jake. "Yes, what's going on with the two of you?"

She exchanged a glance with Jake and nodded slightly.

"We're exploring the possibility of a relationship," Jake said delicately.

Pem slung his arm around Jake's shoulder. "It's about time you made a move, old man."

Jake reached for Pem's hand on his shoulder and walked him to the new sofa. "It's a little early in the day to be drinking, don't you think, Buddy? Let's take it easy this afternoon, watch the movie and relax."

He sat down with Pem next to him. Then he felt his pocket. "Hey," he said, pulling out the paperweight, "I found this at a new antique store in Oak Bluffs today. Does it look familiar, Denise?"

Denise picked it up from his hand. "Why, this is mine! It went missing over the winter when someone broke in. Where did you find it?"

"At that new antique store Pem sent Greta to today."

Pem's face darkened. "Oh come on, it can't be the same one. These paperweights all look alike."

"No, Pem," Denise said, "this is from my desk. I'd know this pattern anywhere!"

"Don't be ridiculous!"

"No, they're all unique." Denise turned it over and over in her hand. "I can't believe it. Jake, I'm so grateful that you saw it and got it for me. Let me pay you back."

"Consider it a gift," Jake said. "Returned to its rightful owner."

"What does that make me?" Pem said, rising up from the couch. "You calling me a liar?"

"Pem," Denise said, "be happy I have my paperweight back. No one's accusing you of anything. I'll put it in the library, and we'll forget about it."

She turned and threw a desperate glance at Greta.

"I'll make some sandwiches for lunch," Greta offered.

"There's some kale soup on the stove," Denise said, as she walked to the library.

"You guys start the movie and I'll bring everything over when it's done," Greta said.

Pem sat down, but he was scowling and his dark eyebrows were knit together in a permanent frown. It was going to be a long rest of the day.

Sheets of spray from the ocean and driving rain covered the house as the wind pushed forcefully. Pem knocked back several more beers and thankfully fell asleep halfway through the movie and Greta, tucked into Jake's side on the other end of the sectional, was fighting sleep herself.

"Why don't you take a nap?" Jake whispered.

"I feel unsettled," she whispered back. "Something feels wrong."

"I'm right here. Go to sleep."

When she closed her eyes she kept seeing the ugly bruise and cut on Denise's foot, and the angry, awful look on Pem's face when he saw the paperweight. What did this mean? She lifted her head and opened her eyes to look around. Indeed, everything felt different, changed.

Even the interior of the house, which was turning out so beautifully and brought her such joy to look at, no longer felt light and bright or warm and welcoming. All her work meant nothing in view of the ugliness within Pem.

It was almost dinner time when they roused enough from sleep, and the movie, and the subsequent sports on TV to talk again. The rain was still coming down, though not as hard.

"So much for our surf and turf dinner on the grill," Greta said.

"We can eat at my house and grill on the stove," Jake offered.

"Your fancy stove even washes the dishes, doesn't it?" Pem said, stretching as he stood up.

"Not yet." Jake got up and went to the kitchen and began to pull out the food they had brought for dinner.

"Let's make dinner special," Denise said. "Greta, we'll dress up and Jake, if you don't mind we'll use your stereo and record collection and have dinner with candlelight. With the rain and the wind outside it will be divinely romantic! Especially now that you two are taking things further."

Greta tried to give a cheerful smile, "That sounds like fun." She looked at Jake. "I'll go change and be back to help you with the food."

Thankfully, Greta had a burgundy sweater dress in the closet that she'd worn on her flight in from work in Chicago. It was hardly romantic but it would do. She put it on and then twisted up her hair and tucked in some bobby pins. She looked in the mirror. The last time she had worn her hair up she had been with Aidan. She brushed it out and put in a small headband instead. A spritz of perfume, a little extra lipstick and she was good to go. She hesitated at the doorway of her room and looked at the keys on her dresser. What if she stayed late at Jake's? She might need them to get back in. The way Pem was acting lately she didn't trust that the doors would be unlocked as usual. She grabbed them and tucked them into the pocket hidden in the side seam of her dress.

Denise came downstairs in a black lace dress. It was low-cut and fit her beautifully. Tendrils curled around her face and for the first time in Greta's presence, Denise was wearing makeup. Greta was in awe of her transition.

So were Pem and Jake. They couldn't help but stare.

Denise cooly ignored them all. "It looks like it stopped raining, but I think we should take some jackets just in case."

She found them all jackets and with food in hand they took off across the yard and down the path to Jake's house, running as the rain began to come down once again.

"Ouch, that's hail!" Greta shouted.

Sure enough, pea size hail began bouncing and stinging as they ran as fast as they could.

Once inside, Jake lit every lamp to dispel the gloom. He lit the fire in the two-way fireplace between the living and kitchen areas. The house glittered and glowed.

Pem mixed drinks at the bar and Denise put on jazz records while Greta made a salad and Jake took a quick shower and changed. He came out in a smooth dress shirt, white with thin burgundy stripes, with his sleeves rolled up and the shirttail tucked into his navy jeans. His hair was still wet and he looked incredibly sexy. He turned on the magnificent stove she had not been able to figure out for herself.

"You smell great," she said.

"Good," he smiled. "Would you please get me an apron from that drawer?"

She unfolded a heavy red apron and looped it around his neck and then tied it at his slim waist. His hands rested on hers for a brief, reassuring moment as she tied the apron and then he resumed cooking.

As she set the table and lit the candles she was equally distracted by the gray tossing ocean with lightening dancing across the sky above it and the vision of Jake at his magnificent stove pan-searing scallops and turning steaks. The man could cook.

Despite the fact that Pem had already had at least one if not two martinis, when Jake called them to the table Pem went to Jake's refrigerator and pulled out the beer.

"Can't have steak and scallops without a good beer," he said, and passed them all a beer. They toasted Jake's stove, rainy Saturdays and a good nor'easter.

As they cleaned up, Pem slammed another beer. Denise sorted through more albums and soon Carly Simon's rich golden voice filled the room.

"Dance with me, Pem!" Denise said, her eyes beseeching him as she reached out her hands. He took her hands and they moved together as one across the floor, Denise so slight and small that Pem practically carried her with his movements. She was wooing him, enticing him, with all she had to offer.

Greta looked at Jake as they finished loading the dishwasher. If they were going to dance, it would not be with an audience. He smiled and slightly shook his head. "Thank you," she mouthed silently.

She settled on the leather sofa closest to the fireplace. It wasn't long before Jake finished turning off several of the lights and sat beside her. "You can put your feet on the coffee table," he said as he lifted his legs up onto it. "I always do."

She laughed and joined him. They watched Pem and Denise dance and dance. James Taylor's voice replaced Carly's and they danced some more. The way they were looking at each other made the ugly scene between them the night before feel like a bad dream.

Jake got up and put another log in the fireplace and sat back down, pulling her into his side again. She looked up at him, wanting nothing more than to be alone with him. He kissed the top of her head. "We'll have our time," he said softly.

The music changed and Frank Sinatra took his turn crooning. They looked up from the fire to see Pem and Denise still dancing strong, no matter the song they were equal to it. It was quite unique.

"Shall we talk about the future?" Greta quietly asked.

"I've been sitting here thinking about us. I have no easy answers," he replied. "I just know we have to make each other the priority."

"Do we set aside certain weekends to meet? You could come to Chicago, I could go to New York?"

"I have to spend more time onsite in Switzerland and Japan. My teams are reaching critical points and I need to be there."

"I can see visiting you in New York, or even in California to meet your parents," she said dubiously, "but I don't see myself interfering with your work outside the country."

"I would love it if you would simply come with me. Come see my work, meet my teams, join us."

"I have several obligations still in Chicago that I have to fulfill. People have been incredibly patient. I work hard there when I'm not here. I need to get those jobs done."

A particularly loud crack of thunder made her shiver and move even closer inside Jake's arm. The air felt charged with electricity. She glanced at Pem and Denise. The easiness between them was gone. Even Jake was aware, as he could only stare at Pem and Denise.

The two dancers were getting tired. Their oneness had dissolved into a strange sort of competition, neither one willing to stop. They moved with a determination that spoke nothing of love or romance or even dancing. Denise did not want to let him go, and Pem did not want to be out-controlled.

Another song came on and they continued. Pem's moves became defiant and angry.

Jake got up and turned off the stereo. "It's about time for some fresh air," he said. He slid open the patio door and chilly, damp air rushed in on a strong wind.

Greta walked over to look at the ocean and the sky. The last rush of rain was already dissipating but the clouds coming at them again looked dark and nasty.

"I need another beer," Pem said.

"Sorry, I'm all out," Jake replied, closing the glass door.

Pem walked to the bar. "Line up, I'll play bartender. What'll it be?"

Deftly Jake intervened, "We're going to keep it light tonight. We've all had enough."

"I don't need your liquor, I have my own. Where's my jacket?"

"Stay here," Jake said. "We're having a good time."

"You're having a good time," Pem said, his face dark with anger, "while my wife embarrasses herself."

Denise laughed nervously and took Pem's arm. "Come on, Pem, it's like old times. We're having a romantic evening."

"How could I be attracted to you?" he said thickly. "You're a leech I can't pull off of me. You hold me back from everything I've ever wanted."

"Pem, I've given you everything you've ever wanted!"

He spat the words at her, "I hate everything you've ever done for me."

Again his eyes were dead, flat, cold like a dead fish.

Jake stepped between Pem and Denise. "Cool it off," he said to Pem. "There's no need for this."

"Leave me alone," Pem pushed Jake aside. He slid open the door and stumbled out.

Denise gave them each an embarrassed, tearful smile and ran after him.

They followed her outside and from they patio they watched her run across the lawn towards the path.

"I've never seen it this bad," he said

"What is it, Jake? What are they talking about?"

"Money."

"I thought Pem and his family were successful bankers?"

"They're dependent on their connections to Washington. The bank merger this summer was heavily dependent on Washington and Denise's father."

"I had no idea."

Just then a strike of lightening lit up the sky, followed quickly by a clap of thunder and a rush of wind and hail. "Whoa!" she cried, running inside. "That was close! I hope they're okay out there."

He closed the doors and stood behind her just inside the doors, arms wrapped around her. They watched in awe as huge black clouds swirled and the ocean curled with the wrath of the wind. The steel and wood and glass of the house stood resilient against it, even as hail again pelted it mercilessly.

"I hope Denise got inside before the hail started," she said. "She's so vulnerable and she doesn't even seem to know it."

"There's nothing we can do about it. We can't pick her up and take her away. She would hate us if we tried."

"Maybe we should try," Greta said. "Maybe that's what it takes."

"She would just go back to him. We would lose her trust and friendship."

"This is true."

He held her tightly. "Let's think about us for a while. This is our night, too."

They stood there, his arms around her, and despite her fear for Denise and the raging storm outside, she tried to focus on them. "It's quite a night."

"It's quite a storm. God likes to put on a good show. It reminds us how small we really are."

"You mean nature puts on a good show," she said.

"Who created nature? All the precise atmospheric conditions that have to be in place to create this storm are not random, they're a clear indication of God at work. Every single thing has its purpose, everything is exactly in its right place. I can't create without a strong appreciation for what God has created. I might not be a practicing Jew, but I have a very healthy respect for God."

She turned around in his arms. "I hadn't thought of it like that."

He kissed her softly. "Do you know how much I wanted to be alone with you? I'm sorry for Denise, but I'm very happy to be with you."

"We have a lot to figure out."

He kissed her again. "Not tonight."

"Before we get any further down this road."

He kissed her yet again. "We are already far, far down this road,

Greta. Don't you see that?"

She did.

Finally the storm passed over. Jake got up from the couch and opened one of the patio doors. Cool ocean air filled the room again. While the rain had stopped, the waves were still especially loud from the storm. He closed the door and returned to the couch and laid beside her.

"I don't want you to go back there tonight."

She closed her eyes at the thought. "I don't want to either."

He kissed her face and neck.

"This is surreal," she said. "I can't believe this is happening."

"I feel like I've been waiting for you my entire life. When you introduced yourself to me back in August and I recalled you from our original meeting three years prior, I could only think that you were and are, incredibly beautiful. I knew last summer I wanted you in my life and I would do whatever I could to get you. I want you with me wherever I go."

She fingered the color of his shirt. "I still can't imagine how it works long term."

"Other couples make it work. We will, too."

"If we are that far down the road, then work this out with me. Let's talk about your bank in Switzerland. It will take at least two years to build, right?"

"More like three or four."

"What's in Japan? How long will that take?"

"A resort hotel. It's just begun. It could be three or more years as well. But I don't live there, Greta. I have this house. I have a house in California so I can be close to my parents, and an apartment in Manhattan.

"And in France?"

He tapped her nose. "You're really smart."

"I know."

"Yes, I still have a place there."

"Why didn't you mention it first?"

"It's hardly an apartment, a set of rooms is more like it. I haven't lived in it for years."

"But you use it sometimes with your ex-wife."

"How do you know these things?"

"It just seems to fit. The rooms will have to go."

"Consider it gone."

"What about living in Chicago? Would you be open to it?"
"Would we want the expense of another home?"
"If I work there then I want my home there."
"You could work anywhere."
"I'm established in Chicago."
"You of all people, with your inquisitiveness and level of excellence, you'll find opportunities everywhere, Greta. Come with me, work with me for a while or find your own niche. The experiences will open your eyes to how limitless your possibilities are."
"I understand that, I do. It's just that I don't know if I want that."
"What do you mean? You would love the exposure to international design. I know you would."
"I would love it, I don't doubt that for a moment. I just don't know that it's right for me right now."
"When you said you were on the cusp of change, what did that mean?"
"I've been thinking a great deal about it. I was wondering if I should have my own firm. I would like that. When I'm done with this job, I want to find my dad and I also have a half-sister whom I've never met. I want to spend time getting to know them if I can. I don't know how they'll factor into things."
"What about having children, have you considered that?"
"Good grief, that's serious."
"I'm serious."
"I'm scared to death to be pregnant and give birth, but I would like a family. Two or three children."
"When?"
"That's a hard one. Knowing me I would procrastinate until it was absolutely necessary. So maybe four or five years. What about you?"
"I would want you all to myself for at least a few years. And then we could start. Two or three would be nice."
Her heart skipped a beat. "But how do we know it will work, Jake? Can we make it last?"
"If we try very, very hard, yes, we can make it last."
And she believed him.
It was almost midnight when they left the house. Jake found another flashlight so they could find their way back down the dark path. The storm was over but the patio and grass and bushes were still dripping water.
"I'll go in with you," he said. "If there's any sign of chaos, you're

coming back with me."

In the black of the night his flashlight was a welcome guide. They were halfway done the path when Jake stopped suddenly, "What the —"

She bumped into him and tried to peer around him and then she screamed. In a crumpled mound before them on the path lay Denise.

In horror, they knelt to gently turn her over. She was still wearing her black lace dress. It was soaked with water and her forehead was a contorted wet mass of flesh, dirt and blood and hair.

Jake spoke first. "Does she have a pulse? Check her breathing; I'll check her wrists."

"She's not breathing. Nothing. She's cold, Jake! So cold!"

Jake straightened Denise's head and immediately began CPR.

Greta stood up, "I'll call for an ambulance." For a moment she hesitated, which house was closer?

Jake lifted his head. "Go to my house, the emergency number's on the phone." He then continued to count as he pumped Denise's chest. "Wait, take the flashlight," he said, counting as he talked.

She ran faster than she knew she could. Inside she dialed emergency. A woman's voice on the other end answered. Greta interrupted her, "Our friend has been badly hurt. She's not breathing. We're giving her CPR but there's no response."

"I'll send an ambulance. Where are you located, ma'am?"

Greta gave the address. "Her name is Denise Arthur. We found her outside on a path between the Arthur house and the Bernstein house. I'm worried her husband, Pemberton DeWitt may have hurt her. They live next door. He was drunk and dangerously angry at her."

"The ambulance and the Duke's County sheriff are on their way. Where is the husband now?"

"I don't know. We were just going over there—we were next door—when we found her."

"Do you need instructions on CPR?"

"No."

The calm voice went on, "Are you safe? Do you want me to stay on the line with you?"

"No, I need to go back outside and help with her."

"I understand. Be careful. First, please tell me what the husband looks like."

She gave a brief description. "Now please, hurry!"

She ran back outside only to see Jake running up the path towards the patio, Denise's limp body in his arms. "Pem is out there! I heard him calling for her. Get in the house!"

She tore back up the steps to open the door for him and then quickly locked it behind them when he entered with Denise. He carefully laid Denise on the floor and began again to breathe in her mouth, willing her to live with every compression of her chest.

Greta knelt down in front of him, helpless. In the brighter light the extent of the wound on Denise's forehead was horrifying to see. Out of nowhere, Greta found herself whispering over and over again, "Please God, don't let her die, please don't let her die, please God. Help us! Help her, God!"

When she looked up, outside the doors Pem stood there watching them. She screamed involuntarily. When her eyes met his, he pounded on the door. "Let me in! What's going on?"

"What did you do to her?" she yelled, standing up. "What have you done?"

Pem shouted through the doors, "I don't know what you're talking about! Let me in! What's wrong with Denise? Let me see my wife!"

Sirens filled the air. Greta saw a wild look of panic flash across Pem's face. She ran to open the front door. Medics rushed in and took over with Denise while Jake moved aside.

Two officers entered as well. "Please identify yourselves," the taller one said.

"I'm Jacob Bernstein, I own this house and this is Greta Little."

Greta said, "I've been staying with Pem and Denise. I'm an interior designer, hired by them. Tonight the four of us had dinner here."

She pointed to the patio doors, where there was no sign of Pem. "He was there a minute ago, Pem was. They left here earlier, about three, maybe four hours ago. Jake was just taking me back," she looked at Jake, "ten or fifteen minutes ago?"

Jake nodded. "I was taking Greta back there when we found Denise on the ground on the path between the houses. I tried CPR but it wasn't working. Then I heard her husband yelling for her. I did not trust him, so I brought her, Denise, inside here and again tried to give her CPR."

Greta went on, "Her husband, Pem, just at the door there a minute ago, was pounding the glass, telling us to let him in. He was drunk and angry at his wife earlier. I'm worried he did this to her."

"We have police outside searching the grounds," the taller one said. "I'm Sheriff Webster and this is Sgt. Price."

Greta turned to see the medics wheeling Denise out on the gurney. Though the medics continued their efforts even as they ran with the gurney, Denise's body, slack, her hair wet and sticky with blood and dirt, moved only when the gurney bumped slightly as they exited the door. Greta dropped her head in her hands at the sight.

"Tell us again what the husband looks like," Sheriff Webster said to Jake.

"He's about six feet tall, lean, brown curly hair. He's wearing jeans and a long sleeve polo shirt. I think it's black."

The sheriff walked outside while Sgt. Price said, "You wait here."

Only a moment later the sheriff returned. "We'll need to get statements from you both. You'll need to come with us."

Just then another officer came in and went straight to the sheriff and said lowly in his ear, "We have him."

The sheriff nodded, "Sergeant, keep these two here for now." Then he went outside.

Greta and Jake sank onto the sofa, anxiously watching the scene unfold.

More people came in, some in uniform, some wearing latex gloves and others taking photos of the floor where Denise had lain as well as photos of the rest of the kitchen and the living room. One of the photographers took a quick photo of her boots, and Jake's shoes, which Greta hadn't even realized they had kept on when they came inside.

She began shaking. This was not Jake's home anymore, this was a crime scene.

Jake picked up a throw from the back of the sofa and wrapped it around her. They both sat on the sofa while the sergeant remained just a few feet from them.

"Excuse me, sir," a woman in uniform said to Jake. "Is there an electrical outlet outside that we can use?"

Jake got up.

Greta looked at the sergeant, "May I go, too?"

"Yes, I'll go with you both."

Greta watched as floodlights instantly lit the path from one end to the other. Then she saw Pem just outside the path in Jake's yard. Webster and another officer stood by his side. Pem's hands were handcuffed behind his back.

Greta sat down weakly on the damp deck, the thick throw beneath her. "I can't believe this is happening."

"Ma'am, I would like to ask you your version of what happened here tonight and how you found the body." It was Sheriff Webster again.

Jake came back but the sheriff held up his hand. "Sir, thank you but please, stay up by the house for now. I'll be with you shortly. I'd like to finish with Ms. Little first."

She started with the night before, when Pem threw the crystal tumblers at Denise. She told him how he drank so much that afternoon and then how he and Denise danced and how odd it was. Then she shared how Denise was sure there was another woman, and how she had tried to woo him back that night and how, despite that cold, dead look in Pem's eyes, she had run after him even after he said he hated her.

She watched from a distance as the sheriff talked to Jake next. Then he came back to her. "We need you both to come with us to the Island Communications Center at the airport in Tisbury. There is no police station here in Gay Head so we need to get official statements from you both there. Sgt. Price will take you."

They were not allowed to go back down the path to where they had found her. Nor were they allowed back in Jake's house for the time being. They followed Sgt. Price to his car.

The Island Communications Center was an old building, clean and neat but aging badly. Surrounding it was an airfield, the only airfield on the island. A kind looking woman let them in through the door just down the hall from her window through which she greeted everyone who came in. As they entered the larger room, Greta could see women answering the phones. She wondered which one had taken her call. Whoever she was, she had done an excellent job. Sargent Price led them to a small room just a few doors down from the holding cells, one of which, they realized, held Pem.

They gave their official statements. Sheriff Webster came in once they finished.

"You're free to go back to your house, Mr. Bernstein," the sheriff said. "The police are done there. But Ms. Little, the DeWitt-Arthur house is off limits for now."

"Everything I have on the island is in there," she said. "Can you at least get my clothes and purse? My room and office are in the wing off the kitchen, in the maid's quarters."

"I'll see what we can do."

Jake asked, "Is Pem going to be released?"

"I'm sorry to tell you that Denise Arthur is dead. Her husband is being held for questioning. That's all I can tell you for now."

    Greta and Jake held each other and cried long hard sobs of disbelief and horror.

6

Bright sunshine and an unruly crowd of reporters and photographers greeted them outside the Island Communications Center. Overhead an airplane was coming in for a landing on the airstrip.

"What can you tell us about the murder of Denise Arthur?"

"Is it true you were with her last night?"

"What was your relationship with the senator's daughter?"

"Have you spoken to Senator Arthur?"

They put up their hands to push away the microphones shoved in their faces and made their way as quickly as possible down the steps and to the taxi waiting for them in the parking lot alongside dozens of cars haphazardly parked.

Jake held her hand tightly as they sat in the back of the taxi during the drive back to his house.

Once there, he tentatively opened the front door. They stepped inside, both struck by the silence. All either could see or hear was the swarm of men and women that had been there last. Surely it had been an eternity since their dinner, since they ate with Denise and Pem and watched them dance and then stayed behind after they left, making out on the sofa. How could that possibly have been less than twelve hours ago?

Jake grabbed a mop and bucket and washed the marred floor tiles which were covered with pieces of grass and drying clumps of mud. Greta vacuumed the area rugs and polished the tables. Then Jake sat down at the dining room table and began to make phone calls.

She went into one of the guest rooms and looked at herself in the mirror. Her hair was flat, bedraggled, her face was still white with shock and her eyes were vacant, sunken. She looked as awful as she felt. She walked into the bathroom and turned on the shower.

Clean and wrapped securely in a thick white cotton guest robe over a t-shirt and pair of shorts she'd found in the dresser, she made coffee for them both, then wrote her own list of calls to make and things to be done.

Still not done with his phone calls, Jake took a break and gave her the phone while he showered.

She dreaded calling Carol but it had to be done. "Carol, it's Greta. I have some terrible news."

"I've been trying to reach you all morning. It's all over the television," Carol said. "CNN is playing the footage of you and some guy leaving the airport. You looked like death warmed over. They say it's murder. Is this right? Have you spoken with the father, the senator?"

Greta closed her eyes. "I haven't seen any sign of him."

"He's there, they keep playing the clip of when he arrived at the airport. I've been calling the number you gave me but all I get is a voicemail."

"The police won't let me go back to their house. My office is set up there, my clothes, everything is there."

"Where are you now?"

"I'm next door. With the neighbor."

"Is that the man on the TV with you?"

"I can only guess you're talking about Jacob Bernstein, the architect. He's a longtime family friend of Denise's. We walked out of the Communications Center together. The Center, it's like their police station for this part of the island. I haven't seen the footage."

"Jacob Bernstein is the Arthur's neighbor? You're staying with Jacob Bernstein? Just how involved in this are you?"

"I was staying with Denise and Pem. You know that. I'm involved but I have no idea what happened to her last night. I wasn't there when that happened."

"You need to be extremely careful how you exit this situation. When will you be leaving?" Carol asked.

"I haven't even thought that far," she said.

"Considering the circumstances, I can understand if you need another day. Clearly you are in this up to your neck. Have you talked with the media at all? Has Fitz & Winton Design been mentioned? We cannot afford any scandal. I want to know exactly what's been happening out there. I've already talked with Vinnie Morales, the mayor's attorney, and he wants to meet with you right away. His law firm will be handling this for us."

"A scandal? This is what you're worried about? You think I would endanger the firm?"

"Think about it, Greta. This has to be managed carefully. Our reputation is at stake. Everything you say and do right now will reflect on us. You can either make this an opportunity for our firm or put us in a negative light. I need you back here right away so we can spin any involvement the right way. Morales is the expert we need. We can't afford a mistake."

"I've never done anything to compromise the firm and I'm capable of deflecting any negative reflection, but I'm telling you, it has nothing to do with us. There are different mistakes, personal ones, I'm more concerned about them. Those are the ones that are life and death."

"What are you saying? Are you responsible in any way for this woman's death?"

"I should have done more. I should have gotten more involved and maybe I could have saved her from an abusive husband."

"Oh, I see what you're saying. Everyone says that. You're in shock, Greta. Get yourself straightened out and get back here. I have an appointment for you at the Morales firm in two days. Do you hear me?"

"Wait. There's something you just said a moment ago. What was it? About making this an opportunity? I understand you have to make sure your business is protected, but you said you want to spin this. Spin this?"

"It's good business. Can't you see that?"

"I can't—I can't even begin. I—you—you just don't get it, Carol. I'm not okay—not that you asked me how I'm doing—but no, I'm not okay with Denise being dead, nor can I even wrap my head around how you are looking for the opportunity in this and trying to spin it to our advantage. I am, quite honestly, *horrified*."

"Be smart, Greta. I get the sentiment, the emotions, I understand that. But you have to look past this to the interests of others. I have the firm to think about. Do you even realize all the ramifications of your involvement?"

"What particular ramification is so critical right now?"

"I can start with profit. Any profit you have brought in has just been consumed in legal fees. We need to turn that around."

Greta pulled the phone from her ear and stared it. "I can't do this."

She held it to her ear once again. "Carol, I quit. I just—I'm quitting right now. I can't do what you're asking on top of everything that has just happened. You have crossed a line here that is just too cold. I will submit an official resignation in writing when I return, whenever that may be." Without another word, she hung up.

She walked out to the patio and sat down to listen to the loud, angry waves and try to calm down.

Suddenly, two men burst through the scrub bushes and began snapping pictures of her. She screamed in surprise and scrambled inside, locking the door behind her. Shaking, she ran to the inside hall where there were no windows and sank to the floor, screaming, "Jake!"

He came running out of his bathroom, dripping, a towel around his waist. "Are you okay?"

"They're out there, taking pictures of me! They came out of the bushes and scared me to death!"

He swore and turned around to turn off the shower. He came out again, dressed but still dripping. He walked around the interior of the house, checking to see the doors and window were all locked. He drew the long dark drapes that hung hidden in the corners of each room. An unnatural darkness filled the hallway where she sat, still sobbing. He sat down beside her on the floor, pulled her to him and let her cry and cry as he rocked her back and forth in his arms.

The senator came late that afternoon to talk with them. By then Greta had changed back into her dress from the night before. Her head was throbbing from the lack of sleep and all the layers of stress, yet she wanted to bring her best to her meeting with Denise's father.

Senator William Arthur was an older man, tall with thick, straight silver hair parted sharply, his military background clear from the erect way he walked. The hollows in his cheeks and the circles under his eyes reflected the dark grief he carried with him. He shook hands with her, and he gave a warm hug to Jake. They exchanged looks that spoke of years of memories.

With him was another man who looked to be in his fifties.

"This is Steve Baker," the senator said. "Steve is a close friend of mine. We've had a chance to look at your statements, but we would like to go over the details with you. Exactly what you remember."

Jake gave a tired sigh. "I would be happy to do that, Bill, but we're exhausted right now. It's difficult to talk about and we've been over it so many times with the police. I'm so sorry. I'll call you in the morning and we'll go over everything; we'll answer all your questions then."

Steve Baker stepped up. "Now is really the best time to go over the details, while they're still fresh. There may be something you recall, something small even, that could help us down the road."

"I understand. We are just so tired right now, I don't think it would be wise. We cooperated fully with the police and gave our statements already."

"We understand. We're just asking as family."

"Sure, and we're so, so sorry. I loved Denise and my heart is breaking. We just need to get some rest."

The senator looked at him closely. "You aren't protecting Pemberton are you?"

"If he did this to Denise, I hope they hang him," Jake said evenly.

Steve set down his card on the coffee table and the men walked out.

Greta exhaled. "That was not what I expected."

"It's not what we would want, but it's what has to be."

"It's so strange. Usually when people die, everyone just comes together. This, it's like everyone is guarded, circling or something."

"We have to be careful."

"Do we need lawyers now, already?"

"I've got two lawyers on their way to the island right now. Their plane should be in by five o'clock. They'll tell us what to do."

"You took care of that first thing when we got back," she realized.

"Yes, it's the wisest thing to do. Steve Baker may have been Bill's friend, but he's also a lawyer. Take a look at his card."

"I get it." Her head was beginning to feel like a vise was closing in on it. "It's just that as her father, there must be so much the senator wants to know."

"I can't even imagine what he's going through. What a nightmare."

She sat down slowly on the sofa. "It's strange, how before you can console a man you have to consult with a lawyer."

He sat down beside her. "I invited him, Greta. We extended our condolences. But the moment I saw his lawyer, I knew that we couldn't have the conversation I wanted to have. I had to protect us first."

"Us?"

"By bringing Denise in here, I don't know if I've endangered us without realizing the consequences. That is my first concern. If Pem is charged with murder, his lawyers may do all they can to implicate us. We need to prepare for that. My lawyers are going to want to protect my firm. You will need to speak to your firm's lawyers right away, too."

"I talked with my boss already. She has informed me."

"That you need to speak with her lawyer?"

"Yes, and how my first priority is to protect Fitz & Winton and look for opportunity here to make the most of this and not make it a liability."

He put his hand on her shoulder. "She said that?"

"It's all about spinning and recouping costs. She's hired the law firm of the mayor's lawyer to help with that. They're experts on spin *and* the mayor is friends with Senator Arthur. That connection is how I ended up here in the first place."

"This could quickly become complicated for you. Bill will want to be informed on every angle of this. That's going to include your involvement and that of your design firm."

"Of course, he should know all there is to know."

"People quickly become controlling. My lawyers will help you for now, but you will need to secure your own lawyer so you're assured your best interests are being addressed, not just Bill's and not just your firm's, or my firm's."

"I've managed to make it even more complicated. I quit my job this morning. Just before I went outside and the paparazzi terrified me, I told Carol I was done. I'm not spinning anything for anyone. On top of that, not once did she even ask how I am. She has no compassion, her first thought is for herself—". She broke off in order to rub her temples in an effort to release the strong grip of the descending migraine.

"You don't need to explain your reasons to me," he said. "You made the right call."

She shook her head. "I feel sick right now. My head is going to explode if I don't get some rest. I'm going to see if I can at least close my eyes and maybe even sleep."

"Is there anything I can do? Do you need anything?"

"No," she shook her head and walked down the hall and pulled back the luxurious black silk spread on the guest bed and slipped between black linen sheets. With the heavy drapes across the window, the room was a sheltering cocoon. Mercifully, she fell asleep in just seconds.

When she woke up, the room was so dark that it had to be dark outside, too. The still pounding waves were relentless. As she turned over to face the ceiling she opened and then closed her eyes again. She wanted to be back in Chicago, sleeping in her own bed in her carriage house where the waves of Lake Michigan broke gently in the background, where clients were alive and busy with their kids and jobs, excited about working with her, like Denise had been back in July when she first spoke with her. As intense as her life had seemed at the time, looking back it had been so simple.

On the chair in the corner she could see a pile of her clothes. She investigated further and was thrilled to find her purse and makeup in a large plastic bag on the floor. She changed into her favorite sweater and a pair of jeans. Her hair was a mess. She brushed it out gently, hoping to not bring back her migraine in full force again.

Two men sat on the sofa opposite Jake. All three men stood up when she walked into the living room.

A man about her age, with dark rimmed glasses stepped forward. "Hello, you must be Greta Little. I'm Matt Phelps, Jake's attorney. I'm so sorry to hear of what you've been through in the last two days. My condolences."

"Thank you," she said. His hand was warm and firm in hers.

Jake introduced her to the older, balding man next to him. "This is Aaron Fielding, he's a criminal lawyer and a good friend of Matt's."

Aaron pressed the fingertips of her hand while he cooly assessed her. He looked every bit the shark she hoped he was if they needed him.

He said, "You have been through a great deal, Ms. Little. Is there anything we can do to help you through this?"

"No," she said, "but thank you for asking."

"Your well-being is our first concern," he said, his eyes steady on her.

"Thank you."

Matt stepped forward again, "I assure you, we've talked with Jake to see if you're up to this. We want to help you. Naturally, we want to protect you both. If at any time you feel uncomfortable, just say the word. You're not obligated to participate here, though we think it will be to your benefit."

She nodded, "I'm okay for now. I'll let you know if I need to stop."

"We've been talking for a few hours already," Jake told her as they all sat down, Greta close by him on the sofa, opposite the two men on the other sofa. "An officer came by with some of your things; I see you found them. There's some takeout in the kitchen. I can heat it up for you if you like."

"No, thanks, I just really want to try to get up to speed with where you're at. Do we have more details of what happened?" she asked.

"The police are keeping silent," Matt said. "We're waiting along with everyone else to hear if charges will be filed. For now we can only talk potential angles. Are you comfortable talking about what you think happened to Denise?"

She looked at Jake. "Have you talked about it yet?"

"I wanted to wait until you were here." He took her hand.

"I'd like to understand this process a little better," she said to the lawyers. "You mentioned angles. Right now I can see several possibilities. It could have been an accident, it could have been Pem, or it could have been a stranger. But, as Jake told me earlier, if Pem did it, his lawyers might try to say that he's innocent but that we did something."

The men all nodded.

"Are there any other angles?"

Aaron said, "This is a criminal investigation involving very powerful, very wealthy people who need to protect their interests. There are definitely other issues at play here."

She looked at Jake. He glanced at her and looked back at the lawyers.

Aaron spoke again, "For one thing, we understand the relationship between Senator Arthur and the DeWitt family is complex. The senator is senior on financial committees that oversee banking concerns. It's rumored that favors have been called in and certain things overlooked in a recent merger between two major banks. The DeWitts were directly involved in the merger. What will happen now that the senator's daughter is dead, quite possibly at the hand of her husband?"

"I see," she said, knowing she was only beginning to really see the many aspects at play. She thought hard for a moment. "How do you happen to know this about them?"

Jake spoke up. "My parents know Bill better than I ever will. They told me about the merger and questionable actions when I told them I was coming out here in the summer. When I called them this morning, they reminded me of the details."

"But how does that affect us? We can't control that. It doesn't touch us, does it?"

Aaron spoke up, "It will be a problem if you want to see justice done and believe it's being averted. For instance, the senator could make it look like he has new information about the banking deal and cause an uproar if Pem doesn't come clean or plead guilty. Or, the DeWitts could threatened the senator if they have something on him, and ask him to pull some strings. Charges could be dropped or maybe Pem just gets a slap on the hand. It depends on who has the most to lose. We don't know which party that is."

Matt explained further, "If you're personally upset about the injustice in that, your reaction to such a scenario could have consequences. Those pulling the strings will want to make sure you can't make a fuss."

"Okay, then it comes down to being careful about what we do and say publicly," she reasoned.

"Right," Aaron said. "However, that's not all. The other major consideration is if Pem is charged with Denise's murder. They may try to implicate you or Jake as part of their defense strategy."

Jake said, "You're confirming that by bringing Denise in here, I opened the door for deeper scrutiny into our involvement."

Aaron was quick. "Pem's lawyer is going to be all over that."

"But there had to be blood left on the grass," Greta said. "She was so white and there was so much blood. It must be clear that she was originally lying there."

Aaron went to the dining table and took a legal pad and a pen from a briefcase. "I'm going to take notes while you talk." He took out a small recorder, too. "Are you okay if I record this? I can only write so fast."

They agreed.

She squeezed Jake's hand. "Are you up for this tonight? You haven't slept in a day and half."

"It feels like jet lag. I'm used to it."

"You have both given your statements to the police," Aaron said, "the facts of what happened as you witnessed them. I'd like to hear exactly what you told them, and then have you brainstorm. What I'm hoping to hear are particulars you may not have realized are important."

They each went over the facts of their accounts yet again.

Aaron's pen never stopped writing. "Now, let's go with some general questions to get you thinking more broadly. Do you think it could have been an accident?"

"No," Jake said. "I didn't see anything in the grass that may have tripped her or that she landed on. Did you?" he asked Greta.

"No. But she was off to the side. Do you think there could have been a large rock in the dirt by the bushes? Or maybe she got hurt a few feet from where she was lying and we didn't see the rock because it wasn't in that spot?"

"Was there anything in the path when you were heading to your house with the food?" Matt asked.

"Nothing," Jake said. "I've walked it thousands of times. If there was anything with that potential, I would remember it."

Greta said, "We told the police there was a huge clap of thunder and hail started just after she left us. We were worried about her then. But even a huge piece of hail wouldn't have done that."

Aaron reminded them, "The autopsy will tell us how she died. We're assuming what hit her, killed her. That looks most obvious, but we just don't know for sure."

"What if she wasn't running from here, but back to us?" Jake said. "What if she came looking for him, or what if she was afraid of him and came here for help but something happened on her way back here?"

Greta felt sick. "That could be. He may have followed her and killed her. Her head was facedown but she was kind of facing their house and to the side," she recalled. "It's hard to say which direction she may have been going." She paused. "But she was still wearing her dress. She hadn't changed into her nightgown."

Jake looked at Aaron. "For some reason their worst fights were usually late at night, after they had gone to bed."

Aaron nodded and kept writing.

"Or," Greta said, "what if Pem killed her at their house and brought her out to the path to make it look like an accident or that someone else did it?" A heaviness of horror settled on her as she said this. This wasn't a murder mystery they were talking about, this was real, this was Denise and Pem.

They all fell silent for a moment, and even Aaron's pen stopped. "Let me switch this up again," he said after a moment. "If for any reason Pem's lawyers try to frame you, do you see any weaknesses in the collaboration of your stories?"

Greta answered, "The only thing we didn't both experience was when I ran to phone for the ambulance and Jake heard Pem calling for Denise. Even then, our stories jived."

"Let's explore that further," Aaron said.

Jake leaned forward. "I was giving Denise CPR. Even though I was concentrating on trying to get her to breathe, I was well aware that whomever had done this to her might not be far away. I had this heightened sense of awareness, so when I heard movement in the bushes and then heard Pem calling for Denise, I wanted to get her out of there. The last thing I needed while trying to give her a chance to live was to deal with Pem. Was he trying to look like the caring husband? Had he come back to finish the job? If he killed her, would he kill Greta or me? All of that went through my mind in a split second. That's why I picked her up and ran back to my house. Greta was just coming outside."

"Yes," Greta concurred. "I had just made the call for the ambulance and was outside running to help Jake. When I saw him, I ran back to open the sliding door for him and once he was inside I locked it behind us in case Pem was out there."

"Did you see him?"

"Not at first. I was more concerned about Denise. When I did look up, he was standing there watching us. He hadn't tried to open the door, he hadn't knocked, he was just watching us. I'll never forget how crazed he looked. Only when I saw him and screamed did he pound on the glass and shout to let him in."

Aaron asked, "Jake, you seemed intent on giving Denise CPR; was there any indication of life at that point?"

Greta and Jake stared at Aaron. Jake spoke first. "I—we had just seen her alive. How could we not?"

"I'm just asking."

"It didn't seem possible that she could be dead," Greta said. "It was just instinct, the right thing to do. I checked her pulse and Jake started CPR."

Next to him, Greta felt a tremor run through Jake's body. "I do think she was dead. She was lifeless. But if there was any chance of saving her, I had to do whatever I could to increase her odds," he said.

Aaron made more notes. He looked up again. "I want to rewind the clock. Go back to the moment when she ran out the sliding door after him, after he had been so hurtful."

Jake said, "In that moment, I believed Pem was capable of anything. I didn't understand how Denise could go after him. It made no sense."

Greta shook her head. "I can't fathom why she loved him so much. Jake, you used the word addiction when you first tried to explain their relationship to me. I think that's exactly what it was. She was sure she couldn't live without him, even though he looked and acted in such frightening ways. I know he hid it well, but clearly not from her."

"He made her believe she couldn't make it without him. He beat her down emotionally," Jake said. "He told her she was repulsive, worthless. She believed him."

"That would be classic. It wasn't just about following him outside that particular night," Aaron said. "It was about all the other days and nights she believed that what he said about her was true. Her dependency on him was built over time, as he abused her."

"That's it," Greta said, taken aback at the truth of their words.

"He did it deliberately," Jake said.

"Killed her?" Greta asked.

"I think he did, but I was referring to what I believe was intentional behavior on his part to make her dependent upon him. I watched him do it."

"Why would he do that?" she asked.

Jake replied, "It gave him power and control. It was a game to him."

Greta looked at Matt and Aaron and then back at Jake. "You all get this, don't you?"

They nodded in one accord and looked down.

"This is what men do?" she asked.

"Abusive men do this," Matt replied. "I think we've all seen it. Some men boast about it."

"I can't believe what I'm hearing," Greta said. "It's so evil."

"I don't think it's always evil," Aaron said. "What Pem did, if indeed he did it, that was evil. Sometimes, however, women choose to be blind when it comes to men. I think Jake and Matt would agree, women give that power to men. For instance, and I'll speak for myself, when I was single there were several times I ended a dating relationship and told a woman I wasn't interested, only to hear from her again the next day. She'd apologize for something she didn't even do wrong. Rather than believing the truth, that I just wasn't interested, women often blamed themselves, or believed there must have been a misunderstanding, anything except the reality that I wasn't attracted to them. In the hands of a lesser man, that's power over that woman. The man knows that woman is willing to disregard reality, in my case, rejection, just to be with him. Now imagine that in the hands of a man who wants to use and abuse that woman."

Greta rubbed her temples. "Every woman needs to hear this."

Matt said, "Your mother never told you this?"

"She probably gave me some version of it when I was a teenager. I'm sure I thought I knew better. Hearing you in my thirties when I understand what's at stake, it's eye-opening. Not understanding this cost Denise her life."

The truth hung in the air for a long time.

"I don't mean to change the subject," Greta finally said, "but I would like to understand how Denise's death might negatively affect Jake's firm and Fitz & Winton Design. How can we best protect them?"

"As it pertains to you, Greta, at this point in time, the fact that you were staying there and witnessed the alleged violence, drug use and abusive behaviors in your capacity as their designer, will bring attention to your company and your role in their personal lives. I haven't had the chance to talk with you yet about your personal relationship with them, but from what Jake has told us, I can see nothing problematic that could be used against you. If this goes to trial, however, your testimony will be critical. Your testimony will be incriminating. A defense attorney will be eager to cast doubt on your character and the reliability of your testimony. They will do their best to discredit you.

"To some degree," he went on, "again, if this goes to trial, they will do the same to Jake because of his presence that night and because of the longevity of his relationship with Denise. Discrediting both of you could become their main agenda. Will that harm your companies? That will depend on how they try to discredit you. I can't hypothesize on that at this point. Defense attorneys would want to know if there's anything in your past or present that could be used against either one of you."

Matt said, "This will be a high profile case simply because of Denise's father and her husband's family and high profile. You need to be prepared for that media interest. It will rise and fall as this unfolds."

She rubbed her temples yet again as her migraine shot pains behind her eyes. As pleasant a diversion as this job had been, it was now a nightmare.

Matt asked, "Is there anything else either of you think would be helpful for us to know, outside of what's in your statements?"

Both Greta and Jake shook their heads.

"Then let's move on," Aaron said. "If the police don't release anything new tomorrow and we know only what you know so far, then when you talk to the senator and his lawyer you stick to your facts again. Keep your personal perspective out of it. You're simply two caring people who sadly happened to see dissension between a married couple. Your concern is for the grieving senator."

Aaron clicked his pen and set the paper and pen down on the table.

"Senator Arthur is going to want to know everything you know. His lawyer will want you to talk openly to him just like you talked to me. Don't do it. Even if Pemberton is charged with murder, Senator Arthur will want his own investigation. We don't know what that will look like. When his lawyers start questioning you, you stick to what you told the police. If you remember anything else that might be helpful, you let me know first. We'll talk it over and I'll advise you. Understand?"

They agreed.

The next afternoon, at Jake's invitation, Senator Arthur and Steve Baker sat down with Greta and Jake and Matt and Aaron. Because the paparazzi continued to swarm the house, police were stationed at the end of the driveway and on the lawn this time, to ward off those who might come up from the beach. Inside, the drapes remained closed and the phone turned on silent.

In the dark, somber house, everyone did their best to be as warm and kind to each other as they could be in view of the heinous crime and how carefully they had to proceed to minimize any negative reflection on themselves.

Greta, migraine in full force again, joined in where necessary, but sharing the facts now felt cold and empty. None of the details seemed at all congruent with the warmth and laughter and good times they'd shared over the past few months. All the good seemed like a cracked facade. What remained was dark and ugly and she felt almost as if she was betraying Denise as she told the senator what she had witnessed during her time with Denise and Pem.

"I'm so sorry to have to tell you all this, Senator," she finished. "My relationship with Denise was so much more than what I saw happening with Pem. She was warm and kind and outside of the abuse and tension with Pem, I loved every minute with her. She was the heart of that home. When she was there the house came alive. It was a gift to know her."

"Thank you, Ms. Little," the senator said quietly. "She was much more than who Pem made her out to be."

She watched as Jake spoke carefully, too. She tried to put herself in the shoes of these high-powered men who knew so well how to take care of business and keep their worlds protected while trying to be patient and sympathetic conversationalists. Where was the sincerity in that? Where was true kindness? Is that what long time family friends do in their moment of tragedy? It felt wrong.

All she could see in her mind's eye was Denise standing in the kitchen with shards of glass on her feet and all round her, terrified as Pem screamed at her. Denise floating in the ocean, her thin, bony ribs showing through her swimsuit, Denise trying to please Pem over and over, and that last night, trying to be pretty and sexy and entice her own husband away from another woman.

She heard her name mentioned.

"Ms. Little," Senator Arthur was saying, "I want to thank you again for all you've done over the last few months for my daughter. That house meant more to her than anything or anyone, except for Pemberton. I wasn't always there for my family, but I will say that the best of our memories were made out here. She called me weekly to tell me all that you were doing. She couldn't have been happier. The last time I spoke with her she said the remodeling wasn't quite done yet. Under the circumstances, I'm sure you'll understand that I'll need to close up the house, regardless of where you're at with it. I will pay you in full for any outstanding costs involved."

"Senator, it was a joy to work with her and help her vision for the house come about. I completely understand that my work here is done. I'm sorry this is even a topic for discussion right now. Please, there is nothing to settle." She would pay Carol for any expenses out of her own pocket if need be, but she would not be charging the estate of Denise Arthur for anything further.

"Thank you," he said, "but my office will call your firm next week to take care of any loose ends." He pushed away from the table. "Thank you, Jake, Mr. Fielding, Mr. Phelps, Ms. Little."

Greta stood and watched as Jake saw Arthur and his lawyer to the door.

When they were gone, Jake turned to Matt and Aaron. "What's next? What else do we have to do?"

The migraine she'd been trying to ignore pushed hard against her eyes. Greta put up her hand. "I don't want to know. I need a break."

Jake gave her a hug. "I'll take care of whatever needs to be done. Go rest."

Her head was pounding as she walked down the hall to her room. Despite the fact that her migraine would not approve, what she wanted to do was rip open the drapes and doors, let in whatever sunshine was out there along with the fresh salt air and breathe in life again.

Tears streaked out of the corners of her eyes as she sat at the foot of the bed. The future, it was here. It was time to leave the island. It was time to go back to Chicago and meet with Carol and the Morales lawyers, tell them all about her life out here these past few months, all the while no longer employed by Fitz & Winton. If this went to trial and her reputation or character called into questions, Fitz & Winton would distance themselves from her if they felt it was best for the firm, and having quit, she gave them no incentive to do otherwise.

There were no clients to go back to. She had no right to them now. Many would be angry about this and feel let down. Legally, she had no right to contact them to even say she was sorry.

Oh, to go back to a year ago, when she was grieving her mom, whose natural death was so much more *normal* to deal with than a murder. A murder left nothing sane in its destructive past. It was destroying her life and it had only just happened. How much worse was it going to get?

She fell back on the bed. "God," she whispered softly as she stared at the ceiling above the bed, "If you're really up there, I've got a million random thoughts right now and I'm feeling pretty helpless about all of them. I feel like darkness is closing in on me. None of this makes sense and it's all destructive. I don't know what you can do about it, but being God, Aidan said you care about me and have a plan for me and my life. It sure doesn't feel like it."

She searched for the right words. "Denise is dead. Dead! All this time I've been focused on her house and enjoying her friendship and this great opportunity on this amazing island, but look at it all now. None of it is important. Her house is closed up. She's dead. I could have and should have done more. At the very least I could have found out how to help her. If she had a design problem, I would have figured out how to solve it. But I didn't even think to learn how to help her with Pem. I'm disgusted with my selfishness. I have no excuse for that at all. I'm so self-centered. I'm busy doing what I want to do, what makes me feel good and look good and what advances my career. But when it comes to what's really important in life, I'm a failure. I was no help to Denise at all!"

She crawled to the top of bed and cried into her pillow, great heaving sobs that left the pillow soaked and her head throbbing.

"God," she said amidst more sobs, "I hate my own self-centeredness. I hate the darkness everywhere in this house and next door. I hate what Pem did. I hate that people have to worry about their businesses and protect themselves when they should be crying together and grieving the loss of Denise. It's not right! I don't know what or how you can do it, but God, please get rid of this darkness. Bring justice to Pem, whatever he did, expose it. Please help me too, to be less selfish. Forgive me for all the ways I've believed I could figure everything out on my own. I can't figure anything out!"

Sobs took over again. She cried until there was no regret left in her soul, for she had poured it all out to God. Finally, she lay there, breathing through her mouth because her nose was so impossibly stuffy, and she felt empty of the pain and angst, yet strangely at peace. How long she lay there, she didn't know.

At last, with her nose stuffed, there was nothing to do but go find some tissues in the attached bathroom. As she blew her nose and her head throbbed yet again, she suddenly remembered that somewhere in her makeup bag or purse were the remaining samples of migraine medicine from Doc that she had carried with her for over a year now, just in case she might need them. She dug out her purse from the bag on the floor. Sure enough, she found one and wrestled it out of the foil packet. Relieved, she dropped her purse back on the floor. It fell lightly next to the shopping bag.

She swallowed the pill and then picked up her brush from the dresser to make herself presentable. And then she froze.

Her purse, it was too light. *The flashlight. Her purse had been heavy with Jake's steel flashlight.* She threw down the brush and ran to her purse. The flashlight wasn't in there. It wasn't in the shopping bag or with her other things either. It was gone.

She startled the men when she ran into the living room. "The flashlight! It's gone!"

Jake stood up. "What are you talking about?"

"Remember the one you gave me other day in case Pem went crazy again at night, so I could see if I had to come over? I put it in my purse. But it's not there. Either the police took it or someone else took it."

Jake turned to the other men. "The flashlight is steel, it's heavy. If the police don't have it, it could be the murder weapon. I have an identical one just like it. I can show them what it looks like."

Aaron called the Island Communications Center and asked for Sheriff Webster. Less than a half hour later they all stood in the driveway outside the Arthur house, not allowed any closer. When Sheriff Webster came out, his hands were empty. "We don't have it," he said. "It's not on our evidence list and it's not in the house now. Ms. Little, why would Mr. DeWitt go into your purse in the first place? Do you have something of his? Is there anything he could have been looking for in there? How would he have found it otherwise?"

"I don't have anything of his," she said. "He's never given me a thing. I can't believe he'd take money or credit cards, they have plenty of money."

"Greta," Jake said, "you took a map out of your purse the afternoon before she was killed. You said Jake gave you the map. He had highlighted a new antique shop in Oak Bluffs."

The light finally dawned. She turned to the sheriff. "I asked if he knew of any antique shops so I could look for some things for their remodel. He said a brand new one just opened up in Oak Bluffs. He gave me the map and highlighted the route. Then he wrote the name of the store on the top. The Yellow Whale."

"Do you have the map?"

"I put it in my purse and about five or ten minutes later handed it to Jake to look at because I was driving and needed directions. Do you recall what we did with it, Jake? I don't think I took it back inside when we returned and it's not in my purse."

"Where's your car?" Webster asked.

She turned around and pointed at the red rental car. "Right there. It should be locked. I took my keys with me when we went to Jake's that night because I knew I wanted to spend some time with Jake once they left. They usually kept the door unlocked, but I thought I'd bring them with me just in case."

They all walked the few feet to the car and peered inside. There was no sign of the map.

"I'll go get my keys," she said.

"I'll go with you," Aaron said. "Matt, come on."

With the yellow tape now gone from the path, they were able to go quickly back to Jake's.

Aaron said, "Greta, you get the keys and give them to the sheriff. Matt and I are going to head to Oak Bluffs. Matt, do you know your way around well enough to find it?"

"Sure," Matt said. "I've been out here a few times. Jake told me it's on Circuit Ave. The Yellow Whale, we can't miss it if we look for the sign."

Aaron went on, "If Pem knew this shop was open and it's brand new, and he didn't want anyone to know he knew it, we need to find out why."

"You need to check out the owner," Greta said. "She's young and pretty and somehow has enough money to own her own shop fresh out of college. And wait," she added, following them to their car, "there's more. That's where Jake found the paperweight that he thought was Denise's. Pem got all upset when Jake bought it back and gave it to Denise."

The men jumped in their car. "Go tell Webster what you just told us!"

When she returned to the Arthur's with her keys, Jake was telling the sheriff the same thing she had told Matt and Aaron. She noted that the senator and Steve Baker were gone, too. So were several police cars. She handed the keys to Detective Webster.

"What does the owner of the store look like?" he asked tersely.

Jake described her. Webster walked away but from the radio in his car they could hear him shouting instructions to his men. "Dispatch a crew to the store and another to the owner's house. I want her brought in for questioning. I'll wrap up here and meet you back at the Communications Center."

Jake held her hand as the sheriff donned latex gloves and opened the driver's side door and flipped down the visor. Nothing. He checked under the seat. Nothing. He went around to the passenger side and opened the door. To the side of the seat, just underneath it and hidden by the bottom where the door closed, was the map.

Jake pointed at Pem's writing at the top, "That's it."

Greta nodded in agreement. "He wrote that and gave it to me. He saw me put it in my purse. He knew we went there because we had the paperweight when we returned. Denise put it back in the library, on her desk. Pem was getting angry and irrational about it."

Webster nodded at a nearby officer, who nodded back and went immediately inside the house. He returned shortly, empty handed, shaking his head.

"At least we have the map," Webster said. "I'm going to Oak Bluffs. I imagine my men are already there. And so I presume, are the senator and your lawyers," he added dryly. He got in his car and drove away.

She hugged Jake hard. "We're getting somewhere."

The relief on his face was clear to see. Maybe it was the sun shining down on them, maybe it was the darkness beginning to lift. For the first time since the murder, she could see how much he was hurting. His pain hurt her. He was taking this harder than she had realized.

"Are you okay?" she asked.

"Not at all."

"What can I do?"

"Just keep putting together all the pieces," he said. "You're wonderful. You did this."

"It wasn't me," she said, shaking her head. "I had no hope. I think it was God. I just asked for his help."

"Let's go back."

Matt and Aaron returned within the hour with lobster rolls from Menemsha. Matt held up the paper bag. "We come bearing good news and great food."

"I need the good news first," Jake said.

Greta and the men sat down at the table and Matt handed out the wrapped lobster rolls. No one bothered with plates.

"We arrived just a minute or two before the senator and the police," Aaron said. "I asked the girl at the counter if we could speak to the owner. She said she was the owner. I asked if she knew Pemberton DeWitt. She hesitated and then said no."

"Her face went white, literally white," Matt said.

"Then we heard sirens and the girl panicked. She ran for the back of the store."

"Except the police met her out back," Matt smiled. "We came out and watched while they questioned her and then took her away."

"I think it's safe to say you're in the clear, both of you," Aaron said. "There's no way you two are going to be implicated. Clearly there was something going on between Pem and this girl. The police will be able to establish a motive and that will be the end of it."

Aaron rose, wiping his mouth with his napkin. "I'm going to talk to the sheriff to confirm this. By now he's got to know more. He may not be able to share much, but I'll see what I can learn."

He came back with more good news. "They don't have the murder weapon yet but they have enough for the prosector to press charges. Get this—the girl admitted on her own, outright, that she was having an affair with DeWitt. And she admitted she's pregnant. The police have a solid timeline, evidence, motive, everything but the murder weapon itself."

Matt clapped Jake on the back. "They're going to put this guy away. You and Greta may have to testify at the trial but I'm not worried about it. The attorneys, the media, everyone is going to be focusing on the pregnant girlfriend. You and Greta, and your firms are not going to become a focus. The worst is behind you."

Aaron joined in, "Greta, I'm happy to speak to your firm's lawyers on your behalf and bring them up to speed. The same goes for your own lawyer when you get one. If there's anything we can do to help, please, let us know."

The doorbell rang and Jake went to answer. He came back with a broad smile on his face. "The security team I hired is here. They're stationed at the driveway, the path to the beach and around the property. We can open the drapes and begin to live here again."

They all cheered. "It's a new day," Aaron said. " I think it's time the two of you realize you are real life heroes. You did all you could to save Denise Arthur's life."

The smiles dropped from Jake's and Greta's faces. Jake said, "I'm no hero. I should have done a lot more to save her years ago."

Greta fought the tears. "I'm ashamed I didn't do more."

"Hey, I'm sorry," Aaron said. "I realize you have regrets, that's to be expected. But honestly, from my perspective your actions were honorable. You did as much as anyone can do in an impossible situation. You didn't know it, but you were dealing with a man capable of murder."

Matt agreed. "I'm glad you're okay and neither one of you got hurt."

There were hugs of relief all around. Shortly, the lawyers left for the airport. The first thing Jake did was go room to room opening the drapes again.

Greta cleaned up the remnants of lunch and turned around to speak to Jake but stopped. He stood, shoulders heaving, at the spot where he had laid Denise's lifeless body. Then he fell down on his knees and wept like a baby, his face in his hands. She held him while he rocked back and forth.

That night he lit a fire again in the fireplace and the two of them laid side by side on the sofa.

"I'm taking back my house," he said. "We are not going to let that last night with them stop us from living here."

"I understand," she said, kissing him softly. "I can't believe how you took care of so much so quickly. You are incredibly capable in an emergency."

"My mind won't stop. I'm still having a hard time not thinking of all that's happened."

"We're trying to make sense of it," she said.

"Except there is no sense to it."

"None at all."

He kissed her then, and they forgot for a while all the senseless evil.

When Greta woke up the next morning she could hear Jake's shower running. She pulled back the drapes in her room. Fog had rolled in.

She showered and dressed and decided to make Jake a nice breakfast. He was already starting the coffee when she came in.

"Two questions," she said. "Do you like waffles and if so, do you happen to have a waffle maker and a recipe book?"

"I do to both questions," he said. "Look in the corner cabinet."

The smell of the steaming waffle iron reminded her of home. He found the butter and syrup and cut up a muskmelon while she made the waffles.

"This reminds me of home," she said as they ate. "It's comforting. Did your mom like to cook when you were growing up?"

"She was good at making sandwiches," he said. "For everything else we had a cook. Speaking of my parents, they'll be coming in for the funeral. Bill hasn't said where it will be yet; maybe New York, maybe here."

"Do you have anything you need to accomplish today?"

"I wanted to show you the fog," he said. "I think today is it. Let's go."

They pushed away from the table. She pulled on a sweatshirt and he zipped up a windbreaker and they walked down a steep path to the beach below. It did not have the boardwalk that the Arthur's had and was instead rough and more than a little steep. "I appreciate my privacy," he explained. "I don't like to make it easy for people to come up to the house."

He took her hand once they reached the sand. There, guarding the path and access to his beachfront, stood two uniformed guards.

"I appreciate your work here," Jake said.

The two men nodded, "Thank you, Sir."

Visibility wasn't terrible but it certainly wasn't good. She kept her shoes on and they walked close to the shore where the sand was hard from the pounding waves.

"It will be awhile before we can come back here," he said. "The media won't leave us alone. I'm still keeping the ringer on the phone turned off. My voicemail is full, even though I deleted it last night. It will be good to move forward again."

"I have no idea what's ahead for me," she said. "Maybe I can start my own business now. It looks like this would be a good time."

"That makes things interesting." He stopped walking. "Do you want to go back to New York with me for a day or two and then head out to Switzerland with me?"

"Thank you, but no. I feel—how do I explain it—like everything is just a jumbled up mess. If I go to New York with you that will be more new situations and more adjustments. Right now I just need to feel something familiar again, something solid."

"I get it," he said. "We both need the familiar to heal and get over the shock of it all. It doesn't bode well for our relationship, though."

"What do you mean?"

"We're just starting out. We're still new to each other. I don't know if any new relationship can be sustained under this kind of pressure."

"Jake! Don't say that!"

"It concerns me."

"I'll come out for the funeral," she said. "No matter where it is."

"If it's in New York I'll pick you up at the airport. You can stay with me at my apartment."

"But your parents will be with you."

"They still have their apartment on Long Island."

"Oh," she sighed, "I should have guessed."

"You'll get used to it," he smiled.

"I don't know," she said, shaking her head. "Where I come from you were considered rich if your parents owned a cabin near a lake where you could go in the summer. Having homes all over the world, or on each coast, it's such a different lifestyle."

In silence they walked and walked, enjoying the fog and the sounds of the gulls that seemed much more obvious in the absence of visible landmarks. Finally they turned around and headed back. Carefully, they climbed up the rough path that led to his house.

"So what do you think of the island in the fog?" he asked as they stepped inside the quiet house.

"It's moody, it's a little unsettling, but I'm glad to be in it with you."

He helped her out of her sweatshirt and then put his hand behind her head and pulled her to him. He kissed her hard. "I want you, Greta."

She knew as she kissed him back that they were both aware they were standing where Denise had lain. She knew how much he needed her, wanted her to comfort him and share the grief and all the emotions that still inundated them both.

She put her arms around his neck. "If I sleep with you I will not be able to leave you. I know myself too well. I'll go with you to New York and then on to Switzerland and Japan and you will make room for me in your life, you will accommodate me, but we would be cutting short the time it takes to really get to know each other, to build trust and to know for sure that…", her voice trailed off. She swallowed the lump in her throat, "That you are the one for me, and that I am the one for you for the rest of our lives."

His forehead against hers, he asked, "So what's next? We go our separate ways and meet at the funeral? Call each other every night?"

"Yes."

"I don't want to let you out of my sight," he said. "I need you more than I have needed any other woman in my entire life."

"It's Denise's death. It's this horrible thing that Pem has done. We're both in shock."

"Where do you get this self-control to think so rationally?"

She laughed. "I don't know. I'm surprising myself, believe me."

"Does that you mean you want me, too?"

"Of course it does! I just don't have the emotional reserves to handle anything more right now."

"Well, work on that would you?"

They laughed half-heartedly. He sighed as she dropped her hands and disengaged despite his hands and kisses. It was the only way to turn down the heat and they both knew it.

They took turns calling the airlines to make their reservations to Chicago and New York.

She was just falling asleep that night when she heard Jake knocking on her bedroom door.

"Yes? Come in," she said groggily, trying to sit up.

He was still dressed. "I'm sorry to wake you! I just have to tell you. My answering machine has been picking up calls though the ringer is turned off. I was listening to and deleting my messages when I listened to one that is for you. You need to hear this."

She pushed her hair out of her eyes. "Seriously?"

"Come on!" he said. He grabbed the robe from the chair by the window. "Here."

With a sigh she swung her legs to the side of the bed and put on the robe and followed him to the kitchen. "This better be good."

"Oh, it is. Are you ready?"

She nodded.

Jake pushed the button on the machine, "Mr. Bernstein? This is Karl

Little. I understand my daughter Greta is with you. Would you please have her call me? Here's my number."

Her hands flew to her cheeks. "Play it again."

He hit rewind and played it again.

She covered her mouth with her hand. "It's really him. It's my dad!"

"The number he gives is local. He's on the island."

She started to laugh and cry at the same time. "I can't believe it," she said again and again.

"Call him!" Jake said.

"I can't! It's eleven-thirty at night!"

"He's your father! He will love to hear from you!"

She shook her head. "No, I need to think."

"Think about what?"

"I don't know!" She gave a little shout of joy but then she cried some more. "I'm so mixed up right now I can't even think straight."

"My guess is that he saw you on the news or read about your involvement in the paper. My friends are calling from all over the country with condolences after seeing us on the national news. They also want to know who the beautiful blonde is at my side."

"Oh stop," she said.

He shrugged. "It's true."

"I can't leave in the morning if my father is here," she said. "That's for sure."

"I'll cancel my flight, too. If you're okay with this, I'd like to be with you."

"That's fine," she said, "but I have to warn you, it's complicated."

"I can handle complicated, remember?"

"Don't say I didn't warn you."

She could hardly sleep. At nine o'clock the next morning, with some trepidation and a breathless prayer, she dialed his number.

"Hello?"

"Dad? It's me, Greta."

"Greta," was all he could manage before she heard his voice crack.

"I'd like to meet with you," she said. "Are you on the island?"

"Yes, I'm in Chilmark."

"We're just a few minutes from each other!"

"It's so good to hear your voice," he said.

"It's good to hear yours, too," she replied, wiping her tears and nose with her sleeve. "Can you come over? I'm at Jake Bernstein's."

"I know where it is," he said. "I'll be right over."

"There are guards at the end of the driveway. I'll tell them you're coming," she said. "They'll let you through."

Jake looked at her as she hung up the phone. "Are you okay?"

She could only nod. "He's on his way here."

In just minutes she heard a vehicle come up the drive. She ran to the door and walked outside to greet him.

He was an old man, with white, white hair, and his face was a permanent tan, weathered from years of sun and ocean, his shoulders a little stooped. But his blue eyes were still familiar, and though he wasn't nearly as tall as she remembered, his voice still ran through her with a familiarity she could only account to those early years of being imprinted on her brain.

She hugged him hard and he hugged her back just as hard.

"I love you," he said, his voice choked with emotion.

"I love you, too," she said. She turned to Jake. "Dad, this is Jake Bernstein, a very good friend of mine."

"How do you do?" he said. It wasn't until he reached out his left hand to Jake that she remembered his right hand had no fingers or thumb. She remembered countless moments spent studying his hand while he held her, while he worked with tools and still managed so capably.

Jake swiftly reached out his own left hand and the two men shook hands.

"I remember your parents and how your place used to look," Karl said. "Years ago I filled in for your caretaker every so often."

"I didn't realize that," Jake said.

"Oh, we helped each other out back then, the caretakers did."

"Won't you come in?" Jake asked and led them inside.

Greta watched as her father stopped inside the door and looked around, taking in every detail, just as she had done the first time she had entered.

She looked at Jake. He was smiling and looking back and forth at the two of them.

"Dad, do you want to look around? Jake won't mind."

"I would like that," he said, "but first I want to talk with you!"

She sat down next to her dad on one of the sofas. "It is so good to see you again, I can't tell you."

"I thought you might not want to see me," he said.

"Life is too short for grudges," she heard herself say.

"I want to say I'm sorry for leaving you and your mother. I

shouldn't have done that." Intently, he looked at her. "I'm very sorry."

"Can we talk about that?" she asked. "Just kind of go right to the heart of things? You okay with that?"

"Yes, the buck stops here."

"I remember the fighting," she said. "I know you were both miserable."

"It was all my fault. I had two families. I felt guilty no matter where I was or what I did. I assume your mother told you all about that when I left."

"She waited until just before she died. You knew that she died, right? I noticed the deposits into her bank account stopped shortly thereafter."

He nodded. "I did. The bank let me know she died. How did she die?"

"Pancreatic cancer. She didn't want any chemo or radiation. She was gone in seven months."

He absorbed this and then went on, "She told you about my other family then, just before she died? You've only known a little while?"

"Yes, it was quite a shock. I didn't even know about the first time you left, before I was born. I didn't know anything about Bridget."

"Bridget is gone, too. She passed away just a few months after I moved back. She had ovarian cancer. That's why I came back here when you were twelve. She was sick but she fought hard. She was a very determined woman."

"That's why you came back to the island?"

"Yes. I had to do the right thing. Both for her and Mel."

"Mel, she's your daughter?"

"Mel was sixteen, almost seventeen when her mom died. She is an only child."

"Where is she? Is she on the island?"

His eyes shifted away from her, "Her name is Melinda, I call her Mel. She moved to Boston after college. She was out here this summer with her family."

"Are you close?"

He nodded. "Yes, she's my life." He hastily looked back at her.

"It's okay, Dad. You have carried enough guilt around. You don't have to worry. I'm fine."

"Tell me about you," he said. "The news clips said something about you being an interior designer."

"I live in Glencoe," she said, "just outside Chicago."

"I remember the town."

"I rent a carriage house there. I decorated it just like all the bedtime stories you told me about the little house on the ocean. Only mine is on Lake Michigan."

He closed his eyes. "I'm sorry."

"Actually, it's a good thing. It's been featured in *Architectural Digest* and some local magazines in Chicago."

"I don't understand," he said, clearly perplexed.

"She's an excellent designer," Jake offered. "Her work is superb. Several magazines have featured it."

A huge grin broke across Karl's face. "You don't say."

"I'm under the impression I inherited that gift from you," she said. "Mom told me about your dream to be an architect."

Karl couldn't stop smiling. "Maybe you did at that."

"What about Melinda? What does she do?"

"She has her mother's and her grandfather's business acumen. As a caretaker, I used to have to dispose of homeowners castoffs. I would bring them to the dump. As Melinda got older, she began going through the boxes and found topnotch clothing and began selling it. In college she began to rent out formal wear and jewelry to her classmates. The business took off from there. She rents designer wear to thousands of people. She opened a second store in Philadelphia and she just launched a third in Connecticut."

"Where did she go to school?" Jake asked.

"Wharton School of Business."

Greta was surprised. "Wharton?"

Karl nodded. "When her mother died, her grandfather, who used to be my boss, set up a trust fund for Mel. Paid for her college. Originally he said he would disown her, but once he met her, he changed his tune."

"Dad, what about you? Are you okay financially? May I ask that?"

"Sure," he said. "I have everything I need."

"I have to ask you, as a caretaker, how could you afford to send Mom money all those years?"

"I live simply, Greta. I don't need much. When I started out here we did well. I setup the caretaking business and Bridget started a catering business. We always had enough. I loved your mom so much I would have given her the shirt off my back if it came to that."

The tears in his eyes were clear to see. "I just want you to know if you need anything," she said, reaching over and taking his hand in hers, "there is plenty of money from Mom's estate to help you."

He squeezed her hand. "No, no, no. Every penny of that she deserved. And you, too."

"I found the stocks from Atlas that you gave to Mom; I turned them in a month ago. I'm more than happy to share that with you."

"They were never traded in? After all these years?"

"That's right," she said. "They were worth a great deal, Dad."

"Greta, it gives me great joy to know you have that inheritance. I hope you do something that brings you happiness with that money. I want nothing more than to know you're happy."

She reached over and hugged him and they both shed a few tears. He pulled out a handkerchief, bringing back another flood of memories to Greta as he did so, and loudly blew his nose. He sounded like Dad.

"You know," he said, "my old boss really took advantage of me. Looking back I should have quit much earlier and done it right, without leaving your mom. But the truth is, Atlas gave each of my daughters something I couldn't."

She didn't say that she didn't care about the money, that it would never replace what his actions and all the years had stolen from her and from her mother.

"Now," Karl said, "tell me about what happened here with Denise Arthur. Were you harmed in any way? Do you need a lawyer or any help with this?"

"We're fine," Jake said. "My lawyers have been here. We're in good hands."

"I'm glad you have good counsel. Greta, were you a friend of the woman or did she hire you?"

"She saw my work in *Architectural Digest* and contacted me. I started in August and I've come out regularly since then. We're devastated by what happened," she admitted. "But it looks like the police have enough circumstantial evidence to put her husband away."

"It's a nasty business," Karl said. "You sure you're going to be all right?"

"Yes, we really are okay."

He stayed for lunch and Jake showed him the rest of the house. Greta watched in awe as they talked details of design. Never in her wildest dreams had she imagined such a day. Yet here it was. A gift dropped in her lap in the middle of the worst of times.

"Does Melinda know about me?" she asked Karl as he prepared to leave.

"She does. We always thought that when you were ready you would reach out to us. We didn't know if you were angry or what."

"Well, I'm not angry at you anymore, and I would love to meet her someday," she said.

"You look alike," Karl said. "You'll be surprised. I have two beautiful daughters."

"I think I look like you," she smiled. "I know Mom always wished I looked more like she did."

Karl shrugged. "The Jenkins genes will come through in the next generation." He looked at Jake. "Are you going to have anything to do with that?"

"Dad!"

Jake laughed and patted Karl on the back. "I would love nothing more."

"It's getting to be about time, don't you think, Greta?"

"I can't believe you're saying this!" she said. "Is this what I have missed in my adult life?"

"Just making up for lost time," Karl grinned. "Now I better go before you've had enough of me."

Greta and Jake watched him drive away in his old white truck.

"I can't believe this just happened," she said.

"You are so much like your dad," he said. "Even your mannerisms, the way you laugh and move."

"I'm so glad. I feel like a missing piece of me has just been put back into place. What a waste of years."

"Don't dwell on it," Jake said, "just enjoy today."

Reluctantly, Greta went back inside. "I do not want to go back to Chicago right now," she said.

"I'm flying out tomorrow. I can't keep changing my plans."

"Of course," she said. "I just feel strange leaving my dad after finding him."

The rest of the day was lazy and quiet. Jake suggested they go outside and watch the sunset from the patio.

"I have ulterior motives," he said.

"Like what?"

"I would like to try one more time to talk about our future."

She looked at him warily. "I don't think I have much emotional wherewithal left in me right now to deal with this."

"I know, I know," he said. "I just have this gut feeling that if we don't have a real plan in place, we'll be headed for trouble. I'd like to talk through some options."

They moved the chairs on the patio so they could face each other. The sky was a pale bluish gray and dimming quickly. The waves were calm once more.

"Option number one," he started, "is you go back to Chicago and I go to New York then on to Switzerland and we call each other each night until we have the details of Denise's funeral. Then we meet either back here or in New York for the funeral, and then you go back to Chicago and I get back to my work and we resume the phone calls at night or whenever our schedules match and we do this relationship long distance for as long as you need.

"Option number two, we get engaged and set a date. You decide whether you want to buy a house in Chicago and set up your own design firm there or open one in New York. Whichever one of those you choose becomes our home base. I will be home every possible weekend.

"Option number three, we get married now and you come work for my firm and we work happily ever after until you're ready to have those children your dad was kidding us about. Then we pick a city and make that our home base."

She could only stare at him.

"Which will it be?"

She dropped her head in hands and tried to think. She could not. She looked up. "I don't know. I honestly and truly don't know."

"What other options are there? We're both good at strategizing. Tell me what you think."

"I don't know."

"That's because there aren't any other options. We could tweak them, but basically, that's it."

She tried. "The first one sounds impossible long term. Option two sounds the most sensible, but it's also quite a commitment."

"I'm ready for that, because that's what it will take."

"You would make our home wherever I want it?"

"Yes."

She closed her eyes. "Option number three is the craziest but it also sounds like that's what you want the most."

"Only if you do, but I think working together would be the best thing for us. I've hired dozens of people and I know who will work well on our teams. You would be an excellent addition. You'd love the opportunity to create on this scale. It is more satisfying than you can imagine."

"What if I'm not as good as your first wife?"

"Apples and oranges. Now, what other options do you see?"

"I don't see any, but I need time to consider yours."

"Greta, if we don't know now how important it is to love well right from the start, after losing Denise and seeing all the wasted years of lost time with your father, then something is wrong. Either we are in this for keeps, or not. I told you, I can't have a casual affair with you. I mean it. And, I don't think we can survive under the pressure of what has just happened without a firm commitment to each other."

"I tried to ask you before," she said, "how do we know that this is it? How do you know that you can trust me? How do I know that I can trust you?"

He grabbed her hands. "After what we've been through, don't you see that you can trust me? I will take care of you. I will never cheat on you or leave you. I will keep your best interests in the forefront of our lives always."

"I don't know if I can fit into your life," she said.

"No offense, but that's ridiculous," he said firmly. "You are smart and capable. You're a highly gifted designer. You know you can have your own design firm if you want it. You can set up in Chicago, or New York or even L.A. or any other city in the world. I'll help by making all the contacts you could possibly want. Given enough time in any city you could make them yourself. You can go anywhere and do anything, Greta. Don't you see that?"

She shook her head. "I know the Chicago market. I have a reputation there. I can build on that. If I go elsewhere it's like starting all over."

He released her hands and sat back. "It's because you don't want it."

She looked at him, puzzled.

"It's more than that, you don't want me."

"What? That's not true. We're too new, Jake. You're asking too much too soon."

"I can see it," he said. "You just don't know it yet." The tremor in his voice was unmistakable. He looked out at the ocean.

"What are you doing?" she asked, completely dumbfounded.

"You've seen into my life. You know now how much it demands, how complicated things get so quickly. You're scared. But I handled it. I took care of everything."

"How do you do it, Jake?" She got up and sat on the arm of his chair so she could put her arm around him and lean her head on his shoulder. "I watched you these past few days, I listened as you had this vast knowledge of all that was going on and all that had to be done, including all the underlying circumstances and relationships. I saw the responsibilities on your shoulders and on your mind. It's so much."

"It's just always been a part of my life, knowing what I know and what my parents know about politics and money and people in high places. You get used to it."

"It feels dark. It's ugly."

"Not usually."

"You deal with rules and regulations for building in multiple countries. You must see these same powers at work wherever you go. They must be a part of your everyday life."

"That's why I come out here to recharge. This is my safe place."

"But it came here, too."

He leaned his head against hers. "But you were here with me. You brought light and life to me here. Look how everything has turned around so fast."

She closed her eyes. "It wasn't me, Jake."

"Of course it's you."

"I tried to tell you, it was something more. I prayed an incoherent prayer of regret and agony in the midst of all that darkness and I don't know how God did it but everything began to fall into place."

He sighed. "Tell me that you'll try to make us work. Please. Pray a prayer for us."

"I'm trying to figure this all out. I wasn't raised like you were. It's like being on guard all the time, thinking harder than I've ever thought about people's motives and who's connected to whom and what's really going on underneath it all and how that will influence an outcome. I just want to love someone and do my thing. I want to create homes that bring people happiness."

He lifted his head. "Are you forgetting you work in Chicago? Talk about dark politics."

She laughed. "You're right about that, though it's on a smaller scale there. I don't have to deal with it either. I got pulled into this without realizing it. I'll be much more careful in the future, believe me."

"I fear we're back to you not wanting me and my world." He pushed himself out of the chair. "I need to go for a walk."

"Sure,' she said, getting up. "To the beach?"

"I need to walk alone for a while. Clear my head."

"I feel like you're distancing yourself, deliberately."

He shrugged. "That goes for both of us."

"Are you pulling away from me, from us?"

"I think you are. You're not willing to find a way forward for us."

"Jake, you're putting way too much on the line here. We both care for each other a great deal. We're just not ready for more right now. It's the stress of everything, it's just pushing us too hard and too fast. You said yourself that we would have a hard time because of the stress of everything. We just need to take a deep breath and breathe again."

"The more you breathe, the farther away from me you will go. I will want you more every day."

"Just give me time."

"I'm not sure how long I can put myself out there for you day after day while you take your time realizing you're going in the opposite direction." He walked down the patio and towards the lawn.

She felt her footing tilt, her world tipping yet again. "I have to go home," she said softly.

He turned around and swiftly came back to her. "Home? Why do you say that?"

She felt so, so tired. "I'm feeling overwhelmed again. Between Denise and my dad and now us, right now I just need to try to clear my head and think straight again."

"Home. Is that where your other relationship is? That flirtation you mentioned?"

"No! Where did this come from?"

He just looked at her.

"I don't know what to say," she said. "Why do you even bring him up? He has nothing to do with us. What do you want to know? He doesn't live in Glencoe. He has nothing to do with my home and my world. Nothing at all."

"My gut is telling me he has everything to do with us."

"No, it's not true."

"Convince me otherwise."

She tried to think past the last few days, to Aidan, to his face, their last conversation. It felt like forever ago. "I grew up going to school with him. I ran into him when I was back in Wiley, at the beginning of summer. I was having a rough go of it, and he listened. We had some meals together a few times and talked about things. That's it. That's all there was."

His eyes narrowed, "What about the flirtation part? You left that out. Are you going to talk about that? Because not once in all the times you've been here with me, have you ever flirted with me. Not once."

She bit the inside of her lip. "I didn't realize that. I was being cautious. I have to be. I don't want to get hurt again." The moment the words came out of her mouth she regretted them.

"So he didn't return the sentiments."'

"No."

For several moments he remained silent. "I don't want a part of you, Greta. I want all of you."

"I know," she whispered.

"Even if you do get over him, I will wonder why you aren't attracted to me like you are to him. I don't blame you, now is when these things need to come out. I'm just incredibly sad."

"Jake, we have a different dynamic. Isn't that okay? The love you had with your ex-wife—what was her name?"

"Margot."

"Margot. Okay, so how you loved Margot and who she was—is—is completely different than how you feel about me. How long did you date her before you married?"

"A year or more. The circumstances were quite different."

"All the differences make for quite a different relationship. Of course we have different feelings for different people."

"Giving one hundred percent, Greta. That's what I'm talking about. Will you give me that?"

"I keep thinking it's too soon, and yes, I'm afraid of your world. It's so much bigger than mine."

"You don't want it. We're back to that, see?"

She stepped forward and took his hands in hers. "I don't know where this is coming from, but I want to reassure you that I want us to work. I'm just asking for time to build this relationship and figure this out."

"Maybe you aren't as good at looking down the road as you think you are."

"Ouch."

They stared at each other.

"I'm not ready to walk away from this relationship," she said.

"Neither am I. But I'm a realist."

"Can we just wait until after Denise's funeral to have this talk again?"

He closed his eyes against her pleading eyes. Finally he opened them again but did not look at her. "Yes, I will wait until then."

"Are we okay?"

He stepped back. "I need to take that walk." With that he walked away.

The sun, she realized looking after him, had set and they had not noticed.

7

Seeing Jonathon pull up to the curb at Arrivals in O'Hare warmed her heart. She really was home.

"Thank you so much for picking me up," she said, as he stepped out and hugged her.

"Thanks for letting me pick you up," he replied. "I'll help you with your bags." He looked around. "No sample books, nothing along those lines?"

"No, I still can't get to my office on the island. Everything will be shipped back once they release it."

"How are you really?"

"As well as can be expected," she said. "I think that sums it up. I feel like I've been away in another world. I'm so glad to be back in Chicago."

They got back into the car and pulled out into the circling traffic.

"I can't imagine what you've been through," he said. "Reporters have been calling the firm nonstop looking for a story."

"I had one incident with photographers that was fairly traumatic," she said. "But I've been sheltered these past few days. We had the phone's ringer off and security around the property after that."

"I hope you're not harassed here."

"I don't have a whole lot to tell anyone."

"Knowing how close you get with the people you work with, there's bound to be a story there."

"You know how it is," she admitted. "They open up their lives to us and while we're there we're practically family. It was even more so with this couple. They were kind and generous, you would have loved them, too. It makes it all so much worse now."

"You make it easy for people to treat you well," he said. "You have a gift for that."

"Jonathon, I failed this client miserably. There were deep problems in her marriage and I just didn't want to see them. I was so busy with the house and how wonderful they were that I wasn't the real friend I should have been."

"It sounds like you didn't really know how bad it was."

"I should have. I was warned."

"You're human, Greta."

"Well, I feel terrible about it."

As they entered Glencoe she noticed the trees towering over the streets were past their peak of fall color, any remaining leaves offered only a half-hearted show of contrast to the vivid blue sky beyond them. She regretted missing the height of their beauty this year.

"Dare I ask if you're going to see Carol this week?"

"I'm hoping to avoid going in," she sighed. "Any chance you're willing to clean out my desk for me?"

"Your office is already boxed up. Carol had Sophie do it."

Greta whistled. "I hate to burn bridges but it looks like this one is incinerated."

"Office gossip has it you hung up on Carol. That was a bold move."

"For a long time I've had the feeling she only tolerates me. It's been tense."

"Further gossip says she's threatened by you. She knows you've outgrown the firm."

"Really?"

"You had to know that," he said in that quiet, no nonsense but inherently kind way he had.

"I wondered at times. I didn't want it to be that way. Funny, I guess I didn't want to see that either. But Carol has nothing to fear from me. She will alway be the design matriarch of Chicago, the great Fitz of Fitz & Winton Design."

"Her micromanagement is destroying the firm," he said as he pulled into her driveway. "I signed on again at the end of summer but it's for just one year. I'm definitely leaving after that. I had a difficult time getting rid of the noncompete clause in my contract this time. Jacqui is already looking elsewhere."

"What about the new girl? What's her name?"

"Her name is Paige Stiller. She worked for Snowden Design before coming here. She still has stars in her eyes but it's just a matter of time before she begins to see the truth."

"Snowden is our biggest competition. Things must have been really bad for her to come to us. What about Edward? What's the latest on him?"

"He's back in Paris again. More gossip says he wants a buyout. Carol can keep his name on the firm if she pays him his share of the company."

"What does gossip say when it comes to whether or not she can afford to buy him out?"

"Sophie overheard Carol talking with the accountant. Apparently she's barely making payroll. Without you there, Greta, I don't know if the firm can survive. She needs you."

"Well, I'm not coming back. She will bounce back, she always does. I never knew if she was going to be kind or controlling. Any kindness feels disingenuous now."

"I think she wants to be kind but her need for control takes over. It's choking the life out of us. You were the breath of fresh air we all needed. We're going to miss you. Do you have plans?"

"Beyond arranging to have the boxes and my personal office furniture moved to storage, no. I'm really glad you mentioned the noncompete clause. I had forgotten all about it. I need to review my contract and see if I can get out of it. I'm also anticipating another trip out to the island or New York for Denise Arthur's funeral, but after that, I honestly have no idea. I need to get my world straightened out again. It's been upside-down."

He pulled into the driveway and drove past the large main house to the gravel driveway of her carriage house tucked under a grove of trees. "This is just so magical," he said. "I love coming here."

"I'm looking forward to some peace and quiet, I can tell you that."

"What's up with your front door?" Jonathon asked.

Amassed over the carved walnut door and stuck in the doorjamb were dozens of sticky notes and odd scraps of papers along with business cards, too.

She lifted them off while Jonathon carried her luggage inside. "Requests for interviews," she said. "My landlord, Avery, must be going crazy if this many people have been in and out in the last few days."

"I'm here if you need to talk, and so is Sophie for that matter."

She gave him a hug. "I'm so grateful for you, Jonathon. Thanks for everything."

It took too little time to put away her things. She made her way to the answering machine and listened in amazement to a wide spectrum of callers, both friends and clients who had her personal number. It was most disturbing to hear how excited some sounded over seeing her in the news. And then there were the calls from the media. TV stations, magazines, news anchors and journalists, they had all found her unpublished number.

The only truly kind message she heard was from Aunt Charlotte. "Honey, you're in our prayers. Please let me know that you're okay. Aunt Ruth and I are worried about you. I also want you to know that Aunt Ruth was moved to a nursing home just a week ago. She fell and broke her hip. She needs surgery but I think she's more worried about you than her fall. Let us know how you are. We send our love."

She made a quick call to the florist and had a bouquet sent to Aunt Ruth. She threw out all the notes and cards and papers from her front door and cleared her answering machine. But after that there was little to do. The house felt dark, the air stale. She opened the doors to the red brick patio and stepped outside. So much better to be outside with the sun shining down, the breeze off the lake fresh and crisp. The small waves of Lake Michigan reminded her how far she was from the island. The lawn was beautifully manicured. The gardeners had already cut back any summer flowering plants and bushes. There were no scrub bushes, no rustic paths, no washboard roads to maneuver.

She walked back inside. Room to room she walked, trying to get a feel for her home again. For the first time in all the years she lived there, her house, beautiful as it was, did not seem to welcome her home. It seemed airless, despite the open patio doors, despite the beauty around her, despite all the efforts of her hands through the years. Flat, meaningless, much she imagined, like Denise Arthur's house stood right now, a thousand miles away, empty of life, just another building of wood and stone and a million other little things that held no real meaning at all now that she was gone.

The phone rang and went directly to the answering machine. It was Aunt Charlotte.

She picked up the phone. "Aunt Charlotte?"

"Greta! I'm so glad I got you. Are you okay?"

"Yes, I'm fine, really."

"You'd tell me if you were otherwise, right?"

"Of course." She sat down on the kitchen chair. "It's a long story."

"I'd like to hear it but I can't today. I'm afraid I have some bad news.

Aunt Ruth passed away this morning."

Greta swallowed hard. "Oh, no. Was it the fall? I just listened to your message not an hour ago."

"The fall started it. Her hip was badly fractured. The doctors knew that sedation for surgery was a risk to her weak heart but the alternatives didn't leave a choice. They operated this morning but it was too much for her heart. "

"I'm so sorry, Aunt Charlotte. Are you okay?"

"I'm busy making phone calls. It will hit me when I stop."

"You'll let me know the details of the funeral?"

"It will be in Indiana. It looks like next Monday. I'll call you back when I know for sure."

"Okay. Whenever it is, I'll be there."

Jake called almost immediately afterwards. "I have bad news," he said.

Greta tried not to hold her breath. "What is it?"

"It's about Denise's funeral. Her father wants it private. It will be in New York on Monday, but only family and close friends are invited."

"I'm not included."

"Correct. He doesn't want a circus so he's keeping it as small as possible."

"You and your parents are going?"

"Yes, our families served together through several administrations. The ties go deep."

"What are Pem's parents doing? How are they reacting to all this?"

"His father is keeping a low profile. He's made a generic statement to the press regarding cooperating with the investigation and seeing justice done. That was it. They won't be there, at the funeral, if that's what you mean."

"I wouldn't expect them to be."

He went on. "Details of what happened that night are starting to come out this morning. *The Times* did a piece on it. Have you contacted a lawyer yet?"

"No, I've only been home an hour or so."

"The phones here at my office are starting to ring. You should be prepared."

"Where does this leave us?" she asked.

Silence.

"Jake?"

"I don't know where it leaves us. I was going to ask you. You wanted to wait until after Denise's funeral to talk. Well, we're not going to have that opportunity."

"I have another funeral, too, I just got word my Aunt Ruth died today. She was my mom's sister. I was worried that her funeral might conflict with Denise's, but now it looks like each of us will be at a different funeral on Monday. Let's give it a few days and we'll talk."

"I'm sorry to hear about your aunt. Was it unexpected?"

"She had a bad fall and the surgery was too much. She and my Aunt Charlotte have been so good to me."

"I'm really sorry for your loss. It looks like we'll need more time to figure things out."

"I think so, too."

"I think I know you well enough to tell you that you need to get to work. You need to be creative and produce. Keep moving forward."

"I know; I will."

"I love you, Greta. Now get to work."

"Love you, too."

Jake was right about the calls. It was one thing to hear all the voicemails and another to be there as the calls came in. One in particular stood out: "Ms. Little, I'm Freda George. Our news magazine is running a story on physical abuse in high profile marriages. Denise Arthur's recent death highlights how critical it is to know the warning signs of abuse and not excuse harmful behaviors just because someone is famous or wealthy or in a position of power. If abuse can happen to a senator's daughter, it can happen to anyone. Would you please consider helping us with this story?"

When she finished listening to the message she did not erase it as she had the others, but there was no time to even contemplate following up. It was time to contact Vinnie Morales' law firm and get a lawyer of her own.

After grueling meetings with Carol and Vinnie Morales, who insisted on personally handling the case for Fitz & Winton, and her own lawyer, Peter Lefler, an older man who came highly recommended and had quite an impressive list of famous clients, the weekend was a welcome relief from legalities and reporters and even well-meaning friends who kept checking in on her.

On Sunday morning she packed a bag and headed out to southern Indiana for Aunt Ruth's funeral. When she pulled into the hotel in the small Indiana town, she was surprised to see some of her cousins piling out of a car as well. There were hugs and greetings and then more family arrived and there were introductions to new spouses and new babies and toddlers and she felt giddy with the sense of family she had missed more than she realized.

At the visitation later that afternoon, friends and more family came and went through the receiving line, which consisted of Aunt Ruth's children and Aunt Charlotte, since Uncle Chuck, Ruth's husband, had long since passed. When Aunt Charlotte got tired, she kindly took Greta's arm. "Come sit with me. I need a break."

From the last row of padded chairs in the room of the funeral home where Aunt Ruth was laid out, they sat and watched the crowd of family and friends.

"How do you keep track of everyone?" Greta asked.

"Word got around that I try to keep track of the family tree. I seem to be the unofficial family historian. I do my best to keep up with it all but I had to check it twice last night to remember which grand-niece had what babies. I won't have Ruth to help me keep track anymore."

"I can't imagine how hard it must be without her."

"She was with me almost my entire life. We talked on the phone every day of our married lives and visited back and forth whenever we could. I always thought of her as a second version of me. I knew this day was coming, but I'm not ready for it. I'm the only one now, the only one who remembers Mama and Papa and how things used to be."

"It will be the end of an era when you pass," Greta said, putting her arm around her elderly aunt. "I don't want to think about this world without you in it. You've always been here for me, for my mom and Aunt Ruth, and clearly for others, too. Thank you for that."

Aunt Charlotte patted Greta's knee. "Someone in this family needs to keep the connections going, Greta. That someone could be you. My kids don't pay attention to that kind of thing. I haven't seen Ruth's kids try either. But you, you'd be good at it."

"I'm so out of touch," Greta protested. "I'd be terrible at keeping track."

"I notice you still haven't put your mother's house on the market. Ruth's house went on the market three days after her children put her in the nursing home. It's for sale as we speak. My children won't be any different. It's not all about the money, though I know that's often a factor. No, Ruth's kids, my kids, they aren't interested in preserving anything from the past. But you're different. I think you understand how important our past is. We have to keep connections alive and pass along all the good things."

"Good things?"

"You know, who we are and what we value. Such as how Mama, your grandmother Greta, knew the importance of praying for her daughters. Mama prayed over us girls all the time. So did Papa. We sisters grew up valuing family and doing our best to raise the children God gave us. These children and grandchildren have been prayed over more than they can imagine. And that includes you. We women sacrificed a great deal to give our children the best childhoods we could. Your mother had a hard time with Karl, but God watched over you and Ellie. Ellie came back to God at the end. He answered Mama's prayers. Just like he will for you, Greta. Have you seen that yet?"

Inexplicably, tears filled Greta's eyes. "What do you mean?"

"Why, how everything in your life and your mother's life has its place. How God answers prayers and gives order to our footsteps. The circumstances of your life aren't some random accident. No matter how bad things get, God can make them work out for your good and his glory. His goodness pours down like rain."

Her breath caught in her throat. "Actually I'm beginning to see, a little bit. In the midst of the bad, I've seen good come out of it."

She patted Greta's knee again. "You think about it. Someday you're going to have children just like we did and you're going to see just what's important and you'll understand what I'm saying. This applies to everything in your life. And one more thing, I've been keeping up with the news about what happened out there on that island. God had you out there for a reason, and that's the truth. You just need to figure out what it is and do something about it."

Greta studied her aunt's face.

"You're smart, Greta. God's got plans for you. Don't ever forget that. You pay attention to what it is he wants for you. He will help you make sense of what happened. And I don't just mean about recent events. My children had a perfectly fine upbringing. But they didn't have the struggles you had when your father left. You, my sweet girl, have a lot more going for you than you realize. You are stronger and smarter because of what you've been through. Don't let it go to waste."

"I don't know what God wants right now. I have no clue."

"You'll figure it out. Just don't compare yourself to those powerful people you've been rubbing shoulders with lately. You are just as bright and smart as any one of them. That doesn't mean you should become like them. They're just people and they're just as messy as everyone else. You be true to who and what God made you to be. Do you hear me?"

"They are no different from us, you couldn't be more right about that, Aunt Charlotte. They have problems too, that's for sure."

"Don't you forget that." With that, Aunt Charlotte patted her knee one more time and stood up, leaning heavily on the chair in front of her. "There's Cousin Aggie. I haven't seen her in years. Excuse me."

The next morning at Aunt Ruth's funeral service it seemed everyone had a unique story of an act of kindness Ruth had done for them out of the limelight, quietly and selflessly. As Greta listened she could not help but wonder how this simple church setting and the lives of these mostly small-town farm people, compared to Denise's funeral at a cathedral in New York with powerful, wealthy people in attendance. What were people saying about Denise's life? Surely it was just as meaningful and significant a life as Aunt Ruth's, wasn't it? How does one measure these things?

That night she called Jake at their usual time. "What was Denise's funeral like?"

"Small, sad, the press did not stay away, and I missed you every minute. I left feeling cold and, I don't know, empty."

"Did she have a lot of close friends?"

"Some coworkers and classmates came. I think some of their friends stayed away because they're unsure of Pem's guilt or innocence. Bill's tight circle of friends was there."

She heard laughter in the background. "Are you alone?"

"No, my parents are here with some old friends."

"Anyone I know?"

"You've probably heard of them."

"I don't need to know," she said. "I just got back from Indiana and I think I have some hay my hair. I would feel more hick than ever."

"I won't ask how it got here," he laughed.

"Only you would think of that!"

"I love you. I'll talk to you tomorrow. "

"Love you, too. Good night."

Over the next several days she got a great number of things done, including finding her copy of her contract with Fitz & Winton. She brought a copy with her to an appointment with her lawyer, who had agreed to look it over for her.

Thankfully, Peter Lefler's law firm was as different from Vinnie Morales and his law firm as one could get in Chicago. There was nothing flashy about their offices, rather they were decorated simply and everyone she encountered was friendly and professional.

"These non-compete clauses have always been difficult for me," she told him. "I signed this with the understanding that I wouldn't take existing customers if I had to leave. I also asked that their standard agreement of not competing within fifty miles be reduced to twenty-five miles. And instead of a five year non-compete, I had it reduced to one year."

Peter looked it over. "Yes, it's as you say. Are you hoping to get out of it?"

"I don't think it's ethical to take my clients with me but I would like to see if I can stay in the city and I would like to begin right away."

"Would you say you're a low-paid employee?"

"No, I couldn't say that."

"Would a delay of a year cause you financial hardship?"

"At this time, no, it would not."

"Then I don't see how you can avoid your legal obligation as stated in this contract. You are free to work 26 miles from the city, and you are only limited to not competing for one year at that. In one year you can do business here as you please. I'm surprised your employer agreed to this. Most are much stricter. You must have had some bargaining power."

"I try to be a tough negotiator, but I don't enjoy it," she said.

"Few people do," he said. "Is there anything else we can do for you? When you were here last you mentioned the possibility of setting up your own firm. While you clearly can't compete right away, we could get everything in place for you to work outside the city."

"I'm going to need to rethink my plans. I'm just not sure of what I want to do yet."

"Have you heard any further details regarding the murder case?" he asked.

"No, I haven't. It's rather nerve-wracking."

"Be patient. These things take time. I'm keeping tabs on it, but I haven't heard anything new, either. I will definitely let you know if I do."

"Thank you," she said.

As she pulled up to her driveway, she saw an unfamiliar car pull in after her. When she put her car in park, a woman got out of the car and ran to her car.

Through the closed window she heard, "Ms. Little, I'm Freda

George. I left you a message the other day about helping us with our report on abuse in high profile marriages."

She took her time gathering her things and then got out of her car. "Ms. George, I have no comment. This is private property. Please leave now."

"Who will speak up for Denise if you don't?"

"I will not jeopardize an ongoing investigation. That's how I'm protecting and speaking up for Denise. Do you understand that? This is for her. Now I have nothing further to say."

"You lived with them, isn't that right? You must have seen something, some ongoing behaviors that led to Pemberton DeWitt killing his wife. Please help us warn other women. Women of all socio-economic classes need our help, Ms. Little."

"No comment. Now please, respect my privacy, and go."

Freda nodded. "I understand. At the same time, I want to help hurting women. Don't you? Please, when you're ready to talk, talk to me. This isn't about selling a story, this is about helping women be safe." She handed Greta her card. "Thank you."

Greta watched her walk away.

Though she tried to sleep that night, sleep would not come. Tired and frustrated, she called Jake early the next morning. "I wanted to catch you before you left for work," she said. "I'd like to come out to New York for a week or so."

"I'm leaving for Switzerland tomorrow."

She sighed.

"I'm sorry," he said, when she said nothing. "What's going on?"

"I'm trying to figure out what to do here. I can't compete for a year, and I don't want to open up a new business outside the city. I thought it would be smart to go to New York and see what options I'd have there."

"I'm going to be in Switzerland for two weeks and then Japan for another two weeks. Then I'll likely go back to Switzerland for much longer. You're free to use my apartment here in New York while I'm gone. I'll arrange to have an assistant from my office meet you and show you around. Anything you need, I'll make sure you have it."

"Thank you, but I think I'll pass. Without you it would be pointless."

"You can always come with me to Switzerland."

"I'm not ready for that."

"Then we'll stay in touch. It won't be as regular or at the same time, but we'll talk, I promise."

"I understand," she said. "It's what I wanted, after all, right?"

"I didn't say that."

"I know. I'm just acknowledging it out loud, that's all."

"I love you."

"I love you, too, safe travels."

This was dismal news and left her face to face with her ongoing restlessness and nowhere to go. The wind off the lake was cold and the early afternoon rain felt even more melancholy. It was time, she decided, for a distraction. Yes, it was the perfect time for the annual ritual of the first fire of the season. From within the stone fireplace she removed the picture perfect birch logs she kept just for looks, put them in garage, retrieved the basket of kindling she kept for starting the fire, and brought in several logs from the woodpile. In just minutes the flames were crackling consistently.

The thought occurred to her that this would be a perfect time to start her journal. When would her schedule be so open again? Then again, perhaps a cup of tea would be comforting as well. She put on the tea kettle. Then she pulled out a cookbook. Some gingerbread would be delicious. Deep in the directions, she only gradually noticed the increasingly heavy smell of smoke.

She ran to the living room. A cloud of smoke grew along the hearth and spread upwards. Quickly she opened the patio doors and checked the flue again, but it was open. It made no sense until a horrible smell began filling the room, too. An animal, it had to be an animal stuck in the chimney. She ran to get some water to put the fire out. The ensuing dank smoke was thick and black. With dismay she looked at the mantle. Her mother's painting wasn't even visible. She reached for it, knocking over a vase that crashed on the hearth. She ignored it and ran the painting to the garage. She came back and opened the front and back doors and all the windows in the house. With a large towel she fanned the smoke towards the open patio doors.

Avery Thomas, her landlord as well as a former client and a good friend, came running in. "Greta! Are you all right? Oh!" She stopped and covered her nose and mouth. "What is that awful smell?"

"I think the chimney is clogged with a cooked animal," Greta said. "I started a fire for the first time this fall. The fire's out but the smoke is just beginning to dissipate."

"I was at my kitchen sink when I saw the smoke coming from your windows. I didn't see anything come from the chimney," Avery said, her hand still over her nose.

"I don't think we need the fire department, but that's your call."

"It looks like it's under control," Avery replied, looking around. "I'll call the chimney sweep and ask him to come right over. He's already scheduled to come tomorrow for the yearly maintenance."

"You're kidding?"

"I wish I was. I completely forgot it in September and when I called last month the earliest opening was tomorrow. I should have told you but it's never been an issue. I'll go call them now and see if they can come over to at least let us know exactly what's going on."

It took a good hour before the smoke cleared. The horrible odor was stronger than ever.

Avery returned. "They tell me they'll come out sometime this afternoon, though they can't give me a time frame. I'll pay for the cleaning of your drapes and upholstery and any damages," she said. " I don't see anything else damaged except that vase."

"I knocked it down getting an oil painting from the mantle," Greta said. "It's nothing. And the painting is fine. I can clean it myself. I think the renter's insurance should cover any cleaning expenses. I'll be fine."

"Are you sure?"

Greta nodded. "I'm just so sorry this happened."

"Do you want to stay next door with me for a few days until this is cleaned up? You can pick whichever guest room you like. After all, you decorated them," Avery smiled.

Greta thought a moment. "That's so generous of you, but I think I'll go down to my mom's house—my house—in Wiley for a few days and stay there. I haven't really closed it up for the winter yet. I could do that and be out of your way."

"I'll call you when it's done then."

"Thank you."

When Avery left, Greta stood for a moment looking at the smelly mess, bewildered. *Back to Wiley, God? Really?*

Because she could think of no better solution, within the hour Greta found herself on the road, once more, to Wiley.

8

The phone was ringing as she unlocked the back door.

"Greta, it's Avery."

"Hello, I just arrived."

"The sweep just left. He says the fireplace needs to be rebuilt."

"All because of an animal's nest?"

"That was a raccoon and it looks like it did a significant amount of damage to the interior. Some of the bricks had fallen in on the nest and it looks like the raccoon couldn't get out fast enough."

"Ugh."

"Yes, but there's more. Because it's an old chimney, they tell me it wasn't built with a liner and because we're right on the lake and we get so much moisture and gases it should be done right."

"You're calling to tell me it's going to take awhile, aren't you?"

"I'm afraid so. It will be two weeks before they can get back here to rebuild it. The work itself should only be a few days. That guest room offer is still open if you need to come back."

"I'll keep it in mind, thanks."

The first thing she did was turn up the thermostat and walk through the house, turning on lights. Crazy how it just sat there, day after day, nothing changing, just a man-made building meant to serve at the whim of its owners.

Dubiously, she looked at the flagstone fireplaces in both the living room and the family room, and she even went downstairs to look at the big brick one in the spacious old recreation room. When was the last time her mother had even used these fireplaces let alone cleaned them?

Greta went back upstairs and made a list of things to do. It wasn't nearly long enough to keep her busy. Something would have to be done about that. Again the thought of starting a journal and sorting through her thoughts about recent events went through her mind. No, she shook her head, not now. For now she needed a shower.

Scrubbed clean after a shower, she began the laundry and soon the wash machine swished and before long the dryer hummed. She replaced batteries in the clocks. They began ticking once again. She got the furniture polish and dust cloths and just because it made her feel much better, she dusted everything she could find. Then she washed again and brushed her teeth and got into her old familiar bed.

Outside, a low rumble of thunder rolled through followed immediately by the sound of rain. She loved falling asleep to the sound of rain on a chilly night. A satisfied feeling came over her. She breathed in the familiar scent of her house. The angry memories of the past were gone. What was that Aunt Charlotte had said about goodness? It rains down? Despite everything, this moment was good. Perhaps because of how crazy everything else was, it felt even better than good. In the midst of this storm, she was safe. She fell soundly asleep.

Sometimes the next best thing to do comes to you with a knocking at your door, she thought as she opened the front door in her robe at eight-thirty the next morning and saw Trista standing there, grinning.

"You gave me a bike!"

Greta's face lit up. "I did! Do you like it?"

Trista hung her head. "I dented the fender when I gave a ride to Kalee, my new friend at school. We thought she would fit on the fender but she didn't."

"I can see if it can be fixed," Greta offered.

"My mom tried. It's okay."

"Do you ride it to school?"

"No, someone might steal it. Sometimes Kalee comes to my house and we can ride, but mostly I go to her house. Her mom watches me after school."

"Well, I'm so happy that you like your bike."

"Thank you," Trista said shyly. "I was so surprised."

"You're welcome! You know," Greta said, looking at the clear skies and warm sun, "I have to get dressed yet, and I have to go to the grocery store, but I'm going to be outside this afternoon to get some raking done. There are a lot of leaves around here. Would you like to help me?"

"Rake?"

"I'll rephrase that. I will rake and you can jump into the big piles of leaves, how is that?"

Trista grinned. "I'll be ready when I see you raking!"

"See you then!"

The front door closed, Greta leaned against it. What joy that little girl had over a gift that had cost very little in time and effort and money. What if, like Aunt Ruth, she began to do kind things like that more regularly? How many more Tristas were there in Wiley who needed a bike, or shoes, or food? In fact, what about their mothers, what did they need? What did Trista's mom need? The words of Freda George flashed through her mind. "Women of all socio-economic classes need our help."

In the garage she found the same old rakes she remembered from years of raking every fall.

"Hello!"

She looked up to see a young woman probably in her mid-twenties, wearing scrubs and standing in front of the garage, with Trista at her side. "Hi, there!" Greta said. "Are you Trista's mom?"

"I am," the young woman said. "My name is Kim. Trista tells me you've invited her over to play in the leaves. I just want to make sure that's okay with you."

"It sure is, if it's okay with you."

"It is. I wanted to check with you first. I have to leave for work in about a half hour, so she can't play long. I have to drop her off at my mom's."

"I'll be sure to check the time," Greta said. "It's so nice to meet you. Have you lived next door for a long time?"

"We've been here two years now. We're just renters," she said, almost apologetically. "I also want to thank you for the bike you gave Trista last year. That was such a surprise!"

"It was fun to do. Trista has been a delight to get to know."

Kim tousled Trista's hair. "She loves bike riding, that's for sure! I think you've gained a lifelong admirer," she said, looking up at Greta. "I'm chopped liver now, compared to you."

Greta laughed. "I had a favorite neighbor growing up, too. The Browns used to live across the street and Mrs. Brown would come out watch me ride my bike when she saw me playing alone outside in the summer. I was devastated when they moved away."

"That about sums up how Trista felt when we didn't see you for several months. Every day she'd look over here and ask me if you're coming back."

"That is so sweet!" Greta exclaimed, taken aback. "I'm not sure how long I'll be here this time, but it looks like about two weeks."

"It's nice to have a neighbor here again," Kim said. "It's comforting."

Meanwhile, Greta could see that Trista was getting bored. She handed a rake to Trista. "Would you like to start that pile of leaves?"

"Yes!" Trista ran off to the yard with the rake.

"Well, I should go. I have to finish getting ready for work," Kim said.

"Do you work for a doctor or a hospital?" Greta asked, looking at her scrubs and walking out of the garage with her.

"I work at the Fairfield Nursing Home," Kim said. "I'm just a CNA but I'm working on getting my nursing degree. I got a little distracted when I got pregnant with Trista."

"A baby is a very understandable distraction!"

"Yeah, well, I made a lot of mistakes early on and I'm finally getting my life on track."

"That can be hard to do," Greta replied. "Good for you."

Kim shrugged. "As a single mom, I didn't have much choice."

"Do your parents help you out?"

"Just with babysitting. They live in the trailer park on the south end of town."

"Trista seems to be a very happy little girl."

"Oh, she is. I think I was lucky that way. She's smart, too. My last boyfriend taught her how to play chess. I don't even know how to play."

"Chess? How old is Trista?"

"She's eight now. He was around last year, so she was only seven then. He's been gone for a while now, and she keeps bugging me to play."

Greta held up her hands. "I am not a chess player. A friend taught me during study hall in high school and I've never played since!"

Kim laughed and turned to go. "Don't worry, she's happy just playing in the leaves with you! I don't care if she forgets all about the game, in fact, the sooner she forgets all about my former boyfriend, the better! He was a piece of work."

Greta took a sharp breath. *God, please, not again.* "I'm sorry to hear that. It sounds rough."

Kim hesitated. "It was. He's gone now. I'm much better off. Just need to stay focused on my own goals and stop getting distracted! I've got to run now. Bye!"

Quickly Greta joined Trista with another rake and soon they had a big pile of leaves and Trista was flying through the air and landing in the center of the leaves, laughing and giggling as she did so. Greta laughed and brushed her off and started all over again and again. All the while she wondered how rough it had been with the former boyfriend. Had he hurt Kim? Had he hurt Trista? And then, as Trista ran circles around her and the leaves flew this way and that, she knew what she would do next.

On Monday morning she stood outside the door of the local women's shelter, knocking. Through a small tinny speaker, she heard a woman's voice. "How can we help you?"

"I would like to learn about helping women in abusive situations," she said. "Is there someone I can talk to about this?"

"Someone will be with you shortly."

The woman who came and unlocked the door had gray curls closely cropped to her head and her green eyes were bright and strong. "Come on in," she said. "Follow me."

Greta stepped up her pace so she didn't fall behind. The woman led her to a sparsely furnished office with white walls and a gray metal desk and sat down behind the desk while Greta sat in one of two metal folding chairs.

"I'm Elaine," the woman said. "How can I help you?"

"I would like to learn more about how to help abused women."

"Do you like to read?"

"Yes."

"There are quite a lot of books on abuse available."

"I'll have to find some. What kind of volunteer positions do you have?"

"You want to get involved here?"

"I'm not qualified, I'm sure, but I would like to learn more about it."

"You need training before you can be of any help."

"I understand that," Greta said, looking hard at the woman. "But I would like to learn more about what you do here."

"I'm just here to greet the new clients," Esther replied.

Greta tried a different tack. "If I came here today because I'm being abused, what exactly would happen?"

"A trained staff person would take an assessment. Your situation would be evaluated and we would recommend next steps."

"And what might they be?"

"It would depend on your situation."

Greta smiled brightly. "I see. Well, it sure would be nice to talk to your boss. I have just oodles of friends who love helping out organizations such as yours. Oh, the fundraisers we get invited to, you just wouldn't believe!"

Elaine stood up. "Is that right? If you can just wait here a moment, I'll get the director. She'll be happy to show you around."

"Thank you so much!" Greta smiled. Elaine left and Greta's smile disappeared. This was appalling, absolutely appalling.

In less than a minute Elaine returned with another woman. "I'd like to introduce you to our Director, Gail Sessions."

Gail shook her hand warmly. "I have a meeting in just a few minutes," she said, "so I must be brief. I apologize for that but I would love to have you come back another time."

"That's okay, my visit is unexpected. I'm hoping to learn more about how to help abused women; a Cliff notes version of what an abused woman goes through when she comes here is just fine."

"Sure. You saw our reception rooms. The women come in and are interviewed. Sometimes they have children with them and sometimes they need an interpreter."

Gail led her down a hall and then unlocked a door.

"This is the living room, if you will. There's a TV and a sofa and chairs, some books." Gail kept walking through the room and into the next doorway. "Here is where the women and children stay," she said. "We just remodeled it and have all new bedding and toys."

The walls were white but the room was bright and clean. Rows of bunk beds lined the walls and the half shelves under the windows had several books and toys. The bedding was in bright greens and blues and red. There was little privacy for the dozen or so beds.

"How long is the typical stay?"

"We don't encourage them to stay long. Just a night or two, three at the most but that's in extraordinary cases. We don't have enough funding to extend their stay more than that right now. Our goal is to help them take next steps."

"What would those be?"

"We recommend they reach out to family or friends for help. Many need direction to get legal help, such as orders of protection. We offer men's groups for the husbands or boyfriends who are willing to come in for help. Some of the men are Spanish speaking so we're always in need of interpreters."

"Do the women get counseling?"

"We have a weekly support group for them."

They headed back to the reception area.

"That's really all to see," Gail said. "I must get to my meeting. But first, here's my card. In fact," she stopped at the counter outside the offices and flipped the card over and wrote something. "Here's my personal phone number. I would like to see what else I can do for you and your friends."

"Thank you," Greta said, and tucked the card inside her purse. She tried to keep her disappointment and frustration out of her voice. "I've learned a great deal today."

"There is a great deal more we want to do," Gail said evenly. "This may not look like much yet, but we have come a long way from what we started with ten years ago. I think that in another ten years we will have doubled our space and we can offer housing for a week or even a month or more, to the point of providing safe apartments and homes for women and children. We dream big but we work hard. There are lives at stake."

"Yes, there are," Greta said.

Once home, the pacing began. Where was the warm welcome abused women sorely needed? Where was the comfort of a shelter? How could they even use that word if they didn't care to make it more than just the bare minimum of a home? One or two nights? That was it? What about the women who didn't have family? Who was there for them? And legal fees, who could afford them if they weren't wealthy?

The phone rang, interrupting her internal rant. "Hello?"

"Greta? Aunt Charlotte. Ben came by your house to rake leaves but he called me to say they're all done and the lights are on. What are you doing home? Is everything okay?"

"I'm fine," she said. "Just fine."

"I hope you don't mind this old busybody, but you don't sound fine to me."

"I'm upset right now."

"Why's that? And what are you doing at the house?"

"A raccoon took up residence in my chimney back in Glencoe. It caused quite a stink and a lot of smoke and destroyed some brick and now the chimney has to be repaired. I came here so I don't have to live with the mess. Meanwhile, I just went to the county women's shelter, and I feel sick to my stomach!"

Aunt Charlotte's voice grew sharp. "Who hurt you? What happened?"

"Oh no! I'm fine, no one hurt me. I went because of my friend, my client out on the island who was killed. Her husband was abusive and I want to learn more about it and how I might help women in need."

"What do you mean you're sick to your stomach?"

"I envisioned something more helpful, something more, I don't know, involved. They're literally just a place to stay and they don't even want you there for more than two nights. The director said that's all the funding will allow. It's bare bones."

"I'm disappointed to hear that. I've recommended that place more than once. It may not be their fault though. I think they haven't been getting the funding they need."

"You know about it?"

"There's a lot you don't know, Greta. I'm not going to names names, but it's closer to home than you realize."

"Abuse? You? Aunt Ruth?"

"Thankfully no, but some of your extended family found themselves in difficult relationships. That's all I'm going to say about that but I have recommended that shelter."

"Did they go?"

"Yes, but come to think of it they said it wasn't much help at all, but I thought it was because they didn't want to cooperate."

"Cooperate?"

"That's not quite what I mean. *Ready* might be a better word. They just weren't ready. Leaving their marriages isn't easy, Greta. With the ones I'm familiar with, there are kids and very little money. They're so locked into their situation they can't see a way out. They're just beaten down and don't have the strength. I thought their dislike of the shelter was just because they weren't ready to make some difficult choices."

"Are there any alternatives for now that might be better?"

"The church."

"What? Going to church?"

"I don't mean on Sunday mornings. I mean a woman could go to her church and ask for help. Personally, I think it's the church who should be there for women in these situations. Our church pays for a hotel room for the woman so she's safe in the short-term and they can help her make a long-term plan. Sometimes someone at the church will know of a job opening or they can help with the kids for a while. One time people chipped in and helped furnish a new apartment for the mom and kids. It's messy, getting involved in people's lives, there's always a whole lot of *he said she said*, but who's the most vulnerable, who has the most to lose? The women and children. They're the oppressed ones. These are the ones God asks us to take care of."

"Huh."

"You know, my memory is getting worse every day, but I'm pretty sure I said something to you at Ruth's funeral about God bringing something good from the tragedy with your friend. Your new interest here might be a part of that, Greta. Did you think of that?"

"I know it's a result of what happened to Denise," she said, rather startled, "but I didn't think God had anything to do with it."

"Huh."

Greta couldn't help but laugh.

"Let me know where this goes," her aunt said.

"I will."

The chimney sweep came that afternoon. "All done," the young man said as he folded his tarp on the linoleum floor of the rec room. "Just some webs and dust. It looks like they were cleaned out several years ago and they haven't been used since. Of course, it's always a good idea to have them checked before you light them for the season."

She just smiled.

He picked up his tools. "I have to ask, did you just buy this house?"

"No, I grew up here."

"It's really cool," he said, looking around. "My wife would love this."

"It's pretty special," she said.

"Yeah, that bar is cool, too. Must have been some fun parties down here back in the day. And what's the game marked out on the linoleum?"

"Shuffleboard. This was quite the space for parties. It was mostly used for holidays," she said. "One of my uncles would always dress up like Santa. The good old days," she smiled.

"Are you going to sell it?" he asked. "My wife and I might be interested."

"No," she said, not even pausing. "I'm not selling."

How she came to that conclusion so readily she didn't know. But that night when she put some newly delivered logs in the grate in the family room with its flagstone surround, she found comfort in remembering all the times she had shared a fire with her parents or her friends. The flames grew as she gently blew on them and soon the fire was coming along just fine. She sat back on the sofa and relished every minute of the cozy glow.

The ringing phone brought her back to reality.

"Jake! You got my message!"

"I did. You're in Wiley?"

She explained why.

"I thought you were going to stay busy and work."

"I'll be busy. First I want to reach out to my dad again. I have an idea I want to float by him. And then," she looked at the pile of books she'd brought home from the library that morning and added, "I'm going to study up on abuse."

"That would mean a lot to Denise," he said.

"I don't want to ever let another woman down."

"I respect that. What happened to starting up your firm?"

"I'm considering waiting out the year of my non-compete clause. I have to be more than 25 miles outside of Chicago but the truth is the closer to the city, the more advantageous it is. It really would be worth it to wait."

"You won't be working at all?"

"The next magazine feature is coming out in the spring. It's not associated with Fitz & Winton, so this time around I need to be prepared for the response and figure it all out on my own. I've got a few months yet to do that, but preliminarily I expect most of these people to fly me out to their homes. I'll still need to have my business set up legally, but I won't need a physical office yet."

She waited for a reply. "Jake, are you there?"

"I won't ask you again," he replied. "I'll just say that you have other options, options that include me. Your intention to study up on abuse is noble and I can't say a thing against it, but what happened to us?"

"You're still in Switzerland, right? How is everything going?"

"Very well, but the resort in Japan is having problems. I have to leave in the morning and sort things out there."

"I don't want to tag along, Jake."

"A wife doesn't tag along, especially when she's working with her husband. You'd be an important part of the team."

She looked at the books and the fire and all the familiarity and comfort around her. "I'm not ready."

"Do you even know what you want anymore?"

"I thought I did. But things keep turning upside down. I'm adapting to keep up with it all."

"Maybe we should talk when you do know what you want."

"I thought we agreed to give this time."

"We're doing exactly what I didn't want. We can talk on the phone indefinitely, but it's not going to bring us closer. You have an opportunity to be with me, to commit to us, and you're not ready."

"I've been through a great deal lately. I have work to do here that is helping me heal."

"I wish you would let me help you heal. I wish you would help *me* heal."

"What about the holidays?"

"I won't make it back for Thanksgiving. It's in less than two weeks. I have too much going on."

"I'm trying here. What about Christmas?"

"I don't know yet. It could be tight."

"Why not just schedule it in?"

"Things are fluid. Besides, I have to consider my parents."

"When will you know?"

"I'll be in touch when I know. I have to go now."

"Goodbye."

She cradled the phone and waited for the sting of tears. It didn't come. With the poker she broke the burning log into coals and added a fresh log on top of them.

"I'm going to lose him." Saying it out loud helped. There was just no way around it. For a long time she stared into the fire and thought and thought and thought. Then finally, she prayed.

It's me, God, Greta. You helped me the last time I talked to you back at Jake's house when I asked you for help. I don't know how you did it but right after I talked to you, when I got up to take the migraine medicine, I realized the flashlight was gone. That was you, wasn't it? You showed me that.

Well, I need you to show me a few more things. Please. Jake is right, I don't know what I want anymore. It doesn't make sense to me at all. Nothing is going the way I wanted it to, nothing. I'm back in Wiley. Strangely, it feels quite good this time. I hope to learn more about abuse and help women, but at the same time if I stay here I'm walking away from a man who really loves me. He's everything I ever wanted. He's running out of patience with me. How can I love him and be okay with this?

Are you doing this, too? Is there something I'm supposed to do with all this change? Is this craziness part of your plan? Why do you care about me? I've never done anything except purposefully disregard you. And make fun of those who believe in you. How can I even have the right to talk to you? The bigger question is, why would you listen? Why answer my prayers?

The enormity of all the times and ways she had ignored God and had chosen to remain naive or had denigrated those who believed in Jesus hit her hard. All the times she ignored her own conscience and did what she wanted to do to get her own way and do what felt right at the time, only to feel guilty about it later and worse, the times she'd laughed at her conscience and instead found joy in the freedom of choice to do whatever she wanted, that hit her harder, deeper still.

"I'm so, so, sorry," she said, head in hands. "Please forgive me. Please help me. Show me what you want me to do."

9

"I have a request, Dad," she said.

"What's that?"

"Would you please come out for Christmas and bring Melinda with you?"

"What are you talking about?"

"Are you okay flying?"

"Sure, what's the deal?"

"A family reunion of sorts. I'll invite Aunt Charlotte and Uncle Irv, and all their kids and Aunt Ruth's kids, too."

"At the house in Wiley?"

"Yes, we can hold it downstairs in the rec room, like old times with a retro theme. I thought I'd even ask Uncle Irv to dress up as Santa again. He fits the part well these days."

"Didn't Ruth have six kids? Charlotte, too? How many kids did those kids have? This might be too much for Mel."

"We can make it an open house so it's not too crowded at any one time."

"I haven't been to a party in at least a decade."

"It would be the perfect time to meet Melinda and make her feel welcome."

"Anyone there have hard feelings towards me?"

"Aunt Charlotte and Uncle Irv are the sweetest people. They don't hate anyone. You know that."

"They're older than I am."

"Will you do it?"

"You call Melinda and ask her. If she'll do it, I'll do it."

"I'll call you back and let you know."

Without thinking about it too much, she dialed the number her dad gave her. She couldn't help but picture that little girl in the pink dress that her mom had painted. How painful it must have been to paint that, how generous and forgiving.

"This is Melinda."

"Melinda, hi, it's Greta Little."

There was just the slightest of hesitations. "Greta! Sister! It is so good to talk with you!"

"It's good to talk with you, too!" she said, heartened at the warmth in her sister's voice. She had to blink through the tears. "Do you have a minute to talk? I know it's the middle of the day but I wasn't sure when would be a good time."

"It's fine! I just grabbed lunch and am walking back to my office."

"Where is that?"

"Downtown Boston. Just walking in the door of the building now. You work in Chicago, right? I confess I did some research after you talked with Dad and I found the magazine with your house in it! It's beautiful! You're amazing!"

"Ah! Thank you," she laughed. "I can't believe I'm really talking with my sister! Now I want to see where you work and live! I want to see your family! Tell me about yourself!"

"I've been married for six years now, he's the best husband a woman could want and his name is Howard. We have two kids, Karl who is four and Anna is three."

"You must be incredibly busy."

"Hold on. It's the 3rd floor please. Thank you. I'm back, sorry about that. No, just a normal family, the kids are adorable and they're driving me nuts. My husband works just down the street from me and the kids are in daycare in his building. We have a home which I would love for you to help us decorate! Can you come out? We'd love to meet you."

"That's one of the reasons I'm calling. I just talked with Dad and I'm hoping you and your family and Dad can come to Wiley for Christmas, Christmas Eve more precisely, though you're welcome to come early and stay as long as you like. I'm having an open house for family. A kind of reunion for all of us. I'd love to meet you and have you meet this side of the family here. I know they're not exactly your relatives, but they loved Dad and would welcome you with open arms."

"That's quite an invitation! Thank you. I'll have to talk with Howard. We did have some plans. May I get back to you?"

"Of course. I told Dad I would call him back and let him know if you're coming. He said he will come if you come."

"Give me a few minutes and I'll call you back."

"Take your time, there's no rush."

"Dad will be getting all worked up over it, trust me. I'll call Howard now and get back to you shortly."

True to her word, she called back in less than 10 minutes. "We'll be there. We cannot wait!"

Both women screamed into their phones at the same time. Greta started crying. "I can't tell you how happy this makes me. What's your email address? I'll email you all the details."

"I feel the same way. I can't wait to meet you!"

She called her dad. "Dad? It's a go."

"I knew she would. I better get a haircut and some new clothes."

"It won't be fancy. And don't forget, it's retro, so a button up sweater vest would be just fine."

"I can dress myself, thank you very much."

"Now that's the dad I remember. Do you happen to have email?"

"I'm computer literate, I'll have you know."

"That's great. What's your email address? I'll email you the details."

"Do you think I forgot how to get there? I lived in Wiley—how old are you?"

"Thirty-two."

"Well, I lived there longer than you've been alive. I think I can find my way back."

"I'm sure you can. My apologies."

"You could email me the names of all the cousins. I remember Stevie, but for the life of me, I can't remember all the other ones."

"I would be happy to. In fact, I'll ask Aunt Charlotte for a copy of the family tree she made. You could fill in some of your side for me."

"I would like that. Thank you."

"Love you, Dad."

"I love you, too, Greta."

One in Four Journal
December 5, 1995

Considering how often I've found excuses for not starting to journal, I should have known it would take something coming out of left field like this to make me start. I'm still in shock. I didn't even know it was abuse. But every single one of these books says it was. They also say it happens to one out of four women. I'm calling this the One in Four Journal *so I can remind myself*

I'm not alone.

I don't know how this will go, but I realize I can't be the first woman to find this out after the fact, and I would like to learn from it when I look back. I thought I would learn about abuse so I could help other women and make right in some small way what happened to Denise. I realize now that I can't help anyone if I don't recognize and deal with what happened to me.

I think I'm ready to begin processing all that I've read. It's a lot. I have no idea where this will end up, but I'm starting. I'm scared, but I want to be honest with myself. It's about time.

Before I get into what happened with Geoffrey, I must start at the beginning. The older boys in the neighborhood who bullied me. The cousin who forcefully kissed me when I was 13. My junior high school teacher who whistled at me every time I had to walk by him. The boy I wouldn't date who stalked me. The guy in college who regularly called me without talking but breathed heavily and scared me. The crazy man who walked by me and squeezed my breast while waiting in line at the restaurant before he disappeared in the crowd. The men, all of them, who have stared at my breasts instead of my eyes.

Dare I start with the women? The girls on the bus who called me fat. The teacher who criticized me every single day in sixth grade. My boss who tore up my drawings when I was an intern because they were so "terrible" and told me I would never amount to anything without her name behind me, who lied about my work those times and said it was hers.

You people did these things. I'm calling you out now. I don't feel sorry for myself, I just want to acknowledge these things happened. I blamed myself for most of these things. Somehow they were my fault. I should have seen it coming. I should have been smarter. I should have figured out a way to make it stop. But none of that is true.

It was never about me. They would have done it to anyone else in their path. They look for people to take advantage of and abuse. They're always all about them, all about meeting their own needs.

But I'm real. I'm a woman to be valued. I was a child and a young girl to be valued and protected, not hurt. Their actions didn't happen to a mannequin, they happened to me. It hurts. Trying to move on and forget it doesn't stop the pain, it just delays the real healing. I can't help anyone if I can't even deal with my own abuse. I need to figure this out. This seems like the safest place. It feels so good to get this out. I wish I had started this sooner.

One in Four Journal
December 6, 1995

On to Geoffrey.

How can I even go there? I don't know how or where to start. Did I know what I was walking into? No. Did he know what I was walking into? Oh, yes. He was charming and handsome and so incredibly sophisticated and talented. How could he be interested in me? I didn't see all that I gave him, my innocence that I was so eager to get rid of, my young body that he used. I was a plaything, a toy. He became the envy of his friends. Now I wonder if they pitied me or laughed at me.

He opened doors for me, at a price. What I thought was a generous gesture on his part, introducing me to Carol and Edward, he used against me. "You have that job because of me, not your talent. You're average, nothing more." I never saw that he took away my self-esteem. I kept thinking that he loved me, that he didn't realize how hurtful his words were. The truth is he knew exactly how hurtful he was and he said those things deliberately. I was easier to control if I lost my confidence. Then I became more dependent on him and his approval.

My friends warned me about him. He said they were jealous. My mom didn't like him either. He said she was trying to control me. I lost touch with my friends and I lost several years of a relationship with my mom. I will never get those years back. He did that to isolate me so he could control me better.

If I disagreed with him about anything, he got in my face. I'd give up and say fine, whatever. He wouldn't let it go. He'd follow me from room to room, shouting at me nonstop. I couldn't get away from him. I have learned that's emotional abuse.

The sex got rougher. No one talks about that, either. It's scary, having your boundaries pushed over and over. How many times did he try again? And again? I was glad when the alcohol and drugs took their toll on him. At least then he would leave me alone. That wasn't love.

I kept thinking if I could figure out why he did these things to me, I could help him. He would pour out his heart with sad stories of his own abuse, and I would cry with him, but it was never enough. He could go on for hours about himself. He would listen to me about my job but only enough to keep me hooked. Also, he never just listened, somehow he would turn it around so that if I complained that something had gone wrong, he made it my fault. I had done something wrong to cause the problem. It didn't matter if it was an issue at home or work, it was always because I had done something wrong. I didn't even realize that until I read in one of the books about another woman who experienced the same thing. I can't believe I missed that, but I did.

He lied about the women in his life. "I'm not flirting. Stop being so insecure." He lied about the money I kept "misplacing". "You're careless with your money. You didn't put it there. You just forgot you spent it." No, he stole it. Because he could. I lived on pennies so when his paintings weren't selling, he could use my money for women and drugs.

The worst part is that when I caught him with that woman the first time, I apologized to him for not being enough for him! I begged him to stop the affair. He grudgingly accepted my apology. And never stopped the affair, though he said he did.

I just didn't see how deliberate it all was. He set me up and used me. Nothing I did was right. When I threatened to leave his apologies and tears seemed so real. I think now he was just waiting for his latest girlfriend to agree to move in with him. When she finally did he picked a fight with me, saying I was late from work and hadn't called him to let him know where I was (always with the double-standard). Then he literally threw me out of his apartment. I had several bruises from that and he had the nerve to call the police and say I attacked him. He was just guaranteeing that I wouldn't try to come back and upset his new life and girlfriend.

It took me years to get over it. I was so lucky that Avery happened to be my client at the time and offered me the carriage house. I worked nights and weekends and used vacation time to do the design work for her home so I could live rent free that first year.

I've never talked about most of this with anyone, not about what really happened with Geoffrey. Part of me thought that it was just normal. Besides, people don't share the reality of their relationships, it's no one's business. There's an intimacy that is personal, between just those two people that is for no one else to know. Right? Or wrong?

If it's abusive, how do you get it to stop? In order to get help you have to be able to talk about it. If you don't go there, if you don't share the embarrassing, intimate details, how can anyone help you?

For me it was too embarrassing to admit what happened. I've felt so much shame about it. When I tell people that I had a relationship with him, they always say, "Oh, him." Like they could see exactly what he was and they know how stupid I was to have been his lover. It reminds me of how Jake knew who Pem really was but I didn't see it. I don't think I'll ever be able to just look at a guy and take him for face value ever again. That's just not smart.

But I wasn't stupid, I was manipulated. Geoffrey (and Pem) was filled with an evil that I could not imagine. As smart as I am about what I know, he was smarter about things he knew. It's okay to be less smart than he is when it comes to that kind of evil. He abused me and tried to destroy me through emotional, physical, sexual and even financial abuse. It happened to me. And I am one in four.

* * *

One in Four Journal
December 8, 1995

I'm exhausted from everything I wrote in my last entry. Reading it over is incredibly painful. I want to write more, process more, but I'm just so sad. I feel like I'm grieving yet again. I think of the young girl I was out of college and all that he stole from me. I'm grieving her, aren't I? Somebody should. I wonder if my mom did. She must have missed me, too. I was terrible to her then. She must have felt so alone. I'm so sorry, Mom. I didn't realize what my choices must have done to you.

One in Four Journal
December 9, 1995

Today I'm feeling angry. I'm angry at what he did. And, rational or not, I'm feeling angry at Jake. I haven't heard from him now in weeks. If he really wanted to spend Christmas with me he would have reached out. On the other hand, I haven't contacted him, either. But he said he would be in touch.

I need to explore the similarities between Jake and Geoffrey. It's so weird how I gravitate to older men who appear stable and secure. Probably because my dad left and I do crave stability. I guess that's a no-brainer. But Jake did not control me. On the contrary, he's been very supportive. He took over when Denise died, but I don't think that was meant to be hurtful, he was just taking care of things. I do think he would protect me if I needed that. I believe he has my best interests in mind.

Still, he seems to trigger in me the whole affair with Geoffrey. I don't want to feel "less than" in a relationship again. I'm hoping for equality. I think Jake thinks of me as an equal, or he said he did, but I don't think I'll ever feel as if I measure up to him. Also, I want to accomplish things on my own, things that are important to me. I think that his priorities, because of all he does and the extent of the responsibilities he has, would take precedence over my own. I'm not comfortable with that right now.

One in Four Journal
December 10, 1995

I went to a local church here in Wiley. I think Aunt Charlotte goes there. I didn't want to mention it to her as I didn't want to disappoint her if I didn't like it. I like that the church tries to help women in abusive relationships. I wonder if they do a better job than the shelters? Do they have more funding? Thankfully, I didn't see anyone I know. I think I'll go next week and just sit in the back row again. I'm not ready for the whole getting friendly thing. I did buy myself a Bible. I'm starting in Genesis.

One in Four Journal
December 11, 1995
The stories of these people—talk about dysfunctional—there's abuse—murder in the first family on earth! How did I not know the details of these things? I get emotional reading them. They are real people with real lives and their lives are horribly messy, just like mine. Here, in the Bible of all places, are the intimate details of people's lives. The stuff we don't talk about today. We watch movies about other people's lives, but we don't really share our own details. If the Bible talks about it, why aren't we talking about it?

One in Four Journal
December 12, 1995
I put on my big girl pants today and called the church. I explained that I'm hoping to learn more about how to help abused women. They connected me to their women's director. Her name is Lana Capsell. I think that's how it's spelled. Anyway, I'm meeting with her tomorrow to see what she can tell me.

One in Four Journal
December 13, 1995
Lana turned out to be a such a nice woman but her office needs some fresh paint and a soft touch. I think it was furnished in castoffs. I got depressed just sitting in there. I was itching to offer her help but I didn't want to offend her. I must be going through design withdrawal.

Anyway, she was quite nice. Says the church attendance is about two hundred a week. Also says there's usually one or two flare ups of abuse a year that she's aware of, though the pastor probably knows of more than she does. Most often they're the same couples, just a different year.

I didn't plan on telling her what happened with Geoffrey, but I did. She was kind and didn't seem shocked and didn't make me feel like a victim or a dumb blonde. She even prayed with me, which I found comforting.

Still, I was surprised to learn she didn't have a lot of experience with abused women. If half of the people attending are women, there are approximately one hundred women. Divide that by four, and that's twenty-five women who have been abused. Of those twenty-five, how many are in an actively abusive marriage or relationship? And what about the teens? I forgot to ask about the size of their group for teens. Because abuse happens to teens, too.

So where are the other women in the church who are being abused? One in four? Where are you?

Lana did say that women who come in are helped as much as possible and they can get pastoral counseling for free if they need it. I asked what that looks like. She said it's essentially marriage counseling. The pastor gives the wife work to do and he gives the husband work to do. That way they're equally accountable for improving the marriage.

That makes no sense at all for abused women. If the woman is afraid of her husband can she even be honest with the pastor to tell him how bad it really is when the guy is right there? Wouldn't she pay for it later? I knew better than to say anything in front of Geoffrey's peers. I think Denise knew the same. I know I was shocked when she told me the little she did, but I think she only told me because I was there when it happened. I don't think she would have told anyone. It must have been harder for her to tell me than I realized.

What abuser is really afraid of his wife or girlfriend? If he's an abuser, he's going to lie and make it look like it's all her fault. How is the pastor to know who's telling the truth? How can the woman be given work to do when she's the victim—here's a list of ten ways not to take responsibility for your abuser's behavior? Like that's gonna fly with her husband.

I explained my perspective about the marriage counseling and Lana seemed to agree with me. I think she was surprised by what I said. I don't mean to be casting doubt on the pastor, I don't even know the guy, but it can't be okay to counsel a woman with her abuser right there. I asked Lana if she interacts with the abused women and she said a little. They usually come to her first but she doesn't have experience with abuse, so she can listen and pray with them, but she passes them on to the more qualified pastor. Maybe a women's director should get training on how to help abused women—one in four????

I wonder, are pastors trained in how to handle abused women? They must have a class on it in college. Right? I sure hope so. Better check that out, too.

One in Four Journal
December 14, 1995

I just called half a dozen universities that offer divinity degrees and none of them offer classes on abuse. Not a single one. I was told none of the divinity schools in the entire country do! Are you serious?

Who actually helps these women? Who is really there for them? A psychiatrist, a psychologist, a counselor? Does a male professional get it? Surely a woman counselor would, if she was abused. I would never want to go to a guy and share my heart like that. But, I think if a compassionate male counselor understood how an abuser thinks, he would be a true resource for abused women. What if an abused woman can't afford counseling? I keep coming back to that. I had no money when I first left Geoffrey. I was broke! It took months to get back on my feet financially. Of the one in four, how many get good counseling that helps them heal? How many, one in four?

She threw down her pen and wept.

Christmas greenery and poinsettias filled the sanctuary of the small church. They were, to Greta's eye, simple but well done. She settled into one of the rows towards the rear of the church.

Lana saw her. "Greta! I want to tell you how much I enjoyed our talk the other day. You really got me thinking about the whole issue of abuse and how we can help women. Things are a little crazy here with Christmas but after the first of the year let's sit down and talk again, okay?"

"I would like that," Greta said. "I'll call you and we can set something up."

"Thanks!"

Greta smiled and took off her coat as Lana walked away.

Then she heard Lana say, "Oh, hi Aidan. Nice to see you."

How many Aidans were there in Wiley? She didn't want to look and see if it was him. As much as she did, she didn't. Not once had she driven down his street or even looked at the street sign when she drove past it. Every beginning of a thought about him she had quickly quelled. Though it felt like she and Jake were on rocky ground these days, thinking about Aidan would only cause confusion.

"Greta?"

She closed her eyes. Where were those big girl pants? The jeans she had on were not cutting it. She looked at him out of the corner of her eye. He hadn't changed a bit.

The music started and Aidan set down his coat on the chair next to her and at least had the decency to stand in front of the next chair over, leaving his coat between them.

She stood up but refused to sing. Somehow she did not want to give him the satisfaction of hearing her stumble over the words.

Inadequate, Less than. Angry.

Aidan wouldn't think of me like that at all, she thought. Not at all. How much, she wondered, of what I do and think and feel is because of how Geoffrey treated me? What would a relationship be like if I had not been hurt by him?

She sat down and tried to focus on the service instead of Aidan's presence so close to her. But little by little it was coming back. What it felt like to be near him. She tried not to notice his black boots and jeans and the white shirt and the black leather jacket. Truth be told, it kind of matched the one she wore to church, only her leather jacket had a hood rimmed with fur.

What, she thought as she bowed her head at the close of the service, am I supposed to say to him? *God?*

She smiled wanly as she bent to pick up her coat.

"Aren't you even going to say hello?"

"Hello," she said and put on her coat.

"Nice jacket," he said, putting on his.

"Mutual."

He grinned. "Are you busy for lunch?"

She shook her head. "Not a good idea."

He put his hand on her arm, his grin gone. "Please?"

"What's the point?"

"I don't want to hurt you. I really don't. I'm just asking as a friend who cares. Please?"

"A friend? Really? You mean that this time?"

"I'm so sorry for hurting you. I really am. I was confused and I should have been upfront with you about that from the start."

She looked at him closely. They might still be at least friends had he been upfront the start. He was right about that. "Apology accepted."

"Would you like to do lunch, today? Now?"

"Actually, it would be good to get out."

"Where would you like to go?"

"The Diner?"

"Sure."

"I'll meet you there."

The parking lot was jammed. Apparently going out to lunch on Sundays after church was a big deal. She pulled up beside the Buick and rolled down her window. "I made a pot of soup yesterday and I can offer a salad and grilled cheese to go with it."

"I'll meet you at your house."

He followed her in through the back door and then stopped to take off his boots and coat, as did she.

He looked around. "The house seems so different."

Surprised, she looked about. Piles of books were on the coffee table and on the floor by the couch and on the end table. On the other end table were her notebooks, pens and the *One in Four Journal*. The fireplace still had the ashes in it from the night before and the smell of the beef barley soup still permeated the house.

"It's real life," she said.

"Things have changed," he said, looking at her.

"Very much."

He made the grilled cheese and set the table while she heated up the soup and tossed together a salad.

"Do you want to talk about it?" he asked.

"I don't have to talk about it, but I can talk about it. I don't mind. But don't you ever get tired of listening to people's drama? Or the difficulties in their lives? Or their aches and pains?"

He cut the oozing sandwiches into triangles and arranged them on their plates. "I don't get tired of it. When I listen I learn about who they are. I like that. I really do care. When I listen as a doctor I discern whether they just need me to listen or if I can help in some way. Most doctors prescribe anti-depressants instead of listening to their patients. It's a disservice to them. They don't all need drugs, they need someone to genuinely care and listen."

"And you can do that for all of your patients?"

"No, I can't. It's a huge frustration for me. I'm locked into short segments of time with each patient. I hate it. I do try to listen but I wish I could do more of it."

"I can hear the frustration in your voice."

"There's no solution for it." He sat down opposite her at the formica table in the kitchen.

It felt familiar, like old times, only better somehow.

"Are you okay if I say grace?" he asked.

"That would be nice."

"God, thank you so much for the great service today. Thank you for this time with Greta, for the opportunity to apologize to her, and to spend time with her again. I pray you would bless our time together, bless this food, and bless our conversation. May it honor you and encourage each one of us. Amen."

She told him about her house in Glencoe and how she came to be in Wiley. He told her that Doc Peterson had begun dating and had cut back his hours again.

After lunch she moved the books off of the coffee table so there was room for their feet while they sat on either end of the sofa.

"What is all this?" he asked, looking at the books.

"I'm studying up on abusive relationships."

"That's a heavy field of study."

"I think that's why it's coming along so slowly."

"Do you want to talk about why you're studying it?"

"Do you want to tell me if you might be able to guess why?"

His blue eyes studied her. "I understand you were working for a couple when the husband allegedly killed his wife. I don't know all the details, other than you were their designer and apparently you were next door at a party or something that night with them. You and the guy next door found her and tried to resuscitate her but she was pronounced dead at the hospital. Most of the reports said alcohol and drugs likely played a part, and it looks like her husband killed her. Her father is a senator in New York. The guy you were with is some famous architect. The woman's name was Denise and she worked as an editor, but I can't recall the publisher. I think that's about it."

"Just for curiosity sake, what's the name of the architect?"

"Jacob Bernstein."

She let out a deep breath. "You sure you don't know all the details?"

"It's not every day someone you know is in the middle of a murder on a famous island with famous people."

She shook her head. "In many ways they're just people, just like you and me. They have addictions and messed up relationships and they're abused and lost and yes they may be successful, but when it comes down to it most are lonely and hurting and focused on careers and things that aren't important, just like us."

"Well said."

"It's true. It's just that Denise's husband was evil. His eyes were like those of a dead fish. I've heard that expression but I saw it for myself."

"Are you okay?"

"I am. So much has changed since that awful night. It was the worst night of my life. I'm trying to trust that God will help me figure it out. I just do what I can each day. It's always different, and it's always stretching me, but I feel good about it."

"I can see how different you are. I'm shocked at what you've been through, but as hard as it is to hear it, you seem to be okay."

She shrugged. "I can only control me. Everything else is just out of control and I'm getting used to that."

"One thing," he said. "What's going on with your job?"

"I quit. When I called to tell my boss about Denise, Carol was worried about what the whole thing was going to cost. She wanted me to make sure it had a good spin for the company. She didn't care about

Denise, her client, let alone me. I was just done."

"No regrets?"

"Just that I didn't do it sooner. I have a non-compete clause so I can't work in the city for a year, well, eleven months now. So I'm studying up on abuse in the meantime to see if I can make a difference."

"Do you have any ideas yet?"

"No, just a growing list of glaring needs."

"May I see it sometime? I may be able to give you some input or help in some way."

She looked at him for a moment before it dawned on her. "Aidan. It didn't occur to me that some of your patients might be abused."

He nodded.

She put her hand over her mouth and just sat there, shaking her head. "This is so crazy. I can't believe I ran into you and here you are again, let alone we're talking about abuse and it's familiar to you, too."

"They lie about it at first. They say they ran into the door, or they tripped, or it was an accident. Always their own fault. Sometimes X-rays show old fractures that never healed properly because they never got help for them. Should they finally tell the truth, I have to report it. They don't come back."

She thought back to some of the horror stories she had read. "You've seen even worse, haven't you, that you can't tell me?"

"I have."

And then she remembered something else. "You said your dad smacked you. It wasn't just once, was it? Abuse—it's personal, too."

He nodded.

"Oh, Aidan. Who do you talk to about it?"

"I never have."

"I'm so sorry."

"My mom is okay now, that's the important thing. As far as my patients, it's difficult to see."

"Your mom. I'm so, so sorry. That must have been awful."

He looked away.

"Who do you talk to about it when a victim comes in? I mean for your sake, not for reporting it."

"At Rush we talked with the other doctors about our cases. Here I talk to Doc Peterson."

"Is it often?"

"I'd say at least once a week I'm seeing something I suspect is caused from abuse. Often it's not physical, but emotional."

"Kids?"

"Yes, but don't ask me to talk about that. I can't."

"One in four girls is sexually abused by the age of 18. One in four women is abused in a close relationship."

"That's just the ones that are reported."

The ringing phone interrupted them.

"Excuse me," she said and walked into the kitchen to answer the phone on the wall. "Hello?"

"It's Jake. I tried calling your Chicago number but I got your machine. I thought I'd try this number. You're still in Wiley? Is everything okay? How are you?"

She tried to keep her voice normal. "I'm fine. I just decided to stay a bit longer. How are you?"

"I'm doing great. I'm finally able to get back to New York. Do you have plans for Christmas?"

"Melinda and my dad are coming to Wiley. I invited all my relatives. My uncle agreed to dress like Santa again for the little ones. Would you like to come?"

"I was hoping you could meet me in New York. We could spend some time together for a few days and then fly out to California. My sister is flying out there, too. I hoped you could meet them."

"I could make it after Christmas."

"I have to be back in Switzerland on the 28th."

"I don't know what to say."

They were both silent. She turned her back on the family room and leaned against the warm stove.

He spoke first. "I'm disappointed but I guess we both assumed plans without checking with each other."

"I hadn't heard from you."

"My schedule just opened up so I can confirm plans. I didn't dare try before today."

"I would love it if you would come here."

"My parents are expecting me. My sister and I are all the family they have."

"I'm sorry I can't meet them. I hope you have a good time," she said.

"That's it then. Okay. Goodbye."

Aidan was engrossed in one of her books when she returned. Instead of sitting down she decided to get a fire going. She swept last night's ashes into the pail and put in fresh logs and starters and it lit quickly.

"It sure is cold," she said as sat back down.

"Usually is this time of the year," he said, putting the book down.

She gave a nervous laugh. The awkward silence that followed didn't help.

"I'm going to go there," he said at last. "I'm guessing that was the architect."

"Yes."

"May I ask?"

"I'm not sure. I hadn't planned on talking about him, but I might be able to go there. I'll let you know if it gets uncomfortable."

"Is it serious?"

"It was. It's strained right now."

"Strained?"

"Strained as in we haven't spoken in a few weeks and out of the blue he wants to spend Christmas together."

"Here?"

"In New York and in California."

"He can't fit into your life but he expects you to fit into his?"

She opened her mouth to reply and closed it again. The fact that he had just summed up what she was feeling and hadn't yet articulated would never do. No one could know her that well.

"Obviously, I heard you," he said. "The kitchen's less than 20 feet away."

"He has to leave for Switzerland on the 28th."

"Where is he now?"

"Last I knew he was in Japan."

"Wow."

"These people do not live like we do."

"I'm still trying to assess how serious is serious and I'm trying to take in this new information, too," Jake said.

"I told you it was serious."

"You're repeating that so I believe you." He paused. "I think I'm beginning to get it. You really—you and this guy—you're really *serious*."

"You wanted to know. You went there."

"I did. I asked."

It took him a moment for him to meet her eyes again, but when he did, she said, "I haven't talked to anyone about what really happened out there with my clients."

"I'm here if you need to talk. I won't say a word to anyone."
"You promise?"
"Of course."
She hesitated for a moment. "I think you'll understand this new relationship much better if I tell you some facts. Jake was their neighbor and their friend. He and Denise grew up together. He arrived on vacation just after I arrived to work. When I wasn't working, we hung out together, the clients and Jake and I. It's another world out there. It's not as glamorous as you would think, not at all. It's all very natural and unfussy, simple really. It's hard to remember what people do for a living and who their parents are and how different their lives are away from the island. We had a lot of good times together over meals or on the beach. Pem and Denise were both incredibly kind and invited me to stay with them after the first week. With Jake next door, coming in and out all day long, it was just the four of us and it was like we were a small family. It was a very special time."

Aidan's eyes were steady on her.

"Jake warned me about Pem and there were some curious moments here and there, but nothing horrible. Then things changed. Jake told me he had feelings for me, and I knew then things would be different. I didn't realize how much that was true, but not because of Jake. That very night I woke up to hear Pem screaming at Denise. He threw some heavy crystal tumblers at her feet. One hit her and cut her and that's when I came in and helped her. That's also when I realized that underneath the nice guy facade he was crazy. I saw a cold, dead look in his eyes. It was terrifying. Thankfully he went off to bed when I showed up."

She got up and began to pace to calm down the anxiety rising in her chest. "Jake and I tried to calm things down and deflect some of the tension by making dinner for them at Jake's house the next evening, but it didn't help. Pem was drinking heavily and he blew up at Denise and ended up getting belligerent, hateful really. He left. Denise ran after him, and then later, when Jake walked me back there, we found her dead. That, in a nutshell, is what happened."

She realized she was shaking from nervous tension. She stood by the fireplace, her arms crossed around the front of her sweater. "There were a thousand emotions going on inside of me at the time. I feel them again, telling you about it."

"Did you get any counseling? You've been through quite a traumatic event."

"No, I didn't even think about it."

He went and stood by her. "Would you think about it? I can recommend a woman you might like. She's in the city though."

"Chicago?"

He nodded. "It's hard to find good counselors. She worked with Travis years ago. She's a Christian."

"I don't know, I've never talked with one before." She tried to reassure him. "I'm okay. Really I am. I just haven't talked about it since I got back. You're the first person I've told."

"I'm glad you're okay and you didn't get hurt by Pem."

"I'm going to make some hot chocolate. Would you like some?" She headed to the kitchen. "I think I was hurt by Pem," she said over her shoulder. "Not physically but emotionally, by witnessing him be so hurtful to his wife. It hurt Jake, too. For me, being able to focus on abuse and figure out how I can help other women is helping tremendously."

"It's the best thing for you," he replied, taking a seat on the red stool.

"I didn't tell you, but I met my dad again." She put a mug of milk into the microwave.

"Greta! That's fantastic! Was he out there on the island?"

"He was. We spent the afternoon together just before I came home. I think we've said all the difficult things that needed to be said."

"What a reunion that must have been."

She thought of how he and Jake had hit it off so well. "I told you things have changed. Now I just have to meet my sister. Her name is Melinda but Dad calls her Mel. She's known about me for a long time. We've talked on the phone but meeting her will be the last piece of the puzzle I need to fit together."

"Puzzle?"

"My life has been turned upside down since my mom died." She opened the microwave and took out the steaming mug, opened the packet of chocolate mix and began to stir it into the milk. "Remember when you told me to trust that God has a plan for my life? I'm trying to look at all these things that have happened as puzzle pieces that make up a picture of my story, my life."

"How did this change happen?"

She set the spoon in the sink. "I think it was the day after Denise died, or maybe the day after that, after we sat down with the lawyers to figure out what we should say or shouldn't say, and who we could trust or couldn't trust. It was all getting so heavy and dark. Yet, in the middle of that darkness I prayed, and it's like God heard me. Right after that I realized there was something missing, what could be the murder weapon. From there all kinds of things came to light and I went from being afraid that Pem would get away with her murder to having good reason to believe that justice will be done."

She handed him his mug and began making her own. "I may not have all the answers yet for my own life, but for the first time in a long, long time, I'm really happy just being here and studying and working on my own stuff."

"I'm so glad you've found some peace here."

His blue eyes still got to her. "Thanks," she said evenly. "I want to keep it that way."

"I do not want to trouble you in any way," he said. "I will leave now if you think otherwise, to reassure you I don't want to hurt you again."

"What is said here stays here."

"I promise you that."

"That's all I'm worried about right now," she said, sipping her hot chocolate. "But I'm done talking about it for now. I need to calm down."

"I understand," he said, and followed her into the family room. "Did you hear our class is having a fifteen year reunion this fall?"

One in Four Journal

December 18, 1995

Talking with Aidan has made me realize that I've been focusing on abused women and not the abused male. How young was Aidan when his father first hit him in anger? What was it like seeing his mom get hurt? How much of their drug use was their way of coping with the abusive behaviors going on in their home? As far as I can find, the most recent statistics say that one in seven men is abused before 18. I don't know what to do about this. There's so much abuse. So much. I'm feeling overwhelmed again at how widespread it is. The ramifications, when do they end? Do they end? How can I possibly make a dent in this?

10

The white flocked tree with silver and pastel ornaments revolved slowly on the color wheel tree stand that changed colors as it revolved. Dozens of crisp gingerbread and sugar cookies stood piled high on card tables along with a dozen tubes of frosting and a box full of different colored sprinkles, crystal sugars, and nonpareils.

To the side of the immense brick fireplace stood a big cardboard box covered in brick patterned paper for the grab bag gifts. It was already stocked with plenty of gifts for adults and children who forgot to bring one. The built-in record player with her dad's stack of old Christmas albums stood at the ready. Peanuts and pretzels filled the little bowls that dotted the bar, side by side with every variety of old-fashioned Christmas candy she could find.

The long polished bar was stocked with vintage soda bottles and pop of all kinds. Her mother's punch bowl was center stage, the ice cream floating in the mix of red Hawaiian punch and lemon-lime pop. TV trays were set by the chairs and the sofa was filled with pillows made from vintage Christmas tablecloths.

Upstairs the house was decorated with real greenery and flocked red bows and poinsettias and forced paper-whites and amaryllis. A real pine tree took centerstage in the front window in the living room, decorated with her parent's vintage tinsel, ornaments and colored bubble lights. The green felt skirt her mother had sewn with sequined trains and toys circled the floor around the tree. The scene made for a warm Christmas greeting.

Several pans of lasagna were warming in the vintage O'Keefe stove, and salads filled the pink and white Pyrex bowls. On the table in the kitchen were several pound cakes from her mother's family recipe, and a special chocolate Christmas cake Greta always made had its place, too. Mounds of homemade cookies were tempting her minute by minute.

Her own outfit was a red silk dress with capped sleeves and a matching slim belt round the waist. Her collar was a large bow that ran low across her shoulders with a silver buckle in the center. Her hair, teased at the crown and curled to flip at the ends, gave her a bouncy, energetic look that she hoped would fool her guests into thinking this was all fun and no work at all.

It was time to turn the lasagna off and start the music and light the candles and the fireplace. The doorbell rang. In poured cousins and their families, and more food and presents. Aunt Charlotte and Uncle Irv arrived and half the little ones ran from her uncle dressed as Santa and the other half followed him wherever he went. He was a huge hit. Finally, the bell rang again, and she checked her watch. Their flight must have landed on time. She ran to the door.

Her heart felt like it would explode with joy as she looked at family she never knew she had. They stood on the doorstep smiling and clearly more than a little nervous, which hurt just to see it. "Welcome!" she exclaimed. "Come on in!"

A quick glance at each other and Mel and Greta embraced and laughed and cried, held each other at arms length, hugged again and laughed and cried some more.

Greta hugged her father, too, but his nervousness did not ease as Mel's had.

Howard got a hug too, and Greta knelt down to greet Anna and Karl at their level. Karl was a miniature Howard and Anna could have been the model for the little girl in her mother's painting. They warmed up quickly when she took them downstairs and showed them the tables with cookies for decorating. In no time they were playing with the other little ones as if it was the most normal thing in the world. Which it was.

Greta took Mel's hand and introduced her to Aunt Charlotte and Uncle Irv and their three daughters and the two of their three sons who could make it. Then there were Aunt Ruth's children and the grandchildren, too. As Mel and Howard greeted them, Greta went to Karl, who was still standing by the stairs, taking in the scene.

She took his arm in hers. "I know it must be hard to be here. Thank you so much for doing this."

"I never expected to be here again," he said, the words catching in his throat. "Not a thing has changed."

"We have changed. We're not the same."

He took a deep breath and ran his hand across the side of his already neat hair. "I'm ready."

There were hugs all around and everyone was gracious and warmly welcomed Karl, as Greta knew they would. But it was afterwards, when the pans of leftover lasagna were reduced to an orange mess, when nonpareils and sprinkles crunched underfoot, when the wrapping paper from the grab bag gifts littered TV trays and the floor and no one could eat one more cookie, when the rest of the family left in carload after carload with warm wishes for a Merry Christmas, that's when the real reunion began.

They were upstairs in the living room with just the tree lights on. Anna and young Karl were asleep in Ellie's old room with the door just partially shut should they awaken. A fire snapped and crackled in the fireplace and on the stereo Doris Day was singing Christmas carols.

Mel and Greta sat side by side one the sofa, heels off, feet tucked under their dresses. Their matching pearl necklaces and earrings had brought smiles to everyone. Mel's long blond hair was twisted up in a bun, and her blue eyes, so like Greta's and Karl's, were gorgeous under the fake lashes she had worn as part of her vintage look. She wore a sleeveless royal blue bouffant dress in velvet; the epitome of elegance.

"Your house is just fantastic," Mel said. "I can't believe how well it's preserved."

Greta looked at Karl as he settled into what had been his chair a long time ago. "Tell her about it, Dad."

"There's not much to tell," he said. "The subdivision was going up without too much variation in the houses but I told the builder I wanted to customize ours. He let me make some changes, and after we moved in I did the rest. The built-in stereos, the speaker system, the fieldstone fireplaces in here and in the family room rather than brick, like in the rec-room. Oh, and that bar in the rec-room took me awhile to build, and those heaters in the wall opposite all the toilet seats were a pain to install."

"How about you show me how you did that?" Howard said.

Karl got back up. "Sure."

"So," Greta said to Mel as the men left, "how are you doing after meeting everyone?"

"They're all very nice," Mel replied. "Watching them welcome Dad was heartwarming."

"He is so brave," Greta said. "He still seems a little nervous, but I think just being here again is bound to do that. What do you think of Wiley? Have you been to Illinois before?"

"I've visited my mother's family here in Wiley a few times," Mel said. "We came back here when Dad left us. My grandfather wasn't welcoming but my grandmother was nice enough. They never did forgive Mom for disgracing the family. They punished her for it up until the day she died."

"It sounds like there's quite a story there," Greta said.

"Oh there is," Mel said with a little laugh. "Unfortunately, it's a familiar one. My mom was the youngest after five sons. She wasn't supposed to want to go into the family business. When she insisted, her father allowed her to be a secretary. She was supposed to work her way up, though her brothers were put in management right away. Her father controlled every aspect of her life. Her affair with Dad was one way to get back at him. I was another."

"She told you that?"

"Mother was transparent about everything. There's hardly a detail of her life she didn't share with me."

"My mom was private about everything. We were close, but looking back she was always more interested in my world. I was so self-centered that I didn't realize how much of her own life I didn't know."

"Consider yourself fortunate," Mel said. "When Dad left, I heard every detail of their messy breakup."

Though Greta was dying to know the details, she didn't say a word.

Mel went on, "Mom was smart and ambitious. She started her catering company while she was still pregnant with me. Her only downfall as far as I'm concerned, was men. She would chronically get distracted trying to fix their problems. Dad wasn't the only man in her life. She went on to have several affairs both before and after Dad left. She constantly said it was a double-standard, how it's expected that men will have affairs but women shouldn't. With that kind of attitude, Dad ended up being the stable one in our home. Mom was the workaholic. Problem was, you didn't know if she was working late or if she had another boyfriend. I couldn't blame Dad when he left us."

"How did you handle all that?" Greta asked.

Mel tucked a stray stand of hair at the back of her neck into the bun. "Not well. I had my own rebellious years as a teenager. When Mom got cancer and Dad came back, I gave him a really hard time. He saved my life. He gave me rules again and discipline, grounded me when I needed it. It took me almost twenty years to realize what he did for me."

"I've had such a hard time trying to put myself in their shoes now that I'm an adult," Greta admitted. "It really helps to hear your perspective. You really needed him. I'm beginning to see that I'll never fully understand what happened. I'm trying to let that be okay, but sometimes I'm still curious."

"Between Howard and the kids and my work, I have little time to dwell on the past. But enough about me! Tell me about you! But wait— I have to tell you that back in high school I went to lots of beach parties in the summer and I remember Jake Bernstein well! I was a great deal younger than he was, my mother never noticed who I hung out with, so my friends and I crashed parties and no one really cared. I understand he's a good friend of yours and you were with him that terrible night the woman was murdered."

"I wondered if perhaps you knew him!"

"I'm sure he doesn't remember me, but I do recall seeing him and thinking what a good-looking guy he was. He was so quiet, though, and serious. Who knew a brilliant architect was in the making?"

"I'll have to tell him," Greta laughed. "Yes, we're good friends."

"Dad hinted you might be more than good friends?"

"I think good friends is the most accurate description," she said.

"I'm getting an idea of how private your mom was," Mel said with a smile. "It's okay for now. But I hope someday you're comfortable sharing more details."

Greta blushed. "I'm sorry. It's just that there aren't a lot of details to share these days. His work takes him all over the world. My world keeps getting smaller and smaller. It's hard to grow a relationship long distance."

"Is he worth chasing down?"

"I don't usually chase down guys," Greta said. "Are you serious?"

"Sister, of course I am! Subtlety is prime but if you want him, go get him!"

"It's not that easy," she tried to explain. "It's who I am when I'm with him that's the issue."

Mel shook her head. "I'm lost."

"I've been trying to figure out my hesitation to pursue him further. I have my work, which is my priority right now, but I'm realizing that it comes down to what he brings out in me. Do I like who I am when I'm with him? Do I like what we as a couple would look like and how we would live? Is that what I want for me?"

"Oh, I see," Mel said. "Like who am I with Howard versus other guys I dated."

"Yes," she said. "What is it Howard brings out in you that you like?"

Absently, Mel fingered the velvet nap of her dress. "Hmm, Howard makes me feel beautiful because he's always telling me I am. He's committed to the kids and our goals. I love having that sense of being on the same team. Our jobs overlap so we can discuss complicated work issues at night after the kids are in bed. He lives and breathes the same work and the same world that I do. He's in marketing and helps me tremendously with my business. We thrive on that intensity and that oneness. There were a lot of guys I dated who would never do that. They completely disconnect after work and their expectations would have been quite different. Is that what you're talking about?"

"It is. At first Jake's passion for architecture and mine for design drew us together. Then we realized we have the same eye for things. I just get him, I just do. And I think he gets me, too. Well, at least that part. The thing is, I'm backing off from design and focusing on my relationship with God and abusive relationships. These aren't just fleeting interests. What happened on the Vineyard, it's changed me. I don't think Jake realizes just how much I've changed."

"Every guy brings out something different in us," Mel said. "However, it's not just about what you have in common, is that what you're saying?"

"Yes, and that's where I'm trying to figure out what I really want."

"Where do you start? What are your must haves?"

Greta leaned back on the sofa. "That's so hard to define. I love humor, and fun, and I like to talk about people and relationships and things that are important in life. I used to think I needed to figure things out by myself, but I realize that talking things out with someone can be helpful."

"Howard and I do that all the time," Mel said. "That is crucial to both of us."

"I hate to break up this reunion, but I'm ready to head back to the hotel. I'm beat," Karl said as he and Howard joined them again. "Can we pick this up in the morning?"

Greta jumped up. "Absolutely! Come on over just as soon as you wake up. I have food for an army at the ready and can do breakfast, lunch and dinner for weeks if need be!"

Mel hugged her. "We have presents for everyone and the kids will be dying to open theirs! We may be over before it's even a decent hour!"

"You're welcome anytime. I'll be ready!"

They shared hugs all around. Karl warmed up the car while Howard and Mel gathered up Anna and Karl in their arms and walked out into the cold December night. Greta watched them drive away, trying to take it all in.

Christmas morning, after opening presents and a light breakfast of egg casserole and mimosas, Greta enlisted everyone's help in the kitchen to make lunch. Howard peeled the potatoes and Karl prepared the ham, encrusted with cloves, pineapple slices and red cherries. Little Karl helped mash the potatoes and Anna stirred the mini-marshmallows into the pineapple, pistachio pudding and topping to make the Watergate salad. Everyone was in charge of something. They all enjoyed the meal but no one as much as Anna, who was essentially covered with the fluffy, gooey salad she had helped to make. It took Mel several wet paper towels to get it all off her hands and face.

As lunch ended, Greta served the dessert, a huge white coconut cake with red sprinkles on it.

"Mommy," Anna said, disinterested in the cake. "I can't get it."

"What's that, Honey?" Mel asked.

"Up nose."

Mel and Howard gave their full attention to Anna.

"What's up your nose?" Howard asked.

"Mallow," she said, poking her finger in her nostril.

Howard was at her side in an instant. "Look up, let us see!"

Mel held Anna's hand while Howard looked up her nostril. "It's in there all right," he said.

Greta handed them a clean napkin. "Make her blow her nose."

They tried and tried. Anna started to cry as Howard tried a light pressure on the top of her sinus in hopes of working it down.

"You're just pushing it in even worse," Mel said.

Anna cried some more and little Karl was getting upset, too.

"Dad, take Karl into the living room with the toys," Greta said. "I'll get some tweezers."

The tweezers were too wide and not long enough.

"I think it's just going up further and further," Howard said, after what seemed like an hour of working at it. "It's too slippery."

Mel looked at Greta. "Is there an emergency room nearby?"

"There's one in Carleton, it's about ten miles." Then she thought of

Aidan. "Hold on. I'll make a call."

She looked through the phone book, picked up the phone and dialed his number. A woman answered. "Hi," Greta said. "Is this Mrs. O'Sullivan? This is Greta Little. I live a few blocks away."

"Why hello, Greta, Merry Christmas."

"Merry Christmas to you. I'm sorry to bother you, but is Aidan there please? We have a small medical emergency at my house."

"Sure," she replied. "Aidan! It's Greta!"

"Hello?"

"Hi, it's Greta. I'm sorry to bother you but can you come over? My three year-old niece has a marshmallow stuck in her nose and we can't get it out."

"I'll be right there."

She put down the phone. "I have a friend two blocks away who is a doctor. He'll be here in just a few minutes."

"Thank goodness," Mel said, breathing a sigh of relief. She kissed Anna's head, which was getting sweaty with the agitation. "You'll be just fine, Sweetie. Just a few more minutes and you'll be all better."

Greta waited at the front door. Aidan had on a black crewneck sweater and a pair of jeans. He hadn't bothered with a coat. It was the first time she saw him with his brown leather doctor's bag. "Thank you so much," she said. "She's in the dining room. Her name is Anna."

Aidan put his bag on a vacated chair. "Hi, Everyone! Merry Christmas! And who is this with a marshmallow up her nose? Mommy? Is it Mommy?"

Anna giggled and shook her head. "It's me!"

Aidan laughed. "You! You don't need a marshmallow up there! Let's get that out for you one, two, three! Mommy, can you hold her lengthwise, like this?"

With a long, slender pair of tweezers, he deftly retrieved the marshmallow. "Ta-da!"

Anna looked at it and then hid her eyes. They laughed and Aidan got up and threw it out in the garbage under the sink in the kitchen and rinsed off the tweezers and came back to the dining room.

"Thank you so much!" Howard said with great relief. "You've done this before!"

"Oh yes, peas, diced carrots, small toys, gum, you name it!"

Anna wriggled off of Mel's lap, "Go play!"

"Go on," Mel said and stood up to shake Aidan's hand. "I can't thank you enough."

"Everyone, this is Aidan O'Sullivan. Sorry, Dr. O'Sullivan," She glanced at Aidan. It was the first time she'd ever said that, too. "Aidan, this is my dad, Karl, and my sister, Mel and her husband, Howard."

They all shook hands.

"Aidan, please join us for dessert," Greta said. "It's the least we can do."

Howard asked, "What do you charge for emergency house calls on Christmas? We're happy to pay you."

"Oh, no," Aidan said, "no charge at all. I'm happy to help. But I will take you up on dessert."

Howard pulled in a chair from the kitchen. "Here you go. You know, my brother is a firefighter with the Boston Fire Department. He tells stories about this kind of thing all the time. It's always on that one day of the year he's finally off and he gets a call like this. I can't believe it just happened to us. One minute everything's fine and the next I'm worried my kid's going to have a decaying marshmallow in her brain!"

Over cake and coffee, the men began sharing crazy stories of emergency rescues. Greta and Mel began to clean up.

"Okay, I have to ask," Mel said in the kitchen, her voice low and quiet, "who is this gorgeous guy? He clearly knows his way around your kitchen."

"Ugh!" Greta said, just as softly. "I'd rather not go into it but I feel this obligation to tell you because you're my sister!"

"If we want to get to know each other, we have to ask personal questions!"

"Asking is much easier than answering!"

"Not for me," Mel laughed, as she put the leftover potatoes into a smaller bowl. "So come on, tell me you've at least dated this guy. How could you not? I'm not seeing a ring on his finger."

Greta began scraping the plates. "We grew up together, I ran into him again after my mom died, and I had a crush on him. I thought he was flirting, and he was, but he didn't want to go further."

"You're kidding? What's his problem?"

Greta paused. "Truth?"

"Of course."

"He's a Christian and I'd been angry at God my entire life and just not interested. Aidan said that was going to be a problem, because we didn't share the same faith. I'm actually, I don't know, growing I guess you could say, in that area. I'm learning a lot more about God and

Jesus, and I'm actually praying now and reading the Bible, but I don't want him to think it's because of him, because it's not, and I don't appreciate the way he flirted with me even though he knew we had different perspectives about that. If he knew all along our differences were an issue, he should have backed off earlier and he didn't. I don't like that at all."

Mel sat down on the little red stool. "You mentioned something about God last night. It must be important to you. Religion is important to Howard, too. He asked me to convert to Judaism. I was happy to do that. That's why I don't understand why, if you're converting to Christianity, you don't want him to know it? Why not?"

Greta rinsed the dishes. "Because it isn't about Jake. It's about me."

"You mean Aidan."

Greta froze. "I said Jake?"

"Uh huh."

Greta sighed. "I meant Aidan."

"You want to talk about that little sister?"

"Slip of the tongue."

Mel slapped a towel over her shoulder and stood up to help again. "Sure it is. Or maybe you really have strong feelings for both these guys."

"Aidan and I are friends."

"So," Mel said, ignoring this, "what about Jake's faith? Isn't he Jewish?"

"He is. He said he's not a practicing Jew but he does believe in God."

"What about you becoming a Christian? Is that going to be a problem with Jake?"

"I'm afraid it will be down the road."

"How's that?"

Greta opened the dishwasher and began loading the dishes. "I'm getting serious about my faith. Say we get married and have kids. How will it impact our kids to have me trying to pass along my faith all the while Jake's Jewish heritage is a part of who they are, too, only Jake doesn't seem to care about it? What happens to the kids? My relationship with Aidan showed me how many differences there really are. I'm fine without agreeing on everything in our lives, but I'm beginning to see how important it is to be in agreement when it comes to faith."

Mel began soaking the pots and pans. "Howard says the same thing. What our kids believe is our responsibility up to the point where they become adults. I had never given it any thought until he brought it up. Then I realized we needed to be in agreement on this. Because he's the one with a strong belief system, I was happy to go along with it. You're sure Jake wouldn't want you to convert to Judaism?"

Just then Karl came in, "Here's one more plate and fork." He stopped and looked at the two of them. "You girls have no idea what this does to an old man's heart."

The sisters stopped, looked at each and then gave Karl a big group hug, wet hands and all.

"Hold that," Howard said, coming in but turning around again. "I need to get my camera."

He came back and took several candid shots.

Aidan, Greta noticed, stood in the background, taking it all in. "Here," he said when Howard was done, "I'm happy to take some of all of you together."

They gathered in the living room around the tree with the kids and Aidan shot many frames.

"I should get going," he said then, handing the camera back to Howard. "It's been great meeting you all but I need to get back to my family."

Mel grabbed the camera from Howard. "Let me take one of two old friends, of you and Greta."

In such a good mood, it was hard to say no. Greta stood beside Aidan in front of the tree while Mel snapped several shots.

Greta walked Aidan to the door with a wrapped platter of cookies, "Please tell your mom I'm sorry to have had an emergency today of all days. Wish her a Merry Christmas for me." She handed him the cookies. "Thank you."

"I'm glad it worked out as it did. Are they going to be here long?"

"No, they leave town tomorrow morning."

"You all seem so comfortable with each other. Literally like a genuinely happy family. I'm so glad I could meet them. It seems providential," He leaned over to kiss her cheek and then stopped. "Oops! Is it okay? Just want to say Merry Christmas."

She laughed and proffered her cheek. "Absolutely!"

Softly she closed the door after him and walked back to the warmth of her very own family, literally gathered around her Christmas tree. *Merry Christmas, indeed.*

* * *

Jake called her the following day. "A belated Merry Christmas! Is your family still in town?"

"Well, hello!" She tried to keep the surprise out of her voice. "They left for the airport early this morning. Merry Christmas to you, too. How was your day? Do you and your family celebrate Christmas?"

"Somewhat. It wasn't too bad. And yours?"

"Amazing," she said. "My dad didn't entirely relax but considering everything, I think he did well. I've never been happier. By the way, my sister remembers you from beach parties years ago."

"You're kidding?"

"Nope. I told her I'd tell you. She also said something about how good-looking you are."

"I have no idea who she was."

"Well, if you happen to have any old photos of friends on the beach, you'll have to look for her in them. She has blonde hair and blue eyes like me but she's taller by several inches and has a gorgeous smile and is extremely outgoing."

"It's not ringing any bells."

"Well, she was pretty young so maybe you didn't notice her. How are your parents and your sister?"

"My father seems to think that because I travel a lot, I'm interested in world politics. I'm not. I had enough of that growing up. That didn't stop him from sharing his view on all the latest news."

"And your sister?"

"Eva likes to provoke my parents by discussing feminist issues. She writes for Ms. magazine."

"I didn't realize that was still around."

"It's changed hands a few times, but yes, it's still around."

"Sounds like a lot of stimulating conversations around the dinner table."

"Exactly, which is why I wish I had spent the day with you."

"Are you saying I'm boring?"

"No, it was meant to be a compliment! Anyway, I thought I'd try to at least redeem one day."

"Oh, how's that?"

"I flew into Chicago this morning. I'm driving down to see you now. I bought one of those new cellphones."

Her heart skipped a beat. "Are you really on your way here?"

"I am. I'm due in about an hour."

"Ahhhh!"

"My thoughts exactly," he laughed. "I'll need directions once I leave the highway."

She gave him directions and then hung up the phone. In a daze, she looked around the kitchen. It wasn't too bad, but then it wasn't too good, either. Within minutes, for the third day in a row she cleaned the sink, emptied garbage cans, vacuumed and cleaned bathrooms.

He rang the bell and she flew to the door. "Hello!"

He kicked the door closed behind them and kissed her thoroughly, all the way to the sofa. And then he kissed her some more.

"Do you know how much I have missed you?" he said, looking at her beneath him on the sofa.

"I'm getting a good idea," she said. "Wow."

"Merry Christmas," he said.

"Merry Christmas, Jake."

He released her and took off his coat. "It's as cold as Switzerland out here."

"I don't even want to know how wonderful it was in L.A." she said. "Are you hungry? I have a lot of leftovers."

He pulled her up. "Show me the way. I'm starving." As they walked to the kitchen he looked at the house. "Very nice," he said appreciatively. "This is a classic."

"My dad would be happy to hear you say so," she said. She opened the refrigerator with its V handle. "We have ham, mashed potatoes, cranberries, sweet potatoes, green bean casserole, the works."

"What's that green stuff?"

It was hard to look at it. "Watergate salad. Basically it's a dessert."

He began to take some dishes out. "A little of this, a lot of that," and he made himself a plate. She heated it in the microwave and sat down with him in the living room by the tree.

"Tell me about your family while I eat," he said.

She filled him in on all the details. "By the way," she finished, "Mel's husband, Howard, is Jewish. She converted to Judaism before they married."

Jake nodded and kept eating.

"What do you think about that?" she asked.

He wiped his mouth with the napkin. "People do that."

"Has it happened in your family?"

"I thought you didn't believe in God."

"I'm changing my mind on that," she said. "Actually, I'm reading the Bible, started with the Old Testament and I'm praying to Jesus."

Jake reached for her hand. "Does it make you feel good?"

"Feel good? It's humbling and gratifying. I'm learning a great deal."

"Well, it doesn't matter what I think. It's your relationship with God. People always want to complicate things with religion. I try to keep it simple. God exists, I acknowledge God, but I don't think he is still asking us to follow all the laws and traditions. It just doesn't make sense to me. If I happen to be with my parents on a Jewish holy day, I'll observe it out of respect for them. Otherwise, you do what is right for you, and I'll do what is right for me."

He wiped his hands and tossed his napkin on the empty plate. "I wouldn't ask you to convert if that's what you're asking. Come on, let's go back to that living room sofa."

She followed him to it. "Did Margot convert?"

"No."

"How were your parents with that?"

"They were not happy. I can live with that."

They sat down and he reached over to pull her closer. "Now, is that all?"

"I'm guessing Margot didn't care what your parents thought."

He laughed. "Margot never cares what anyone thinks!"

She noticed a few more gray streaks by his temples. Lightly she touched them. "How is your work? Has it been terribly stressful?"

"Yes," he said. "I have needed you more than I can say."

He kissed her then and they were back on the island, just the two of them on his black leather sofa.

"You sure you want to stop?" he asked.

"My body is saying one thing and my head is saying another," she said, looking up at him.

"We need this, Greta." His eyes examined every inch of her face and hair. "If we don't do something soon we're going to lose each other. You know I'm right."

She crinkled her nose to stop the tears. "I know. I'm so glad you're here and we can have this time, but I'm trying hard to be wise and not get carried away in the moment and then have consequences down the road."

He kissed her again and again, "What consequences?"

"I've told you. I get distracted too easily. I would forget my own life and immerse myself in yours."

"And I've told you, I want you to have your own life. Where our lives overlap, that's the good part, we need to make that happen, too. That's what sex is meant to do."

"It's one way," she laughed softly. "But if it's the only way, sex would become the glue that holds us together, not our commitment to each other, not a common faith. I want to know I'm ready for that commitment."

"Making love will hasten that," he said, and kissed her neck and shoulders.

"You're very tempting," she said, kissing him back. "But I need more time."

She felt him sigh and try to back off.

"Thank you," she said.

"You're worth it," he whispered in her ear. Then he pulled back. "Wait a minute. What do you mean about a common faith?"

She knew she shouldn't have let that slip out. "I've been trying to consider how having different beliefs might impact us."

"I told you, it doesn't have to be an issue. Why can't we each just do what works for us?"

"We'd be split in our faith."

"Greta, I'm not going to hold it against you that you're not Jewish, and I would hope you'd do the same not holding it against me that I'm not a Christian."

"I'm beginning to see why this ends up being a big deal."

"How's that?"

"I was about to bring up the subject of children and how we're not really teaching them a common faith if we're both split on what we believe. That's so confusing for the kids. But then I realized people have had this conversation for centuries and there really is no easy resolution."

"I wish you wouldn't overthink these things."

"I'm not making it complicated, it just is complicated."

"I sit corrected." He kissed her again. "Can we just agree to disagree for now?"

"Yes," she sighed. "I have no further insights."

Late into the night she listened as he stretched out on the sofa, his head in her lap and talked of the layers of difficulties he faced in building in Japan. The months upon months it was taking just to get the construction permits. The diplomacy needed, the right connections in the different trades and the knowledge of their culture and practices to keep building trust and show the proper respect.

In Switzerland it was much easier, but there was ongoing controversy over the design itself. The criticism of his peers stung.

"Someday," he said with certainty, "they will see I'm right. It will stand the test of time. No, it's not another glass building. We don't need more of them. The granite of this bank is bold. Inside, it's seductive. And the vault, you should see the plans for the vault, Greta. It's like a church down there, sacred, somber and glorious at the same time, as it should be."

"Help me understand seductive while at the same time sacred."

"It's enticing, it draws you into its holy places. Like my house draws you in. Only with the vault, it's the most private and intimate place in a bank."

"How do you leave one amazing project to go to the other when they're just fledglings?"

"It requires a great deal of faith in the people that work for me. I keep in touch with each team daily. I'm not taking on anything more until I'm done with these. Though I am considering a project in Spain. It's an urban high-rise. You would love Spain."

"I can imagine you at eighty and ninety saying the same thing about another conquest in another country."

"I hope I'm still doing this then, don't you?"

"You love it so much, I do hope so."

"I just can't keep doing it alone, Greta."

"Years ago I read about Frank Lloyd Wright and his lover," she mused, stroking his hair. "It's good to know genius architects need love, too. It sounded pretty complicated, though."

"I'm not going to cheat on you like Wright did with his wife, I can promise you that."

"People always say that at the beginning."

"All I can tell you is that I won't."

She continued to stroke his hair. "I don't know if traveling the world is the best lifestyle for children."

"People do it all the time. I think you're underestimating me, and maybe even yourself. Besides, I'm happy to have you pick a city and we make that our home base."

"You're so sure of everything, Jake. Everything fits in your world, everything has its place. Mine isn't like that anymore."

"I think the bottom line here is whether or not you know what you want yet."

She looked at the bubbling lights on the tree. "Having my family here for Christmas made me realize how much I ache to have my family around me. I come alive when they're around. I feel connected to them and the past and the generations that came before me. It's powerful."

"Family will always be a priority with me. What else?"

"I love design, I can never stop that. Even though I'm not working on a project right now, I threw myself into Christmas with a retro theme. I love doing things like that. My family loved it. You should have seen everyone's outfits and how much they enjoyed all the details; it was so much fun.

"As much as I loved that, I couldn't wait to get back to my books on abuse. I borrowed a bunch from the library and ended up ordering most of them from the bookstore so I can have a library on abuse for myself. There is such a need, Jake. Abuse is everywhere. I want to invest myself and really make a difference."

"Abuse is rampant in every single country. It's part of human nature. You can help others anywhere."

"I want to start out with practical ways here, where I understand the culture and I can start small and perhaps build."

"Such as?"

"I'm thinking about offering to decorate shelters for women," she said. "I know it's not much, but making the places warm and welcoming is the least we can do for them. I might go back to school and get a masters in social work so I can counsel women, too."

"All this because of Denise?"

"It's triggered some memories about a past relationship," she said.

He pulled himself up next to her. "A past relationship of yours?"

"I told you about him, Geoffrey Tate. I've always blamed myself for the times he hurt me, physically or emotionally, and even financially. I kept telling myself I was young and naive and if I had only been sophisticated enough or smart enough, he wouldn't have done that. Now I know it had nothing to do with me. He was the one with the problem. He knew what he was doing the whole time I kept trying to help him. He loved controlling me."

Jake squeezed her hand. "Just like Pem wanted control over Denise."

"Denise did the same thing I did. She kept thinking she could fix Pem if she just tried harder. It was never about her. Pem didn't love her. Or even if he did, he loved himself more. I don't know about their earlier years, but if I'm right, Pem was like this all along. He didn't change suddenly. He may have gotten worse over the years, but his selfishness was longstanding."

"You're right about that," Jake said. "I ran into Pem in downtown Manhattan one night, at a restaurant with another woman. He and Denise had been married less than a year. I never told her. He was chronically unfaithful to her. Everyone knew it."

"Do you regret not telling her?"

"Do you think she would have listened to me? Denise didn't change either. She never wanted to see the truth. Surely she had clues that he was unfaithful. How do you go about helping someone like that?"

"I don't know," she said. "But I want to learn. Maybe if I can learn better, I can help better, too."

He put his arm around her and pulled her to him. "You're going to save the women of the world and leave me in the process." He kissed her. "I'm not so noble. I want you in my world, helping me, letting me help you."

"Who are you with me?" she asked, searching his eyes to see if she could see it herself.

"What do you mean?"

"How do I make you feel? What is it you like about being with me that makes you want to spend your life with me?"

His smile was so big she almost wanted to cry. "You make me feel all kinds of things. I feel like I'm the luckiest guy in the world. You have this presence about you that is strong and beautiful, almost forceful. It makes me want to work with you, be a part of your strength and at the same time give you my strength. I think of all we could accomplish together. At the same time, you're so beautiful. I enjoy just being with you and enjoying you. You make me want to achieve great things and enjoy every minute of it with you."

"What about Margot, who were you with Margot?"

His smile dropped. "Don't ask me that."

"It's who you were, not necessarily who you are today. I get that," she said. "I'm just curious."

He thought for a moment. "Can you handle the truth?"

"I think so. I really want to understand you."

"Margot is incredibly sexy. She made my knees weak. She could distract me from my work and make me forget about everything. Then she would go into my office and look over the projects on my table and tell me everything I was doing wrong. I felt belittled and afraid of her half the time. I kept trying to measure up in her eyes."

"Do you ever find yourself still trying to measure up in her eyes?"

"You really need to stop that," he said, removing his arm from around her.

Her back ached. She nodded and got up from the couch to stretch. "Because I'm right and you know it?"

With one move he grabbed her waist and pulled her down into his lap. "You are right and when I catch myself wondering what she would think I give myself a firm talking to and I get over it."

"Ah, but do you ever get over *her*? That's the real question."

"I'm over her."

"Is that, what did you call it—*a set of rooms*—in France gone?"

"It was gone before I left the island."

"When is the last time you spoke with her?"

"She called me yesterday."

"She wished you a Joyeux Noelle?"

"I thought you didn't know French."

"I've forgotten most of the French I took in high school," she said. "Random bits and pieces remain."

"Yes, it's a tradition with us."

"I think I'm sensing a loyalty here."

"Loyalty?"

"Well, if it's not lust anymore then what is it?"

He was silent.

Her eyebrows raised significantly. "Love? Is it still love?"

He looked away. "Loyalty, maybe that's it."

"You love her."

He looked back at her. "I married for life. She left me for another man. We were disastrous together, but still, it hurt."

"I couldn't get far enough away from Geoffrey," she said. "It hurt but I wasn't about to go back for more once I realized he had moved on. It's been ten years for you and Margot."

"And the times since then that we've connected. Margot and I didn't mistreat each other, not really. Yes, she could be critical and hurtful and taking a lover was the last straw for me. But we didn't part in anger. It was actually rather sad, for both of us."

"So you turned into one of her lovers. Don't you think it reaches a point where it's not healthy for either one of you to have those meetings in France every so often to keep things going?"

"The last time we were together was before I met you. No, it wasn't smart," he said. "I admit that not meeting with her this year has lessened my feelings for her."

"I would assume that your feelings for me lessened your feelings for her."

"Of course, you are foremost in my mind! I thought we were acknowledging the power of sex between two people."

"Yes, and I'm also acknowledging the power of your love and sense of loyalty to her, still. At the same time that you have all that, you're asking me to consider marrying you."

"I don't know how to explain it, Greta. I will always love her. But it's different now." He searched her eyes. "You know, I could ask the same of you and your feelings about former relationships but I'm afraid of what you'll tell me."

"There's nothing to fear," she said.

"You've been in Wiley for almost two months now. Have you seen him, the flirtation?"

"Technically, yes, I've seen him. We ran into each other at church and had lunch here afterwards. We talked about abuse from his perspective. He's a doctor and helped with a situation here yesterday and that was it."

"Yesterday? A situation?"

"My niece got something stuck up her nose. Aidan lives just a few blocks away so I asked him if he could come by. He had a piece of cake with us and he left. I haven't contacted him other than that and I haven't heard from him."

"Then my competition is your work? That's it?"

"I'm worried about faith, too, that it could come between us. I've been trying to tell you that," she said. "But I confess, my brain is getting tired. I have a spare bedroom you can sleep in tonight. When do you need to leave?"

"My flight is at three o'clock tomorrow afternoon."

She calculated backwards, "You should leave here about ten o'clock then." She frowned. "We'll have time for breakfast and that's it."

"I'm missing you already," he said and kissed her again.

She showed him to her mother's room and put some fresh towels in the adjoining bathroom.

"I'm here if you want to join me," he said, kissing her one last time.

"Stop! Good night!"

She turned out the lights in the kitchen. She checked the fire to make sure it was out. The last to go out were the bubble lights on the tree. As she stood up after unplugging them, she caught the tail lights of a familiar old Buick driving by. She stood there a moment, hands on hips, wondering what this meant. Had he seen Jake's car?

She and Jake lingered over coffee, waffles and fried ham the next morning.

"The forecast says snow today," she said. "You should make it back to the airport before it hits."

"Oh!" He reached into the pocket of his jeans. "I completely forget to give you this last night," he said, holding out a small square box wrapped in gold paper.

"I didn't know you were coming. I have no gift to give you."

"That's okay. I envisioned giving you this on a snowy night under the stars. Clearly that didn't happen. Open it."

"I don't know that you can get snowy and stars at the same time," she smiled as she opened the box.

Two round diamond earrings set in yellow gold twinkled up at her. "Oh, Jake."

"I hope you will wear them and think of how much I love you and remember our nights watching the sun set and the stars come out. Let me see them on you," he said. "I want to remember you wearing them."

She complied. He leaned over and kissed her, "Don't let work or religion come between us, Greta. Please? And as far as Margo goes, if you want me to cut off all communication with her, I will. I realized last night that I should have done that a long time ago. Just don't take too long sorting us out, okay? We can't go on like this indefinitely."

"I'll do my best," she said.

She repeated this as she walked him to the rental car in the driveway, "I'll give you a definitive answer soon," she promised.

"That sounds like a yes or no," he said, setting his bag in the back seat. "I'm hoping for some plausible options on how to make this work long term."

"Yes, of course," she said, kissing him goodbye. "That's what I meant."

She waved as he drove away. But as he turned the corner and disappeared, a more honest answer came to her. "A yes or no is what I really meant," she said aloud, sadly, as she fingered one of her earrings. Then she turned and walked inside.

After all the work of recent days, she cleaned up the kitchen, threw sheets and towels in the wash machine and then declared a rest. It was time to just chill.

For a while she read before eventually falling asleep on the sofa halfway into an old movie. She woke up just as it was getting dark. Slowly, she got up and went to the tree to plug in the lights. The memory of the Buick's red tail lights flashed through her mind. What was Aidan doing out so late at night, driving by her house? What had he thought when he saw Jake's rental car? Perhaps he would assume the car in the driveway belonged to her dad or her sister. But then she remembered she had told him her family was leaving in the morning. Well, whatever he thought, there was nothing she could do about it.

11

One in Four Journal
> *January 1, 1996*
> *I'm starting out the new year with a different approach to my journal. I've gotten so much of my anger out on paper that I'm ready to start to do some more work. I hopes this helps.*
>
> <u>My Thoughts Today</u>
> *After the warm fuzzies of Christmas and family, and Jake, New Year's Eve was hard. I tried to tell myself it's just a few hours. If I didn't know it was December 31, it wouldn't have mattered at all. It was a lonely few hours, that's for sure.*
> *Meanwhile, it's snowy and beautiful and I'm already lonely and I'm wishing Jake was back here. I'm almost tempted to buy a ticket and go visit him in Switzerland. Swiss chalets, ski slopes, gathering on a long winter's night around the fire with friends, surely there would be some of that along with work. Why not go? If not now, when my work is on hold, then when? What if the opportunity never comes again? What kind of regrets will I live with for the rest of my life if I say no to Jake? I can't believe I'm saying no, if even for today. What is keeping me here?*
> *What I'm learning about abuse in this season is healing me. I know that. It is so satisfying to have answers, to be able to make sense of what made no sense at all. It's painful to examine the past, but I feel stronger now seeing the reality more clearly. I can speak up now, which I couldn't do before because I had no reference points. I was trying to survive a relationship that threatened my entire world. Then running from it and pouring myself into my work and creating a safe world for myself, that took up so much energy.*
> *I'd rather pour my energy into healing right now. If I go see Jake, I'll be*

tempted to consider staying with him. I'll cut short the work I have to do for me. I need this. At some point my life has to be about what I want, not what my mom wanted, or my what my dad did, or what Geoffrey did or even Carol. All that micro-managing was nuts. She really is a self-centered person. Why is it self-centered people are so hurtful? She kept trying to make me fit into her agenda.

Jake's description of what our life could be like sounds so good, but it's his description, his agenda, not mine. Do I want to fit myself into someone else's life? I've done that so often and turned into a victim. I want out of all these people's agendas. I feel badly saying that about Jake, but it's honest. I want to be honest here.

That reminds me, Jake said something about relationships and love being what matters, not a person's religion. Is that true? When things went south with Geoffrey, I was consumed with trying to make it better, which was so futile. Actually, I did the same thing with Aidan. How often did I think about him after realizing the relationship wasn't going to go anywhere? Way too much. I kept sifting through the details and sorting out the truths from the mistakes. He was right about a lot of things, but so, so human. Then again, I am, too.

Relationships come and go. They cannot be my entire world. But I do need God. It's not about feeling good, like Jake thinks. I do believe God loves me, and being right with him and learning more about Jesus, that is satisfying in a way I've never felt before. My life is meaningful with or without a man in my life because I am loved by God, who I may not understand completely, but I do know he intends good for me, that his ways are so much better for me than what I thought was okay. His ways are actually for my good. I don't know that any man will be—is capable of being—that unselfish. I'm certainly not capable of it either! I don't think it's humanly possible.

<u>My Work Today</u>
Figure out my agenda. What is it I want for me?
My Agenda
1. *To heal: because I've been deeply hurt.*
2. *To learn: so I can do better in all my relationships, and so I can help others who are hurting.*
3. *To grow: in the Bible, God picked people and pretty much said, "You're mine." The ones who returned that love did amazing things. They often became leaders or influenced people on a scale that's hard to imagine. The ones who didn't, they self-destructed. I don't know why God answered my prayers, but he did. I get it that he forgives me for what I've*

done. But now what? What does that mean going forward? What does loving God and being loved by God really mean? I want to continue to figure this out.

My Prayer Today

God, thank you for being here for me to talk to. I need a lot of help healing from abuse. I have so much to learn yet, too. I want to grow more in ways that are important to you and figure out how I can help others. I feel so alone in that.

I also ask that you would please continue to help me see the differences that could be problematic in my relationship with Jake if I marry him. Conversely, if there are more reasons why I should marry him, please show me.

Hmm...hmm... Deep breath. Okay, God. Do you want me to marry Jake? Yes, I think that's the real question I need answered. Your will is always about what's good for me and honors you at the same time. So, what do you want me to do?

12

Just as she entered the church to attend the second service on Sunday, she heard Aunt Charlotte's voice, "Greta! Wait for me!"

She turned around to see Aunt Charlotte coming up the wide walkway. "Fancy meeting you here, Aunt Charlotte!"

"One of us is a surprise here and I'm sure it's not me," Aunt Charlotte said, and gave her a hug.

Greta held open the door for the couple coming in behind them and then followed Aunt Charlotte inside. "Where is Uncle Irv?"

"He had cataract surgery on Friday," Aunt Charlotte said. "He's taking it easy. Now come sit with me and keep me company."

Between the door and the chairs inside the worship center, well-connected Aunt Charlotte introduced Greta to at least half the people in attendance. On the way out after service, Greta was sure she met the other half. She might not be able to remember a single one of their names, but they sure were friendly.

"What do you think of our pastor?"

Greta took Aunt Charlotte's arm as they walked the snowy parking lot. "He seems nice enough but I'm no expert on pastors."

"He's a real shepherd, sincerely cares for his people. Teaches straight from the Bible, too. We need that."

"Aren't they all supposed to do that?"

"We briefly had one pastor who was afraid to tell people they need Jesus. He said he might offend them. I suppose I shouldn't tell you that, seeing you're new to church, but if you're not prepared for the reality of what church is and what it isn't, you'll run from it at the first hiccup."

"Hiccup?"

"You know, when you see someone at church and think they're wonderful and then you see them at the store shoving people aside to get to the blue light special."

"That's a hiccup?"

"More like a hypocrite than a hiccup. But you get my point. Not everyone sitting in church is really living out what they're taught. We're all on a journey, don't get me wrong, no one's perfect, but you'll find some people are serious about their love for Jesus and some just like to think they are. You just can't let them rattle your faith when you seem them sinning."

"I'm just learning for myself what God considers right and wrong, Aunt Charlotte. I'm a long way from judging anyone else."

Aunt Charlotte stopped just a few feet from her car. "It's one thing if someone doesn't know better, but a church attender who claims to be a Christian should know better. God calls Christians to judge each other. We shouldn't judge people who don't know better, but we should speak up loud and clear when a Christian is sinning."

"But how do you always know if they are or not?"

"That's the thing. We don't always see people up close and personal, do we? We can't always sort the wheat from the chaff, only God can do that."

"Excuse me? What's that supposed to mean?"

"We just have to wait until the end of time when God sorts out the good from the bad. I have to leave an awful lot up to God to decide whether those around me at church are worthy of my love as a true brother or sister."

"So you trust those you don't know in church and hope they're really sincere and doing good?"

Aunt Charlotte laughed, "Our pastor and elders see me coming and they know they're going to get an earful of the truth if I think something's wrong! I believe in bringing things to the light. Remember our conversation about abuse? All those churches with abusive leaders, it's shameful what they've done to cover it up. I'm not talking about those kinds of things. I'm talking about giving Christians the benefit of the doubt but doing so wisely. People need to earn our trust. Sometimes Christians are foolish and are too ready to come to the defense of another Christian. We need to lovingly correct someone who's in the wrong. Do it nicely. Gently. They may not like it, but if it's done in love, that's on them."

"Okay, I think I see what you mean."

"A Christian is going to let you down, Greta. We all let each other down in one way or another, sooner or later. Jesus didn't trust himself to any man, because he knew what was in the heart of all men. He trusted God and God alone. We must do the same. "

"Aunt Charlotte, did someone just hurt you? You seem really adamant about this and I'm not sure where it's coming from. No offense, but it's intense."

Aunt Charlotte looked down and fumbled with her keys. "I just know you're going to get let down one day by a Christian and I don't want that to turn you away from trusting God when that day comes. Christians will fail you, they're human, but God will never fail you."

"I'm taking that as a yes." Greta kindly took her aunt's keys and unlocked the car door and helped her in.

Aunt Charlotte set her Bible and bag on the seat next to her and then looked up at Greta, her gray eyes brimming with tears. "This past week I was disappointed by a friend I've known for more than forty years. I won't say more than that, but I've been feeling blue ever since. But you know what? I saw you today walking into church and everything changed. You have no idea what joy you have brought me today."

Greta leaned down and kissed her soft, wrinkled cheek. "I love you, Aunt Charlotte. I'm so sorry you were hurt."

Aunt Charlotte brushed away the tears that fell. "I love you, too. I guess I still need to work on forgiveness. Not that my friend deserves it, but I'm no more than a hypocrite if I can't turn the other cheek."

She had no sooner say goodbye to her aunt when Lana drove up with her car window open. "I'm so glad to catch you. Are you free for lunch this week? Tuesday at noon at The Diner? Something's come up and I'd like to talk with you about your interest in abuse."

"Sure," Greta said. Then she remembered how crowded The Diner could be at lunch time. "You're welcome to come over to my house for lunch," she said.

On Tuesday afternoon Greta opened her front door to Lana.

"I love your house," Lana exclaimed as she stepped inside. "What a gem!" She wriggled out of her jacket. "Meeting at people's home seems to be going out of style these days. Yours is the first invitation I've had in a long time."

"I think most people are afraid their house doesn't measure up," Greta said. "It's a shame, because relationships are so much more important than how a house looks."

"You are so right," Lana said. "I admit I feel insecure about my house. There's always something to be done." She looked around. "Your house is like a movie set. Everything is done to perfection!"

"I can't take credit for it; it was my parent's. I have days where it's a mess, believe me."

Over a simple lunch of pumpkin chili, Lana shared her news. "A woman came to me last week asking some questions about what is and isn't abuse. I immediately thought of you. Would you be interested in talking with her?"

Greta's eyes widened. "I'm not qualified to talk to anyone."

"But you already know so much more about it than I do."

"Having information and actually being able to help someone are two different things."

"I agree. That's where your heart for women and your own experience with abuse comes in. You have a natural compassion and ability to relate that I will never have. That's a gift you have, even if you don't realize it."

Greta's left toes in her warm socks started silently tapping the table leg. "I really don't know. I wouldn't want to say something wrong."

"What if you just say that you've been through some painful situations yourself, and you're there to be a friend?"

"Lana, I'm going to be blunt. Aren't there professionals who should be doing this?"

"She has a counselor. What she needs is someone who can just be there for her. Meet for coffee, listen to her story, help her trust that good people, who have been in her shoes, care for her."

"That's all?"

Lana leaned forward, "That's everything."

Her toes stopped tapping. "I can do that."

"Thank you. I'll be praying for you and for her and for your meeting. You won't be alone. God will be with you, too."

She raised her eyebrows. "Thanks, I'm going to need it."

"Her name is Autumn, Autumn Gifford."

She tried, for two weeks, to meet with Autumn. Last minute Autumn canceled, time after time. Then, one Friday night Autumn called her back. "Can you meet me tomorrow morning? At the coffee shop on Main?"

"Sure. What time?"

"Nine o'clock."

"I'll be there."

Breathing a prayer, Greta walked into the warmth of the small shop. The smell of rich coffee beans permeated the air and cases full of baked goods beckoned her. She was early, so she found an empty table along the wall in the back, away from others so they could have some privacy.

Looking back, she realized she had expectations about what Autumn might look like. They were not realized. The pretty young woman who walked in the door looked like any new mom with a baby in a seat swinging from her elbow. Autumn wore jeans and a puffy jacket, a cute pair of boots, and the highlights in her hair were gorgeous.

"Hi," Autumn said as Greta approached her. "Are you Greta?"

"Yes, hello! Please, come sit down. What can I get you? My treat."

"I can't drink coffee, I'm still nursing. Just an herbal tea, ginger."

"Sure. Anything to eat?"

"I would love a cinnamon raisin bagel with cream cheese."

"You got it."

When she came back with their orders, Autumn had the blanket pulled away from the baby's seat just enough that Greta could see only a tiny amount of pink skin and some soft eyelashes.

"You're a brand new mom! Congratulations!"

"Thanks," Autumn said, putting the baby's seat on the empty chair between them. "This is Samantha. She's six weeks old today. She's sleepy right now because she didn't sleep a wink all night."

"You must be extremely busy."

Autumn took off her own coat and brushed back her hair from her shoulders. "I'm a hairdresser. I just opened up a salon in the basement of my home for clients. I thought it would be easier than trying to get a babysitter full-time and going back into the salon. It was a crazy idea. I should have known better. I'm so exhausted that I canceled my appointments for today. I haven't slept in six weeks. My husband says I'm losing my mind." She shrugged, "I don't care."

"Sleep is crucial." Greta said.

Autumn sipped her tea and met Greta's eyes. "Lana recommended I talk to you. She said you've been through some tough things."

"I went through a really painful relationship when I was in my twenties."

"Painful? What happened?"

"Well, I had moved in with him, and in just a matter of weeks he completely changed."

"How's that?"

"He would get drunk and say really hurtful things. Sometimes when I asked him to stop, he would just get louder. When I tried to get away from him, he would follow me from room to room. He wouldn't let me close a door, he'd kick it open. Sometimes when I asked him to stop, he would escalate it."

"How's that?"

"Pushing, shoving, grabbing my arm at times to get me to go where he wanted—I had plenty of bruises. He would get in my face and scream at me. It really scared me, but I thought I was tough, that I could take it."

"How long were you with him?"

Greta began to wonder who was there to help whom. "Six years. They were the worst years of my life."

Autumn was chewing on her lip. She set her tea on the table. "When Brian learned I was pregnant, he threatened to kill me and the baby."

Greta's heart skipped several beats. "Did he try? Are you in danger today?"

Autumn shook her head. "No, that was months ago. He apologized. He said he didn't mean it."

"Do you think he did?"

"I think he meant to scare me."

"Why does he want to scare you?"

"I don't know. I think he's got mental problems. I've asked him to get help. He won't. He says I'm the one with the problems. I'm beginning to think I am."

"Why is that?"

She gave a short laugh. "For starters I'm still with him. I keep pretending everything's fine, when it's not. I'm scared to death half the time. Now I'm frightened for my baby."

"Has he hurt her?"

"Last night she was fussy and crying and I needed a break and I just asked him to hold her for a few minutes so I could go to the bathroom. He walked around the room two times and gave her back to me, while I'm still in the bathroom! He said she's my problem, not his. He needed his sleep."

"What about that made you feel frightened for Samantha?"

She reached out and put her hand on the little bundle that was Samantha. "He's come after me before, punched me, hit me, but last night, when he was holding her and she was crying, it was like he hated her, like he was going to shake her. His eyes were dead, cold. As tired as I was, as much as I needed a break right then, I took her back. I walked her all night long. I put her in the swing. I sang her songs. I will do anything, go to any lengths no matter how tired or exhausted or whatever I am, I will do it. I don't want him holding her ever again."

Greta breathed a silent prayer to God for wisdom. "Autumn, do not ignore your mama's heart for your baby. You hear me? You do whatever you have to do to be safe with her."

"I can't see any options at this point."

"What about a safe place to live?"

"I sank every last penny into remodeling the basement so I could work from home. I wanted to stay home with her as much as possible. Now I think he wanted me to do it so I wouldn't have any money to leave."

"What's the safest thing for you and for her today?"

She shook her head. "If I leave now, I will have nothing."

"I hear you. I understand that it seems impossible. But you and Samantha are precious human beings. You are worth whatever it takes to be safe and secure. It will help if you have a safety plan."

"That's what my counselor says," she replied. "I'm working on one with her. Did you have a plan?"

"I wish I could say I did, but no, not all. I couldn't see any options, only my worst fears. At the time I lived in the Hancock building in Chicago with my boyfriend. It was way beyond my means. I kept telling myself that financially I couldn't afford to live on my own in the city. I had already been mugged once and I was afraid that anything I could afford would be in a bad neighborhood. I thought that if I stayed and fixed Geoffrey, figured him out and loved him well enough, that we would be fine. I became more focused on fixing him and being who he wanted me to be to keep him happy, than being who I needed to be for me and fixing myself so I could get out of the craziness."

Autumn leaned forward. "That's exactly how I feel right now. I've been so focused on surviving that I can't figure out how to take care of me! On top of that, because I've been pregnant and now I'm nursing, my body isn't my own right now. I can't imagine taking care of myself. I can't even remember what it was like before Sam and she's only six weeks old!"

"I can only imagine how much being pregnant and having a baby takes away from your sense of self."

"What does it even mean to take care of yourself? I don't want to—what is it some women say—*find myself*—as if I'm bored or disappointed in my marriage. I mean it more like I can't even think straight or make a decision anymore. I find myself stuttering when I talk to Brian or try to explain something to someone. Everything I do is wrong, and yet when I try harder it just seems to make things worse. I find myself acting like Brian expects me to act, stupidly. I feel like I've lost every ounce of intelligence I might have had. I look at myself and wonder who I've become. I don't recognize myself. I used to be able to think logically and carefully. That's all gone. My only relief is when he's gone during the day. The closer it gets to when he's due home, the more frantic I get. I dread it. I'm trying to troubleshoot anything that might upset him, and address it before he gets home. Trying to keep him happy is consuming me so I can't even think straight."

"He wants it that way, Autumn. From everything I know so far, abusive men don't want their women to think straight. They want power over us so they can feel like they're in control of us. If a man can keep a woman off kilter, he owns her."

"But why? Why would someone do that?"

"They're usually insecure men who think they are far superior to those they control. That makes them feel good. They believe their superiority entitles them to do it. It's heady stuff. They don't want to give that up."

"Meanwhile, I feel completely worthless." She stared at the coffee bar, seeing but not seeing. "I feel like I'm nothing. As if he wants me to be nothing at all. He finds me disgusting, especially now that my body has changed from being pregnant. I can't lose the weight fast enough for him. The names he calls me, and that look in his eyes, it makes me feel dead already." She turned to Greta. "What would you do if you were in my shoes?"

"I've seen that cold look in someone's eyes before. That really scares me. It's dangerous. Knowing what I know, I would get as far away from that person as I could."

"Yeah, but how?"

"If family and friends aren't able to help you, go to Lana and tell her you need help from the church, you need a safe place to stay. Try the local shelter if only for a few nights and see what the church can do after that."

"I'm afraid the church will tell me to stay with him."

"Why on earth would they do that?"

"That's what happened to my friend."

"What happened?"

"She lives in Peoria and goes to a church there. Her husband, they weren't even married a year and he was hitting her and worse. She tried to leave and her pastor told her she had to stay, that she had made a vow and she had to stick it out because then her husband might believe in God."

"I don't even know where to start with that," Greta said. "Maybe with the fact that her husband made a vow to love and to cherish her and he broke that? And to stay could mean her death?"

"That's a good one," Autumn nodded. "I'll have to remember that."

Greta rubbed her temples, trying to think. "I'm pretty new to Christianity, Autumn, but I can't see why God would want a woman to stay with a man who is trying to destroy her. That is antithetical to who God is. He delivers us from evil. I'm not talking about a relationship where someone is annoyed or irritated with their spouse. We're talking people intentionally out to hurt us. Are you sure that's what your pastor thinks?"

"I don't know. I've never talked to him."

"I may be out of line here, but what does your pastor even have to do with your situation? Do you need his permission to get help from the church?"

"I think so. I can't imagine the church would be willing to help me out financially without making a call on whether or not they agree with what I'm doing. But there's something else, too."

"What's that?"

"I want to please God. I don't want to do the wrong thing. The pastor can tell me if it's right or wrong. I think I'm right but I want his reassurance. But if I go to him, I'm afraid that he'll want to talk to Brian. Somehow Brian will use the pastor to make me stay. He'll tell the pastor that I'm the problem. I won't be safe there either."

"He's threatened this?"

"I just know he's turned everyone against me. My parents even think I'm to blame for what's gone wrong. How he turned them against me, I don't know how, but he did."

"I'm so sorry, Autumn. So sorry."

Autumn looked at sleeping Samantha. "This is the longest adult conversation I've had with anyone since she was born. I tried calling my counselor twice now to talk and I've gotten like ten minutes in and Sam woke up screaming. Usually when she sleeps I'm running around like a crazy woman trying to get a shower or clean the kitchen or give someone a cut and color." She looked back at Greta. "Thank you for being willing to talk to me. I feel safe, for now, like I can just be me around you and that's okay."

Greta's eyes filled with tears. "You're welcome. I'm here. Anytime. Just please be careful. Please. Okay?"

Autumn's eyes filled with tears, too. "Thank you." She stood up and began to gather her things. "None of my friends at church understand me. They keep second-guessing me. They want me to stay no matter how bad it is. I end up feeling like I'm trying to convince them of something they don't want to believe. I keep thinking if I just say the right thing they'll get it. But no matter how badly Brian treats me, they think it's wrong to leave him because he hasn't cheated on me. I kind of wish he would, so I could go with a clear conscience, but then I think, no, I have no money, and nowhere to go. I'm better off with a roof over our heads."

"You're better off alive, Autumn. Safe."

Autumn nodded. "I know, but it's easier said than done."

The two women hugged.

"If you want to meet again, or just talk on the phone, once a week or whenever, I'm here for you," Greta offered.

"That is so nice of you. Thank you. I'm so crazy busy with the baby and the salon, but if I can find the time, I'll try to stay in touch."

"I understand," Greta said. "I'll be praying for you."

The next day Greta called to make an appointment to meet with Gail from the women's shelter. She was put on hold.

"Hello," Gail said a minute later. "This is Greta Little?"

"Yes, I'd like to come by and talk about some possibilities of helping out the shelter," she said.

"I'm available now if you're free," Gail said.

"I'll see you shortly."

Gail's office was painted a dark green with white trim. The burgundy sofa and navy blue pillows completed the traditional look. Her desk was a dark cherry. The papers on it were neat and organized. "I appreciate what you do here and I would like to offer some help," Greta began. "I'm a professional interior designer and I would love nothing more than to offer the shelter my skills at no charge."

"Are you able to be more specific about what you would like to do?"

"I understand how a person's living space or work space can impact them in ways they may not even realize. For women seeking safety, it would make sense to make their space as warm and welcoming as possible. However, I'm sure that simply maintaining the shelter and providing for salaries of employees, etc., must take priority over fixing things up. That's where I would like to help. I'd love to spend time with you hearing about each space and how you wish it could look, if you had the resources. Then, I would like to see how much of that I could make happen for you, at no expense to you."

Gail blinked. "Are you serious? You do this?"

"Well, I haven't offered to design at my own expense very often but yes, I've worked with homeowners around the country, hotel owners, management companies of office buildings all over Chicagoland, and elsewhere. To be able to make that happen here, for women and children who need it most, well, it would be very satisfying."

Gail was clearly excited. "Honestly, how it could look, I have no idea. Now, if you need to know how to fundraise and make this place run, I'm your woman. But decorating? I would have to depend on your input for that. However, I do have a board that I answer to. They will want to review any plans and monitor this. People say a lot of things, but following through and the liabilities of it all, that's where the board will need to meet with you and approve this."

"I understand and that's not a problem. I'm used to this. I'll submit my credentials and give a list of references for them to check. Whatever I need to do for them, I'll do it."

"May I ask why you're doing this?" Gail said. "Is it personal?"

Greta thought for a moment of all she had been wrestling with recently. Her thoughts came out in what felt like a jumbled up rush. "It's not easy to talk about, but I guess I'm doing it for several reasons. In November I lost a friend who was in an abusive marriage. She was killed. I began to read more about abuse and I see things so differently now. I recognized abuse in a past relationship I was in. Now I realize that just like predators look for vulnerable children, some men look for vulnerable women. They find her weakness and exploit it for their own selfish reasons. I never imagined it was so common. Maybe I wasn't ready to see it, I don't know, but it took God to open up my eyes! I used to tell myself I was just young and stupid. But that was just more denigrating self-talk. Now that I've learned, I've got a lot more to learn, but I'm beginning to think that every woman needs to be helping other women, no matter how little we think our help is. We need to teach our daughters this compassion from day one. We need to warn our family and girlfriends about hurtful people. We need to be looking out for each other, looking for ways we might be able to help. I have the resources right now to do this much, to make this offer today. Honestly, it feels small, like it's not really much at all. I was hoping you wouldn't think I'm just frivolous or focused on something that's unimportant. But I know how important it is to feel safe and welcome, even comforted by our surroundings, especially when we're traumatized. I think the truth is it's what I've been given to do, I can do it, and I need to do that much, little or not. It's my way of honoring my friend and doing what I can for our sisterhood of women." She paused. "And to be completely honest, I think it's honoring God by loving each other well."

Gail sat there silently for some time. Finally she spoke. "Frankly, I'm very moved by what you just said."

Greta looked at her in surprise. "I'm sure you know this so much better than I do!"

"I likely do, in fact I'm sure I do, but the reason behind why I do it, that's not easy to articulate so passionately. You've encouraged me. This isn't easy work, yet you've reminded me of all that's good about it and I'm encouraged to keep fighting the good fight. Thank you."

Greta's eyes stung with tears. Her voice came out small and timid but it was really because she felt such awe at what was happening. She pulled a tissue from her purse. "This is it," she said, wiping her eyes. "This is exactly what I was trying to say. I share my little bit with you and then you encourage me, and we both walk away feeling so blessed."

Gail smiled. "You're so right." She stood up. "Now let's go take a walk and show me some possibilities for what this place can look like."

"I'd love to!"

Gail opened the office door and then stopped and turned back to Greta. "I just thought of something. Our annual fundraiser with community leaders and business owners is coming up next month. I'd love to have you attend and share from the front what you just said to me."

Greta swallowed hard. "Me? Share that? Why, I don't know if I can even exactly recall what I said."

"Would you please consider it?"

"Why, yes, I—I would. Thank you!"

"Thank you," Gail said quietly, and together they toured the building yet again.

Lana called three days later. "Autumn is at the shelter. I talked to her less than an hour ago. She wants you to know she's going to be okay."

Greta sat down on the kitchen stool. "That was fast."

"She had to call the police two nights ago. Her husband punched her stomach. He said she shoved him and he was just protecting himself."

She felt sick. "She's probably just beginning to heal from giving birth."

"Apparently the police believed her when they saw her throwing up. They called an ambulance and she was admitted to the hospital with internal bleeding. She's doing better now and she was released this morning to the shelter."

"They don't usually stay away. They go back."

"Who?"

"The abused. They go back multiple times."

"We don't know that Autumn will go back. She's highly protective of her baby."

"I know, but the likelihood is there. Is the church able to help with housing? She said she didn't know where she would live."

"She hasn't asked for anything."

"Maybe it could be offered, to reassure her?"

"I think we usually help when they ask."

"I didn't know how to ask for help when I was being abused. I was so scared and so worn out, and humiliated, that asking for anything was really hard."

"I didn't realize," Lana said quietly. "I'll see what we can do."

"Thank you for letting me know."

"Pray for her, Greta. Pray hard."

"I will."

She found her journal and her pen.

One in Four Journal

January 20, 1996

How do I pray for Autumn? What does she need? What does every abused woman need?

Pray for her safety.

Pray for a place for her to live without abuse.

Pray Samantha will be kept safe.

Pray her financial needs will be met.

Pray Autumn won't go back to abuse.

Pray she will heal emotionally and physically.

Pray that she will trust God more than hurtful people.
Pray that God will show me if I should offer her more help.

How would I have prayed for Denise?
  That she would see what Pem was doing and disengage.
  That she would be able to see how dangerous Pem was.
  That she would protect herself.
  That she would be happy without him.

How would I have prayed for me?
  That I would have valued myself.
  That I would not let myself be used.
  That I wouldn't have wasted those years on a man who was so selfish.
  That I could see I didn't need to be afraid of being alone.
  That I would have loved my mom and the people who loved me more than I loved an abuser.

An hour later, Lana called her back. "Confidentially, the church is going to provide her with enough to cover expenses for the next three months. And, amazingly enough, a retired missionary couple happened to be in the pastor's office when I called. They had just offered up the lower level of their home to be used down the road for any visiting missionaries, and they said they would be honored to have Autumn and her baby there instead."

She sank onto her mother's bed. "I'm so relieved. She'll be safe there. I wasn't sure how involved I should get."

"I know what you mean. I was feeling the same way," Lana admitted. "It's always hard to figure out where to draw the line when helping someone."

"I'll keep praying for her," Greta ended. "I know I can do that much."

She set down her pen and walked away from the journal. It was late afternoon, almost dinner time. Outside the front window the street light went on, and in its light she could see snowflakes swirling. On a whim she went to the back door and donned her snow boots, a warm coat, hat, scarf and mittens.

It was crisp and cold and the snow came down heavily as she walked another block and then another. His car was in the driveway; she had timed it well. With her mittened hand, she pushed the bell.

"Hello?" She had Aidan's blue eyes and dark hair, though it was streaked with gray.

"Hi, Mrs. O'Sullivan. I'm Greta Little from a few blocks over, a friend of Aidan's. Is he in?"

"Why, Greta! Come on in."

"No, that's okay, I'm all snowy."

She opened the door wide. "Don't be silly. Please, call me Mary. Aidan!"

The house smelled rich with dinner. "I'm so sorry, I wasn't thinking that I'd be interrupting dinner."

"We have plenty. Would you like to stay?"

"Oh no! Really, I'm so—"

"Hey, Greta!" Aidan's smile was warm as he walked into the front room.

"I'm sorry, I just wanted to ask you a few questions about a situation. I was hoping you'd be home but I forgot it's dinner time. I apologize."

He continued to smile. "Stay for dinner. Please, Mom always makes plenty."

"Irish stew," Mary smiled. "Aidan's favorite."

So it was Greta found herself seated at the cozy kitchen table next to the patio doors that were warbled this time not with rain but with steam from the warm oven. It felt as if no time had gone by at all.

"I do recall meeting your mom at one of those neighborhood watch meetings," Mary said, "though I'm sure we probably crossed paths at least a few times when you two were growing up."

Greta poured gravy over the potatoes and carrots. "Is there still a neighborhood watch group?"

"Sure" Aidan said, "I take a turn driving around late at night to check the streets. They say it really does help reduce crime."

Thoughtfully, she set the gravy down. "So if I happened to see your car driving around late some random night, that's what you'd be doing?"

"Yep, that's right." He went on eating without looking at her.

"Well, it's good to know we have good people watching out for us here. That's quite reassuring."

"I admit that having Aidan living here has been more than nice," Mary said. "I'm gaining weight from cooking for him, but I enjoy having someone to cook for again."

Greta sighed. "I try to be good about making meals for myself, but today was one of those days where it's too easy to just eat a yogurt or some cheese and crackers. This stew is a treat, thank you so much."

"You're welcome," Mary replied. "Do you remember the old couple from the corner, Ida and Henry Mitchell? Once Henry died, Ida became a recluse. When they took her to the nursing home they found canned peaches and preserves decades old still in her fruit cellar. Some of us would drop off groceries or meals once in a while, but I always wondered what she ate the rest of the time. We never saw her go out. I have always wondered if she was eating her way through those canned goods."

"She would have died a lot earlier from botulism had she been eating them," Aidan said.

"Maybe she was working backwards with them. She lived to be a 101," Mary said. "Just goes to show how the body can live on very little that's good for it."

Dinner ended with coffee and homemade peanut butter cookies. They were delicious.

"Now you two go, while I do the dishes," Mary said, shooing Greta away from the sink where she was rinsing her dishes.

"I'm happy to help," Greta said.

"You wanted to ask Aidan about something. Go have a talk."

"I think I'll walk her home," Aidan said, drying his hands on a towel. "We can talk as we walk."

"Sure," Greta said, trying to remember what she wanted to talk to him about.

The snow was fine but still heavy. The air was thick with it as they walked up the middle of the empty street.

"So what's your question?"

"Honestly, it's not so much a question as a need to process some random thoughts I have about helping the abused."

"Okay. Such as?"

"I talked with an abused woman the other day. She broke my heart. She's spunky and intelligent, capable, beautiful, you name it. She has a professional counselor, but she was hoping to find another woman who could just be a friend, who would understand her and connect with her. Lana at church connected us. Financially, the woman's money is tied up in the family home. I found out that after we talked her husband hit her again, badly, and she was just released to the shelter. After I spoke with her the first time and then again after talking with Lana today, I wondered if I should take her in. It turns out she was offered another option, which I imagine she'll take, but it's really given me something to think about. Should I offer up my house to another woman in that situation? Especially with a child?"

"What would you want someone to do for you if you were in her shoes?"

They crunched on through the snow as she thought about it. "I would want to be independent. I wouldn't want to live with anyone. I wouldn't mind some money to put towards renting an apartment, but I'd want to try to make my own way. The mom I'm talking about could do it. She wants her own business, and even if she can't do that, she has skills and could get a job."

"Is that your answer?"

"I don't know. The baby brings a different dimension to abuse that's a game changer. While I think a mom would want to get away, from what I'm learning they're more likely to stay because they can't manage everything on their own."

"Are you afraid the woman you met will go back home?"

"I'm not sure now. She's been offered the lower level of someone's home, so it sounds like it could work unless she gets manipulated by her husband again and goes back."

They walked on in silence for sometime before she spoke again. "What if I give a woman the money for a deposit or to live on for a few months, and she decides to go back home and uses it on something else? I can't make her do what I hope she'll do. I want to give dignity to these women. I want to encourage them to believe they can make it, that God can help bring light and purpose to their lives again. But what if they're caught up in their worst fears? What if it doesn't really help at all? It just brings me back to feeling helpless. How can I really make a difference?"

"You haven't seen that counselor for yourself yet?"

"I forgot all about it. But I did start journaling. It's a tremendous help. Why?"

"I bring it up because your feelings of helplessness around the death of your friend on the island are certainly going to be triggered while you're helping this new woman. That's going to be painful right now. It will be until you've had a chance to heal. Right now I would think you're still emotionally charged from what happened."

She swiped at some snow on the bridge of her nose. "So if I heal, I'll have better answers?"

"No," he said slowly, "I think when you heal the reality that you want to help and yet you can't control the outcome won't be as painful or difficult to wrap your head around."

She sighed. "That's the truth I needed to hear."

"That said," Aidan went on, "I think you're hitting on a real problem. The options for women in volatile situations are limited."

"Including their options for financial support. They also need good counseling. By the way, have you ever heard of a pastor telling a woman she has to stay in an abusive situation?"

"I know of a priest that did."

"Tell me it wasn't your mom's priest."

"It was. You know how people expect a doctor to have a good bedside manner? I think we do the same with pastors and priests. That particular priest had no skills in helping hurting people, in fact, I think he did more damage than good."

She shook her head in anger. "I called some different seminaries, and after getting a master of divinity to become a pastor, a student would then need two more years of education to get a biblical counseling degree. How many pastors are willing to do that?"

"How many pastors even have a passion for counseling? I imagine most like to teach or evangelize."

"That's a good point. Counseling may not be their thing. But with abuse so rampant, wouldn't pastors and priests do well to get training? That's not even taking into consideration all the other kinds of related issues that come into play, like anger or depression, anxiety or addictions. We all have our issues, right?"

"Right, but is the pastor the right person to expect that kind of expertise from? He's there to address the spiritual side of the issues."

She slowed down. "So what would the spiritual side look like?"

"That would be a discussion around right and wrong, around what the Bible says about abuse and one's response to it."

"What does the Bible say about abuse?"

"You mean other than it being wrong? I wonder, if we went through the entire Bible and noted every single incidence and how God dealt with the abusers, how big a notebook we would need."

"I'm not even a third of the way through the old Testament right now, and there's the guy in the first family who kills his brother, there's a guy whose brothers sell him as a slave, there's a brother who rapes his sister, and that guy's dad, a king, makes a woman sleep with him and then sends her away, and when she finds out she's pregnant, he kills her husband. I made my way through all the laws, and many of them deal with forms of abuse, including murder, which is rampant, too. I can't get over how many times God just strikes down nasty people. I can't wait to see what the red words say, the words Jesus actually spoke. What blows me away is when some of those victims forgive their abuser. Oh—and when God forgives them! It blows me away."

"That's where the pastor would be able to speak into one's response."

"Like forgiveness."

"Exactly. And he might encourage them to get away from the abuse, but forgive, not become bitter, or to not try to get vengeance, and he could give the woman hope for her future, for her own walk with God, for—."

Greta interrupted, "For how things could change if she stepped out with strength and courage to stop the craziness. If she trusted that God would open doors for her that she can't even imagine, even if it is difficult to leave."

"Yes."

"Of all those things, it's still forgiveness that really gets me. In one of the Bible stories, the one about the brother sold to slaves, he forgives his brothers. I about cried when I read what he said to them later, when he forgave them. It was so beautiful. Maybe I'll get there someday, but right now, I can't imagine forgiving Geoffrey for all he did to me."

"Tate? He abused you?"

"Yes."

"That's awful! When you mentioned him before, I didn't realize he'd been abusive."

They reached her street. The snow falling thickly, the warm lights in the houses looking inviting and snug, everyone safe in their homes for a long winter's night, it made her heart ache it was so peaceful and pretty. The last thing she wanted to do was talk about Geoffrey right now.

"This is gorgeous," she said. "Like a painting. "

He looked at her and then up at the snow. "I love how still it gets."

She stopped walking for a moment. "Let's just listen."

He took off his hat and she took off hers and they stood still and just listened. In a swoosh of wind swirls of snow spun for a moment, and then it grew quiet again, with just the silence of snow falling on snow.

In the distance a snow plow drove by and then away. Greta smiled and began walking again. "Thanks."

"Thank you."

They walked up the driveway to the back door. "You're welcome to come in for some hot chocolate," she invited.

"I can help you shovel your driveway."

"No sense in that. We're supposed to get a few more inches tonight. I'll wait until morning."

"Okay. Well, it was good to see you."

Snow flakes were melting on his long black lashes. "You don't want to come in?"

"Are you sure you want me to come in?"

"Last time I gave you hot chocolate from a box. I told myself I'd make some homemade good stuff next time."

"You don't have to."

"I enjoy it. Having you here is a good excuse to make fun stuff."

"You and my mom."

They shook out their coats and boots and laid their gloves and hats on the hearth. Aidan started the fire while she melted the bittersweet chocolate and stirred the sugar, vanilla and milk in the pan her mother had always used to make fudge and hot chocolate.

"Anything I can do?"

"There are marshmallows in that cupboard," she pointed.

He poured several marshmallows into the mugs she had set out. Once hot and well-blended, she poured the chocolate liquid into their mugs and they sat down together on the sofa by the fire.

"I didn't tell you about Geoffrey because I didn't realize it was abuse at the time. When I began to study the books on abuse, it hit me hard. I was reading over a checklist for abused women to identify the different types of abuse, and all of a sudden I realized I was mentally checking every single box. Then I couldn't *not* see it." She stopped and looked up at him. The look on his face was one of pain and anguish. She rushed to reassure him, "I'm okay! Really I am."

"I feel sick knowing that someone you trusted did that to you," he said.

"I have felt all kinds of angry at him. I'm trying to journal about it, to get it all out. I see how it led to all kinds of insecurities and fears and lack of trust. It will probably always have some sort of impact on me. It doesn't define me, but it does explain a lot. I—," she smiled, "I think it probably has something to do with how driven I am. He belittled me so often that I tried all the harder to prove I'm not stupid. I think I had the tendency before that, but I think he made it worse."

"Your perfectionism is no more?"

"I wouldn't go that far. I did feel like I had to show you I could do better than just hot chocolate from a mix."

"Less than a half hour ago you said making this hot chocolate was about making fun stuff!"

"I know. I think I lied. I didn't realize it was more about proving myself until now."

They both laughed and sipped their hot chocolate.

"I like this new side of you," he said. "I liked the old Greta, too, but you seem much more reflective and easy going."

"Really?

"Don't just take my word for it, what do you think?"

"Guys think, women feel," she said. "I feel like I've tapped into a whole new side of me by studying abusive relationships. Things are starting to make sense. It helps that I'm not working crazy hours all the time. I don't have deadlines or thousands of dollars on the line; I'm home, with books, reading and learning and I love it."

"You don't miss going into work every day?"

"I don't. Not that I'm walking away from it, no way. I can't imagine doing that. I still have to make a living; I don't want to live off my mom's money. I'll keep moving forward so I can support myself, but I don't want that to be because I'm driven."

"Your contentment, it shows."

She looked at him. His blue eyes were so intense. She quickly looked away. But she wanted to know what he saw. "How is that?" she asked, as she looked into the fire.

"When you first came back you were tense and on edge. I don't see that now."

"That's good to know."

"Do you want to know what else I see?"

A quick glance was all she could manage. "Sure."

"I see a woman who is happy. I see a woman who is healing, who is enjoying her home and her life and isn't driven by someone else's definition of success anymore."

She thought of Switzerland and Japan and New York. All that she and Jake could do together. Success on a scale that would dispel any doubts that she wasn't good enough.

"Success doesn't just happen, it takes drive and hard work," she said quietly, more to herself than to Aidan.

"What does that mean?"

She looked up at him while she struggled to put her thoughts into words. "I don't want to work that hard ever again. Not for someone's house, or office, or bank or resort. But I think I can still be successful."

He waited.

"I've done enough. I really have. I could always do more, in fact I've been tempted to," she paused and looked away and then back at him before she went on. "I've been tempted by an invitation to design internationally. To work with Jake in Switzerland and Japan. To join his team. Or I could set up my own firm in Chicago, or New York or L.A."

She put her mug on top of a book on the coffee table. "I feel like I could just reach out my hand," which she did, "and take all the opportunities for success and walk into the perfect future." Her hand grasped the empty air.

"That's the problem," she said, looking at her empty fist. "There's nothing to hold on to. Will I be more successful if I own my own firm? I don't think it would take away the restlessness I used to feel to keep moving forward, to do more. Will I be successful if I design interiors with teams of brilliant architects? Or marry a genius or have kids that travel the world with us? What is the ultimate success? No matter what it is, when someone dies, like Denise died, I have to consider what purpose all that served. All the successes Denise had in her career, and her husband's successes, her father's, none of it helped her. It made no real difference when it came down to it. Her struggles were the same as mine, the same as millions of abused women who for one reason or another are locked into an abusive relationship."

She looked over at him again. "The woman I talked to who is now at a shelter, she would think that at least Denise had options and resources. But Denise didn't have the ability speak up and get away from her abuser. This girl, she does, she got help. At least for today she's keeping herself and her baby safe. She spoke up and said no more. That's success."

"If your old life no longer embodies success for you, what do you want going forward?" Aidan asked this quietly, as he set his hot chocolate on a coaster on the coffee table.

"I'm going to contact some colleges and see what it will take to go back to school to become a licensed counselor. I'm also going to start calling shelters and offering my services as a designer."

"What about starting your own business?"

"I'm going to do that, too, but it will be part-time for now, until I can get my degree."

"And will part-time really mean part-time?"
She grinned. "I won't guarantee that."
"It sounds like a lot of work."
"I enjoy it all!"
"Sure, but what about your personal life?"
"What do you mean?"
"It's a general question."
"Lately, I've been productive, and that feels good. Every day I try to write three things. First I get out my thoughts, so I can continue to get used to being honest about the real stuff going on inside me. Then I try to give myself a goal for the day, something little or big, to give me a focus, a sense of purpose and accomplishment. Then, I try to be completely honest with God. I'm trying to learn to talk things over with him and believe that he is really listening and more importantly, caring about me and looking out for me. You know," she said with surprise, "I keep coming back to what you told me about all those medical people who helped Travis learn to heal and then to live on his own after being paralyzed. You talked about how they just showed up every day and did their thing, and what a difference it made for Travis in the long run. That's how I feel about God. Like I'm completely inadequate and can't possibly do all the good things that good people did in the Bible, but every day I just do a little thing, like continue to talk to God, and read some verses, and try to think about them and apply what I'm learning to my life or offer up what little I have to offer someone, and it's enough."

"I think that's quite a good summation of what God asks us to do," Aidan said. "Anything else?"

"What do you mean?"

"What about your personal life?"

"Okay fine, yes, I would like to have a family of my own and I know that life can get crazy difficult in a heartbeat, but I want to keep it as simple as possible. I need," she didn't want to say Jake's name, but she thought it, "I need someone who gets that, too."

"It's not all that common."

"What isn't common?"

"To have simple dreams, to walk away from the world's definition of success."

She gave him the side eye. "You kind of did though, didn't you?"

"I work on it every day. It's a battle, I can tell you that."

"How did you not get pulled into believing the standard definition of success?"

"I think God used what happened to Travis and Davey to show me how important each choice we make really is. If I want my time on this earth to matter, I need to obey God and love others well. That focus keeps my life simple."

"That makes sense," she said. In fact, it all made very good sense. His words settled into her, down deep, and she felt a sense of peace as she thought of how simple Aidan's life really was. "It's a lot like what I'm trying to do."

"You think so?"

She looked at him carefully to see if he was being sarcastic. She couldn't read a thing from his face, but it really was true.

For sometime they sat there listening to the fire crackle, sipping their hot chocolate.

"I could put a record on," she said.

He shook his head, "No need."

She looked at him yet again. He wasn't striving, he wasn't focused on achieving, he was living out his life purposefully, intentionally, every day.

"What?"

She shook her head and looked away, "Nothing."

"Are you okay?"

She shook her head.

Aidan waited a few minutes and then got up and turned the logs and added another one to the grate.

He came back and sat down, one leg tucked under him, his elbow bent on the back of the sofa as he faced her. "What else do you want?" he asked.

She shook her head and looked at the fire.

They sat there for a long time, listening to the wind blow and the fire snap and burn. To Greta it felt like an ancient evening, one that had gone on for centuries before them, a man and a woman sitting together in front of a fire on a cold and snowy winter's night, quiet, listening to the wind blow and the fire snap, watching the excited flickering flames, talking now and then; a night that had been and would be for millennia to come.

His eyes never left her. At last he spoke. "I think we want the same things, don't you?"

She kept staring at the flames. "I just wanted to talk to you tonight. I wanted to bounce things off of you and get your feedback."

"And I just wanted to help you."

"You understand abuse."

"I've been abused and I am healing from abuse. It hurts my heart to think you've been abused. But this is more than that," he said.

Yes, it was. The truth came out, unbidden, "You get me, Aidan. Like I understood Jake's house when I walked in the door, that's how well you understand me." She looked at him in amazement.

"I don't know anything about the guy's house, but I do understand you. I also don't know exactly where you're at with him at this moment, but after what happened between us last summer you need to know my feelings for you are growing again every time we're together. I want you to know this upfront. Only this time," he took a deep breath, "I think not only do I get you, you understand me much better now."

She sat up a little straighter. "I do, I really do. I understand why you thought we wouldn't work if we didn't have the same faith. I get it now. I understand why you didn't want to make love with me that last night. You understood the bond that it makes and how difficult it would be to walk away from that. I thought about that a lot and realized how true it is. I also understand how grateful you are to God for giving you hope again when everything looked hopeless with Travis. God gave me hope that it would all work out after Denise's murder. I haven't stopped thinking about everything you said and did. I had no idea at the time what an impact you were having on me."

"I will do whatever it takes to rebuild your trust in me."

"I do trust you."

"My life gets messy sometimes. Emergencies come up when I'm on call. I come home upset some nights because I can't shake off a patient's issues. Sometimes I have to spend an inordinate amount of time on research to figure out how to best help someone. Sometimes I have to keep secrets about patients and won't be able to share with you why I'm so upset. You will understand if you help the abused, you'll understand that weight like I do."

"I understand, and I will handle that. I have to tell you, Jake is waiting for an answer from me. He's waiting for me to tell him what I want to do so that we, he and I, can spend the rest of our lives together. He will go anywhere I want. He just wants me with him. He's been good to me, so good to me. He's done nothing to deserve being hurt."

"I can't help you with that."

She bit her lip. "I don't want to hurt him."

Aidan's eyes grew wide. "Are you serious right now? Are you second-guessing everything we've just said to each other?"

"I can't hurt him. You don't know what a really, really nice guy he is."

He stood up and walked over to the chair with his coat on the back of it.

"Stop! Please understand what a difficult position I'm in right now!"

He turned around, hands on his hips. "You just happened to be in the next chair over when I found a seat at church. When the restaurant was crazy busy, you invited me over for lunch. You called me on Christmas Day for help. I got to meet your family, and see a whole new side of you and your life. Tonight you showed up at my front door. I walked you home and you invited me inside to sit in front of the fire and have really good hot chocolate. I offered to stay outside and shovel your driveway, but you invited me in yet again. What do you expect me to think?"

"You think I'm the one leading you on now? Is that what you're saying?"

"I thought you were being genuine about it. Now it seems you're genuinely confused."

"I'm not confused. I know what I want—who I want. It's all falling into place so honestly, so easily, I know it's right. But I also have to let go of Jake."

"So the question is, do I walk out of here and give you all the time you need to make that break or do I ask that we start now?"

"I don't know."

He stood there, waiting.

She looked up at him. "You don't want to go?"

"Are you crazy?"

For one long moment their eyes held. A log spontaneously popped, sending sparks into the air. They met halfway and the kissing took over and the cocoa got cold and the fire in the grate burned out while the fire on the sofa, where they quickly ended up, was kept, barely, under control.

She sat up on the sofa and straightened her hair. The pile of gray embers in the fireplace looked depressing. As much as she wanted to add another log and start it again, let this night go on forever for her and Aidan, she couldn't do it.

"I have to tell Jake."

He brushed his hair out of his eyes. "Yes."

"I don't know how to tell him."

"This isn't something you want my help with. Trust me."

"Just over and done, end of story?"

"The guy doesn't want your pity. He wants the truth."

"Jake, his name is Jake."

"Whatever." He sat up, looked at his watch and groaned. "I need to head home."

"Is something wrong?"

"I have an early start tomorrow."

"Do you want me to drive you home?"

"No, if I run I'll be home in five minutes. It'll be good for me." He leaned over and kissed her again. "May I invite myself over for dinner tomorrow night? I'll pick up something if you like. Chinese? Pizza?"

"I've got plenty of food. I'll make something."

They kissed more at the door until finally, with a sigh, he left.

She closed the door behind him. Life as she knew it, she suddenly realized, was behind her. Beginnings were all around her. She smiled weakly. It was what she wanted. He was what she wanted. A simple life, a good life doing meaningful things, that is what she wanted.

"God? I've got tell Jake. Help me with this. I don't know how to do it. Hold his heart, help him forgive me, and may he be drawn to you somehow through it."

For a moment she debated waiting until tomorrow. "No, I'll never get to sleep if I do that."

She sat down on her mother's bed, where Jake had slept not so long ago. She dialed the number he had given her for Japan.

His voice was warm and eager. "Good morning!"

"Hi! Is this a bad time?"

"Not at all. So you heard from your lawyer?"

"My lawyer?"

"I just got off the phone with Aaron Fielding. I thought maybe your lawyer called you, too, to let you know."

"Let me know what? I haven't heard a thing."

"Pem is going with a plea bargain! He's afraid of a trial. The property was searched again and the missing flashlight was found in a paint can in the garage, along with that paperweight. There was still hair lodged in the flashlight. Forensics identified it as Denise's. The perky girlfriend also came forward with more information about that night."

"She knows details?"

"She knows everything. Her name is Dana Armstrong. She said Pem called her twice that night using a cellphone he had just gotten. The first call was about ten o'clock. Pem told Dana that Denise confronted him, saying she knew he was having an affair and she threatened to tell her father. She told him that her father would, as we guessed, jeopardize the DeWitt's financial empire."

"Do you know exactly how yet?"

"I do. My parents shared more with me at Christmas. I should have told you when I saw you but it wasn't the time. Prior to the merger, the DeWitts were taking irresponsible risks with other people's money with no accountability. Several other banks in New York were doing the same thing but they went under. Bill Arthur made sure the DeWitt's bank did not. This helped set up the DeWitts for a merger with another big bank. With the merger the DeWitts acquired more assets than ever before. It doesn't stop there. Bill is one of the key senators that helped in passing a new act that enabled big banks to increase their power even more. The DeWitts are now among the wealthiest bankers in the country, and they're beholden to Bill Arthur. If Bill found out how Pemberton treated Denise after all he's done for them, he would have been livid. There is no doubt in anyone's mind that Bill would have taken them down."

"Without implicating himself?"

"Bill Arthur is too smart for that. Besides, even if he somehow missed completely covering his own tracks, he is owed favors by every political entity out there. Repercussions wouldn't touch him, his friends in high places would see to that."

"Pem knew that, so he figured by making it look like an accident he could fool Arthur?"

"Pem told Dana he was going to make sure Denise never found out the truth. He said he was going to destroy any evidence that linked Dana to him and shut up Denise permanently. That scared Dana. According to her, she tried to reason with Pem but he hung up. About an hour later, Pem called Dana back and said it was done. Dana asked him what he meant. He said, 'She'll never get the chance to humiliate me again.'"

"Oh, Jake."

"Dana asked him if he had hurt Denise. He then told her the truth, that he rounded up any evidence that might tie Dana to him. He told her about the missing map and how he found the flashlight in your purse, and then frightened Denise so that she'd come running over to my house. On the way, he hit her repeatedly with the flashlight."

"My prints were on that flashlight," she realized.

"I know, mine, too."

"They couldn't survive a paint can, though, right?"

"I guess they could if the can was fairly empty, depending on where the prints were. He might have easily implicated us."

"I don't want to think about that," she said, her knees involuntarily shaking. She crossed her legs to stop them. "What else did Dana say?"

"Pem told her he had to get back outside in case we came out. He wanted us to think he was worried about her."

"You knew it right away."

"Pem's actions were pure evil."

"Did Aaron say why Dana didn't come forward on her own?"

"Are you ready for this? She claims she woke up the next morning thinking it was just a bad nightmare. She says she didn't watch the news that day and had no idea what happened. Except we all know that news spreads on the island like wildfire."

"Let's hope she's not a complete liar and is at least telling the truth about what Pem did."

"The good news is that we won't have to be witnesses in a trial."

"It's going to take some time for this to sink in."

"We can put the worse behind us and focus on us."

"Oh," she said, sharply brought back to the present reality.

"Oh?" The enthusiasm in his voice disappeared. "That doesn't sound good. What's up?"

"I—I have to tell you something difficult. I hate to do it on the heels of finding out what happened to Denise."

"What is it?"

"I need to tell you that I've decided that I think you were right. We can't make this work."

For a moment he said nothing. "You're calling to tell me it's over. We're done."

She winced. "I have nothing but gratitude for our time together. But you were right all along."

"What really happened? I know the run around when I hear it."

Her eyes closed and she came clean. "I talked with Aidan tonight. My feelings for him are back again."

"So he was interested after all."

"I'm so sorry. You did nothing wrong."

He was silent for a long time.

She tried again, "Thank you for all you did for me."

"It doesn't seem to have made much difference."

"Your kindness and support during that time, it made all the difference to me."

"Kindness? Support? You're better than that, Greta. I love you. Remember that. Remember the truth. Don't spin it."

Her cheeks turned red from shame. "I did. I'm sorry."

"What's the truth? Is it physical, your bond with him? Is that what it's about?"

She thought hard. "It's me. I've changed. What happened to Denise, it didn't happen just that one night, it was day in and day out. That's where she really needed help, day in and day out, little by little. I put all my effort into making her house beautiful, every day I was there, and so little effort into really helping her. I want to be prepared and knowledgeable next time I encounter a woman in her situation."

"Their house is already up for sale by the way. I don't understand what this has to do with us."

"It's all so senseless. I get the practicality of what I do, our homes and spaces need to be livable and safe and attractive if we can afford it. But in the long run, it's a fleeting pleasure and to me, it just feels empty now. I can't keep looking for happiness or success in the same places anymore."

"Are you walking away from your career in design?"

"No, but it won't be the only thing I do. I want to figure out how to be less self-centered and help others in ways that really impact them longterm."

"I hear what you're saying, but I still think it comes down to who you want, not what you want. I was willing to meet you on your terms, anywhere you wanted."

"You would have settled for that, but you really wanted me to come alongside you in your work, and make your goals my goals."

"We could have been a team at work and at home. What is wrong with that? By the way, you know I put you before my work for three months. Those three months were critical to my work, but I put you first."

"I know you did. I am more than grateful and honored that you did that. I also want to be a team at work and at home. Only my dream is to work helping the vulnerable among us. We have different dreams."

"I love you, Greta."

"I have sincerely loved you, Jake. I will never forget what we had together. But ultimately I would not have brought you lasting happiness.

"You're saying that I would not have brought you lasting happiness."

"I'm saying I can't fill the most important void in your life, no more than you can fill mine."

"Yet this other guy can."

"No, he won't either. I'm not asking him to and he's not asking me to fill his." She paused. "Jake, I'm going to be gut level honest with you. All my life I've been dismissive of God. I had no need for him. I realize now that the more I trust God with the details of my life, the more I see him helping me. At the same time, I still get so easily caught up in being in control and doing things my way that I know it's going to be a constant battle for me to continue to keep my priorities in line. I need to grow as a Christian. This guy will cheer me on as I work out my faith. And I will cheer him on. I don't want to be at odds about that with my spouse. That's where I really need someone who will walk that journey with me side by side. That's the kind of team I'm talking about."

For a moment she thought he had hung up. "Jake?"

"I'm here. I don't know what more you want me to say. I am who I am and clearly that's not fitting in with where you're headed. I'm not going to convince you otherwise. You've made your choice. I wish you well, Greta. I hope you get what you want."

With that the phone went silent until the dial tone kicked in. Slowly she hung up the phone.

She cried then, great heaving sobs for all the good they'd had together, for all the hard things they'd been through, for the distance that was between them and would remain forever, and the dance she had thought was their destiny that would never be.

When at last she stopped crying, she got up and got some tissues in the bathroom to blow her nose. Why, she thought, as she blew her nose, is getting a tissue always the next thing to do that gets me moving when I feel utterly bereft?

The house was silent, except for the furnace and the ticking of the clock on the wall. She walked over to the fireplace and put her hand on the still warm flagstone. It felt comforting. She closed the flue and pulled the wire screen across the opening. Next she picked up the mugs of cocoa, rinsed them out in the sink and put them in the dishwasher.

Thoughtfully, she washed and dried her mother's old fudge pan and then put it away inside the pink metal cabinets.

As she turned off the lights in each room, her fingers trailed along the chairs, touched the trim around the doorways, lingered on the doorknob of her bedroom door. Her parent's loving hands had touched these same things through the years, all to make a home, a home for her, for them as a family, failures and all. And now it was her home, more than ever.

She stood still for a moment as it came to her. It was her responsibility now to pray for those who would come after her, and to be content with what she had, and what she had not. She closed her eyes for a moment and tried to take it all in. She could hear her grandmother's prayers, and her mother's too, before she died, coming to terms with loss and forgiveness at last. It was her turn, her time now, to live the rest of her life fully, giving, taking, loving sacrificially, learning how to forgive things she didn't want to know about ahead of time, finding out what good boundaries looked like, learning at last the real meaning of love. Somehow it didn't frighten her, no, it felt right and good and even exciting.

Like rain, she thought, God's goodness, it pours down like rain. She opened her eyes and gave a short, surprised laugh. "*Restore*. Is this what it means, God? Have you restored my soul?" She smiled and looked up. "Thank you."

Getting Personal

Getting Personal
Need Help Now?
Call the National Domestic Violence Hotline at
1-800-799-7233 (SAFE).

From the Author

One in Four Journals

My friend, I hope you've found some of the truths in the pages of this book to be encouraging. If you have been in an abusive relationship, or if you are in one now, you are one in four. You are not alone. There is hope for you!

One in four women is abused by an intimate partner in the United States. Worldwide that statistic increases to one in three and we are rapidly on track to reach that soon in America. A quick search of the internet will also bring you more painful statistics with the same ratio of 1:4. For instance, one in four girls is sexually abused by the time she is eighteen. Once these statistics sink in, it's hard not to look around at a family gathering, or at the grocery store or at church or at school or at work or the beach, and have our breath taken away by the sheer number of women close to us who have been gravely wounded.

Our wounds need not define us. With healing comes strength and the ability to speak truth with courage. It also brings relief and restoration, not in old ways, but in new strength and new hope for a future where God's provision is enough. Putting off healing only increases the layers of unhealthy coping measures and prolongs the bitter consequences of abuse.

Healing often starts with an honest look at what is happening or has happened. Journaling is an excellent way to begin. Reading back our own words is sometimes the first affirmation we will get that what we are experiencing or have experienced is real and painful.

Because of the need to have a safe place to journal that won't bring unwanted eyes, I thought you might find it helpful to have some pages here where you can write and begin to process, to grieve, to work on healing and to grow. The pages are set up like Greta's journal in the story. I hope you will use them safely and well. Those pages come at the very end of this book, just before the list of recommended reading.

Exactly What Qualifies as Abuse?

The unique dynamics between each couple are such that abuse may pop up at any moment in innumerable ways that others may not even perceive. You are the best judge of what is abusive. The categories below are meant to be a starting point for those who are unfamiliar with abuse and need help identifying the different types.

While any one of these as an infrequent event may be considered abusive and life-changing, the impact of multiple abusive behaviors over time is staggering.

Also consider that the impact of abusive behaviors is magnified by the degree of power someone has over their victim. That power may increase through the abusers physical size and strength, the victim's emotional or financial or even physical dependency upon the abuser, and their perceived need to maintain a relationship with them.

Remember, abuse is never okay. It is never deserved, or justified. God hates violence and through the Bible instructs men to love their wives as themselves and to treat all women well. Please note that while in intimate relationships women can be abusive too, most abuse comes at the hands of men. That is why I have chosen to focus on abused women.

Verbal Abuse:

Name calling, insults, raised voice, belittling, cursing, ridiculing, raging

Emotional Abuse:

Fault finding, blame shifting, gaslighting, denying your reality, denying their actions or words, stealing, lying, cheating, causing fear, threatening suicide, threatening to hurt you or others, following from room to room relentlessly, stalking, tracking your phone, making you account for every minute, using GPS to track your whereabouts, ignoring, shaming, turning friends and family against you, turning you against your friends and family, isolating you, endangering your job, not letting you sleep, hurting pets or children, destruction of your property, displaying weapons, threatening with weapons

Financial Abuse:

Sole control of finances, lack of disclosure regarding all accounts, restricting your spending and not restricting his, tracking your purchases and or receipts, going into your purse/wallet to track your cash or credit cards, withholding money, hiding their spending or savings accounts, making large purchases without your input, purposefully putting you in danger financially, making you ask for money

Physical Abuse

Slapping, punching, hitting, biting, pinching, squeezing hard, causing accidents, choking, kicking, stepping on, shoving, pushing, dragging, hair pulling, burns, causing bruises, throwing objects at you

Sexual Abuse

Forcing sexual advances on you against your will, purposefully painful sex, ignoring pleas to stop, rape, using your body while you're sleeping, abusing you verbally during sex, adultery, sexual addictions, forced use of pornography

Spiritual Abuse

Using Scripture to force submission or to intimidate or get "obedience", a self-righteous lording over, accusations of biblical disobedience either in the abuser's eyes or supposedly in God's eyes

What is a Safety Plan?

A safety plan is a predetermined set of steps to get you out of danger when necessary. Implementing a safety plan means there has been an abusive incident. Your first reaction must be to get to safety. You may also feel anger, fear, or indignation. They are all justified. HOWEVER, DO NOT retaliate. Do NOT become the crazy person your abuser wants you to be. Get safe. Be calm. Be strong. Speak the truth quietly and rationally. Your credibility as you interact with police or authorities of any kind will be much more convincing if you have responded without actions that may appear irrational and your anger or indignation are under control.

A critical portion of a good safety plan may include using a women's shelter. *Uncommon Dreams* takes place in the 1990s, when women's shelters had limited funding and few resources. ***Today's shelters are much better funded and can be one of your best resources! Memorize the contact information for your local shelters. Visit them ahead of time to find out what they offer.***

A good safety plan will include resources set aside that you can access quickly. Here are some important steps to consider:

• Keep an extra set of important keys on hand that only you know about. *Always* bring your first set of keys with you in case you need to get away on your own when you are out with the abuser or

if you might be forced out of the house.
- Keep your vehicle filled with gas whenever possible.
- Have an emergency or "burner" phone available and programmed with important numbers.
- Set aside cash or credit cards out of reach of the abuser so you can afford a safe place to sleep and groceries.
- Visit a local woman's shelter and become familiar with their procedures and how they can help—*before you need them. Don't let unfamiliarity keep you from getting the help you need!*
- Get a lawyer or ask at the shelter for information they may have on how to get an order of protection. If they cannot point you to the correct help, contact your county courthouse and ask what free legal help is available for women in abusive relationships. Know your rights ahead of time!
- Keep a private record of the abuse, including days and details and photographs if possible.
- Get copies of important documents, including a lease or deed to the house, social security numbers, court decrees, financial records, passports, children's immunizations, etc., and keep them in a safe location outside the home or with a highly trusted individual outside your home.
- Have extra clothes and things your children will need available outside the home.
- Create a Plan B for how you will live if you cannot go back home, including how to support yourself, a budget and how to get plenty of emotional and spiritual support.
- Have a designated person who will give you sound advice should you consider returning to a dangerous situation. Know who you will call when feeling weak or tempted to return to the abuser.
- Be aware that after an explosion of abuse an abuser will often express remorse and promise not to do it again. They know exactly what to say and do to entice you back. But abuse is a cycle, and after the remorse the tension builds again and the dread increases and then the explosion comes again. *Real change is not possible in the short term.* Lasting change takes years and improved actions tested by time.

Maintaining Hope

Daily, victims are killed in domestic abuse. Yet every day there are also miracles as abused people escape and get help and grow and heal.

I have never seen an abuser change overnight, but I have seen God intervene by providing a way out for the abused and the children, by giving courage, wise insights and providing help in simple and drastic ways.

Do not forget that while the enemy may be winning, while the police may not believe you, when the lawyers are not helping, when you aren't believed, when your partner has lied and hurt you and "won" yet again, all is not lost. The enemy may win the day, but your life is more than just a bad day, a bad month or even a bad year or years. Life can be good again, and even better. Good things will happen to you again. You will laugh again, and you will breathe again, freely. Draw close to God, and trust that as you draw closer to him, he is trustworthy. He will never leave you or forsake you. He knows the losses you've endured. He is loving and kind and wishes to give good things to those who love him. As you grow closer to God, he makes the following grow inside of you: love, joy, peace, patience, kindness, goodness, faith, gentleness, and self-control. Don't these sound wonderful after the craziness of abuse? What a contrast! What a hope!

Helping Abused Women

I highly recommend learning more about helping the women around you who are being abused or are in need of healing.

Women in your family, church and community need supportive friends who understand the dynamics of abuse. Too often those sought for support do not understand the dynamics of abuse, and in an effort to keep together a marriage, which most in the church see as an absolute must, they minimize the abuse, or blame the woman for not being godly enough or submissive enough, and often they encourage trust in an abuser who does not deserve it.

Here are 3 way to help:

1. **Believe** - *The most important thing you can do to help a woman who is being abused is to believe her.* Do not question or doubt her. Rare is the woman who will lie about abuse. Give her the benefit of any doubt, and trust that she is doing the best that she can, though you may not agree with all of her choices. Do not try to fix her, you will just push her away and quite likely you are unaware of all that is going on in her situation and she knows much better than you do the dynamics at work between her and her husband. Keep encouraging her to get professional help and to believe that God is for her, not against her. Ask her how you can help and be prepared

to follow up as regularly as she will allow. Remind her that God loves her and sees her as precious. Someday, she will find her voice and use it again to say, "Enough."

2. **Learn** - On the last two pages of this book is a list of books that I and many other women have found to be insightful and helpful. Some of them are eye-opening! Shining light on confusing dynamics, they offer insights that will surprise you. You may find insights into situations that you have experienced as well. Learning from experts is critical before you attempt to listen. As well-meaning as you may be in listening before you've studied up on abuse, you may do a great deal of damage in trying to give advice when you don't understand the situation. You will inadvertently wound the abused even more. Even if you think you know enough to be helpful, learn some more!

3. **Help** - Become an advocate through your church or local shelter or even through your workplace. Please advocate that your church have a fund set aside specifically for helping abused women who need shelter and safety. Encourage abuse training for your church leaders. Visit your local shelter and find out how you can help. Most shelters have lists of needs and take donations of toys, clothing, women's toiletries, and of course, financial donations. Do you have a legal background? Consider volunteering legal aid to women who have neither the financial resources or mental wherewithal to figure out the court systems. Does your office make donations to non-profits? Consider supporting a shelter!

One Last Encouragement

Change. We all hope abusers will repent of abusive behavior and realize that their sense of entitlement and desire to have power over someone is wrong. We hope they will follow through with a commitment to make it right with those they've abused.

We hope the abused will realize their compassion and desire to help their abuser will never be enough to bring about change. We hope the abused will see how precious they are and how they deserve to be protected and sane and at peace in their home or environment.

The Bible says that nothing is impossible with God. Trusting that a man or a woman will change in our timeframe and according to our wishes is futile. Trusting that God can and will change those who trust in him and allow him to work in their hearts and lives is the only wise option. Is your loved one able to do this? On their own, no. With a dependency on God, yes. Are you able to do this? The degree to which one moves towards God will determine one's future on this earth and in eternity.

True peace and life comes only through faith in Jesus Christ. No matter how bad one's circumstances, the inner peace given us by the Holy Spirit, who works in one accord with God and Jesus, passes all understanding. Trusting our future to him means that no matter what happens to us, we are secure in him. Each one of our lives and all of our actions are accountable before God, and God will see that justice is done. As the good shepherd described in Psalm 23, God will provide for those who love him, he will refresh and restore their souls, provide for and anoint them with oil. Surely goodness and mercy will follow those who love him, and they will dwell in the house of the Lord forever.

May it be so in your life.

To God be the glory,

Love,

Jill

Journaling

One in Four Journal

While I would love to have endless pages for you to write in, sadly, it's not feasible. Feel free to copy this format into a password protected app or notebook of your choosing.

Journaling here begins with "Topic for the Day". This is where you can begin to express your feelings and identify the reality of your situation. Clarity will come as you're able to see on paper what is true.

The second half of the journal pages begin with "Ready to Move Forward". This starts with a place to write what is on your mind each day, followed by action steps for that day, simple or big, and then ends with a prayer for that day. You decide how simple or how difficult each of these will be.

Don't forget that at the very end of these pages is a list of recommended reading! These books are very helpful in learning about abuse and healing from it.

Topic for the Day

To get you started, here are some helpful topics to address in your journal, *if this is a safe place to do so!* If you have cause to believe this will be read by anyone who will hurt you, do not write here.

Today I'm feeling…
   Today is…
   I've been abused in the following ways…
   I've been abused by the following people…

The first time I was abused…
The last time I was abused….
The worst time I was abused….
It is not okay that….
I think God is….
I am…
I believe…
I can….
I need help with…
I need to grow…
I need to heal from…
God sees me as…
God promises…
This just happened…

Date:

Topic for the day:

Date:

Topic for the day:

Date:

Topic for the day:

Date:

Topic for the day:

Date:

Topic for the day:

Date:

Topic for the day:

Date:

Topic for the day:

Date:

Topic for the day:

Date:

Topic for the day:

Date:

Topic for the day:

Date:

Topic for the day:

Date:

Topic for the day:

Date:

* * *

Topic for the day:

Date:

Topic for the day:

Date:

Topic for the day:

Date:

Topic for the day:

Date:

Topic for the day:

Date:

Topic for the day:

Date:

Topic for the day:

Format Change - Ready to Move Forward

Date:

My thoughts today:

My goal today:

My prayer today:

Date:

My thoughts today:

* * *

My goal today:

My prayer today:

Date:

My thoughts today:

My goal today:

My prayer today:

Date:

My thoughts today:

My goal today:

My prayer today:

Date:

My thoughts today:

My goal today:

My prayer today:

Date:

My thoughts today:

My goal today:

My prayer today:

Date:

My thoughts today:

My goal today:

My prayer today:

Date:

My thoughts today:

My goal today:

My prayer today:

Date:

My thoughts today:

My goal today:

My prayer today:

Date:

My thoughts today:

* * *

My goal today:

My prayer today:

Date:

My thoughts today:

My goal today:

My prayer today:

Date:

My thoughts today:

My goal today:

My prayer today:

Date:

My thoughts today:

My goal today:

My prayer today:

Date:

My thoughts today:

My goal today:

My prayer today:

Date:

My thoughts today:

My goal today:

My prayer today:

Date:

My thoughts today:

My goal today:

My prayer today:

Recommendations

Reading Recommendations

Holy Bible - NIV version is excellent

Lundy Bancroft - *Why Does He Do That?*, Inside the Minds of Angry and Controlling Men.

Pamela Cooper-White - *The Cry of Tamar*, Violence Against Women and the Church's Response

Beverly Engel, *The Emotionally Abused Woman*, Overcoming Destructive Patterns and Reclaiming Yourself

Patricia Evans - *The Verbally Abusive Relationship*, How to Recognize It and How to Respond

Brad Hambrick - *Becoming a Church that Cares Well for the Abused*

June Hunt - *Domestic Violence*, Assault on a Woman's Worth

Gregory L. Jantz,- *Healing the Scars of Emotional Abuse*

Mary Susan Miller, *No Visible Wounds*, Identifying Nonphysical Abuse of Women by Their Men

Chis Moles - *The Heart of Domestic Abuse*

Jeremy Pierre and Greg Wilson - *When Home Hurts*, A Guide for Responding Wisely to Domestic Abuse in Your Church

Tammy Schultz and Hanna Estabrook - *Beyond Desolate*, Hope Versus Hate in the Rubble of Sexual Abuse

Dr. Kevin Skinner - *Treating Trauma from Sexual Betrayal*, Overcoming Destructive Patterns and Reclaiming Yourself

Dr. Steve Stephens and Pam Vredevet - *The Wounded Woman*, Hope and Healing for Those Who Hurt

Steven R. Tracy - *Mending the Soul*, Understanding and Healing Abuse

Leslie Vernick - *Emotionally Destructive Relationship*

Leslie Vernick - *The Emotionally Destructive Marriage*

Leslie Vernick - *How to Act Right When Your Spouse Acts Wrong*
Susan Weitzman - *Not to People Like Us,* Hidden Abuse in Upscale Marriages

Made in the USA
Monee, IL
17 July 2022